SETTLE MY HEART

ALENA MENTINK

ELECTRIC
MOON
PUBLISHING

www.emoonpublishing.com

DEDICATION

For my family–Dad, Mom, Kailey,
Caleb, Aiden, Annika, Asher, Abigail, and Lillian–
who have supported me through
each step of my writing

TABLE *of* CONTENTS

CHAPTER

1

Des Moines, Iowa, 1881

"Do you really have to go?"

Brittany Haines barely managed to restrain a sigh at her aunt's question. They had already been over this too many times in Brittany's opinion. Far too many times. Her aunt should have realized by now that Brittany had no intention of staying in Des Moines. Not when she had already given her word that she would be arriving at Fort Laramie by stage on September first. Not with her bags packed and her tickets already purchased. Not when she had already gone through the pain of saying goodbye to the friends she had made over the years here in Des Moines. Double-mindedness had never been one of Brittany's faults, and when the train pulled out of the station in just twenty minutes, she would be on it. Couldn't her aunt understand that?

Rather than looking at Aunt Ida, Brittany turned her attention to the two children fidgeting on the bench beside her. "Lars, Brenna, sit still. I don't want you getting dirty before we even board the train."

They both nodded, looking up at her with matching pairs of blue eyes that danced with an excitement not even her scolding could quench. They considered their trip away from Des Moines an adventure, starting right here at the train station. Brittany wished that she could see this trip like her younger siblings did—without worry or fear.

"I still think carrying through with this plan of yours is reckless," Aunt Ida said, her tone insistent. "I don't see what made you suddenly decide to run off like this, leaving civilization behind."

Brittany tightened her grip on her reticule, knowing Aunt Ida thought she wasn't thinking clearly, that she hadn't weighed the costs of leaving Des Moines. But in truth, she had put plenty of thought and prayer into this decision. Surely her aunt couldn't think it was easy for her to leave Des Moines. The city that had been her home for years now ever since Aunt Ida became her guardian and that of her three siblings after their parents' deaths. It had been hard adjusting to the city after living all her life on a farm, but over time, she had come to love Des Moines, and few things would have persuaded her to leave.

Brittany drew a deep breath. "You've always emphasized to me and my siblings the importance of family. You, of all people, should understand why I'm going west. Our family has been given an opportunity to be together again, and I cannot turn it down."

"You shouldn't need to go west for your family to be together." Aunt Ida's back was ramrod straight. "If that brother of yours would just get himself back here to Des Moines instead of rubbing elbows with those uncouth westerners—"

"Clem isn't coming back." How Brittany wished he were! If only her older brother would leave the Western range and come back to Iowa. But now she was thinking like Aunt Ida. Judging from his all-too-short letters, Clem was happily settled in Wyoming Territory and had no intentions of coming home. He had been out West for five years already, and Brittany had long ago given up hope that he would become disillusioned with the cowboy life and return to Iowa.

"We have to face reality. Now that Clem's courting a girl out there, he has less reason than ever to come back."

Aunt Ida's silence said Brittany had scored on that one. Brittany thought back to Clem's last letter, the one with the shocking announcement that he was calling on a girl who lived near the ranch he worked for. Brittany had known for some time that there was little possibility of his ever coming home again, but that letter slammed the door on even the slight chance he might change his mind. Her brother was one stubborn man.

"I do wish you would at least leave the children here," Aunt Ida said, breaking through Brittany's thoughts. "There's no need for them to be dragged along on this—this Western spree of yours when you know I would be happy to keep them here with me."

Leave Lars and Brenna here, when the very reason she was leaving Des Moines was so they would have a chance to meet their older brother?

"The children will be fine with me." Brittany worked to keep her voice even.

"You can hardly think that a ranch teeming with barbaric westerners is a good place to raise children. What kind of an upbringing will they have in such a filthy atmosphere?"

"I agree with you, and that's why we will only stay for one year before coming home. I assure you that I will be careful who I let Lars and Brenna associate with."

"But–" Aunt Ida adjusted her wire-rimmed spectacles, a nervous gesture of hers, Brittany knew. "If you take them to this ranch, they're going to lose a year of schooling."

"No, they won't. I'll see to that. I packed their schoolbooks in with their things." Brittany didn't mention how she had packed and repacked, trying to squeeze the books in. Nor did she mention how they had cut severely into the twenty-five-pound weight limit for baggage per person that was the rule of the stage company in Cheyenne. Every pound over would cost an extra dollar, and she didn't have the money to spare for that.

"The children are coming with me," Brittany said firmly. That was one point she refused to change her mind on.

For a moment, she thought her aunt was going to protest further, but then her shoulders slumped. "I worry about you," Aunt Ida said, her voice softening. "If–if something happens to you, I'll never forgive myself."

Brittany felt tears rush to her own eyes. "Oh, Auntie." She wrapped an arm around the older woman, who had become like a second mother to her. "This is only for one year, remember? Then I'll be coming straight home again."

"Unless you marry some westerner." Aunt Ida made a face. "Dear, please remember: westerners are nothing but trouble— and don't let any man fool you into thinking differently."

"You can't lump all westerners into one group."

"Now, I know you've been rather sheltered, but you must be aware that there are people out there who will take advantage of you given half the chance." Aunt Ida peered at her over her spectacles. "I've heard that Western men will do anything to get a wife—anything at all. You be careful, Brittany."

"You shouldn't believe everything you see in print."

"And you shouldn't be so quick to push good advice aside." Aunt Ida frowned. "A least you'll have Clem with you. I know he'll take good care of you. You *have* heard from him since his last letter, haven't you?"

Brittany hesitated, unwilling to admit that Clem hadn't responded to her letter telling him that she was coming. Was he just too busy to write? Or was he upset with her?

She was spared from replying when Lars said, "Here comes Pastor Brown!"

Brittany looked up, and sure enough, crossing the crowded station platform was Pastor Brown, his wife, and their son, William. She was surprised to see them, especially since she had seen them just the day before at church, and none of them had mentioned any plans to see her off at the station.

"I hope you don't mind, dear, but the Browns wanted to see you one last time," Aunt Ida whispered, leaning in close.

"Of course, that's fine. I'm glad to see them." Brittany inwardly wondered if this was another ploy of her aunt and Mrs. Brown to thrust her and William together. Ever since she had arrived in Des Moines five years earlier, she and William had been close friends—even though William was several years older. It was partly because of him and his easygoing way that she had fit so easily into Des Moines society. The only shadow on their friendship was that Aunt Ida and Mrs. Brown refused to let things rest as they were. In more recent years, they had taken to pushing William and Brittany together in an obvious attempt at matchmaking, an idea that did not appeal to her. William was a dear friend, but that was all. Brittany feared that if the two older women kept at it, the friendship between her and William was going to unravel.

The one good thing about my leaving is that I'll be able to escape their scheming, she thought. *At least until I come home next year.*

"Brittany, dear, how good to see you." Mrs. Brown bustled over to her, beaming. "It's hard to believe that your day of departure is already here! We're going to miss you terribly. Our sewing circle isn't going to be the same without you."

"Of course, we will miss her, but we'll look forward to next year when she returns." Pastor Brown smiled down at her in a fatherly way, and Brittany felt a lump form in her throat. She was going to miss these dear people.

"Hello, Brittany," was all William said. He smiled, but his blue eyes failed to light up like usual.

"Hello, William." Brittany was aware once more of just what a fine-looking man William was. It was no wonder all the girls around were wild to catch his attention. He was tall, standing over six feet, with straight blond hair, a dimple in one cheek, a charming smile, and impeccable manners. And the fact that he would be ordained as a minister in a few months only added to his appeal.

"I think it's so sweet that you're going west to be with your brother." Mrs. Brown smiled broadly. "There aren't many eighteen-year-old girls who would travel so far from home, and with two siblings in tow. I must admire you, Brittany."

"Thank you," Brittany said, her mind racing off to Clem again. Was he happy she was coming or had their childhood bond dissolved over the years? Had his young woman changed things between them? If only she could stop these agonizing doubts!

A train whistle wailed in the distance, and Brittany felt her heart start to pound. The time to leave was fast approaching, and soon the train would be carrying her far, far from Iowa and everything she had ever known.

Pastor Brown seemed to sense her mounting fear. "Let's pray," he said, and forming a circle, they all bowed their heads.

"Heavenly Father," Pastor Brown began. "We come to You with thankful hearts for the opportunity You have given Brittany to join her brother out west, but also with heavy hearts as we prepare to see her off. We know that You will be watching over her every step of the way, and we ask You to give her peace that comes from You alone. Please, bless this journey and bring her safely home to us when that time comes. We ask these things in Your Son's name. Amen."

Pastor Brown squeezed Brittany's shoulder. "And that is only the beginning of our prayers for you."

Brittany felt unwanted tears sting her eyes. "Thank you."

The sound of the approaching train grew louder, and across the platform a stirring passed through the crowd as travelers prepared to leave.

"Do you have all your baggage?" Aunt Ida asked, hands pleating her handkerchief.

"Yes." The single word was tight with all the emotion Brittany felt.

The train pulled into the station with a loud screeching of iron wheels on iron tracks, and with a great sigh it shuddered to a stop. The conductor came to the passenger car door, and Brittany knew that it was time to go.

"Be careful, Brittany." Aunt Ida hugged her tightly. "Remember what I warned you about."

Brittany nodded and wondered which warning in particular she was speaking of. Maybe all of them.

Aunt Ida then turned to Lars and Brenna, and Mrs. Brown took her turn to claim Brittany. "Goodbye, dear," she said, embracing her for one instant. "Hurry home. We'll all be eagerly waiting."

She beamed, and Brittany cringed, suspecting that Mrs. Brown was thinking of her and William again.

Pastor Brown hugged her next, saying, "Remember—we'll be praying for you."

Then there was no one left but William. He smiled again, but it looked forced.

"Have a good trip," he said, extending his hand.

Brittany accepted it, feeling her chin wobble. "Study hard. Just think: by the time I come home, you'll be the *Reverend* William Brown! It's going to be a bit confusing with two Pastor Browns."

"I hope I'll always just be William to you, Brittany." He hesitated, then said in a rush, "Would you—would it be all right if we wrote to each other while you're gone, Brittany? A year is a long time to be apart."

What will his mother and Aunt Ida think? Brittany felt an instant of panic but found herself nodding. "I'd be glad to keep in touch with a friend. I'm not sure how often Northridge gets mail, but that doesn't mean we can't write when it works."

"Good." William's shoulders lost some of their tension. "I'll get the address from your aunt."

He started to say more but was cut off by the conductor calling, "All aboard!"

"Oh, my!" Brittany glanced around, checking to make sure she had everything she needed. Nothing remained on the bench.

Taking Lars and Brenna by the hand, Brittany made her way to the train, Aunt Ida and the Browns following along. There was a final round of hugs, and Aunt Ida began to cry. Brittany's heart ached at leaving them behind, but there was no turning back now. The conductor helped her up the train steps, then boosted Lars and Brenna up after her. They waved once more to the small group gathered to see them off, and Brittany tried to commit every detail of their faces to memory. She wanted to be able to vividly recall each of their features in the following days when homesickness struck and she was surrounded by complete strangers.

Then she entered the passenger car, Lars and Brenna trailing along behind her. As she lowered herself onto one of the worn leather seats, the train whistle blew, and with a lurch the train began to move. She pressed close to the window and caught a fleeting glimpse of Aunt Ida, Pastor and Mrs. Brown, and William standing on the station platform, still waving. Then the train carried her away from them, from Des Moines, and from everything else familiar.

CHAPTER

2

Eastern Wyoming Territory, September 1, 1881

She sure wasn't in Iowa anymore.

Brittany stared out the stagecoach window, her feet braced against the stage's floor to keep her seat on the upholstered leather bench. The land beyond the stage window seemed empty to her—empty and absent of life. No farms or fields broke the expanse of grass and sagebrush. No houses lined the rutted road they traveled; no people were in sight. Nothing moved except the grass waving in the unceasing wind.

Brittany couldn't bury her sigh. *What have I gotten myself into?* she wondered. Clem had written of how open the land was, of how the hills seemed to rise right up to touch the clear blue sky spread over it like a great bowl. He had also mentioned how isolated the region was and that neighboring ranches were often a couple hours ride apart. Somehow she had brushed that fact aside in her decision to come west, and now she found herself completely unprepared for the loneliness she saw imprinted on this land.

This is silly, she scolded herself. *You've only been away from Des Moines for a matter of days, and you already want to turn tail and go home? You can't do that; you're already too far into this adventure to turn around.*

Still, the thought of Aunt Ida and her motherly concern for the Haines children was hard to push aside. How Brittany missed Aunt Ida! At that moment she gladly would have gone through one of her aunt's worry-induced lectures just for a glimpse of the dear woman's face. Brittany missed the snug house that she had learned to call home, the friends she had made, the church she attended. She missed Des Moines and its familiar, bustling atmosphere, and William.

Brittany had treasured Clem's letter when it first arrived, but now she wondered if it would have been better had Clem never penned it. If it hadn't come, she was sure she wouldn't be here now.

It started when Brittany read Clem's letter aloud to her family as they always did when one of his rare letters arrived. Aunt Ida had cried over the idea of Clem being old enough to think of marriage, and Brittany, too, had felt a little teary. But Lars and Brenna didn't seem very interested. *They ought to be interested in what's going on with their own brother,* Brittany thought but then realized, *Why should they be interested when they don't even know Clem?*

The thought jolted her. It seemed wrong that Lars and Brenna didn't know their own brother. Family was important, a gift straight from God, her parents had taught her, and not knowing your own brother seemed almost a sin to her.

But it wasn't the children's fault. Brenna was only seven, and

Lars just one year older; they had both been too little to remember Clem before he left five years ago.

They already lost their parents. They shouldn't lose their brother as well, Brittany thought but felt helpless. Clem had already made up his mind that Wyoming Territory was home, and he wasn't coming back to Des Moines.

She was still wrestling with the problem the next morning when she reread Clem's letter, trying to commit every detail of it to memory. One line in the middle seemed to leap straight out at her.

Tim Myers, my boss, is looking for someone to come out here and help his wife with the housework. They've had a hard time keeping help around for more than a few weeks, and I know they're anxious to find someone reliable since Mrs. Myers struggles with her arthritis. If you happen to know of anyone who might be interested, have them drop a line to the boss. He's getting mighty fed up with this whole problem of finding good help.

It was the perfect answer. Brittany had run straight to her desk to "drop a line" to Mr. Myers, asking for more information about the job. Maybe Clem wouldn't return to Des Moines, but what was stopping her from joining him out West?

Mr. Myers responded quickly, writing that if she were to come, she would be given room and board along with a small wage, and her travel fares would be covered. He also agreed that Lars and Brenna could come with her, although it seemed he was reluctant about that. And best of all, she would be living on the very same ranch Clem worked for.

Due to the cost in both time and money, and to make sure that my wife and I are not left in difficult circumstances, we'll need you to sign a contract agreeing to stay and work for us for one year, Mr. Myers had concluded his letter. *And within that time, you won't be allowed to be either engaged or married, so if that is your idea in hiring on with us, stay home and don't bother coming.*

Brittany raised her eyebrows at his strong emphasis on the no-marriage policy, but she wasn't bothered by it. The only reason she wanted to work at Northridge was to be near her brother, not to find a husband. Goodness, if that were why she wanted to go, then she most certainly would stay in Iowa! A westerner was not high on her list of marriageable men.

To commit to a whole year at Northridge was harder, but Brittany figured she could do it. For one year she could tolerate Clem's "wild West," but the day that contract was up, she was coming home. She would see to it that Lars and Brenna had a proper upbringing and was convinced the West was not a suitable environment for children to grow up in.

Quickly Brittany wrote first to Clem, telling him of her intentions to come to Wyoming Territory, and then to Mr. Myers, agreeing to all his terms. Then she set about convincing Aunt Ida that she wasn't making a fatal choice in going West—

Brittany blinked back tears. She had to stop thinking like this, or her emotions were going to unravel. They would be arriving at Fort Laramie soon, and the last thing she wanted was for her face to be splotchy and tearstained when she met Mr. Myers, who had said he would be at the fort when she arrived.

Purposefully, Brittany turned her gaze from the window and instead looked at her two younger siblings seated across from her. Lars and Brenna had both been wonderful throughout the trip. No complaining. No begging to go back home. Nothing but their best behavior. Now the two children sat quietly on the bench, swaying along with the stage and looking as tired as Brittany felt. The long days of travel were taking their toll on them all. The stage's cramped quarters, wedging all nine of the passengers hip to hip and knee to knee, not allowing enough space for them to so much as stretch out their legs, was wearing everyone's nerves thin. That and the lack of sleep they all faced. Sleeping upright on the stage's leather bench and getting jerked awake whenever they hit a bad rut was not at all restful, Brittany had discovered.

As soon as I get to the ranch, the first thing I want to do is sleep, in a real bed, for hours and hours without getting bounced around the whole time, Brittany thought. Or would she want a bath first? It would feel wonderful to be clean again, to wash off the layer of dust that stuck to everything in the coach, including her clothes, her skin, and her hair.

But it was the thought of seeing Clem that took complete control of her thoughts. To see her older brother again, after so many years of separation, would be best of all. He was the reason she had braved all this hardship, all these long, arduous miles. How many times throughout the trip had she found the strength to keep going just by reminding herself that Clem was at the end of the journey, waiting for her arrival. Clem, with his laughing blue eyes, his teasing smile, his gentle, caring ways. Oh, she couldn't wait to see him again! Fort Laramie was only a few more miles away. How far it was to Northridge Ranch, Brittany didn't know, but it surely couldn't be that far. Before the day was over she would probably be seeing Clem. And that thought alone was enough to drive away some of Brittany's weariness.

I just hope he isn't mad at me for coming without waiting for his reply—"Look! Deer!" Brenna's voice broke through Brittany's thoughts.

"Pronghorn, not deer." Mrs. Munson, an older woman Brittany had befriended during the trip, smiled as she spoke, taking any sting out of her words. Brittany knew that Mrs. Munson's husband was an officer stationed at Fort Laramie and that she was rejoining him after a brief trip back East. She had a wealth of information about life in Wyoming Territory, information she had been more than willing to share with Brittany as the stage rattled its way toward the fort. Her presence was a great relief to Brittany since the stage's five other passengers were men. The men had been polite enough to Brittany, but their rugged appearance and some of the words Brittany overheard them use made her keep her distance from them—at least as much as could be managed on a stage.

"How can you tell they're pronghorn?" Brenna asked Mrs. Munson. "They're a long way off."

"Just look at them closely." Mrs. Munson pointed toward them. "You'll notice the white fur on their throat, their sides, and their rump. That's what gives away that they're pronghorn."

"I see. They are pronghorn." Brenna looked so pleased with herself that Brittany couldn't keep from smiling. Leave it to her little sister to find something to be excited about in that tangle of sage-dotted hills.

Brittany glanced at Lars. He had been quiet for some time, but the smile on his face assured her that he was enjoying himself. He, too, seemed greatly interested in the view outside the stage window.

So you're the only one complaining. And how many times have you told Lars and Brenna to have a cheerful attitude both inside and out? Seems like you're the one who needs to take a lesson from them just now. How Brittany wished that nagging voice would leave her in peace!

"Bridge up ahead," one of the men called out.

"Already? We're closer than I thought." Mrs. Munson turned to Brittany and said, "Fort Laramie is just across the North Platte. We're almost there."

Almost there? Brittany felt her stomach suddenly tighten in a hard knot of fear. The trip, first by train to Cheyenne, then by stage here to Fort Laramie, had gone much as she had expected—but now she was about to step into the unknown. She didn't even know what she *should* be expecting. A complete stranger was meeting her at the fort, then she was traveling to a place she had never been, to help a woman she had never met. Brittany swallowed hard, suddenly terrified.

Trust in the Lord, she reminded herself. She had prayed before making the decision to come here; she had to believe that God was leading her and that He would not forsake her in this Western land. He was the God of Wyoming Territory as well as Iowa, unchanging, unfailing, and faithful in every circumstance. She had to trust Him.

The stagecoach wheels created a different, more hollow sound as they rolled onto the wood-planked bridge. Three pairs of long, iron bows arched up into the air, creating a safe railing between the stage and the North Platte River Brittany could see below. *Safe as any Iowan bridge,* she thought, relieved.

As the wheels dropped off the wooden planks, safely on the other side, the driver called out, "Rustic Hotel up ahead, next stop."

"Will you be staying at the hotel?" Mrs. Munson asked Brittany, stooping to pick her reticule off the floor.

"No. Mr. Myers should be waiting to pick me up." At least, Brittany hoped he was.

"Be glad," Mrs. Munson muttered for her ears alone. "There are people who call it no second-rate affair, but I've heard too many stories about lice and dirty bedding to believe them."

"Then I'll add that to my list of blessings," Brittany whispered in return.

Mrs. Munson laughed. "Now that's a good idea, to count your blessings when you travel. Soon as I climb onto a stage, I tend to forget that there are such things as blessings."

Brittany stared out the window as the stage swayed past a couple of barns and corrals. Then the driver called out, "Whoa!" and the stage slowed to a rattling stop in front of a low, single-story, log structure, obviously the Rustic Hotel. To Brittany's eyes, the building seemed shabby and in need of a good day of repair. Its sod roof sagged, the porch railing was broken in one place, and the curtains at the window were crooked. *I'm glad I don't have to stay here,* she decided.

The stage door swung open, and one by one the passengers began to scramble out. *How am I going to recognize Mr. Myers?* Brittany suddenly wondered, *Suppose he isn't here?*

As Mrs. Munson took her turn climbing down, Brittany knew it was time to leave the safety of the stage. She motioned Lars and Brenna ahead of her; then, drawing a deep breath, she stepped down from the stage herself. Nothing had ever felt so good as the solid ground beneath her feet—and the ability to stretch out her legs. Basking in the freedom to move, she stepped away from the stage and took a good look around her. The Rustic Hotel stood a fair distance from the fort, she realized. Apart from a few outbuildings and the stage company's barns and corrals, no other buildings stood nearby. She could see Fort Laramie farther off, a flag snapping in the breeze above it. Several long buildings dominated the fort, probably for the soldiers stationed there. The sheer size of them made the other houses and buildings seem dwarfed in comparison. It was not the bustling town she had hoped it would be, and Brittany had to swallow back her disappointment. *It's better than nothing,* she reminded herself, but inwardly wondered.

"What now?" Lars asked, his eyes wide as he stared at their surroundings.

"We need to find Mr. Myers," Brittany said, looking around her. The station area was crowded at the moment, making her search more difficult. Mr. Myers—what did she know about Mr. Myers? She presumed he was an older man; a quick glance showed that the station abounded with older-looking men. Brittany bit her lip and raked her mind for any other details about the man. She had none. Mr. Myers hadn't written a full-length description of himself. He'd kept his letter short and sweet, not including a word that strayed from the business at hand.

Just as Brittany began to panic, her gaze met with a man across the station. He looked rather uncertain, as if he were looking for someone. He was an older man—and yes, he was coming her way. He plowed through the crowd milling about the station area and walked right up to her.

"Miss Haines?" he asked, not cracking even the trace of a smile.

"Ah—yes." Brittany pulled Lars and Brenna closer to her. "Are you Mr. Myers?"

He gave a brief nod. "Where's your bags?"

"Got 'em right here," the driver said, coming up behind Brittany. Mr. Myers took them with another nod, and motioning for Brittany to follow, he set off through the tangle of people gathered about the stage.

He certainly isn't much for talking, Brittany thought, taking Lars and Brenna by the hand and hurrying to catch up with him. *Or smiling, for that matter.*

She stumbled after him, noting that Mrs. Munson appeared to have reunited with her husband. She and a man dressed in crisp, blue uniform stood arm in arm with matching smiles on their faces. Brittany bit back a sigh, wishing that she had family here to meet her. Reaching her destination at last was not very rewarding when welcomed by a complete stranger.

This isn't the end of the journey, she reminded herself. *When I reach Northridge, the real end of the journey, Clem will be there, and that will make this whole trip worth the effort.*

But she couldn't wholly dissolve the nagging doubts as she looked at Mr. Myers's rigid shoulders and wondered *what* exactly she had agreed to in signing that contract.

Mr. Myers led them around the corner of the hotel, and Brittany searched for a wagon. There was none that she could see. Several horses stood tethered to a hitching rail, quietly waiting for their owners to return, and an old man leaned against the wall of the hotel, thumbs hooked in his pockets. Mr. Myers steered straight toward him, and the man grinned.

"Looks like you got 'em all right, Timmy," he said, looking at Mr. Myers.

Timmy? Brittany had to hide her smile. The boyish name seemed incongruous with the frowning man in front of her.

The old man came toward her, his grin spreading even wider across his face. "Howdy, and welcome to Wyoming Territory, Miss Haines," he said. "My name's Johnny Myers."

"Myers?" Brittany stared at him, suddenly bewildered. She looked from the weathered face of the old man in front of her to the slightly younger man who also bore the last name Myers. Two Mr. Myers? No one had mentioned this to her.

"So which of you is the man with the wife who needs help?" she asked, feeling the heat rush to her face.

Johnny's eyebrows rose. Then he began to laugh, a kind of laugh that made Brittany feel not as if he were making fun of her but rather that he was simply sharing a good joke.

"I can see how that might be confusing," he said, eyes twinkling. "Timmy's the one who needs help, or rather, Timmy's wife. I'm just Timmy's uncle—and I ain't got a wife."

"Oh." Brittany wasn't sure what else to say. "I–I'm sorry, Mr. Myers."

Johnny's eyebrows lifted again. "For what? Givin' me the best joke I've heard in a long spell? That ain't nothin' to be sorry about. And by the way, just call me Johnny. That's what everyone else does."

"Fine, and you can call me Brittany." She offered him a tentative smile, liking the old man already.

"Better get movin'." Tim Myers made an impatient motion. He then seemed to notice Lars and Brenna for the first time, and he frowned. "Are those both yours?"

The answer seemed obvious to Brittany. "Yes, they're my siblings. You told me they could come."

"Thought there was only one." Mr. Myers frowned at the two children for a moment, making them shrink behind Brittany's skirts. Brittany's chest tightened. What was going through Mr. Myers's mind? Was he thinking of sending them back to Iowa?

At last, Mr. Myers shrugged. "Guess there ain't nothing we can do 'bout it now. The kids will just have to ride double; only brought one extra horse."

Brittany was sure she heard him wrong. "One *what*?"

"Horse." Mr. Myers looked at her as if she were a small child. "Ever ridden a horse before?"

Brittany stared from Mr. Myers to the horses tethered to the hitching rail, the connection slowly forming itself. "No! I–I haven't ridden a horse in years. I–I can't—"

"You're gonna have to," Mr. Myers interrupted. "Part of living out West is knowin' how to ride. Won't get too far if you don't, and you ain't gettin' home today if you don't."

Home? The word made Brittany shake her head. Home was in Iowa, not this rough, horseback riding, Western land, and just now she wished with all her heart that she had never left it. Her gaze slid toward the horses again. One of them stamped the ground with a big, powerful-looking hoof—and all the horses were so *tall*. She swallowed hard. True, she had ridden horseback when she was younger. But the horses she had always ridden were her pa's gentle old plow horses who never went faster than a bone-jarring trot. And always when she had ridden, it was with Clem safely behind her, holding the reins and guiding the animal. She had never been the one in control of the horse—and she didn't wish to be now.

"Look, girl." Mr. Myers's voice cut through her thoughts. "Iffen we don't git movin' now, we ain't gonna make it home today. It's a half day's ride from Northridge to the fort, and we're gonna be gettin' home after dark as it is."

"Don't you worry none about the horse," Johnny said, sounding sympathetic. "Major here is well broke, and he's used to carryin' a lady. He won't give you no trouble."

Brittany wanted nothing more than to run back to the stage and beg for a return trip back East, but she knew that was impossible. She forced a smile, feeling as if her face might crack from the effort. "If you're sure the horse is safe—"

"Oh, he is, he is," Johnny said, leading her over to a dark brown gelding sporting a star between his eyes. "This here is old Major. He'll teach you a whole lot about ridin' in no time."

Brittany could feel her smile tremble. "Hello, Major."

"Stick your foot here in the stirrup, and I'll give you a bit of a boost up." Johnny gave her arm an encouraging pat. The saddle, Brittany noted with dismay, was not a sidesaddle. It was definitely made for a man, not a woman. It hardly seemed proper to sit astride the horse like a man, but it appeared she had no choice. She feared that if she voiced one more complaint, Mr. Myers would lose his temper with her entirely.

Brittany did as Johnny directed and in a moment found herself seated high up on Major's back.

"Good," Johnny said, taking a step back.

Clutching the saddle horn with both hands, Brittany risked a glance at the ground and immediately felt dizzy. Major seemed even taller when she was on him. Her ankles were showing, and she knew she should try to rearrange her skirt so she looked somewhat proper, but just now the idea of releasing her grip on the saddle horn seemed like a bad idea.

"You'll do just fine," Johnny assured her once more before mounting his own horse. Brittany saw that Lars and Brenna were both seated on their horse as well—Brenna in the front, Lars in the back, just like her and Clem when they were younger. Both of them grinned as if they were actually enjoying themselves.

"Time to move on," Mr. Myers said, turning his horse toward the road. Brittany felt a moment of panic. How did she get Major to move? Or turned around in the first place?

Johnny came to her rescue. "Pull gently on the reins and say, 'Back.'"

Brittany nodded and tugged on the reins. To her surprise, Major moved back from the hitching rail with no hesitation. Brittany looked to Johnny for her next direction.

"Use the reins to guide him toward Timmy," he said. "Don't yank on the reins or nothin'. He'll know what you want soon as he feels the rein on his neck."

Brittany was amazed by how quickly Major picked up on what she wanted. *This is actually almost fun,* she thought as Major trotted after Mr. Myers.

"There, I knew you'd get it," Johnny said, beaming as he rode alongside her.

Brittany smiled at him. "Thanks for your help. I wasn't expecting to ride horseback, at least not right away."

"We would've brought the wagon, but it's gone with the boys on the cattle drive. One thing you can be glad of is that the trip is a whole lot faster by horseback than wagon—wagon takes over twice as long, and ain't so comfortable neither."

Brittany disagreed about the comfortable part, but she was glad to hear that they would be at Northridge faster. At least riding horseback had one benefit.

Brittany let a moment pass before she spoke again. "You know my brother Clem?"

"Know him?" Johnny said. "I most surely do. He's a fine man, one of the finest we have at Northridge, iffen you want my opinion."

"He was always the best of brothers." Brittany felt her heart warm at Johnny's praise for Clem. "He was always looking out for me and was always willing to let me tag along, even if he had friends with him."

"He's a good man. And more than that, he's a fine Christian. He knows his Bible inside out, and he ain't ashamed of it like most of the boys. And he don't mind spendin' time with an old man like me neither."

"I can't wait to see him again." Somehow, Brittany knew that Johnny would understand her excitement.

"I can imagine. And he's sure gonna get the surprise of his life when he gets home and sees you."

Brittany frowned, puzzled by his words. "Home? Home from where?"

Johnny looked sideways at her. "Oh, you don't know, do you?"

"Don't know what?" Brittany's heart began to pound.

"He's gone."

"Gone! Gone where?" Panic filled her and made her voice squeak.

"Relax. He's gone on the cattle drive to Cheyenne, but he'll be back in three weeks, Lord willing."

"Three weeks! But—" Panic gave way to helplessness, and Brittany felt tears sting her eyes. After this long trip, covering hundreds of miles by train, stage, and now horseback, Clem wouldn't be waiting to meet her at the end of the journey. How could he do this to her? "I wrote to him, telling him when I would be here."

Johnny cleared his throat. "Ah, yes, your letter—"

Brittany swiveled her gaze to his face. More bad news?

"I'm afraid Clem never got your letter," Johnny said, his voice apologetic. "He'd already left by the time it came."

This can't be happening. Brittany felt as if she were caught in a terrible nightmare, only there was no waking up from this one. Clem wasn't here to meet her—and didn't know she was coming. The trip was fast turning into a disaster.

CHAPTER

3

Brittany didn't dare look at Johnny again as they left Fort Laramie behind and set off for Northridge. To hear that the very brother she had made this trip for was gone and didn't even know she was coming was overpowering news. She stared straight ahead of her, torn between fear over being in an unfamiliar land with two strangers for company and—anger. To be angry at Clem was unreasonable. He had done nothing wrong; it wasn't his fault that she was here.

No, mostly Brittany was angry with herself. Angry that she had put herself in this awkward situation by leaping ahead of Clem and deciding to come here. Now, with time to think as the miles ticked by separating her from Fort Laramie, she began to wonder if she *had* made a hasty decision in coming here. She knew nothing about Wyoming Territory besides what Clem had told her in his brief letters. Nor about what her new job was going to entail. Yes, she had been hired to help Mrs. Myers with her housework, but what did she really know? And, she suddenly thought to wonder, why had the Myerses had trouble keeping help around for more than a few weeks? Clem hadn't given her any particulars; he'd had no clue that she would be interested in coming West to join him. He thought she was still sitting safely at home in Des Moines stitching quilts.

Oh, if only he knew!

Lord, forgive me if I've rushed ahead of You in coming here. Perhaps I was impulsive in agreeing to work for the Myers. But I know that You are able to work even when we make mistakes, and I ask that You would be working here in this situation. Help me to trust in You and to realize that my protection comes not from man but from You. Help me to serve the Myerses to the best of my ability, no matter how they treat me. And, Lord, help me to wait patiently for Clem to return. It's going to be a long three weeks until he comes. Brittany blinked back tears. *Lord, let Your name be glorified in all of this. In Jesus's name I pray. Amen.*

Brittany drew a long breath and looked up at the sky. *This is only the first of many times that Clem and I are going to be apart,* Brittany realized, a truth she had tried to deny up to now. But it was the truth. There would be times, sometimes long stretches, when their jobs would prevent them from seeing each other. And, now that he had a girl, she would claim a fair portion of his time as well. *It's time to grow up,* Brittany told herself. *There will be no more fits because Clem is gone. Starting now.*

With that decision made, Brittany forced her attention away from her doubts and fears. She looked about her, noting that the fort was nothing more than a small dot behind them. *There goes my last connection with home,* she thought, feeling a tug of sadness.

Beyond that, there was nothing else worth noticing. The view was no different from horseback than from the stage window—grass, sagebrush, and open sky. Brittany sighed, wondering if she would ever come to love this land like Clem obviously did.

"This sure isn't Iowa," she whispered.

"Reckon it ain't." Johnny's voice startled Brittany. She hadn't realized that he was still riding alongside her. "Not that I know anything about Iowa."

"Did Clem ever tell you about growing up in Iowa?" Brittany asked, grateful that Johnny was more talkative than his nephew.

Johnny shrugged. "Some. But most of our talk was about the here and now; life here out West, and most recently, about his girl." Johnny grinned. "That young man was bound and determined to become one of us through and through. And I'd say he's managed that pretty well. I can't tell much difference between him and a born westerner, except that his talk sounds a little more educated."

His words sent little shivers of dread through Brittany. Clem was like a *westerner*? But westerners were rough and uncouth—at least in Aunt Ida's opinion. Brittany herself wasn't sure how she felt about westerners. She liked Johnny, rough speech and all. Mr. Myers? Well, she wasn't so sure about him. Every time he looked at her, she felt herself tense, preparing for him to scold her. But he was by no means savage or vicious. When he wasn't giving her the look that plainly said he thought city women were ridiculous fools who knew nothing about anything, he was all right.

But they were only two westerners, not enough to judge all westerners in general. And the idea of Clem being any different than the laughing, teasing, gentle boy she remembered didn't sit well with Brittany. But five years had passed since she had last seen him. Of course he would have changed. Brittany herself had changed. When he left all those years ago, she had been only thirteen, a young girl fresh off the farm overwhelmed by the booming city of Des Moines. And now here she was, an eighteen-year-old young woman fresh from the city and completely overwhelmed by this country life of her brother's. Times had changed, leaving their mark on them both.

Before Brittany could fret more about Clem, Johnny spoke up again. "Pay no never mind to what Clem's already told me. Tell me about yourself."

Brittany hesitated, wondering where she should start. "I grew up on a farm in Iowa," she began. "It was just Clem and me for a while, and we did everything together. He let me go fishing with him, or tree climbing, or sledding." She smiled. "The trouble was that he was always the one who decided what we would do, so I missed out on all the girl things like tea parties and playing dolls. But I liked Clem's version of fun, and we got on well. Then Lars was born, followed by Brenna." Brittany's gaze turned to the two children riding ahead of her. "Mama passed away when Brenna was born. That was a hard blow on all of us, but we made do." Brittany didn't mention the many struggles she had faced as a young girl trying to fill in Mama's place for her father, two brothers, and a baby sister. Nor did she mention the pain of growing into a young woman with no mother to turn to with her questions and problems. Those were things she preferred to leave in the past.

"We lost Papa two years after Mama died. Aunt Ida came from Des Moines to take us to live with her, so we sold the farm, packed up our things, and moved to the city with her. All of us kids adjusted to the city—except Clem. Clem hated Des Moines. He didn't last a month before he began to talk of going West. He was only sixteen, and Aunt Ida tried to talk him out of leaving, but his mind was made up, and nothing could change it."

"That sounds like our boy," Johnny said, smiling. "Stubborn as a rusty old bear trap."

"Some things never change." *And some things do—sometimes more than we like.*

As the miles slowly passed underfoot and the sun dipped low in the western horizon, Brittany felt heartily sick of travel. *I never want to go anywhere again, never,* she thought as the first of the stars appeared in the sky—and according to Johnny, they still were far from Northridge.

If you never travel anywhere again, you'll be stuck here in the West forever, the rational side of her mind whispered. Brittany wanted to groan. Neither the prospect of traveling nor of staying here for the rest of her life was pleasant.

On and on they traveled, mounting one hill only to have another rise up in front of them. Brittany felt as if she were being smothered alive by the winding hills and the dark night. How could Mr. Myers tell where they were going? With the setting of the sun, she had lost all sense of direction.

Sleepiness began to steal in on Brittany as the miles passed by. It became harder and harder to stifle her yawns and keep the waves of weariness from overpowering her. *Focus on something other than how tired you are,* she told herself; but what that would be, she didn't know. It was too dark to see anything past the horses, and there was nothing to think about besides the now-familiar homesickness and longing for Clem. She would have talked more with Johnny, but he was riding up ahead alongside Mr. Myers now. The steady sound of the horses' hoofbeats numbed her senses, making it all too easy to drift away on a cloud of sleep—

Brittany jerked herself upright just in time to keep from falling. *Stay awake,* she scolded herself. *The last thing the Myerses need right now is for their newly hired help to fall off her horse and break her neck before she even gets to Northridge.*

The near fall banished all her sleepiness and gave her a clear mind once again. But after only a few minutes the drowsy feelings returned in full force, and she could feel herself drifting away again.

"Here we are." Mr. Myers's voice roused Brittany from her state of half-sleep. Major was no longer moving and stood alongside the other horses, his head bowed. *We're at Northridge,* Brittany realized, coming fully awake. She looked around her, straining to see what Clem's beloved Northridge looked like, but it was too dark to see any more than the small log cabin in front of them and a few other dim shapes that might have been buildings nearby.

"Climb on down," Johnny said from beside her, and Brittany realized that both he and Mr. Myers had already dismounted while she sat gawking. Refusing to blush, she swung her leg over Major's back, holding her breath until her foot landed safely on the ground. She kicked her other foot free from the stirrup and began to turn around when, without warning, her legs gave way beneath her, and she crumpled to the ground in an unlady-like heap.

"You all right?" Johnny appeared above her, his face concerned.

Brittany's cheeks began to burn, and she struggled to get to her feet again. "I–I don't know what happened. I–I've never done that before."

"Never ridden that far neither, I'll bet." Johnny reached out to help her up. "Don't worry none; a little fall like that is just your muscles' way of sayin' they don't take too kindly to the way you've been usin' 'em. Let me give you a hand."

Brittany accepted the hand he offered her—or, as it turned out, his whole arm. She had to lean on him for support more than she would have liked as they walked toward the Myers' house.

"Where'd Lars and Brenna go?" she asked, looking around for the two children.

"Timmy'll make sure they get in, and he'll make sure your things get in, too."

Brittany murmured a thank you, feeling terribly helpless. As they started forward again, Lars and Brenna raced past, jumping onto the porch steps and turning to wait for their sister to catch up. They seemed to have gained a burst of energy and didn't appear at all sore from the trip. Brittany sighed. Not even Johnny, who must be in his sixties at least, seemed bothered by the long ride.

The door of the cabin swung open as they reached the steps. "Hurry in, everyone," a woman said, motioning them in. She was shorter than Brittany, with silvery gray hair pulled back in a snood, and her face, though seamed with age, shone with a welcoming smile. Brittany stared at her. This must be Mrs. Myers. *The* Mrs. Myers she had traveled so far to assist. Looking at the woman with her crisply pressed calico dress and neat hair, not a strand out of place, made Brittany conscious of her own appearance. Her wrinkled, travel-stained dress, her tumbling hair, the layer of dust that covered every inch of her. But there was nothing she could do to change that. Johnny was already ushering her up the steps and into the house.

Mrs. Myers took control. "Sit down at the table, all of you. I'm sure you must be famished."

Her words and the aroma of something cooking on the stove made Brittany suddenly realize that she was starving. Lunchtime seemed to have taken place a very long time ago, and now that she thought of it, she hadn't eaten very much because she had felt so nervous. Lowering herself into one of the high-backed wooden chairs, Brittany wondered how sitting down could feel so good when she'd been sitting all day.

Mrs. Myers set a bowl of stew in front of her, and although somewhere in the back of her mind the thought niggled that she ought to be the one serving, Brittany took it gratefully. She dug into the stew, not paying attention to the voices that hummed around her. But her bowl wasn't even half empty before a wave of sleepiness rolled over her again, making her set down her spoon and blink quickly to keep from giving way to it.

Mrs. Myers appeared beside her. "Come along, dear. You look exhausted."

Brittany had no strength to argue. "I'm sorry. I shouldn't be so tired—" A yawn cut off the rest of what she had planned to say.

"Nonsense." Mrs. Myers led the way into a bedroom just off the kitchen. "You have every right to be tired. It's nearly midnight, and there is nothing so exhausting as travel."

Mrs. Myers tried to strike a match to light the lamp, but Brittany noticed that her fingers shook, making it difficult.

"Let me do that," she said, stepping over.

Mrs. Myers handed her the matches, and Brittany struck one with no trouble.

"My fingers." Mrs. Myers shook her head. "They don't work so well. Arthritis, you know."

Brittany studied the woman a little more closely. She hadn't been sure what condition she would find Mrs. Myers in. Bedridden had been the idea that stuck most in her head. Brittany noticed that Mrs. Myers limped slightly as she walked and moved slowly but still seemed able to get around relatively well. Tomorrow, Brittany promised herself, she would have to talk to Mrs. Myers and see exactly what her new job would entail. But for now—

Brittany yawned again.

"Tim brought your bags in." Mrs. Myers motioned to the corner where her luggage lay in a heap. "There's water in the basin on the dresser, and you can take a bath tomorrow if you wish. I'll send your siblings in when they're finished eating. The three of you will have to share this room; you and your sister can share the bed, and your little brother can have the cot." She pointed to a cot standing against the wall.

"I'm sure this isn't quite what you're used to, but it's our best, and we're glad that you decided to come." Mrs. Myers folded her hands in front of her. "And I'm glad you brought your siblings with you. I'm looking forward to having children in the house."

"I'm glad to be here," Brittany said. That much wasn't a lie. She had never in her life been so happy to have her feet firmly planted on solid ground. "And the room is fine, just fine."

Mrs. Myers's face relaxed into a smile, and she turned to leave. "Just call if you need anything."

Shouldn't I be saying that to you? Brittany wondered as the door shut behind her. She crossed the room to the basin, sitting right where Mrs. Myers had pointed. Using the washcloth sitting beside it, Brittany washed the worst of the dust from her skin and thought longingly of the big, claw-foot bathtub at Aunt Ida's in Des Moines. She didn't have to ask to know that there would be no such tub here at Northridge. She made a face. The idea of bathing in a tiny tub like she did as a child on the farm was not appealing. *But it will at least do a better job than a sponge bath,* she thought, putting the washcloth down in the now filthy basin.

Brittany unpinned her hair next and ran her brush through it, trying to remove at least some of the dust. She was still far from the prescribed one-hundred strokes when she set the brush aside, and slipping into a clean nightgown, climbed into bed, pulling the covers up to her chin. The bed felt every bit as wonderful as she had imagined it would.

I've made it to Clem's West, she thought, leaning over to blow out the lamp. *And now he's farther east than I am. How am I ever going to last three weeks here without him?*

CHAPTER

4

Brittany awakened to the sound of birdsong and the brightness of sunlight streaming across the bed. For a moment she lay still, puzzling over where she was. Certainly not Aunt Ida's.

Then she remembered. She had made it. She was finally at Northridge. She couldn't keep herself from smiling, a feeling of immense satisfaction washing over her. She had traveled hundreds of miles with two children in tow, and, despite Aunt Ida's dire predictions, she was safely at Northridge. For an instant Brittany was tempted to feel proud of what she had accomplished. But remembering how much prayer was going up on her behalf by people such as the Browns and Aunt Ida, she felt humbled instead. *The Lord is the one who has given us a safe journey, and the credit for our arrival here goes to Him,* she thought, running her fingers along the edge of the quilt covering her.

As Brittany came more fully awake, her mind took off. After meeting Mrs. Myers the night before, she was convinced that she would be a sweet woman to work for. *If that's the case, then why so much trouble keeping help around?* she wondered, unease stealing in on her peace. If Mrs. Myers wasn't the problem, then obviously there must be something else that drove the help away. More than ever, she regretted not waiting for Clem's response. He could have answered any questions she had, and he would have stopped her if she were making a bad choice in agreeing to work for the Myerses for a year. Now she was stuck whether the job went well or not.

Brittany pushed aside her nagging doubts, refusing to dwell on them—or the pain that Clem was gone. Today marked the start of her new life, and she would not let her thoughts mar this beautiful morning.

Brittany sat up and swung her feet over the side of the bed, wondering where Lars and Brenna were. Mrs. Myers had said something about sending them in when they were finished with their supper; Brittany must have fallen asleep before they came. The clothes scattered across the floor testified that they had been in the room at one time, but they must have already slipped away.

She paused on the edge of the bed and let her gaze travel around the room, taking notice of her surroundings for the first time. The room wasn't fancy, the furniture consisting of one dresser, Lars's cot, and her and Brenna's bed. The log walls were completely bare except for a row of pegs for hanging clothes on one wall and plain brown curtains around the room's only window. A quilt on the bed and a rug on the floor added a touch of color to the otherwise dark room. It wasn't at all like her room in Des Moines, with its colorful wallpaper, carpet, and drapes. But it was at least clean, and Brittany let herself think that perhaps once she adjusted to its bare simplicity, she might even come to like the room.

Hopping out of bed, she crossed the room to the window, eager for her first real look at Northridge. Immediately her eyes fell on a big unpainted wooden barn. It was shaped much like the barn on the farm where she had grown up in Iowa, hayloft and all, and Brittany felt as if she were suddenly flashed back to her childhood days. She wouldn't have been surprised at all had she seen her father emerge from its door, full milk pail in hand, whistling loudly enough to be heard from the house. Feeling a sharp stab of longing for the big man with the even bigger heart whom she had called Papa, she pulled her gaze away from the barn. There was no use wishing for the past. It was gone, never to return.

Near the barn there was a long, low-roofed building—the bunkhouse, Brittany presumed. That would be where Clem lived when he returned. Not too far from the bunkhouse were two similar-looking little cabins. Brittany had to dig through her mind, thinking of every fragment of Clem's descriptions of Northridge before she could figure out their purposes. The simpler of the two, the one with the big metal stovepipe sticking out of its roof, was the cook shack more than likely. And now that she thought of it, Brittany remembered Clem speaking of a man named Johnny who had his own little cabin on the ranch. The second cabin was probably his place. Brittany felt rather proud of herself for being able to identify each of the buildings—and without ever having set foot on a ranch before.

A rattle from the kitchen reminded Brittany that the morning was wasting away while she still stood around in her nightgown, not even dressed. Yanking the curtains shut, just to be safe, she hurried over to her bags and began to rummage around for a clean outfit.

By the time she was dressed and had her hair fixed, Brittany's stomach began to complain that it needed food. *I hope Lars and Brenna have been behaving themselves,* she thought, crossing to the bedroom door. *And I hope the Myerses don't think I'll be sleeping in every morning like this!*

That thought was enough to make her hurry her steps as she opened the door and entered the kitchen. She stopped, however, when she realized that the kitchen was vacant and that she was alone in the house. She knew someone must be nearby; she'd heard noises in here not long before.

Her gaze wandered toward the clock on a shelf on the wall. It read ten thirty, making her gasp. Everyone must have finished their breakfast long ago while she slept on.

Just then the outside door swung open, and a young woman with brown hair piled high on her head entered the kitchen, humming to herself.

Her brown eyes fell on Brittany, and a smile lit her face. "Good morning! I see you finally woke up."

Who is this? Brittany wondered. She couldn't be the Myerses' daughter; Clem had written that the Myerses were childless. Besides, if this young woman lived here, the Myerses wouldn't have needed Brittany's help. But no other ideas came to mind.

"Have a seat," the young woman said, taking over the Myerses' kitchen with an ease that plainly said she was comfortable here. "I saved you some breakfast; I'll pour myself some coffee and join you if that's all right."

"Sure." Brittany sat as the young woman instructed her. She watched the woman pull a plate of food for her out of the warming oven, still sorting through Clem's letters for any mention of a young woman here at the Myerses.

The young woman set a plate before Brittany and sat in the chair across from her, coffee cup in hand. She gave Brittany another smile. "We've been so eager for your arrival. Clem told me about you, but I never dreamed I'd get to meet you and your siblings. I do believe you could have knocked me over with a feather when Mrs. Myers showed me your letter saying you were coming. It's going to be wonderful to have another young woman in the area, especially Clem's family. And, by the way, your two siblings are just the cutest things. They've been keeping us amused this morning."

Brittany tried to absorb all that the young woman was saying, but it made no sense to her. "I'm sorry, but who are you?" she asked when the young woman paused for breath.

The young woman stared across the table at her, then suddenly burst into peals of laughter. Brittany wasn't sure what she found so funny, but she couldn't help but laugh along. The young woman had an infectious laugh.

"Forgive me," the woman gasped out at last. "I completely forgot to introduce myself. I'm Morgan Norris. My Uncle Dave owns a ranch a couple hours' ride away. And Clem probably wrote to you that we're courting."

Courting? The pieces suddenly fell into place. "You're the girl Clem wrote about. I should have remembered your name."

"Well, I should have thought to tell you my name in the first place." Morgan laughed again. "Clem's already told me so much about you that I feel as if I already know you, and I forgot that you couldn't be expected to know me."

Brittany liked the young woman already, and any fears she'd had about meeting Clem's mystery girl disappeared. She should have known that her brother would make a good choice.

"You said you lived two hours away?" Brittany asked.

Morgan nodded. "Close enough that I'm over here often."

"Two hours seems like a long trip to me."

Morgan shrugged. "Depends on how you look at it. There are more cows than people around these parts, and we're all pretty well spread out. Two hours isn't so far. Besides, I love the ride over here. I'll take any chance to be out in the fresh air on horseback."

"You *like* to ride?" Brittany couldn't quite keep the incredulity from her voice.

"Love it. Uncle Dave taught me to love being up on a horse from the time I first moved out here. I had a wonderful time helping Mr. Myers get Major used to having a woman on his back." Morgan smiled. "Mr. Myers asked if I would work with Major a couple years ago when their first helper was coming. He thought that if Major ran away with her on her first day here in Wyoming, she probably wouldn't be sticking around."

"I knew the Myerses had hired help before—"

"Oh, yes. You're the fourth attempt."

"Attempt?"

Morgan's eyes gleamed. "Two years ago, the Myerses decided they needed some help, so they hired a young woman from New York. She did a good job, but before two weeks were out, she announced that she was engaged to a local cowboy and that she wouldn't be able to work for the Myerses anymore. They couldn't stop her from marrying the man and moving away, but she did give them the address of her sister, saying that she would certainly be willing to come and help out. The Myerses hired her, and she worked out even better than her sister. Only trouble was, she didn't last any longer than her sister—she was married within a month. The Myerses were a bit frustrated by then, so when they next sent out an ad for help in the paper, they wrote flat out that they wanted an older woman. And one who was not good looking." Morgan laughed. "They got a woman who fit their description perfectly. But that woman was only around for a few weeks longer than the two sisters before she was married as well. Mr. Myers was outraged! He vowed that he would never send another ticket to a woman unless she promised not to marry for a good long while, long enough for them to at least feel their tickets had been paid for."

"Well, they needn't worry about me. I have no intentions of marrying anytime soon."

"Given their bad experiences, they weren't taking any chances." Morgan raised an eyebrow. "And you never know. You could change your mind when the proposals start pouring in."

"I hardly think that will be the case." Brittany smiled.

"Better think again. By the end of your year here, you'll have a whole list of men you've turned down."

"Impossible." Brittany stared at her, Aunt Ida's stories of desperate men hunting for a wife to haul back to their cabins leaping to her mind.

"More than possible. It's almost a guarantee."

"How many proposals have you had?" Brittany asked, not caring that her question went against all the etiquette her mother and aunt had taught her.

"I lost track at half a dozen."

It sounded awful to Brittany. Nothing less than awful.

"You could have a nice future here when your year is up." Morgan's eyes twinkled. "Perhaps I could introduce you to a few people. There are a couple of especially nice men who work over at the Bryan brothers' ranch. And then the foreman over at Jones's is a fine man; he has his own cabin at the Joneses', and a good wage, so he's able to support a wife and children. And up at our ranch, we've got the nicest man—"

"No! I'll never marry a Western man."

Morgan's eyes widened. "Why not? Is there a man waiting for you at home?"

The image of William flashed through Brittany's mind, but she pushed it away. She didn't care for William in that way. "No, there's no one waiting for me."

"Then, why not? Don't you want to get married and have children of your own someday?"

"Well, yes. But I'm not going to marry a man who has no sense of manners or—or civilization, or morality, or anything."

"And you think that's what westerners are like?" Morgan raised her eyebrows. "Your brother's a westerner."

"But he—" Brittany stopped short. She sounded exactly like Aunt Ida. In Des Moines she hadn't appreciated Aunt Ida's judgments, but now here she was, citing them right off to Morgan. When had she let Aunt Ida's ideas take root in her mind?

"There are plenty of fine westerners you could marry," Morgan said, her voice allowing no argument. "You'll see for yourself when all the men get back. No, they aren't perfect, and some of them are best to keep away from, but isn't that the case anywhere you go? For the most part, they're just ordinary men like your brother, men who have learned to put in a hard day of work and to swallow the hard stuff of life without complaining. And, let me tell you, not all of them are crazy to find a wife. There are some who really couldn't care less. But almost all of them have respect for women, and they won't overstep their bounds. I can assure you that I feel just as safe in a crowd of Western men as I do in my own house."

Brittany felt that she had been given a good reprimand, and she wondered if she should apologize.

"But let me give you a word of advice." Morgan's smile reappeared. "If Able Zimmerman asks you to marry him, and he will, give him a firm no."

"Who's Able Zimmerman?" Brittany asked. She disliked even the sound of his name.

"Unfortunately, he's your nearest neighbor. He has a claim not far from here, and if there's any trouble around, it can usually be traced back to him. He proposes to every woman who passes through here; he's so quick in asking that once he accidentally proposed to a married woman. Whatever you do, tell him no."

"Does that mean you have some experience in dealing with him?"

Morgan grimaced. "Yes. He comes around at least once a year, just to see if I've changed my mind."

Brittany was sure she didn't want to meet this man. Ever. He sounded like one of the characters out of Aunt Ida's horror stories.

"Who are our other neighbors?" Brittany asked, eager to change the subject.

"There's the Bryan brothers and the Joneses, but no one else close enough to mention."

"Do either the Bryans or the Joneses have children?"

"Oh, yes. Both the Bryan brothers and the Joneses have a whole troop of them."

"Lars and Brenna will be glad to hear that." Brittany suddenly wondered where her two siblings were. It was too quiet for them to be nearby.

"They're out in the barn with the kittens," Morgan said, reading her thoughts.

"And what about Mrs. Myers? Where's she?"

"Resting. Yesterday wore her out, I'm afraid. The dear woman tries to push herself too hard." Morgan looked up at the clock. "Look at the time. I should have had dinner started long ago, and here I am sitting and letting precious time waste away."

Brittany stood with her, picking up her empty plate to put in the dish tub. "I'll help you with lunch."

"Oh, no." Morgan waved her hand. "Why don't you go take a look around the ranch? This is your first day here."

Brittany felt that she had already seen quite enough of the ranch. "I'm here to help, not sightsee. Really, I do want to help. Please."

Morgan shrugged. "Well, if you insist, I won't deprive you of the pleasure. I'm going to grind up some coffee beans now, and you can start mixing up some biscuits."

Brittany agreed, relieved to be given a job that she knew how to do. She'd already displayed her ignorance in Western ways quite enough.

As she began measuring out flour into a mixing bowl, Brittany thought that if she could stay in the kitchen all the time, she would be happy. At least in the kitchen, no one could find fault with her or shake their heads at her city-girl ways. And she could avoid any men desperate for a wife. Maybe Morgan was right about there being plenty of fine men around, but that still didn't change Brittany's mind. She couldn't bear to spend the rest of her life in Wyoming. A year was one thing, but a lifetime? Never. She doubted there was any man worth staying in this land of cattle and sagebrush for.

"Tomorrow we will be having a normal day," Brittany said to Lars and Brenna as they prepared for bed that night.

"Normal?" Lars scrunched up his nose. "What does that mean? What is normal?"

Brittany bit her lip. He had a right to ask the question. She herself wasn't too sure what "normal" meant lately.

"'Normal' means back to school for you and Brenna, mister," she told her younger brother. "Tomorrow we'll figure out what you and Brenna's new chores will be." And for her, it meant that she would be taking over most of the household work. She'd talked with Mrs. Myers earlier that day. Starting tomorrow, she would be the one responsible for putting meals on the table, cleaning the house, washing laundry, and any other odd jobs that might come up. She was confident that her new job would go well. After all, she'd practically taken over running the house when Mama passed away years before.

Lars groaned. "I don't mind chores, but why do we need school? We're in the middle of nowhere out here. Who cares?"

"I do." Brittany arched an eyebrow at him. "And someday you'll be thankful that I made you keep up with your schooling."

Lars shook his head but made no further comment.

"School sure is going to be different now," Brenna said from her place on the bed. "It's just going to be me and Lars, nobody else." She frowned at the flame flickering in the lamp on the dresser.

"It will be different." Brittany sat down beside Brenna and hugged her close. "But we're just going to have to get used to 'different'. Everything is different out here." She amended her words. "Everything is different except for God. He never changes, and He has told us that He will never leave us or forsake us. We have to trust that. Even here in Wyoming Territory."

"We don't have a church near here," Brenna said, still frowning.

"No, but we don't need a building to worship God. We can worship Him anywhere as long as we come to Him with the right heart and attitude. It is how we worship Him on the inside that matters most, not where we are."

"I'm still going to miss our church."

"I know." Brittany smoothed back the girl's hair. "So will I."

"There are things you miss about Iowa?" Lars asked, tilting his head to the side.

"Oh, yes. Many things." Brittany refrained from saying just how many things she missed in Iowa. Or of how homesick she was. They might all end up in tears if she did that.

"It's awful quiet here at Northridge," Brenna said. "Too quiet. The whole place seems empty."

"That's because it *is* empty. Didn't you hear what Johnny said? All of the hands are gone and won't be back for another few weeks. Of course Northridge seems empty." Lars grinned, obviously pleased to be able to share his new knowledge.

"Lars is right. There will be more people around when the hands return." Brittany smiled at her brother. "And today

Morgan Norris told me that some of our neighbors have children. Of course, they still live a ways off—"

"But they're still neighbors." Lars's face brightened. "I hope we get to meet them soon." He looked out the window into the dark night and smiled. "I like it here. I think I might even like it more than Des Moines. Mr. Myers said we could ride anytime we want."

"He did?" That was news to Brittany. She wasn't sure that she liked the idea of the two children up on a horse with no one else around. "If you two do go on a ride, you must ask me first and tell me where you're going, all right?"

Lars frowned.

"All right?" Brittany said again.

Lars sighed. "All right. We'll tell you."

"Good. If something were to happen to either of you—" Brittany didn't finish her thought, not wanting to even think of it. Aunt Ida would never let her forget.

"Time for bed," she said instead. "Into your bed, Lars."

Brenna rolled over to her side of the bed, and Lars climbed onto his cot. "Clem made a good choice in coming here," Lars said, squirming around until he had the blankets wrapped around himself the way he liked. "I would have done the same thing if I were him."

"I'm glad you like it here," Brittany said, blowing out the lamp. *At least one of us does.*

CHAPTER
5

"Well, I reckon today brought us one day closer to Cheyenne." Nathan Lindale balanced his plate in one hand as he eased himself to the ground next to his friend Clem Haines. He sighed, glad to be sitting on something solid after a long day of sitting in a saddle. He loved to ride, had grown up riding almost before he walked, but—all things in moderation. Being in the saddle for stretches of twelve hours at a time was enough to wear any man out. And going for no break seven days a week hit the limit.

"I'll be glad when we're through trailing this herd." Clem nodded toward the shadowy outlines of cattle lying off to the side. "I usually enjoy the trip to Cheyenne, at least for the first few days, but this time I was ready to be home before we even started out."

Nathan knew that before they left Northridge, Clem had asked Morgan Norris if he could call, and she had agreed. He smiled as he remembered when Clem came home that night and how he'd whooped loud enough to raise the dead.

"Hope you didn't carry on like that in front of Morgan and her uncle," Nathan had been unable to resist commenting. "Morgan might regret saying yes if she heard you now."

"Aw, you're just jealous," Clem had said, grinning. Nathan and Clem had known each other for so many years that they could say almost anything to each other's face without either one getting offended.

Nathan took a bite of the beans on his plate and chewed slowly. In truth, he did envy Clem, not because of Morgan, but because he had someone waiting for him when he came home from the trail drive. That was something he would have paid a good deal for.

"By the way," Clem said, breaking the silence. "Did you hear that Scott found a replacement for Hoss?"

Nathan winced at hearing the name. Not many days before, Hoss had been killed in a stampede, trampled to death by dozens of sharp hooves of out-of-control cows. It was a grim reminder of what could happen to any one of them if they ended up in the wrong place at the wrong time. It was too easy to lose one's life on a cattle drive. Too many accidents could end at a lonely grave dug in the middle of nowhere in Wyoming Territory.

"So, Scott found a replacement for him?" Nathan asked.

"Yep. The man was looking for a job. Said that cattle is his business."

"What's his name?"

"Dunno. The name slipped past me."

"Well, an extra set of hands would be mighty welcome about now. Especially if he knows his way around cattle. We've been stretched too thin lately without Hoss."

Clem nodded. "I agree."

Nathan took another bite, casting a sideways glance at Clem as he did so. Clem had done quite a bit of growing up since he'd first come to Wyoming Territory. He was nowhere near as impatient as he used to be, or as complaining. He was quick to pick up on new ideas, and he didn't let himself get intimidated by a challenge. He was also a good listener, and he put into practice the things he was taught. He had matured from a boy to a man Nathan was proud to work with, perhaps even more so because of the hours of teaching time he had invested in the young man.

"Did you write to your sister about Morgan yet?" Nathan asked. That was yet another enviable point. Clem had family, family who cared about him and took the time to keep in touch with him. True, Nathan had family as well, but his relationship with them had ended with his leaving home.

"I did. Haven't heard back from her yet." Clem scraped the last of his beans from his plate. "I think she'll be happy. She's been dropping little hints for some time that I should think about getting myself a wife. And I did think about it—I dreamed about it! I never thought Morgan would give me a second glance, not with all the other men throwing themselves at her. I think every man within a hundred miles was crazy about her."

Nathan raised an eyebrow. "Not quite every man."

Clem gave a little snort. "Let me rephrase that then. Every man except you. But that's just because you're too practical for your own good, and you wouldn't recognize beauty if it came and bit you on the nose."

"I do too see beauty in things."

"I meant besides in four-footed critters and their kind."

"You mean, there's beauty *besides* that?" Nathan put a shocked look on his face.

Clem rolled his eyes. "You're a hopeless cause, Nathan. Better be careful giving girls compliments that compare them with a cow. That's hardly flattering."

"Thanks for the advice," Nathan said, tempted to roll his eyes as well.

Clem missed his sarcasm. "Now, I wasn't trying to discourage you, so don't lose heart. There *might* be another girl out there like Morgan. You've just gotta find her—and be willing to outlast the other men who are watching her. And don't just go for one who's pretty. Go for one who has a real heart."

This was a change, Clem advising Nathan. Nathan glanced at the chuckwagon. Just now he was more interested in bed than in Clem's lecture.

But Clem was on a roll. "I guess most fellas around here liked Morgan because she's so pretty—and because the pickings are pretty slim in these parts. Maybe that was what first attracted me to her, too. But the more time passes, the more I see the *real* Morgan, the person she is on the inside. She's everything I could want in a wife, brave, sweet, plucky—and she's got such a heart for the Lord. That's what I like best about her."

Nathan shifted and eyed the chuckwagon again. He always felt uncomfortable when Clem started talking about his God. And not in the way that the other men in the bunkhouse did. Clem knew that his views about God were different than Nathan's, about as different as Africa was from Wyoming. Over the years they'd had several discussions about their beliefs, all of them uncomfortable. But neither of them was willing to budge. Clem insisted the Lord was a God of love and mercy and forgiveness for those who repented of their sin. Nathan agreed, to a point. But he'd seen too much of life's dark side to believe that just *anyone* who repented and believed on the Lord could be saved. How could people who had done something terrible, something desperately wrong, be cleared of the punishment they deserved, just by saying they were sorry? It didn't add up for Nathan. If Clem wanted to believe all that, then good and fine. But Nathan had no intention of letting himself fall for such nonsense.

Nathan stood abruptly. "I'm heading to bed. Mornin's gonna come all too fast, and there's still night watch in between now and then." Sleep was one thing there was never enough of on a cattle drive.

"Sure, go ahead. I'll be joining you soon. And keep my advice in mind, you hear?"

"It'll give me nightmares." Nathan shuddered, making Clem chuckle.

Nathan set off toward the chuckwagon, not stopping at the campfire longer than to drop off his empty plate. A few men still lingered over their suppers, but Nathan guessed that it wouldn't be long before they turned in for the night as well. Had the men not been so tired, stories would have been flying fast and thick, but as it was, sleep was the only thing anyone wanted.

He turned to the chuckwagon where his bedroll was stored, and pushing aside a few others, fished out his. Tucking it under his arm, he started toward an open space not far off. Coming around the corner of the wagon, he nearly collided with someone.

"Hey, watch it!" The man stepped aside just in time, his fist clenching as if he thought Nathan had deliberately attacked him.

"Sorry." Nathan gave the man a quick glance, not recognizing him. He must be the newly hired puncher Clem had mentioned.

Nathan started to brush past him when a beam of moonlight fell on the man, showing a lined face, dark eyes, and a jagged scar that trailed down one cheek. Nathan froze. Maybe he *did* recognize this man after all. But no, that was impossible. The last time he had seen *that* man was years before, way down in Texas. There was no way that this could be the same man, was there?

The man must have felt Nathan staring at him and glared back. "What?"

That voice. Nathan felt a little shiver of dread run down his spine. He had no doubt about who this man was. "Rueben Pierce?" he said without thinking.

The man stiffened. "Do I know you?" he asked, squinting at Nathan. Nathan saw his eyes widen with sudden recognition. "You're one of Michael Lindale's boys, ain't you?"

Another unwelcome shiver went down Nathan's spine. "Michael Lindale's boys". It had been ages since he'd heard that phrase.

Rueben still stared at him. Swearing softly under his breath, he said, "You're Nathan, ain't you?"

"Yes." Nathan resisted the urge to turn and run, powerful as it was. What kind of ill fate would cause him to run into this man, of all people? The only man Nathan had never been able to tolerate. And the only man who had never been able to tolerate him.

A slow smile spread across Rueben's face. "Wal, now, ain't this a surprise? What are you doin' so far from home, sonny?"

"I really don't see how that's any of your business." Nathan lifted his chin slightly.

Rueben's smile changed to a leer. "You don't seem to have lost your smartness yet."

And you haven't learned not to meddle, Nathan refrained from replying.

"You work for this outfit?" Rueben asked.

"That's the way it appears."

"Where's your folks?"

"I'm old enough to take care of myself, thank you." *Run!* Nathan's mind screamed again.

"But how come you're workin' so far north from Texas? Does your pa still have his ranch?"

"Last I heard, yes." Nathan turned away. Why did that matter to Rueben?

"You ain't makin' any sense! If you could be in Texas partnerin' with your pa on his ranch, why are you here workin' for some other man?"

"That's not your business!"

Nathan fairly ran until he was far enough away that Rueben couldn't call out to him again. He set down his bedroll, realizing that his hands were shaking. Rueben Pierce. Why did he have to show up? Life had been going just fine. He loved his life, his job, the people he worked with. But Rueben had the potential to destroy all that. He knew too much about Nathan, far too much. Nathan feared that eventually Rueben was going to dig for some answers. That was the kind of man Rueben was, a man who delighted in rubbing salt into old wounds.

Nathan ran a hand through his hair, willing his heart to stop pounding so wildly. Something deep in his bones told him that the old trouble between him and Rueben Pierce had not breathed its last. Not by a long shot.

CHAPTER
6

Could there ever be one day in Wyoming Territory when the wind didn't blow?

Brittany pushed the stray wisps of blond hair back from her face and glared at the sheet on the clothesline, whipping in the wind. She had won that battle—barely. The wind had seemed just as determined to keep it off the line as she was to pin it on. Now, rather than cowering in defeat, the wind seemed to know that the sheet hanging on the line was only the first of several, and it seemed to laugh at her, challenging her to try to win the next one.

"I should have waited for a less windy day to hang out sheets," Brittany said aloud. But then the sheets might never be done. The wind never seemed to stop blowing here.

Brittany pushed her hair out of her eyes again, glaring up at the sky. If that wretched wind would just leave her in peace for a few minutes, she could get this job done quickly and move on to something else. She didn't like washday to begin with, but with that wind—

Brittany Haines, you are getting very practiced at complaining. Stop the fussing and be grateful for all God has blessed you with.

Easier said than done. Brittany found it far easier to focus on the hard things lately. Things she never would have encountered had she stayed in Des Moines. Things like mice making a dining hall of her cupboard, hauling water by hand from a well, and wind that threatened to drive her out of her mind.

"Brittany?" Lars appeared at the corner of the cabin. "I've got a question on my math."

"Did you try to figure it out yourself?" Brittany fought to keep the snap from her voice.

"Yeah, I tried, but this problem just won't work."

"I'll help you when I'm done." Brittany turned back to the clothesline. Blessings. Why was it so easy to lose sight of them when problems pressed in?

Brittany picked up another sheet and, trying to keep its end from dragging on the ground, fought it onto the clothesline. The wind seemed to settle down a bit, and if she could just get a clothespin on that edge—

A shrill whistle from behind her made Brittany jump, losing her grip on the sheet. The wind chose that moment to whip up, and without hindrance, the sheet flew off the line into the dust. Brittany felt her frustration on the verge of bubbling over. She spun around, fully prepared to lash out at whoever had caused all the trouble.

"Howdy, there." A man on an ungainly-looking horse grinned down at her. "You sure was focused on what you was doin'. Couldn't hardly get your attention."

Brittany had never seen this man before, and the words she'd intended to say died on her lips. She couldn't dress down a guest, even if he were rude. He hadn't even apologized for startling her. And now, on top of everything else, she would have to rewash that sheet.

The man clumsily dismounted his horse and turned to face her. He appeared to be a middle-aged man, tall with arms and legs that seemed far too long for the rest of his scarecrow-like body. His thin lips seemed to be permanently turned downward, and Brittany didn't quite like the way he looked at her with his faded blue eyes.

"I guess you're the Myerses' new hand." The man puffed out his chest. "Let me be one of the first to give you a proper welcome to the West."

"Thank you." Brittany knew her voice must sound flat, but she couldn't help it.

The man made a motion that may have been a bow and swept his hat off his head, revealing a thinning thatch of gray hair. "Pleasure to meet you, miss. I'm Able Zimmerman. Own a section of land not far from here."

Brittany felt her face freeze. Able Zimmerman? *The* Able Zimmerman who proposed to every woman around?

"It's a mighty fine pleasure to have you here, miss. I heard you was comin', and let me tell you, miss, I was struck right off with admiration for you. It takes pluck to travel far as you have, real pluck, and I knew straight off that you was a girl I would have a lot in common with. Lots of folks 'round here are gonna look down their noses at you because you're from the city, but miss, always remember that you've got a real friend in Able Zimmerman." He patted the faded shirt over his heart.

Brittany had to fight the temptation to flee to the cabin. She forced a smile. "Thank you, Mr. Zimmerman. I—"

"Please, it's just Able." He gave her what was probably supposed to be a charming smile.

"Mr. Zimmerman, it's been wonderful to meet you. I have laundry to do now, but if you're looking for Mr. Myers—"

"Oh, I ain't lookin' for him. Actually, I was hopin' to talk to *you*."

"Indeed?" Brittany stared up into his face. The stray thought came to her that his face strongly resembled his horse's, long and thin and rather flat. Only, she preferred the horse's looks to Able's. At least the horse had a kindly look to it.

"Yes, indeed." Able nodded. "It's about a personal matter. You see, I happen to know your brother, and I think he'd be downright happy about my idea."

"Oh?" *Does he think he knows Clem better than I do?*

Able straightened and tugged at his collar. "Miss," he said, the word almost a croak. "I've never in my life met such a fine lady as you. I'd like to offer you a proposition. I think we get along right well, and I'd like to ask you to be my little bride."

Brittany couldn't keep from gasping. "Oh, no! No–I–"

"What?" Able appeared calm, probably because he'd gone through this before. "Don't you love me?"

Brittany drew herself up to her full height. "Mr. Zimmerman—"

"It's just Able."

"Mr. Zimmerman, how on earth can I love you enough to marry you when I only met you five minutes ago?"

"Women." Able shook his head. He looked back at Brittany. "If you feel we're goin' too fast, I can ask you again next week."

One look at his face told Brittany he was serious. "Mr. Zimmerman," she said in her firmest voice. "Where I come from, before there is any agreement to marriage, a couple gets to know each other, *really* know each other—over several months, maybe even a year. *Not* within a matter of minutes."

Able stared at her, then nodded. "Fine. Next week it is then."

Did everything she said go right over his head? "No." Brittany shook her head hard enough to loosen some of the pins in her bun. "No. Never bring this up again. I have no intention of marrying you—ever."

"Never?" Able chuckled, a raspy sound as if it weren't used very often. "Never's a long time, miss."

"That is my answer, nevertheless." Brittany turned and walked toward the house, barely able to restrain herself from running.

"You'll change your mind," Able called after her, his voice confident. "And I saw you first, so you're mine."

Brittany spun around. "I am *not* yours. You have no claim on me!"

The corners of Able's mouth quirked slightly in what might have been a smile. "Spunky, she is," he said as if to himself.

It's no use arguing with this man, Brittany told herself, and whirling around again, she marched up the porch steps. She was nearly inside when Able called after her, "Say, miss, what is your name anyway?"

Brittany let the slamming of the door be his answer.

"How dare the man." She clenched and unclenched her fists, then turned away from the door. Lars, Brenna, and Mrs. Myers stared at her from where they sat at the table. Brittany felt the heat rush to her face as if drawn there by a magnet.

"What's wrong?" Brenna asked.

"There–there was a man," Brittany began but then broke off, too embarrassed to finish her story.

Mrs. Myers's eyebrows rose, "Able Zimmerman was up to his usual mischief, I take it."

"Yes." Brittany pressed her hands against her cheeks, welcoming their coolness on her too-warm face. "How—how can he be so crude?"

Mrs. Myers shook her head. "Don't let it bother you, dear. Able has a strange way of doing things, is all."

"I should say so." Brittany crossed to the kitchen window and looked outside. Able was quickly disappearing down the ranch lane. She let out a breath of relief. At least he had taken himself away.

That's a blessing, she thought, then smiled. She never would have thought that she would count someone's going away as a blessing.

Now she only hoped that her words would get through to him, and he would realize that she meant every word of what she'd said. But Brittany's hope was only halfhearted. If Morgan's warning were at all true, he would be back soon, undaunted by her rejection. Even here in the relative safety of Northridge, she couldn't hide.

CHAPTER

7

Dear Aunt Ida,

Two and a half weeks have passed since I arrived here in Wyoming Territory. Northridge is a good place, and the Myerses are very easy to get along with. At least, Mrs. Myers is. I still get the impression that Mr. Myers is waiting for me to prove myself. But I trust that with time, he will come around.

Brittany stared down at what she had written, wondering just how much she should tell Aunt Ida about the things that had happened since her arrival. If Aunt Ida knew that Northridge was, at best a half day's ride from the fort, or that Clem wasn't here to look after her, or about Able Zimmerman's proposal— oh, she would be horrified! And no doubt determined to make Brittany return to Des Moines. What else had happened besides all that? Surely there was something she could write that wouldn't send Aunt Ida into a panic.

Abandoning her letter, Brittany rose and crossed the room to the stove. She opened the oven door and pressed on the tops of the baking bread but decided they needed to go a little longer. Shutting the door, she raked her mind for the next thing on her list but could think of nothing that needed doing. It was too early to start supper; the housework had already been taken care of that morning. Mrs. Myers was taking her afternoon nap. Even the mending pile had disappeared over the last several days. The truth was that Brittany didn't have enough work to fill her days. With only three small rooms, the cabin didn't take long to clean. The children's schoolwork required minimal effort on her part. Neither of the children had ever struggled in school, and now, with no distractions from other students, they finished their work faster than ever. Cooking took up some time, but with only basic supplies such as flour, beans, and coffee on the cupboard shelves, the meals she made were hardly creative. There wasn't even a garden that she could vent some of her energy on.

Maybe I should go visit Johnny, she thought. She had already paid the old man many visits since her coming, as had Lars and Brenna. Johnny had a great store of wisdom buried inside him, she had discovered, along with stories that set Lars and Brenna, and even Brittany, on the edge of their seats. And he could play his banjo with a master's touch. Yes, Brittany decided that was what she would do. A visit with Johnny was just what she needed.

Brittany went to the door, passing by the table where Lars and Brenna were finishing up the last of their lessons. "I'll be at Johnny's. Just call if you need anything," she said, untying her apron and hanging it on a nearby hook.

They both gave a brief nod in response and continued with their work.

Brittany swung the door open only to jump back with a stifled shriek. A young boy stood just outside the door, looking just as startled to see Brittany as she was to see him.

"I'm sorry," Brittany said, putting a hand over her racing heart. "I–I wasn't expecting to find someone out here."

The boy dipped his head slightly. "Pardon me. I was just about to knock. Didn't mean to scare you none." He had a pair of the finest blue eyes Brittany had ever seen, framed by lashes so thick his eyes might have seemed almost girlish if they hadn't been set in such a strong, handsome face.

"Don't worry about it," Brittany said, opening the door wider. "Come on in. What can I do for you?"

The boy took a single step inside, his eyes darting to Lars and Brenna, then away just as quickly. "I just thought I'd stop by and visit. Pa said that the Myerses were gettin' new help and that there were a couple kids, too." He glanced again toward Lars and Brenna, who had dropped their books to the table with his coming.

"How kind of you to stop by!" Brittany smiled down at him. "What's your name?"

"Carson," the boy said. "Carson Bryan."

"Nice to meet you, Carson. Your pa is a ranch owner?"

He dipped his head in a nod. "Him and my Uncle Jay. They own the ranch together."

"I see." Brittany glanced at Lars and Brenna. They seemed to have lost all power of speech.

Brenna was the first to speak. "Hi," she said, bouncing out of her chair. "I'm Brenna Haines, and I'm seven. How old are you?"

"Eight." Carson lifted his eyes to her face for one second, then quickly down again, his face reddening.

"Really? Lars is eight, too." Brenna beamed.

Lars stirred and offered the boy a smile of his own. "Hi."

Brittany saw Carson glance at the books on the table. "Lars and Brenna were just finishing up their school. Why don't you two be done for the day and go play with Carson?"

Carson looked at Lars. "You do school?"

"Brittany makes me," Lars said as if apologizing.

Carson said nothing, just moved closer to the table and stared down at the slate and McGuffey Reader lying there. "What's this book about?" he asked, pointing to the reader.

Lars shrugged. "It's got a lot of different stories in it."

"And you know how to read it?" Carson's voice sounded wistful.

"Of course." Lars stared at him. "Don't you know how to read?"

Carson didn't look up, just shook his head. "My pa can—a little. But he don't have time to teach us. Besides, reading and writing ain't too important, he says."

Lars started to open his mouth, but Brittany shook her head, silencing him. "You have other siblings?" she asked, changing the subject.

Carson nodded. "There's four besides me." He looked at Brenna, reddened, and spoke to his boots instead. "Sarah wanted to come, but she didn't get her chores done in time. She's six."

Brenna's face bloomed into a smile. "You'll have to come visit again and bring Sarah. Come on," she said, motioning toward the door. "Let's go outside."

Carson and Lars followed her out, Carson pausing long enough to tip his hat to Brittany and say, "Pleased to meet you, ma'am," before closing the door behind him.

"Now that was one fine boy," Brittany said to herself. "And he certainly is well mannered."

Brittany crossed to the window and watched the three children race of toward the barn; their shyness completely vanished. She smiled. This boy would make a good friend for Lars and Brenna, she was sure.

As they disappeared into the barn, Brittany moved away from the window and headed for the door again. It was time for that visit with Johnny.

"Howdy, Brittany!" Johnny called out to her as she marched down the path to his cabin. He was seated on a rocker on his porch. "I seen you had company."

"A boy named Carson Bryan. Such a nice young man." Brittany climbed the porch steps and sat down in the second rocker.

"All those Bryan kids are real nice. Maybe they'll come visitin' more often now that there's kids their own age around here." Johnny looked over at her. "What brings you over here today?"

Brittany gave her shoulders a slight shrug. "I didn't have anything else to do." Realizing how that might sound, she hastily added. "And I always enjoy visiting with you."

"That's good. Can't say there are too many who would share that opinion. They might find it more of an annoyance listenin' to an old man rattle on."

"Now, Johnny, I'm sure there are plenty of people who love visiting with you. And if there aren't, then westerners are—are—" Brittany searched for the right word. "They're addle-brained."

Johnny chuckled. "Well, I'm glad that's the way you think."

A comfortable silence fell between them. Johnny slapped at a fly lazily buzzing by. Brittany gave a push with her foot that set her chair rocking. From the barn there was a shout of laughter from the children.

"Johnny, can you read?" Brittany asked.

Johnny looked at her from under raised eyebrows. "Sure, I can. Why do you ask?"

Brittany looked away. "Carson Bryan said he can't." She kept her voice matter-of-fact, not wanting to admit how much his words bothered her. Especially the ones about reading and writing not being very important.

"That's none too surprising," Johnny said. "Reckon there's not a whole lot of folks 'round here who have much schooling of any kind."

"But a child has such potential. It's a shame he can't learn to read. He said that his father knows how to."

Johnny shrugged. "Hard to say just how well Grant Bryan can read."

"But if he could at least teach his children what he does know—"

"Reckon he just don't consider reading too important. It ain't like there's a lot to read out here. Long as a man can tally up numbers and read cattle brands, his learnin' is about rounded out."

"But times change. Maybe that's the way things are now. But what if someday reading becomes essential to even a remote area like this?"

"If a fella needs to know something, he can generally learn it." Johnny leaned back in his chair. "Kids ain't the only ones who can learn to read, Brittany. They can learn when they're older if they gotta."

"I know, but—" Brittany bit her lip. "It just doesn't seem right. It seems to me that a child should have at least an opportunity to learn."

"Schoolbook learnin' ain't the only kind of learnin' there is. Some of the best lessons we learn are the ones no book could ever teach us, the ones that only experience can give."

Brittany stopped trying to argue. She stared off to the barn where Lars, Brenna, and Carson sat petting a kitten. The three children seemed to be having a great time together if the smiles spread across their faces were any indication.

"How will he ever be able to read God's Word for himself if he can't read?" she asked. The question hung in the air, and Brittany realized that she had just asked the most important question. What worth was all the education in the world if you missed the true source of all knowledge, the Lord? "Don't his parents care about that?"

Johnny shook his head slowly. "Probably not. 'Round here, there's a real lack of interest in religion of any kind."

"But these people don't need just any religion." Brittany shook her head as well. "They need God."

"I ain't arguin', but most folks believe that God helps those who help themselves. They think either that they jest plain don't need God, or that they only need Him when they're at the very end of themselves and nothin' short of a miracle can help them."

"That's a terrible lie."

"It is, but it's what they grew up believin'."

"It's just too bad." Brittany looked at the three children once again. A deep heaviness tugged at her heart. If only there were a way that Carson could learn to read—and ultimately, how to read the Bible. And not just Carson but any other children around. A verse began to play through her mind. *How then shall they call on Him in whom they have not believed? And how shall they believe in Him whom they have not heard?*

CHAPTER
8

"Knock, knock. Anybody home?"

Morgan poked her head through the front door even as she called, a smile tilting her lips.

Delight at seeing her new friend brought an answering smile from Brittany. "Morgan, how good to see you!" Brittany hurried toward her, drying her hands on a towel. "Please come in. Excuse the mess." She waved toward the dishes stacked on the table and next to the dish tub. "We just finished breakfast."

"Don't worry about that." Morgan gave a little snort. "Life is life, and I came to see all of you, not the house." She turned to Mrs. Myers, who was sweeping the kitchen floor at her own slow pace. "How are you doing, Mrs. Myers?"

"Quite well, thank you. Soon as that young man of yours gets back, I'm going to have to tell him what a wonderful sister he has. She's the best help we've had so far." Mrs. Myers beamed at Brittany.

When Clem gets back— The words made a shiver of anticipation run down Brittany's spine. She had been trying to keep herself so busy that she had no time to think about Clem, but she couldn't deny that she missed him terribly. She had been faithfully marking off each passing day from the calendar, and now he should be returning any day.

Morgan turned to Brittany. "How are you liking it here out West?" The shine in her eyes told Brittany that she didn't believe anyone could not like Wyoming Territory.

Brittany shrugged. "It's all right." *But compared to Des Moines—* She didn't let herself finish that thought. None of the words she would use to describe Wyoming were flattering.

"Able Zimmerman stopped by," she said, changing the subject.

"Ah." Morgan's face took on a knowing look.

"You were right. He did propose."

A little smile played across Morgan's face. "And you told him yes, of course you would marry him?"

"The Myerses would have hit me over the head with my contract if I did."

Morgan laughed, and Mrs. Myers rolled her eyes.

"On a more positive note," Brittany said, "Carson Bryan came to visit us yesterday."

"Isn't he a dear? He takes everything so seriously that it's hard not to smile." Morgan began to clear the dishes from the table.

Brittany wondered if she should share her idea with Morgan and Mrs. Myers. It had been gradually coming together in her mind ever since her talk with Johnny yesterday. Was her idea too crazy to even bother mentioning? And if she did dare to tell it, what would their reactions be? Would they laugh? Be upset? Tell her to mind her own business?

Brittany drew a deep breath, deciding that there was only one way to find out. "I've been thinking that it's a pity none of the children around here can read."

Mrs. Myers shrugged. "It is too bad, but what do you do? It's not like we could start a school here. There aren't enough people to keep a teacher here."

Brittany nodded slowly, wondering if she should just let the matter go with that.

"What are you thinking?" Morgan asked, watching her with raised eyebrows. "I can see your mind is working."

"I just thought that maybe—maybe there is a way they could learn." Brittany could feel her cheeks warming. "Suppose— suppose we were to hold classes somewhere?"

Mrs. Myers and Morgan both looked uncertain. "Who would teach them?" Mrs. Myers asked.

Brittany's face was now painfully hot. "Well, I–I did graduate from high school in Des Moines. I–I'm not a teacher, but—" She looked away, wishing she hadn't brought this up.

"You think you could teach them?" Mrs. Myers's voice held a trace of doubt, but no accusation.

"I think I could. I've been teaching Lars and Brenna."

"Teaching children who know nothing and who might not want to learn would be harder than teaching your siblings, I'm afraid."

It was a good point. "We can only try, can't we?" Brittany forced a smile.

"Maybe you'll wish you hadn't tried." Mrs. Myers's voice was matter-of-fact.

Brittany shook her head slowly. "No. I don't think I'll regret trying. I think that when it comes time for me to leave, I'll regret it if I don't try. Just think of what this could mean for those children. A whole new world of books would be open to them."

"We don't have much for books around here," Mrs. Myers broke in. "There's not much reason for them to know how to read."

"I know. But maybe those children won't remain here forever. Maybe they'll move somewhere else when they grow up, a place where reading and writing are important. And if they know how to read, they'll be able to read the Bible. Isn't that important? How are they to be strong in their faith and to grow if they can't even read God's message to them?"

"That's true," Morgan said.

"It will do them no harm to learn to read." Brittany leaned forward. "It only has the potential to do them good. And if we can do them good, we ought to, by all means."

Mrs. Myers bit her lip. "Where would we hold these lessons?"

"I–I don't know."

"And would you have time to prepare your lessons, teach them, *and* do all your other work?"

"The lessons wouldn't have to be long."

"We don't have much for teaching materials."

"We could improvise." Brittany felt a trickle of sweat run down her neck. Now that her idea was out in the open, she realized just how much she wanted it to work.

"And what about the children and their families? Do you think they would be interested in this?"

That was the real question. "I don't know. You know them better than I do. I've never even met them," Brittany replied. But the longing on Carson's face as he looked at the book on the table was imprinted on her mind. She was sure that she had one student in him, provided that his parents allowed him to come.

"I think it's a good idea," Morgan said. "We should give this some serious thought."

"Yes. It certainly is something to think about." Mrs. Myers still looked uncertain. "I would have to talk it over with Tim and see what he says. And we'd have to talk to the Bryans and Joneses." She gave her hand a little flutter. "Yes, we have much to think about."

It wasn't exactly a yes, but it wasn't a no either. *But with Mr. Myers being given the last word, maybe my idea is as good as dead,* Brittany thought. He probably wouldn't believe she was dependable enough to teach a room full of children.

"Perhaps we should wait to make any decisions until your brother comes home," Mrs. Myers said. "Talk it over with him and see what he says about it. If Tim's estimation is right, it's only a few more days until he'll be here."

He'll be here. Again Brittany felt that little shiver of excitement. "That's a good idea. A few more days won't hurt anything. And it would be good to have some time to pray about this."

"Fine. We'll consider it settled," Mrs. Myers said, returning to her sweeping.

But nothing was truly settled. Her idea was now out in the open, but no decision had been made. Brittany was sure that she would feel restless until the question had been settled once and for all when Clem came. *Clem, hurry back,* she begged him silently. *We need you here to make a decision.*

Then another thought struck her. Suppose Clem didn't respond the way she wanted him to? Would she be able to accept his decision with grace, whether it was in her favor or not?

CHAPTER
9

The sound of hoofbeats coming up the lane caught Brittany's attention as she swept the porch steps the next day. Holding the broom in one hand, she shaded her eyes against the sun's glare to see who was coming. *Please let it not be Able again,* she thought, her chest tightening at just the thought of him. It had been a couple weeks since he'd first come, and every day she'd feared that he would appear again, pressing her to marry him.

But the approaching rider was wearing skirts, and Brittany felt herself relax. *Morgan.* Then she frowned. Morgan had visited just yesterday. What would make her visit again so soon?

"Brittany, I have the best news!" Morgan drew her horse up in front of Brittany, making her horse snort and toss his head. "One of Uncle Dave's men came this morning with the message that our men and the Northridge men are coming home today."

"Today?" Brittany stared up at her. "Do you think they really will?"

"I know they will. Come with me. I want to show you something." Morgan kicked her foot out of the stirrup and held out a hand to help Brittany up behind her. Brittany hesitated, then accepted her hand. She made it a goal to keep away from horses, but as long as Morgan was the one holding the reins, she was confident they would be safe.

As soon as she was settled, Morgan turned the horse and headed back down the lane. Brittany held tightly to Morgan's waist and fussed over her skirts as the wind whipped at them, wishing the wind would give her just one day of peace.

She held on even tighter as the horse climbed a steep hill just beyond the ranch. She could feel the horse's muscles strain beneath her and the power coursing through it. It amazed her that such a strong animal could be controlled merely by a bit and bridle.

At the top of the hill, Morgan stopped him. "Look over there," she said, pointing.

Brittany's eyes followed her finger. Coming in a cloud of dust, a white canvased wagon was lurching its way toward them across the prairie, flanked by several riders on horseback and other unmounted horses. Brittany watched their slow progress for a moment, uncomprehending.

Then it dawned on her. "You mean, those are the Northridge men?"

"Yes. I saw them coming when I was almost here."

Brittany watched the approaching men, her excitement rising as she realized that one of those small figures was Clem. Before she'd had her fill of looking at them, Morgan swung the horse around and took off down the hill back to Northridge.

"What's the hurry?" Brittany asked, frightened at how quickly the ground passed underfoot.

"We're going to surprise Clem. He has no clue that you're here, and I want to give him the shock of his life!"

"Surprise him? Do you think—will he like that?" Sudden fears assailed her as she again remembered how she had jumped ahead of him in coming here. Would he be happy that she was here, or would he have a list of reasons like Aunt Ida that she should have stayed in Des Moines? Would he think that Wyoming Territory was too wild for a girl like her? Worst of all, would he think she had come merely to spy on him and Morgan—and would he care to spend time with his siblings now that he and Morgan were courting?

"Oh, Clem won't mind being surprised. He'll be delighted to see you," Morgan said, and Brittany told herself to relax and trust Morgan. After all, she ought to know how Clem would feel.

When they reached the ranch, the two of them dismounted, and then Morgan set off to find Lars and Brenna, calling over her shoulder for Brittany to go into the house. Brittany was obliged to obey. When Morgan got that look on her face, there was no stopping her.

Brittany passed through the kitchen straight to her room and began to fix her hair again, catching all the stray wisps that the wind had teased loose. She was aware that her fingers were trembling; despite that, her hair didn't look too bad. She noticed a smudge of dirt on her skirt and brushed at it, then straightened the neck of her waist. She heard the door open as Morgan returned with Lars and Brenna, directing them into the room to freshen up. After playing outside all day, Brittany knew the two children would be dirty and windblown.

Within minutes, all of them were ready and waiting in the kitchen.

"I see them coming down the lane," Morgan said, peeking out the front door.

Lars and Brenna dashed to the window to watch. "Look at all those horses!" Lars exclaimed.

Brittany joined them at the window, her hands suddenly becoming sweaty. She still couldn't pick out which man was Clem, but they were close enough she could hear their excited whoops and yelps.

"I'm going to step outside, but make sure you stay here until I bring Clem back with me," Morgan said, her eyes dancing.

"Now, how's that fair, that you get to go out while we're left inside?" Brittany asked.

Morgan grinned and turned to Mrs. Myers, who had just come from her bedroom. "Keep an eye on them, Mrs. Myers, and don't let them break loose."

"I'll do my best." Mrs. Myers rolled her eyes, smiling.

"I'll be back." Morgan disappeared out the door, and Brittany clasped her hands together, praying that Morgan wasn't mistaken about Clem's reaction.

Trying not to be too obvious, Brittany looked out the window again and watched Morgan hurry down the cabin's steps, skipping the last one entirely. She headed toward the barn where the men were dismounting, shading her eyes against the sun's glare.

One of the men waved to her and broke away from the others, hurrying toward her. Brittany felt her heart jump nearly into her throat. Was that Clem? He was still too far off for her to see him clearly, but if it was, he wasn't the lanky kid who had left Des

Moines five years ago. He had filled out and grown even taller. He was a man now.

Morgan reached him, and the two held hands for one brief moment. Brittany watched as Morgan leaned closer to say something, then motioned back toward the Myers' house. The man tipped his hat back and shook his head, looking toward the house. Brittany knew he couldn't see her, but she still inched a little farther back, feeling as if she might go crazy from her curiosity. She had never before so badly wanted to know what two people were saying.

The two of them talked a minute longer, then the man turned and called something back to the hands by the barn. One of them called back in response, then Morgan and the man turned toward the Myerses' house, Morgan taking the man's arm.

Brittany watched the man draw nearer, her fingers pleating the curtains. He laughed at something Morgan said, and Brittany's heart began to pound. This man had to be Clem. She would recognize anywhere the lift of his head as he laughed.

They reached the steps, and Brittany backed away from the window, afraid he might see her. She glanced at Lars and Brenna and pressed a finger to her lips, aware that her hands were trembling. So much hinged on this moment—Had it really been a good idea to give into Morgan's whim and surprise him like this? Surely someone should give him a bit of a warning.

"When that mouse jumped out, you should have seen his face. It was the best joke on the whole drive." Boots clattered on the porch, and Clem's laugh rang out. "Every day after that, Little Joe was real careful when he went to open his saddlebag—didn't want to get a scare like that again."

"You boys have too much fun."

"Now Morgan, it wasn't me who put the mouse in there, so don't give me that look. You know how George and Little Joe are." The door swung open, and Clem's frame filled the doorway. He looked so much like their father that Brittany's breath tangled in her throat, keeping her from making a single sound.

Clem moved into the room, Morgan behind him. He turned his back to Brittany, and she realized that he hadn't seen her or Lars and Brenna.

"Good to see you, Mrs. Myers." Clem tipped his hat to the woman. "Feels like I've been gone extra long this time."

"And it's good to have you home, young man." Mrs. Myers winked at Brittany.

"Now, what was it you wanted to show me?" Clem asked, looking at Morgan.

Morgan's eyes danced, and she grinned at Brittany. "Look behind you."

Clem turned, and at last Brittany got a full view of his face. She noticed the slight cleft of his chin, the familiar twinkle in his eyes. And there was the little scar above his right eyebrow from when he tumbled out of Mama's apple tree, the white line made even more visible by how tanned his skin was. She swallowed hard. This was definitely her brother.

Clem stared at her, and she watched as his blue eyes went wide. He blinked, then lowered his gaze to Lars and Brenna, studying them. He gave his head a slight shake and looked back at Brittany, his face telling her that he couldn't believe what he was seeing.

"I—I don't understand," he said, his voice almost a whisper.

"Don't you recognize your own sister?" Morgan asked, bursting into laughter. "Surprise!"

Clem gave his head another shake. "Brittany? How'd you get here?"

"You asked if I knew of anyone who'd be willing to help the Myerses out." Brittany could feel a smile spreading across her own face. "I did."

"Well, I'll be. I sure wasn't expecting this." Clem stepped forward, gathering her, Lars, and Brenna into one big hug. "But this sure is a good surprise. Better than most surprises around here. I'm glad you're here."

Brittany felt tears sting her eyes as the last of her tension disappeared. He was glad she had come. It seemed that despite their years of separation, they were still a family.

CHAPTER
10

Nathan couldn't resist sneaking a glance at Clem as he and Morgan walked off toward the Boss's house arm in arm. He kept his hands busy unsaddling his horse, Loner. But he'd done the job so many times that he could do it in his sleep, and his mind could occupy itself with other things, other things being Clem and Morgan just now. Those two sure were quite a pair. Their joy at seeing each other again seemed to radiate from them.

Funny, but before Clem announced that he and Morgan were courting, Nathan had never thought about marriage, not once. But lately he had wondered what it was like to be planning for a home and someday a family. A home and family sounded mighty good to him after years of living on his own—where home meant sharing cramped quarters in the bunkhouse with the other hired hands. But Nathan shook those thoughts aside with a laugh. If Clem wanted to get married and settle down, that was fine. But for himself, such a dream was impossible. Why, he doubted he could even find a girl who'd want him.

Nathan pulled his gaze away from Clem and Morgan with a shake of his head. He caught a slight movement off to the side, and he turned to see Johnny Myers making his way toward him. He couldn't keep the smile from spreading across his face.

"Howdy, Nathan," Johnny called out. "You sure are a sight for sore eyes."

"Johnny, good to see you again." Nathan stopped there, not wanting to give away just how glad he was to see the man. Johnny Myers was like a second father to him, or maybe more like a grandfather. He'd done nothing but good to Nathan for all the years he'd known him. And more than that, he'd always seen Nathan's potential and talent, even when others saw nothing but a skinny, lost-looking young boy. Because of Johnny, he was standing here today with a good job and even better friends.

"Been awful quiet 'round here without you boys," Johnny said, reaching his side.

Nathan let out a groan. "Quiet sounds like a piece of heaven about now. There's nothing quiet on a cattle drive, especially not when your friend is all excited about his courtship."

Johnny chuckled. "Clem's been talkin' your ear off, has he?"

"Is that news to anybody?"

Johnny laughed again. "You sure do humor the boy."

Nathan shrugged. "He's better than he used to be. He does let us have an occasional spell of silence." Nathan set his saddle on the ground with a thump. "What's new around here?"

Johnny's eyes twinkled. "You ain't gonna believe this. Guess who the Myerses hired to help them while you were gone?"

Nathan wasn't sure how Johnny expected him to know. "Who?"

"Brittany Haines."

"Clem's little sister? But I thought she was just a kid."

"Think again. She's eighteen and one mighty capable young lady. She brought her younger siblings with her, too, and, boy, do those two keep the place lively."

"Hmm. That sure is some news." Nathan rubbed Loner's forehead, and the horse snorted. "I thought nothing ever happened while we were gone. I wonder if the Myerses will be able to keep them here or if they'll be gone as fast as the last help?"

"Oh, Timmy and Eleanor made sure that wouldn't happen. They made Brittany sign a contract saying she'll stay on for one year—and no gettin' hitched during that time."

"Given all the trouble they've had, it's no wonder." Nathan slipped Loner's bridle over his ears. "How long do you reckon she'll last after her contract's up?"

Johnny grinned. "Not a day, in my opinion. She already got one proposal."

Nathan arched an eyebrow. "Able?"

"You got it."

Nathan snorted. "That's nothing unusual." Nathan set the bridle down on top of his saddle and gave Loner's rump a light slap. "There you go, old boy. You run on now."

Nathan watched as Loner moved away at a lazy trot, pausing to snatch a mouthful of grass before walking on. Loner was his favorite of all the horses in his string, partly because he was his own, while the other horses were ones he borrowed from the ranch. He'd had him since the time Loner was a foal, and they'd put in more hours of work together than Nathan could count.

Nathan picked up his saddle and bridle and started for the barn. Johnny fell comfortably in step beside him. "How'd the trip go?" Johnny asked.

"It was fine." Nathan shrugged. "We lost Hoss to a stampede."

Johnny's eyebrows lifted. "That's too bad. Hoss was a good man. Been around here for a long time."

"I know. It was a bad deal." Nathan let a moment pass, then said, "Scott found a replacement for him."

"Did he? What's his name?"

"Rueben Pierce." Even just saying the man's name set Nathan's teeth on edge.

Johnny must have noticed. "He done something wrong?"

"Not according to the other men."

"But what do you say?"

Nathan looked toward the horizon, taking his time in answering. "Rueben is—is someone I know, from a long time back."

"How long?"

"From back in Texas."

"Oh." That one simple word said that Johnny understood.

They had come to the barn, and Johnny reached out to open the door. The barn was dark compared to outside, and it was a moment before Nathan could see clearly again.

"So this man knows your folks?" Johnny asked as they walked toward the tack room at the back of the barn.

"He worked for my pa. Him and his brother, Dallas." Saying Dallas's name let loose a whole string of memories. Memories of a big man with one of the biggest laughs in all Texas, a temper that flared to life with the slightest provocation, and a loyalty for the Lindale family that was unmatched. Nathan swallowed hard, missing the man who had meant so much to him as a boy—the complete opposite of his brother, Rueben.

"Dallas was a good man," he said, working to keep his voice even. "I owe him more than I can ever repay. Seems impossible that Rueben and him are brothers. Rueben caused all kinds of havoc, and Pa fired him."

Johnny looked concerned. "What do you mean by havoc?"

Nathan frowned, trying to remember what exactly the circumstances had been around Rueben's getting fired. "Rueben had something against Pa from the first day he started working for him. Pa had a talk with him one day; he didn't like Rueben's attitude, or the way Rueben treated me and my brother. Rueben ended up hitting Pa, and he was fired on the spot."

"Hmm. Hope he don't cause no trouble for Timmy and Scott."

"I doubt he will. He's just got something against anyone with the last name Lindale." Nathan hung his bridle on a nail, still struggling with the bitter memories Rueben's presence evoked. "I could forget the nasty things Rueben said to me. That isn't what bothers me. It's what he said to Evan that I can't forgive him for. He hurt Evan, and he still isn't sorry."

Nathan frowned at the memory. He'd long ago told Johnny the story of why he'd come to Wyoming Territory, leaving behind the home and family he loved more than anything else on earth. But there were still things Johnny didn't quite understand. Such as how a single insult against his younger brother would send the blood pounding through his veins and kick his protective instincts into full gear. He would have done anything to protect

Evan, anything at all. The fact that Rueben had added pain to his brother's all-too-short life made him angry even now.

"I cannot stand even the sight of Rueben Pierce," Nathan said, his fist clenching at his side. "He's been a plague this whole trip, ever since the day he signed on with our outfit. I'm sure he goes out of his way to irritate me. He makes sarcastic comments, he pries at my past, and he reminds me of things I would rather forget. He *likes* to know that he can hurt me."

Johnny chewed on the end of his mustache for a moment. "Try not to let him bother you, Nathan. Just forget about what he's done in the past."

"I can't, Johnny. Not when he hasn't changed a bit. He is the one man I will never, *ever* be able to forgive."

"Nathan—" Johnny began.

Nathan held up a hand to stop him. "I know what you're going to say, Johnny, but don't. I know you believe that God can help a person forgive others, and that's fine, but some people are just plain unforgivable. Especially when they aren't sorry for what they've done. What he did was wrong, and he doesn't deserve forgiveness."

Johnny studied him. "Course he did wrong. I ain't denyin' that. But, Nathan, how can you determine what's too far, what's too unforgivable? Truth is, no matter how small the wrongs we do, none of us deserve to be forgiven. That's why we need grace."

"Well, I'm afraid my grace is too small for a man like Rueben." Nathan wished Johnny would agree with him that Rueben sounded like an unforgivable character. He didn't even know Rueben, and here he was telling Nathan to forgive him.

"And that's where you need help, Nathan. You need help from beyond yourself."

CHAPTER

11

"I still can't believe Aunt Ida let you get on the train and come here."

Brittany looked sideways at her brother, trying to keep from smiling. Smiles came easily this evening as she and Clem walked around Northridge, catching up on all the years they'd been apart. This was what she had come to Wyoming Territory for, and at last she felt at peace.

"I can't say that Aunt Ida is exactly happy that I'm here," she said, not mentioning all the arguments they'd had leading up to her departure. "She would still rather have the children and me safe in Des Moines."

"I never did get why people would want to live in a city like that. Des Moines was crazy busy. People dashed from one place to another like chickens with their heads cut off." Clem shook his head.

"Maybe *you* don't, but it makes perfect sense to *me*." After this visit, Brittany vowed that she would never take life in Des Moines for granted again. There she could attend church every

Sunday. There she could visit friends who lived within walking distance, not a long horseback ride away. And there she had reasons to dress up and fuss over her hair. She had brought one dress for good with her but now wondered if it had been a waste of precious space. She hadn't taken it from its peg on the wall even once since arriving, and it didn't seem like she would anytime in the foreseeable future.

Homesickness threatened to overwhelm her, despite Clem's presence at her side, and she looked away from him. "I miss Des Moines."

"Life's been harder here?"

"Harder in many ways." Brittany refused to let herself list all the ways life in Des Moines was easier.

"What made you come here?"

That was a simple answer. "I came because the Myerses needed help, and—"

"I know that. But why did you decide to come here and be that help?"

That answer was harder. Brittany looked at Clem, again wondering how he felt about her coming to Wyoming. "I came here for you. I realized our family has been apart for far too long. Lars and Brenna don't even remember you, and that hardly seemed right. And I guess, after your last letter, I realized that you weren't coming home."

"No." Clem studied the distant horizon. "No, I couldn't go back to Iowa after seeing a country like this."

He didn't seem upset with her, but Brittany had to make sure. "You aren't mad at me for coming, are you?"

"Mad at you?" Clem's gaze swiveled around to meet hers, his eyebrows rising. "Whatever for?"

"For coming here without waiting for your response."

"For mercy's sake, why would that make me mad? I'm glad you're here, Brittany, honest. I've missed you and Lars and Brenna like crazy these last years. Sometimes it gets awful lonesome out here."

"You could have come home."

Clem shook his head slowly. "The farm was home, but not Des Moines. With the farm gone, there was nothing to go back to. And besides, after the homesickness wore off, I fell in love with this land. This is home now."

"I see," Brittany said, but she didn't really. Clem might as well have said he loved sagebrush, wind, and loneliness, and she saw nothing lovable about any of the three.

"How do you like it here?" Clem asked.

Brittany hesitated. "It's all right. Things are rather slow here, don't you think?"

"I don't think that's a bad thing."

Obviously not, since you still live in this forsaken country. "It takes getting used to, I suppose. There aren't many people around here."

"No, but a person kind of gets to like it after a time. And let me tell you, Brittany—when you make a friend here, they'll stick with you through thick and thin. The people are a good sort."

Nothing about Wyoming Territory seemed to bother him, and Brittany felt an urge to argue. "But everyone is so spread out. Even Morgan lives a couple hours away, and the only way to visit people is to ride *horseback*."

"So? I ride horseback every day, and I like it."

"But I don't. It simply isn't proper to straddle a horse like—like—"

"Like any rider with common sense would?" The tilt of Clem's chin said he was beginning to feel annoyed. "Brittany, 'proper' out here is not the same as in Des Moines."

"So I've noticed, but I am not a westerner. If I don't uphold what is proper, Lars and Brenna are going to have no sense of what is right and good manners."

"Manners are important, yes, but proper is flexible. I'm warning you that you'll be putting unnecessary burdens on yourself and the children if you try to live here like it's Des Moines."

"Clem!" Brittany wanted him to agree with her. Instead, he was trying to convince her to live as if she were remaining in Wyoming Territory forever. Johnny's words whispered in her mind again: *I can't tell the difference between him and a born westerner—*"

Brittany glanced at Clem, noticing his clothing: his Stetson hat, high-topped boots with spurs, and leather vest. He looked the part of a westerner, but more than that, it seemed he now thought like one. Clem wasn't going to agree with her, Brittany realized. Frustration with him flared, and she wanted to tell him just what she thought of him acting like the westerners around him, trying to become one of them, but as she opened her mouth to speak, a sudden yell cut through the air.

Brittany's heart began to race, and she looked around for the cause. Another yell followed on the heels of the first, and Brittany grabbed Clem's arm.

"What's that sound, Clem? Indians?"

"Indians?" Clem's lips twitched. "Hardly. It sounds like either George or Little Joe. Those two are always after each other with one prank or another."

His words failed to rid Brittany of her fear. Their walk had brought them in a wide circle around the barn, and now, as they neared the corral, she could see two men standing along the fence. The taller of the two men looked the worse for the wear. He had a large rip down his shirt sleeve, exposing his arm underneath, and he was covered from head to boot in a layer of dust and manure. He spat at the ground, his face screwed up in disgust, and in a voice meant only for Brittany's ears, Clem said, "That's George Maxton."

The other man was doubled over with laughter, obviously amused by his friend's plight, and Clem whispered, "That's Little Joe."

"Would you quit laughin'?" the man named George said, glaring venomously at Little Joe.

Little Joe acted as if he didn't hear him. "I wish you could see yourself! Bet you look even worse than some of those beeves we drove to market, and I bet you smell worse, too."

"This is your fault!" George said, adding a couple words that made Brittany gasp. "You tripped me on purpose."

"Did not!" Little Joe said around more laughter. "You tripped yourself. You just ain't very graceful."

"Quit laughin', would you?" George spat again. "Ugh. I've even got dirt in my mouth."

"Now that's lucky! Dirt's a whole lot better than horse apples."

"I said quit laughin'!"

But Little Joe only laughed harder, and quick as a flash, George leaned over and scooped up a handful of dirt and other less-pleasant material. He hurled it at Little Joe, hitting him square in the face.

Little Joe's laugh dissolved into a fit of coughing and spitting, and he let loose a string of profanity that made Brittany gasp again.

George appeared to be on the verge of blasting back with some choice expletives of his own, but Clem called out, "Boys, best watch your tongues. Lady present."

The two men spun around to face them. The teasing halted, and the anger on their faces melted away, a look of pure shock replacing it.

"P–pardon me, ma'am," Little Joe said, his cheeks turning bright red. "Didn't mean no offense."

"No, no offense." George reddened as well, looking everywhere except into Brittany's eyes. "Dreadful sorry about that."

Brittany forced a smile in response, but all she really wanted was to get away from the two of them as quickly as possible. These were the kind of westerners she had no wish to become associated with.

"You two sure could do with a scrubbing," Clem said. Brittany wanted to shake him. In her opinion, the less said to the two filthy, swearing men, the better.

Clem seemed to catch her urgency to move on, and he turned away from the two men, saying, "See you at supper."

"Those are friends of yours?" Brittany asked as soon as they were out of hearing range. She tried not to sound as disgusted as she felt.

Clem shrugged. "We're not the closest friends. Some days I just plain want to shake those two for all their carrying on."

"You sure seemed friendly with them," Brittany couldn't resist saying.

"We get along. My closest friends are Johnny and Nathan. I know you've already met Johnny, and maybe later this evening I could introduce you to Nathan. He grew up here out West, and he's a wealth of information about everything from horses to cooking over a campfire. He—"

"No, Clem." Brittany's voice sounded hard even to her own ears.

Clem stopped short. "No what?"

"No. I do not care to meet this man you're talking about. I think I've seen enough rough, swearing Western men for one night."

Clem looked genuinely shocked. "But Brittany, Nathan's not like George and Little Joe. He takes things seriously—and he doesn't swear."

"He doesn't?" Somehow Brittany doubted that.

"No. He's as fine a man as they come. Morgan knows him. Just ask her."

Brittany took a deep breath to steady her voice before she responded. "Morgan is free to associate with whomever she wishes. But for myself and Lars and Brenna, I would prefer not to associate with men like–like those two back there." She jabbed a finger toward the corral where George and Little Joe had been.

"Nathan's not like them," Clem said again, his words heated.

Why did he have to be so stubborn? "Let me make one thing clear to you, Clem Haines. Lars and Brenna are only children, and like all children, they imitate those around them. I don't want them around men who are going to have a bad influence on them."

"Brittany," Clem began, but she wasn't finished.

"I am overjoyed to see you again, but that joy does not carry over to any other man here—at Northridge or otherwise. I want nothing to do with *any* other man, and I would appreciate it if you did not try to introduce me around. Or Lars and Brenna. Do you understand?"

"Nathan is not bad association. He—"

"Could you just stop?" Brittany felt close to tears from pure frustration with her brother. "I have told you how I feel; can't you respect that? I don't want to meet this Nathan whatever-his-name-is or any other man. And I'm not changing my mind!"

Clem opened his mouth and started to speak, but then seemed to change his mind. He glared at his boots for a moment, then said, "If that's how you feel, then I shall respect it and not introduce you to any men."

Brittany couldn't miss the coolness in his voice, and she sensed that speaking those few words had cost him a good deal. "Thank you, Clem," she said, releasing the breath she had unconsciously been holding.

They walked on in silence, but the atmosphere between them now felt strained. *Clem has changed,* Brittany thought, feeling more sorrow than anything. *Neither of us understands one another now. Is this the way my whole visit is going to be, bickering over one thing after another?* Brittany could only hope not.

CHAPTER

12

Brittany's first thought upon waking the next morning was of Clem. She lay staring up at the ceiling, feeling again the disappointments his coming had brought. She didn't remember him being so opinionated when they were younger, or maybe she had just forgotten. Either way, he was certainly set in his thinking now, and she realized that unless she wanted to spend her whole visit fighting him, she was going to have to put up with some of his strange notions. It was going to be hard to keep silent when he said something that she didn't agree with, but as long as his ideas didn't affect her or the children, Brittany promised herself that she would not argue with him.

Things must improve today. She didn't want to regret making this trip, and it was up to her to make sure the memories their family made during this visit were good ones, not ones of battles waged against each other.

Brittany pushed aside thoughts of family conflict and instead focused on the day's activities, thinking through the list of chores she would need to accomplish. *Later I'll have to ask Clem what he thinks about me teaching,* she thought. How she hoped that teaching would not be another subject on which they disagreed!

Brittany threw back the covers and climbed out of bed. There was too much to do today without wasting time lying here thinking. Quickly she dressed and fixed her hair and then crept from the room, moving quietly so she wouldn't wake up Lars and Brenna.

She entered the kitchen where Mr. Myers sat at the table pulling on his boots.

"Good morning," Brittany said, pulling on her apron.

Mr. Myers only grunted, his usual response to everything she said.

Usually Brittany gave up after the first grunt, but whether it was because of her vow to make sure things improved today or just plain stubbornness, she tried again. "Did you sleep well last night?"

He half shrugged.

"It's a beautiful morning."

He gave another grunt, the corner of one eye twitching, and Brittany decided it was time to give him some peace.

Mr. Myers had already had the stove going, and Brittany reached for the frying pan. But a glance at the water bucket told her it needed filling, so she grabbed it by the handle instead and started for the door.

"I can do that." Mr. Myers spoke for the first time.

"That's all right," Brittany said. "I don't mind doing it."

She was out the door before he could protest further. As the door swung shut behind her, she heard him mutter something under his breath, presumably about her, but she paid him no attention. *That man knows nothing about what it means to be joyful,* she thought.

She was instantly ashamed of herself. Too often she found herself focusing on Mr. Myers's bad qualities, not his good ones. Maybe it was because he was always fault-finding with her. But just because he frowned at her didn't mean she ought to frown back. *Lord, please forgive me, and help me to love Mr. Myers, even though he is a difficult man,* she prayed, then shrugged the thought of Mr. Myers aside. It was too beautiful a morning to spoil by complaining over a man who just needed to see the positive side of things more often.

Brittany swung the pail at her side and hummed a hymn to herself as she walked across the yard to the well. It would have been handy if Northridge had a windmill like many farms and ranches; hauling enough water from the well for one day was a chore. But Mr. Myers considered that an unnecessary, new-fangled invention. And he said that since the old well worked just fine, he saw no reason to waste good money on a windmill.

Brittany pulled the cover off the well's opening and hooked the well rope up to her bucket. She dropped the bucket down inside, listening for the splash as it hit the water. Brittany tilted her head back and drew a deep breath of the cool, fresh air, glad for a chance to get outside in the open and away from the confining walls of the cabin. The morning was beautiful, with a meadowlark trilling out its first waking notes as the sun began to slowly peek its head above the horizon. The meadowlark seemed to be echoing the music in Brittany's own heart, singing, *All is well, all is at peace.*

And that was true. With Clem safely home, all was truly well and at peace. Even the wind wasn't blowing as hard as it sometimes did.

Brittany slowly drew the bucket up, watching as the sun flung bars of brilliant pink and gold across the horizon. She had to admit that watching the sunrise here at Northridge was better than watching it in Des Moines. Here the wide horizon and empty plains provided a sweeping view with no buildings or trees to interfere. And Clem had one thing right: Des Moines was never a quiet place. Even in the early morning, traffic would rumble its way through the streets, and people would be thumping down the boardwalk. Brittany had not realized how much she missed the quiet of the farm until now, when she stood here with nothing in the background but the song of the meadowlark.

Brittany set the full bucket to the side, pulled the well cover securely back into place, and then turned back to the cabin. Her feet twitched with a desire to skip. *If I were still a child, I'd set this bucket down and dance and twirl until I was too dizzy to do it anymore,* Brittany thought. The idea immediately arrested her. Why *not* dance and twirl around? This wasn't Des Moines, and no one was around to see. The meadowlark sang out again, its notes clearer and more insistent, and Brittany made up her mind. Setting the bucket down, she glanced first one way, then another. No one was in sight.

Brittany gave a little spin, making her skirt flare in a most delightful way, and unable to help herself, she spun around again. And around. And around again.

The meadowlark seemed to be trilling out its approval, and Brittany couldn't help but laugh. She felt like a girl again, entirely freed from all the heavy responsibilities she carried. The world was a whirl of sunlight and color and birdsong and laughter. She twirled around until she was so dizzy that she had to stop, and closing her eyes, she turned to face the rising sun, letting its warmth and light spill over her.

She stood there for a moment, reveling in joy of the morning. She might have stood there longer but for the sudden impression that she was being watched. Opening her eyes, Brittany turned to find an unfamiliar young man standing not far off, staring at her as if he thought she was out of her mind.

Brittany's heart began to race. How long had he been standing there? How had he sneaked up on her so quietly? And why was he staring at her with such a funny expression on his face?

Brittany's gaze darted from him to the cabin. Would it be better to make a run for it or try and act like nothing had happened? It took her only one second to make up her mind.

"Good morning!" she said in her most cheerful voice. "Beautiful day, isn't it?"

He looked uncertain, so she rushed on. "I–I've never in my life seen such a beautiful sunrise. I really do think the sunrise is one of the nicest things about Wyoming Territory. So many colors, and all of them so vibrant and real—" *Stop talking,* she ordered herself. *The more you prattle on, the more childish you seem. He already saw your little dance. You don't need to make yourself look any worse.*

The young man glanced toward the sunrise and studied it for a moment as if seeing it for the first time. "I reckon it *is* rather pretty," he said at last. Brittany found herself strangely intrigued by his accent. He sounded like no one she'd ever met before, not here or in Iowa.

"I—I better go," Brittany said, taking a step back. "Everyone will be wondering where I am. I'm the Myerses' hired help."

"I know." He didn't smile, but his brown eyes were warm. Brittany instinctively felt that he was a man she could trust, a man different than some of the rough, swearing men she'd already met.

"Have a nice day," she said, the words blending chaotically as she turned to hurry away.

She had only gone a few steps when he called after her, "Is this your bucket?"

She skidded to a stop and turned back to him. He was picking up the pail of water she had set down a few moments before, the very reason she had come out here. She could feel the heat rush to her face at the thought of what Mr. Myers would have said if she came back without it.

"Th—thank you," she said, speaking the words to a button on his shirt rather than to his face as he handed the pail to her. She turned back to the cabin, feeling utterly humiliated. She had always flattered herself that she could handle introductions and conversations with ease, but she had entirely *mis*handled that one. She was already at the cabin when she realized, with some surprise, that the fact he was only a westerner did absolutely nothing to appease her. Nothing at all.

Nathan watched Brittany walk back to the Boss's house, mentally scolding himself for a clumsy introduction. He'd gone tongue-tied, something that seemed to be happening to him with dismaying regularity lately. But in his defense, any man would have the words blown clean away, rounding the corner expecting nothing more than horses but to find a girl spinning in the sunrise. Yes, that was a most unusual sight at Northridge. It made him think of his little sister, Maryanne. Maryanne would have done just what Brittany was doing, dancing for pure joy. Only difference was that she would have tried to get him to dance along with her. And he might have, too; although later he would have wondered what had possessed him to let himself get sweet-talked into such ridiculousness.

"Just enjoyin' the view, hey?" a voice asked behind him, and Nathan felt himself stiffen. It was Rueben. Again.

"There are worse things a fellow could do," Nathan said, keeping his voice even. He glanced again at the sunrise and added almost to himself, "The sunrise *is* rather pretty this morning." He honestly couldn't remember the last time he'd thought to pay attention to the sunrise, despite the fact that it painted the sky every morning.

"Sunrise ain't what I meant," Reuben said, grinning. "I meant that." He jabbed a finger toward the Myers' cabin where Brittany had just disappeared.

Nathan felt his face turn hot, much to his annoyance. "The ideas you come up with," he muttered, turning away.

"Not interested, huh? Little Joe and George tell me she's awful purty. You got yourself a different girl?"

"No, and I'm not looking to find one." Nathan didn't attempt to keep the snap from his voice.

"Maybe someday you'll change your mind," Rueben said in a patronizing tone that set Nathan's teeth on edge.

Nathan didn't bother to respond, just walked faster until he had outdistanced Rueben. "That man's got some nerve," he muttered, throwing the barn door open a little harder than usual. *Take a deep breath, and don't let him get you all worked up,* he told himself. He did just that and gained a little more control of himself. He grabbed his saddle and bridle and headed outside again. Why was it that he let the little things Rueben said bother him so much? He ought to just ignore the man—good advice, but impossible to follow.

Nathan set off for the corral where Loner stood waiting for him, his mind still working on the problem. He scarcely noticed the meadowlark singing nearby, its notes ringing out true and clear in the still morning.

CHAPTER
13

The sun hovered close to the horizon, this time dipping low in the west, as Brittany stepped out onto the porch to join Clem. Despite the fact that they lived on the same ranch now, their work took them in separate directions, and Brittany found that evenings were the only time she might have a chance to talk with her brother. All day long she looked forward to the evening and the time they could visit; after all, the reason she had come to Northridge was to be with Clem again. They still had much to catch up on, and Brittany guessed that it would be a long while before either of them had a hard time thinking of what to say.

"You want to walk?" Clem asked. "It's a little chilly out here just to sit."

Brittany was glad that Clem's voice held none of the coolness of the evening before. She pulled her shawl tighter around her and asked, "Where's your coat?"

"In the bunkhouse. This isn't cold enough for a coat. I hate wearing my coat unless I absolutely have to. It's a big, bulky thing that keeps out the cold all right, but makes it hard to move."

Brittany hid her smile at yet another of Clem's strange ideas. She would much rather wear the "big, bulky thing" than be cold. She disliked cold about as much as a kitten disliked water.

"We could go inside," she said, but Clem shook his head.

"This is fine," he said, then added as an afterthought, "unless you're too cold."

"I'm the one with the coat, remember?" Brittany hesitated, then dared to ask, "Is there a reason you don't want to go inside, Clem?"

Clem shrugged. "It's just a little—awkward, you might say. Since I work for them, and all."

"Oh," Brittany said although she didn't see at all. She took Clem's offered arm, and together they walked down the cabin's steps. "You'll *have* to come inside this winter."

"I guess." Clem sounded as if the prospect was a grim one. Then his face brightened. "Or we could meet at Johnny's place. Johnny and I are good friends."

"And you're not with Mr. Myers the younger?" Brittany tried in vain to keep from smiling.

"The answer to that is no." Clem grinned as well. "I always get this crawling feeling on the back of my neck when he's around—as if he's going to pass sentence on me."

"So I'm not the only person who feels that way?"

"By no means!"

The two of them strolled on, and again Brittany found herself enjoying the quiet of Northridge. The quiet and privacy of the ranch almost made up for its faults. Almost.

"I spent some time before supper with Lars and Brenna," Clem said. "I realized that you're right. They don't know me at all. I'm going to try to be intentional during your visit and really spend time with them, you understand?"

"That sounds good." Brittany felt her heart warm at her brother's thoughtfulness, but before she could stop herself, she asked, "It was just you and the children, wasn't it?"

Clem stiffened, and Brittany knew he had caught her meaning. "When I make a promise, I keep it," he said, his voice hard. "No one else was around."

Brittany bit her lip, wishing she had kept quiet. He was so defensive of his Western friends.

They walked past Johnny's cabin, and Brittany noticed that tonight Johnny wasn't the only one sitting on his porch. Another man occupied the rocker beside him. With a start, Brittany realized that he was the young man she had met earlier that morning—the man who had seen her crazy dance. She glanced at Clem, a sudden, horrible thought striking her. Had the man told Clem about what he'd seen? Clem would get a good laugh hearing about that, and he'd never let her live it down. Suppose, even worse, everyone in the bunkhouse knew about it, and she had been the joke of the day? Brittany's face felt suddenly hot, and she could not, for the life of her, look at that man sitting by Johnny.

Then, to her horror, Clem slowed almost to a stop. They couldn't be stopping here, could they? But that was the way things appeared.

"What are you two doing just sitting there?" Clem called out to them, his voice teasing, "Are you so lazy that you can't at least get up and walk while you visit? Don't you have any sense of industry?"

"Clem sure has a knack at makin' people feel good about themselves," Johnny said, raising his eyes to the sky.

"Tell us how walking around in aimless circles is industrious and we'll come join y'all," the other man said, his accent even heavier than before. Brittany couldn't resist taking a peep at him. He was sitting with his hands behind his head, and his legs stretched out in front of him. His gaze caught hers for the briefest moment, and Brittany wondered if it was just her imagination or if there was a little twinkle in his eyes. Hastily she looked away.

"Walking's good exercise," Clem returned. "Real good exercise."

"That's all well and good, but I think I've had enough exercise for one day," the young man said around a yawn. "You get along and walk your circles if you want, but I have no intention of moving."

"He speaks for both of us," Johnny added.

"You two are no fun," Clem said, shaking his head. He took Brittany's arm again and resumed walking. "No fun at all."

The young man murmured something that Brittany missed, and Johnny gave a snort of laughter. Brittany glanced back at them one last time and found them both looking at her. And there was definitely a twinkle in the young man's brown eyes now. *He does have nice eyes.* The thought made Brittany trip, and had Clem not held her arm, she might have fallen.

"Whoa, easy there," Clem said, and Brittany focused her attention on the path in front of her, aware that her cheeks were painfully warm.

"That was a friend of yours?" she asked when she was positive they were out of earshot of the two men on the porch.

"Yep," Clem said. He did not go on.

"He grew up in the area?" she asked, not sure why she was digging for more information about the man.

"Nope."

He was stingier with his words than a miser with his gold. "Well, where *did* he grow up then?" she asked, tempted to stamp her foot.

Clem burst into laughter. "Brittany, Brittany," he said, shaking his head. "How is that one night you're beating me over the head for wanting to introduce you to a couple friends, and tonight you're so curious about one of those very *Western* men?" He gave the word *Western* a little twist that told Brittany what he thought of her opinions.

"I'll tell you what," he said. "If you want any more information about him, you'll just have to ask him yourself. He'll be happy to answer any questions you have." His eyes sparkled with laughter—and a challenge.

If Brittany thought her face was hot before, it was doubly so now, knowing she deserved his scolding. She had told him in no uncertain terms that she didn't want to hear about any westerner or have anything to do with one, and yet here she was asking for information about one. It wasn't like her to be irresolute like that.

Brittany's chin lifted. "Fine. I won't ask you anything else. I was just trying to make conversation."

Clem's face betrayed his doubt about that, and for an instant Brittany feared he was going to start laughing again. But he held himself in check and instead asked, "How'd your work for the Myerses go today?"

Brittany grabbed at the new subject, glad for a reprieve from the teasing. "It went well, as usual. Mr. Myers can't complain that I don't know how to cook or wash laundry."

Clem smiled. "That's a girl. Just you wait, and I'm sure you'll win him over with time. Did you ever hear about the Myerses' hired help before you?"

"Morgan told me a little about them. Why?"

"That whole experience left a bad taste for city women with the Boss. You're just going to have to work a bit to show him that you're not like them and that you won't go back on your word."

Brittany pondered the information. So Mr. Myers's lack of trust in her was the root of the problems between them. He thought she was unreliable because she was from the city. It seemed unfair, and Brittany made up her mind that she *would* win his approval, even if she had to turn headstands to get it.

"Clem, there was something else I wanted to talk with you about," she said.

"Talk away. My ears are open."

"I–I was wondering—" Brittany paused, her mouth suddenly dry. The moment had finally come to tell him her idea about teaching. The moment that so much hinged upon.

"Yes, you're wondering—" Clem prompted.

"I had an idea, you see. There's a little boy, Carson Bryan—"

"Grant's son." Clem nodded. "Sure, I know him."

"Well, he came over to visit Lars and Brenna, which gave me the idea in the first place."

Clem's eyebrows arched. "Sorry, Brittany. You're going to have to stop talking in riddles. Tell me flat out what this idea of yours is, 'cause I'm just not getting it."

Brittany drew a deep breath and let her thoughts come tumbling out in a rush. "He said he can't read, which gave me the idea that perhaps we could open a school of sorts, at least to teach the children around here how to read. We could—"

"We? What do you mean *we*?"

"*We*, singular." Brittany pointed at herself. "*We* meaning *me*."

Clem nodded uncertainly. "Have you talked this over with anyone else yet?"

"Yes. I already talked with Mrs. Myers and Morgan."

"I see. What did they say?"

"To talk with you about it."

Clem looked taken aback. "What do they want me to say?"

"Whether you think it's a good idea or not." Brittany clasped her hands. "Please, Clem, do say it would be all right. I really want to do this, and if you say no, I won't have a chance."

"Are there any hidden strings attached to this?" Clem asked.

"No, not at all. All I need is your approval of my idea."

Clem seemed to think for a moment. "You do realize that this is going to be a lot of work. None of those kids probably has a lick of learning, and they don't know the first thing about what school is."

"I know it won't be easy, but I have to try. Those children are capable of learning; they just need an opportunity."

Clem nodded slowly. "Well, then I guess you can have my approval, for whatever it's worth."

Brittany stared at him. "Really?" she asked. Surely it couldn't be this easy.

"Sure," he said, grinning.

"Oh, Clem, thank you!" Brittany clasped her hands together. "You don't know what this means to me."

"Pleasure to oblige."

"I need to go talk to the Myerses," Brittany said, spinning around and starting for the cabin.

"What's the hurry?" Clem called after her.

"Why *not* hurry?"

Brittany found it hard to restrain herself to a ladylike walk when all she wanted to do was fly across the ground as fast as she could. She nearly leaped up the cabin steps, skipping the last one entirely, and pushing open the door, she flew into the kitchen.

Mr. and Mrs. Myers both looked up from where they sat at the kitchen table, the lantern sputtering between them. Unable to hold the wonderful news to herself one second longer, Brittany said, "I just talked to Clem, and he said that it would be all right."

"What would be all right?" Mrs. Myers asked, exchanging a look with her husband.

"If I wanted to teach!"

Mr. Myers's expression didn't change. "Now, hold on. We never told you that you could teach, did we?"

Brittany felt herself crash back to earth with a jolt. "I—I suppose you didn't. But you said I should ask Clem, and I did."

Mr. Myers's frown deepened. "We hired you to come and help us, not be out gallivanting and teaching school, right?"

"But—" Brittany began.

"We want you here full time, you hear? Why else would we say no marryin'? Teachin' school would take a big chunk of time, and you would be out runnin' all around the countryside, every which way for most of the week instead of bein' here where you belong."

"But it wouldn't have to be that way," Brittany said, speaking more boldly than she felt.

Mr. Myers raised one bushy eyebrow. "How so?"

Brittany willed her heart to stop pounding so wildly. "For one thing, the lessons wouldn't have to be very long."

"They'd still take up time." Mr. Myers frowned and shook his head. "And where would you have these lessons of yours in the first place? There ain't no school building 'round here in case you forgot."

Brittany bit her lip. "I–I don't know. Maybe we could have them here—that is, if it would be fine by you."

"Here?" Mr. Myers exploded. "Here? Do you think that me and Eleanor want to have our place overrun brimful with screeching, running, giggling children? You already brought two here; ain't that enough for you?"

"Tim." Mrs. Myers laid a hand on his arm.

Mr. Myers turned to her. "Now, Eleanor, you just listen to me. We gotta be firm and set our limits, or this here girl is gonna have our ranch turned into an orphanage or somethin' before we can even turn around."

"Tim," Mrs. Myers said again. "Brittany said nothing of the sort. All she wants is to hold a few lessons here to teach children to read."

Mr. Myers let out a huff. "Now look—this here girl is hardly more than a kid herself. Put her in a room full of kids, and she might just set herself down and start playin' games with them, not even teachin' them, and things are gonna git out of control around here."

Brittany clenched her jaw to keep from making a nasty response. Hardly more than a kid? The nerve of the man! She was every day of eighteen years old, plus a little more, and it had been years since she'd romped around as a girl.

Mrs. Myers saved her from needing to speak. "You can't say that, Tim. Brittany is a responsible young woman—"

"Maybe that's how you see her, but that ain't quite how I see her. I think it would be one big mistake to let this here girl frolic around playin' at teachin' school when she should be here helpin' you." Mr. Myers huffed again.

Brittany clenched her fists as well as her jaw. If he dared call her "this here girl" one more time, as if she were a table or chair instead of a living human in the very same room as him, she was going to scream. Playing at teaching school? That was some idea.

"Why don't we talk about this later?" Mrs. Myers said, pressing her lips into a thin line.

"No need." Mr. Myers rose from his seat. "My mind is made up. Nobody is gonna be teachin' no schools around here. Nobody." He stomped off toward his bedroom, slamming the door behind him.

Brittany stared at the door, then at Mrs. Myers.

"I'm sorry, dear," Mrs. Myers said, rubbing her hands together in a way that told Brittany they must be hurting her again. "I would give up on the idea if I were you. Tim surely does have his mind made up this time."

Brittany couldn't reply. Her gaze again went to the closed door, and she could feel tears burn behind her eyes. That was just what had happened to her dreams; a door had been slammed shut on them with no warning. *I thought this was Your will, Lord,* she prayed inwardly. *What went wrong?*

CHAPTER

14

Breakfast was uncomfortably silent the next morning, a heavy tension hanging over the table. Mr. Myers scowled at his bacon, hardly raising his eyes from the plate as he shoveled his breakfast into his mouth. Mrs. Myers looked tense, and even Lars and Brenna, who had nothing to do with the argument, seemed to catch the room's undercurrent and said scarcely a word.

Mr. Myers already gave a decided "no" to my idea. He needn't keep glowering at me as if he wished the earth would swallow me up whole, Brittany thought, making herself take another bite of her food. She wasn't hungry, but she didn't dare leave any food on her plate. Waste was one thing Mr. Myers could not abide.

"Tim, dear, we need to talk," Mrs. Myers said as Mr. Myers drained the last of the coffee from his cup.

Mr. Myers frowned. "Seems to me we've already said all that needs sayin'."

"I think you should reconsider Brittany's idea. I really think we could make this work."

"Now Eleanor, I already told you that if we let this here girl run loose all over the country—"

"Brittany would not be running all over the country." Mrs. Myers's voice took on a determined note Brittany had never heard her use before. "She would have her lessons here."

"Here?" Mr. Myers's voice rose.

"Yes, here. It's a practical solution. And like Brittany said, her lessons wouldn't have to be very long."

"But–but this is preposterous!" Mr. Myers' eyes blazed. "We're hirin' this here girl for money, and she signed a contract that made no provision for her teachin'!"

"But neither did it say she couldn't teach. Please, just give this a trial, won't you? I'm sure Brittany will be able to keep up with her work around here, and if she doesn't, we'll consider the trial over, and we'll set the teaching idea aside."

Mr. Myers seemed to be thinking. "If this doesn't work, the girl will stop teaching right away?"

"Right away."

"I expect you would keep an eye on her, make sure she's doin' what she's supposed to?"

"Of course."

Mr. Myers heaved a deep sigh. "Well, I reckon she's your help. If you want to let her give it a try, I guess you can if the neighbors will let their kids come. But remember I didn't suggest this, so if she quits on us to go become a schoolteacher, just like all those other women ran off to git hitched, don't blame me."

"Thank you, Tim. More coffee before you go?"

He grunted his no, and rising to his feet, he marched out the door. The cabin walls shook as the door shut behind him. Brittany blinked, stunned that Mr. Myers had agreed to her teaching school, and without her even saying a word.

"Tim's a dear, but he gets ideas sometimes," Mrs. Myers said, shaking her head but smiling. "Sometimes, he just needs a good night's sleep to think things over."

Brittany exhaled slowly. "Thank you, Mrs. Myers."

"Thanks for what? I didn't do anything." Mrs. Myers reached out to pat Brittany's hand. "I'd suggest you get the finer details of your teaching plan worked out, like how long your lessons will be, what days, and such. Then you should go talk to the Bryans and the Joneses."

"Today?" Brittany asked, her joy suddenly changing to irrational fear. Everything was happening so fast. Too fast.

"Why not? There's no sense in waiting."

"I–I suppose not. But—" Brittany paused.

"What is it? Are you having second thoughts?"

"It's just, I've never done anything like this before," Brittany sought Mrs. Myers's eyes. "I'm not a real teacher. What if I fail? Is this really a good idea?"

"Brittany, we've been praying about this, right?"

Brittany nodded slowly.

"And I believe that your heart in this is right. I also know this is unexpected to you, but you must not let doubts creep in. Do your best, and remember that your job is not to produce results but to be faithful to the Lord. Understand?"

Brittany could feel the bands of tension around her chest loosen. "I think so."

"Good. Now, let's do some thinking about these lessons of yours."

The world was coated in a layer of frost that glinted in the early morning sun as Brittany made her way from the house to the barn just half an hour later. The morning was chilly, reminding her yet again that winter was fast approaching. She remembered Clem writing of blizzards that whipped through the area. With snow so blinding, a person could easily get lost between the house and the barn, and cold so penetrating that a person might freeze to death with no fire to warm him or her. Brittany grimaced. She had never experienced a Western winter, but it was nothing to look forward to, given what she already knew.

She pulled her coat more tightly around herself and let her thoughts turn from winter back to her mission now. She still had trouble believing that she would actually be teaching school—if the parents agreed, that is. She had a plan for her teaching firmly in mind, and Mrs. Myers had given directions to the Bryan brothers' ranch and the Joneses. She hoped that with Mr. Myers' stubbornness she had already jumped the worst of the hurdles she was going to face, but the knot tightening in the middle of her stomach warned that worse things could happen. She refused to allow her mind to dwell on the meetings that lay ahead of her.

Brittany swung the barn door open and stepped into the gloom of the building. Mrs. Myers had told her to get Johnny or Mr. Myers to help with saddling up Major, but Brittany hesitated to do that. She wouldn't have minded Johnny's help; that would have been a relief, really. But Mr. Myers was another matter. He was already in a bad temper with her this morning, not that his temper was ever overly amiable toward her. He was over at Johnny's now, talking something over with him, and Brittany didn't wish to face him again. He was sure to be irritated by her request, and as anxious as she already felt over the upcoming meetings, she didn't care to endure more of his scowls. So instead of going over to Johnny's to ask one of them for help, she headed to the barn herself. She would saddle Major, and Mr. Myers would have no reason to rail at her over her helplessness. Besides, she was certain that saddling a horse couldn't be too hard. Surely, any intelligent young woman should be able to figure it out without too much trouble.

Brittany had to do some looking before she found a saddle and bridle for Major at the back of the barn. She recognized the saddle as the one she used when coming to Northridge, so she wouldn't be stealing anyone else's saddle. She flinched a little at the idea of using *that* saddle again, the man's saddle, but it appeared she had no choice. She hated to think of the expression on Aunt Ida's face were she to see her, but then, Aunt Ida would be horrified at the idea of her riding a horse in the first place. Brittany grabbed the saddle and bridle and carried them to the door. The saddle was heavier than it looked, with an awkward shape that made it difficult to handle. She tripped several times over the dangling cinch strap as she lugged it outside and dropped it by the hitching rail, panting.

Brittany paused for a moment to catch her breath and gather herself together for the next step—getting Major out here. To her relief, Major was in the corral today, not out grazing. There were a few other horses in with him, horses that Brittany was not glad to see. She knew nothing about them or their temperament, whether they were wild or tame or easily spooked. For all she knew, they could be man killers.

Brittany made her way to the corral gate, trying to ignore her mounting fear. As she drew closer to the horses, she was once again amazed at their size and by the fact that a mere human could control such power. *Perhaps* control *isn't quite the right word,* she thought, slipping through the gate. Direct *is better.* Meaning that while a horse might generally listen to its rider, there could be times when it did not. An idea that Brittany did not like at all.

Brittany made sure to close the gate behind her as she entered the corral. The last thing she needed was to have one of the horses push up against it and escape while her back was turned. Mr. Myers would be really angry with her then.

Major stood with his head hanging low, looking rather sorry, but the other three horses watched her warily, their ears pricked and their heads held high. As Brittany drew closer, they whirled around and bolted for the other side of the fence. Major suddenly seemed to come to life and ran after them, away from Brittany.

Brittany sighed and went after him again, calling in her sweetest voice, "Here, Major. It's time to do a little work now. Come here, boy."

Her words seemed to have no effect on him. He just stared apathetically from under a shaggy black forelock— until the other horses bolted, and he took off with them again.

Frustration welled up inside Brittany, making her want to throw the bridle onto the ground and stomp away. But that would be childish, so, gritting her teeth, she set off toward the horses.

Twenty minutes passed before she finally caught Major. Or rather, he let himself be caught. He could have easily kept her from getting ahold of him, but by then he seemed to be tiring of his little game. He stood still as Brittany fumbled around with the bridle, trying to make sense of the leather straps and the metal bit at the bottom. The bit went in his mouth; she knew that much. But was she supposed to put the bit in his mouth first, or the leather strap over his ears? After a moment's study, she decided that the bit went first, and, feeling well-pleased with herself, turned to put it into his mouth.

Another ten minutes passed before she could get him to accept the bit. He kept throwing his head up in the most provoking way and refused to open his mouth until Brittany wondered if she had it wrong, and the straps over the ears came first. But finally Major tired of that game as well, and heaving a great sigh, he lowered his head and allowed Brittany to put the bit in his mouth.

"You *know* you can get away with such pranks with me, don't you? You wouldn't do all these tricks on Mr. Myers, now would you?" Brittany accused him.

Major's only response was to give another deep sigh and stare at her mournfully.

Getting the straps over his ears took little effort, and in a moment she was leading him out of the corral. Brittany led him over to the hitching rail and tied him up, then grabbed the saddle. She struggled to lift it onto his back, wishing she wasn't so short. Wishing that she were stronger. Wishing that she had never come to Wyoming Territory in the first place! Stray locks of hair escaped from her bun and teased about her face, and all the exertion had made her overly warm—her heavy coat trapping all the heat. Clem did have one thing right: a coat restricted movement badly.

Brittany grabbed the cinch strap and pulled it under Major's belly, fastening it loosely in place. "There," she said aloud, stepping back to admire her work. "I knew it couldn't be too hard. Any intelligent person could do that."

Major only gave a little snort.

"Silly horse. You don't have much appreciation, do you?" Brittany asked, rubbing him on the neck. Despite all the trouble he'd caused her, she was starting to like the old horse, spunkiness and all.

Brittany grabbed onto the saddle horn and stuck her foot in the stirrup, pausing to gather herself together for the jump that would land her on Major's back. "One, two, three," she counted, then put all her strength into a mighty leap upward.

But something was wrong, terribly wrong. The saddle shifted, then began to slip, taking Brittany with it.

"Oh, no, no, no!" She grabbed for something, anything to stop the fall, but her hand closed on thin air. The ground seemed to fly up to meet her, and with a crash, Brittany struck it.

She wanted to scream, cry, yell, anything, but the air seemed to have completely left her, and she was unable to so much as draw a breath. *Breathe,* she ordered herself. *Don't panic, just breathe. Breathe!*

With great effort, she finally managed to take one breath, then another, and her fear subsided. It was then that she heard footsteps coming toward her, quickly. She wanted to turn and see who was coming, but for the moment it seemed wise to just lie still and concentrate on breathing.

"Are you all right?" a voice asked, and Brittany opened her eyes to find a pair of brown eyes hovering above her. Brown eyes set in a face she was beginning to dread seeing.

It's that man again. Brittany felt her heart sink. The man who had witnessed her wild dance. The man Clem refused to talk about. He sure had a habit of appearing at bad moments.

He was still watching her, and Brittany realized she hadn't answered him. "I–I think I'm fine," she said, her voice barely a whisper even though she felt as if she were shouting.

"You're sure?" he asked.

"Yes," Brittany said, her voice sounding more natural now. "I'm fine."

She struggled to a sitting position, but he stopped her. "Just stay there a minute. That was a pretty nasty tumble, and it might be best if you just sit tight a moment longer."

Brittany was willing to do just that, even if she was in a rather humiliating position. She watched the man out of the corner of her eye and noticed the way that he looked at the upside-down saddle on Major's back, his eyebrow quirking slightly.

"I've never saddled a horse before," she said, explaining the obvious. "I–I thought I would try–I was sure it would be easy, but I realized it's not." She could feel her cheeks warm. It seemed that over the past couple of days she had blushed more than she had in years.

The young man nodded slowly, thoughtfully. "Saddling is easy once you get it down."

"Well, I'm not at that point yet." Brittany gave her head a shake that sent several pins slipping from her bun. She reached back and tried to push them into place, but it still felt as if her hair could go tumbling at any moment.

"And there was no one around to show you how to do it?" he asked, his drawl catching her attention yet again. It was a strange accent, but also rather—appealing?

Brittany blushed even more deeply. "I could have asked Johnny or Mr. Myers."

"But?"

"But Johnny was talking with Mr. Myers," she said, not sure why she was confessing this to him, a complete stranger. "And Mr. Myers and I sometimes have a hard time—understanding each other."

"I see," he said, and Brittany got the impression that he really did.

"So I thought I would do it myself and try to–to avoid Mr. Myers. But, well, this is what happened."

Again he nodded, a smile fighting at the corners of his lips.

"It wasn't funny," Brittany said without thinking. "It wasn't one tiny bit funny."

Now a real smile spread across his face, a smile that could dim the sun. "I know it wasn't. When I saw you fall, I had one awful picture of having to tell Clem that his little sister was terribly injured, or worse, and laughing was about as far from my mind as Canada is from the Rio Grande."

"You know Clem?" Brittany asked, again without thinking. The answer was obvious.

"Sure, I do," he said. "He's one of my best friends."

Brittany stared at him. "Who are you?"

"Who am I?" He stared back at her. "I–I'm sorry. I thought Clem—" He shook his head, not finishing the thought. "Sorry. I'm just not good at introductions. My name is Nathan, Nathan Lindale."

Nathan Lindale. The name rang a bell in Brittany's mind. This was the man Clem had wanted to introduce her to, the man she had thrown a fit over meeting. She was sure her face must have drained of color.

"I–I see," she stammered, gathering her scattered wits together. "I'm pleased to meet you, Mr. Lindale."

"Please, it's just Nathan," he said, and Brittany found herself nodding in agreement. Just "Nathan" seemed to suit him better than "Mr. Lindale".

"Where are you from, Nathan?" Brittany asked. The question had been eating at her since their first encounter the day before.

He ran one finger along a jawline strong enough to almost be called stubborn. "This is home now, but I grew up in Texas."

Texas. That explained his funny accent. "Texas is a long way from here."

A little shadow crossed his face. "A lifetime away."

He glanced back at Major and suddenly became all business again. "If you think you're ready to stand, I'll show you how to saddle up old Major."

Brittany couldn't quite hide her surprise. "You'd do that?"

"Of course," he said. "I can spare a bit of time. Besides, wouldn't want you to have to drag the Boss out here for help." There was a glint of teasing in his eyes.

"Thank you." Brittany started to stand. He offered her a hand and helped her up.

"You feel dizzy or lightheaded at all?" he asked.

Brittany shook her head. "I'm fine." For some strange reason, she felt comfortable in Nathan's presence. Perhaps it was because of Clem's praise for him. Maybe even more so because of his straightforward manner and a gaze that held none of George and

Little Joe's ogling or the possessiveness of Able Zimmerman. Just genuine concern for her.

Nathan turned to Major, motioning Brittany over, and with deft fingers, he undid the mess she had made of the cinch. Then he placed the saddle on Major's back where it belonged, just as easily as if it weighed no more than a feather.

"You're going to have to pull the cinch tighter this time so that your saddle won't slip," he said, holding the end of the cinch out to her.

"But won't that hurt Major?" she asked.

"No need to worry about that." He smiled slightly. "Major might look sad about getting saddled up, but he's not in the least bit of pain."

Brittany took the cinch, and following his directions, pulled it tight and fastened it into place. She glanced at Nathan and was rewarded with a nod of approval.

Strangely, her mind suddenly turned to William Brown, and she could picture his blue eyes and winning smile as vividly as if he were standing before her. Why she thought of William, Brittany could not imagine. He bore little similarity to this young man. William was fair; Nathan was darker. William was always dressed immaculately, his suit crisply pressed and every strand of hair in its proper place. Nathan wore a pair of dusty chaps, a blue shirt, rather the worse for wear, and a Stetson that appeared to have seen better days. William smiled and laughed with ease; Nathan was sparing with his smiles, not to mention his laughter. William was a model of perfect manners, a man who always knew just what to say, a gentleman in every respect. But he would have been entirely out of place doing what Nathan was just now—standing beside a rangy old pony on a ranch in the middle of nowhere, teaching her to saddle a horse for herself.

"Now, let's look at Major's bridle and see how you did there," Nathan said, interrupting her thoughts. That was probably a good thing. Thinking of William only brought on another wave of homesickness for Des Moines and the life she knew before coming to Northridge.

She joined Nathan at Major's head and could tell from the look on his face that she had not put the bridle on right. "This strap is twisted," he said, undoing her work. "and you needed to fasten this buckle right here."

"Oh." Brittany's ignorance threatened to overwhelm her.

Nathan fastened the bridle the right way, then stepped back. "You're ready to go."

"Thank you. I—I'm sorry I took up so much of your time."

"No trouble," Nathan said, turning to leave.

"Nathan," Brittany called after him. He stopped and turned to face her again. "You—you won't tell Clem about this, will you?" It was more than a question; it was a plea.

Nathan shook his head. "Why would I?"

"Did you tell him about—about yesterday?" she asked, struggling to get the question out.

Again Nathan shook his head. "There's no reason he needs to know about either yesterday or today." He studied her, one eyebrow arched. "You thought I'd tell him?"

"I didn't know what to think. For all I knew, you might have told the whole bunkhouse."

"I wouldn't do that," he said, his voice quiet but firm.

"Thank you," Brittany said, then wondered why she was whispering.

He tipped his hat to her and again turned and walked away. Brittany watched him go, gratitude welling up inside her. He was different than any other young man she'd ever met, but he seemed nice. And helpful. And considerate. *Clem has a good friend,* she admitted to herself. Even if he was Western.

Brittany thought of the way his face had shadowed when he spoke of Texas being a lifetime away, and she wondered if perhaps he too knew what homesickness was. A lifetime away. That's about how far off her life in Des Moines seemed right now. Brittany absentmindedly rubbed her hand along Major's neck. Maybe there were some things she and Nathan Lindale had in common.

CHAPTER
15

The Bryan brothers sure do have a nice place. Brittany viewed the land spread out before her as Major plodded down the long lane leading to Grant and Jay Bryan's ranch. Every building appeared even bigger than the Myerses', from the barn to the bunkhouse. There were a couple different corrals with horses milling around in them, and two stout cabins flanked either side of the ranch. A windmill whirred in the wind, its blades gleaming in the sun, and judging by how neat the place looked, Brittany guessed the Bryan brothers were doing well in their ranching.

As Brittany rode into the yard, an older boy came running from the barn. "I'll take your horse for you, ma'am," he said, stopping in front of her.

"Why, thank you," Brittany said, looking down at his freckled, good-natured face.

"You're the Myerses' new helper, ain't you?" he asked as she dismounted.

"Yes, I am. But how—?"

"Carson was tellin' us about you." He tipped his hat back to reveal a thatch of reddish-blond hair. "Carson's my kid brother."

"Ah." Now that Brittany thought of it, she did notice that he and Carson shared the same thick-lashed blue eyes. "And what is your name?"

"I'm Everett Bryan," the boy said, sticking out a hand. "Grant and Kate's oldest."

"Nice to meet you, Everett." Brittany shook the boy's hand. "How old are you?"

"Twelve." He nodded toward the bigger of the two cabins. "Ma's in there, iffen she's who you come to talk with. Otherwise, Aunt Allie lives over there." He nodded to the other cabin.

"I'd like to talk to them both."

"Sure." Everett cupped his hands around his mouth and called, "Hey, Billy!"

"Yeah?" a small boy poked his head out of the barn door.

"Go git your ma! Tell her to come to our house, 'cause there's a lady who wants to see her."

"Sure!" The boy took off running, his arms swinging in rhythm with his pumping legs.

"That's my cousin Billy," Everett told Brittany. "He likes to follow me around, helpin' me out with stuff." He gathered up Major's reins and walked off toward the hitching rail. "Just go right on in. Ma will be mighty glad to have company."

Brittany started down the dirt path leading to Kate Bryan's house, mentally rehearsing what she was going to say. How she hoped the Bryans would see the value of what she could teach their children. They obviously were more forward-thinking than the Myerses, with their tall, metal windmill pumping up water.

Brittany reached the door and raised a hand to knock, but the door swung open before she could. Carson stood in front of her, grinning from ear to ear. "Ma, the pretty lady who works for the Myerses is here!"

"Well, by all means, let her in. Don't just leave her standin' there." An apron-clad woman with reddish-blond hair like Everett's came up behind Carson. She smiled at Brittany and said, "I'm Kate Bryan. You just come right on in. I'm afraid we don't git much for company 'round here. Kids git all worked up and forget their manners when visitors do come."

The woman ushered Brittany into a kitchen that looked much like the Myerses', Carson skipping along right at Brittany's side.

"Let me git the coffee brewin', and then we can set ourselves down and visit," Kate said, bustling over to the stove. She waved to one of the straight-backed wooden chairs pulled up to the table. "Help yourself to a chair."

Brittany did just that, Carson taking the seat across from her. No sooner had she sat down than the door opened once again, and a woman entered the kitchen, one small child on her hip and another little boy clinging to her skirts.

"Howdy there!" she said, sending Brittany a smile every bit as welcoming as Kate's. "Billy tells me there's visiting going on over here, so I just thought I'd barge in on you."

"Land!" Kate said from the stove. "As if your comin' would ever be an intrusion. Scarce a day passes that I don't tell my man he and Jay ought to have just built one big house for us all. Would save both you and me quite a few steps goin' between each other's places."

"Kate's husband and mine are brothers, as I'm sure ya know," the woman said to Brittany. "I'm Allie, Jay's wife."

"Pleased to meet you, Allie, and you too, Kate. I'm Brittany Haines."

"Clem Haines's sister." Allie nodded. "I've seen your brother around before. You do look a lot like him, a good thing, of course. Your brother is one mighty-fine-looking man, although not as good-looking as my husband." Her eyes twinkled.

Allie disentangled herself from the boy clinging to her skirt and took a seat. "This feels real good. Thanks for giving me an excuse to sit down. Keepin' up with these two wears a person out."

"How many children do you have?" Brittany asked.

"Two. Nothing compared to Kate."

Brittany looked at Kate.

"I've got five kids." Kate set cups of coffee in front of both Brittany and Allie and took a seat herself. "I've been thinkin' I should git myself over to the Myerses' place and introduce myself to you, but it's been busy around here with Grant gone on a cattle drive, and I just kept putting it off. I'm glad you stopped by to visit."

Brittany smiled and nodded, wondering if now was a good time to bring up her idea. "I actually came to run an idea past you," she said. "I was wondering if perhaps your children would be interested in me teaching them some reading lessons. I have a little time, and I thought maybe–maybe your children would like to learn to read."

Brittany watched the faces of the two women before her, wondering what was going through their minds. Neither of their expressions changed in the slightest.

"It's entirely your choice," she said, laying her hands on the table palms down. "The lessons would only be a couple hours each, maybe Tuesdays and Thursdays And if you don't like my idea, I completely understand. Don't feel any pressure."

"Hmm." Kate fiddled with her cup. "I don't know—"

"Say yes, Ma," Carson whispered loud enough to be heard across the room. The boy's eyes sparkled.

"Hush, son. Let me think." Kate looked at Brittany. "What do you charge?"

"Charge?" Brittany repeated. "Nothing."

"Nothing, huh?" Kate's eyebrows rose. "But surely you wouldn't just do this teachin' for nothin'. I've an idea this ain't gonna be an easy job you're takin' on. Don't you want somethin' in return?"

"No." Brittany shook her head vigorously. "No, all that I ask is that those who do wish to learn work hard and behave themselves."

"Ma, I could do that easy," Carson whispered loudly.

"I said hush, son," Kate said, frowning at him. She turned back to Brittany. "When does this school of yours start?"

"I was thinking next week," Brittany replied. Since one of the men at Northridge would be taking the wagon to Fort Laramie for supplies in a couple days, she and Mrs. Myers had decided that one week would give her time to get some basic teaching materials, such as paper and pencils, and to prepare her lessons.

"What ages are you thinking of teachin'?" Allie asked.

"Six and up."

"Oh. Billy, my oldest, is only five."

"Do you think he's ready to learn to read?" Brittany asked.

"He's a smart boy. He has a good memory, and if I tell him something once, he has it memorized for good," Allie replied.

"Then if you would like for him to learn to read, he may come," Brittany said.

Allie's eyes brightened. "Good. I'll have to talk with Jay, but I'm sure he'll be right fine with Billy going. I always wished I knew how to read."

"Then you come, too," Brittany said, only half teasing.

"Now, Jay might have something else to say about that. Me, a grown woman with children, going off to school to learn to read?" Allie shook her head. "Supper won't cook itself; I've got my hands plenty full without adding a bunch of frivolous lessons to the list." She laughed, but Brittany thought she still looked wistful.

"Ma," Carson said, leaning forward, "can I go too?"

Kate looked uncertain. "I don't know as how readin' and writin's gonna help you at all 'round these parts."

"Can't hurt," Carson said, his eyes pleading.

Kate wagged her head. "Talk it over with your pa when he gets home. I don't care what you do, long as your chores git done on time."

Carson sat back in his chair, beaming. Evidently he was sure of what his pa's response would be.

"How many of your children would be attending—if your husband agrees, of course?" Brittany asked Kate.

Kate shrugged. "Oh, I dunno. Guess I'll leave it up to the kids. And Grant. It'll be all five of 'em at the most."

"I see." Brittany rose from her seat. "Excuse me for leaving so quickly, but I'm still hoping to stop by the Joneses before din-nertime comes."

"Of course. We understand." Kate rose as well. "Thanks for stoppin' by. We'll think on what you said."

"That's all I can ask," Brittany said, making her way to the door. She drew a deep breath of the cold late-morning air as she stepped outside, wondering if she should be pleased or discouraged by the Bryans' response. Allie had been enthusiastic. Kate didn't seem to care much one way or the other.

She started walking toward Major when a voice from the house called out, "Miss Haines?"

Brittany turned. Carson stood in the doorway, grin still in place and blue eyes shining.

"Thanks," he said. Then he ducked his head back inside and closed the door behind him.

That boy must take after his aunt with his enthusiasm for learning, Brittany thought, smiling. If all her students were as enthusiastic as him, teaching wasn't going to be hard at all.

Brittany clung to the image of Carson's glowing face as she sat across from Martha Jones, listening to the woman reprimand her for being "fresh off the stage and already full of highfalutin ideas to change things here out West."

"We got along well enough without no readin' or writin' before you came here," Martha said, her eyes blazing in her angular face. Everything about Martha Jones was sharp: her chin, her nose, her elbows resting on the table, and especially her words. "It's a waste of time, a terrible waste of time to make a kid sit still for a couple hours doin' nothin' but makin' little scratches on paper. Tell me: what's the point of such foolishness? Tell me."

"It's not simply little scratches that the children write," Brittany said with supreme patience. "It's actual words—"

"It's words. Actual words." Martha mimicked her. "And what's the point of bein' able to write words when you can speak 'em a whole lot faster?"

For a moment Brittany was floored, but then she regained her tongue. "The written word can travel much farther than the spoken word. The written word carries new ideas to any corner of the world."

Martha didn't look impressed. "I'm not lackin' for work to keep my kids busy. They don't need to know how to read to keep a house or be a rancher—and I reckon simple folks like us don't got any words worth bein' carried to the corners of the world."

"But even a rancher or a person who keeps a house should be able to read the Bible," Brittany said, straightening in her chair. "That's one of the most important things—"

"Important, huh?" Martha snorted. "The Bible's just a book of made-up stories. Sure, they're good for you, for tellin' kids so they learn how to be good, but it sure ain't the most important thing in life. 'Round here, what's more important is knowin' how to read a brand on a cow and how to use a lariat. This ain't the city, girl. Bible lessons and books just ain't important."

"But—"

"No! I don't want to hear no more. I ain't gonna be sendin' my kids over to the Myerses' place for lessons they don't need when they should be here doin' their chores." Martha thumped the table for emphasis. "Now, no more."

Brittany realized that she had been given a clear dismissal. "Thank you for your time, Mrs. Jones." She rose from her seat. "I'll see myself out."

Brittany started toward the door, trying to ignore the anger simmering inside her. At least Kate hadn't given her a flat-out no—especially not piled on top of insults about being a city girl.

As she opened the door to leave, she thought of one last thing to say. "Mrs. Jones," she said, turning around, "did I mention to you that the Bryans are sending their children over to learn how to read?" A half-truth, in all honesty. Allie was sending Billy over, but Kate wasn't sure yet.

"Really?" Martha blinked, then frowned again. "Iffen that's what they want to do, then fine. But no Jones is gonna darken the door of your schoolhouse."

Brittany paid her no attention. "Their children are so bright, so ready to learn. Why, I'm sure they'll be caught up to Lars and Brenna in no time."

"Humph," Martha said, a heavy frown still in place.

"And the best thing is that after they learn to read and write and do some arithmetic, no one will ever be able to take advantage of them. Or cheat them out of a good deal." Brittany kept her eyes off Martha's face, focusing instead on the dingy-looking lantern on the table. But she was sure that sentence had grabbed Martha's attention.

"When they take over their father's ranch someday, I'm sure they're going to excel. Why, they'll have one of the most profitable ranches around." Brittany wondered if she should have thrown that barb in. It was obvious just by looking at the Joneses' ranch that they were not as well off as the Bryans. The Joneses' ranch looked rundown in comparison.

"I'd better go," Brittany said, looking back at Martha. "I have quite a bit of work to get done before school starts next week."

Martha nodded, her face now appearing more uncertain than angry.

"Have a wonderful day," Brittany said, stepping outside.

As she closed the door behind her, Brittany felt her shoulders sag. She had tried, but some people were hard to argue with. She wasn't sure how well she'd handled the conversation. Now, with the door closed firmly behind her, her mind whirled with responses she should have made, points she should have made more clearly—

Brittany sighed and walked toward Major. It was time to go home. She had done what she could.

She untied Major and had prepared to mount him when the Jones's door opened, and Martha appeared in the doorway, her face flushed.

"Hold on!" Martha called, sounding out of breath. "You know, I was just thinkin', with winter comin' right up on our heels like it is, the kids ain't gonna be as busy now. We might just be able to make a little time for these lessons of yours. When did you say they start?"

CHAPTER
16

"So how many students do you think you'll have?"

"Twelve, I'm hoping." Brittany rubbed at her temples. Three days had passed since she'd last visited the Bryans and Joneses. Three days of trying to plan her lessons without many materials to work with and without knowing exactly how many students were coming. This evening she had put the books away and brought her knitting over to Johnny's. Scott, the ranch's foreman, had taken the wagon into the fort for supplies yesterday, and Brittany had asked him to try and get some paper and pencils for her. She had no clue what the post trader carried for wares and felt on edge as she waited to see if Scott would be able to fulfill his mission. He was scheduled to return this evening. Brittany hoped with all her heart that he wouldn't be delayed.

"You got the Joneses and both sets of Bryans to agree to come?" Johnny asked.

"Well, not exactly. Allie Bryan's boy is coming for sure, and Martha said her four children will come as well. And Lars and Brenna will be there, of course." Brittany ticked the numbers off her fingers. "So that makes seven students for sure, and twelve if Kate lets her kids come."

"I thought you would have more trouble convincing the Joneses than Kate," Johnny said, the smoke from his pipe forming a ring around his head.

Brittany shrugged, not willing to say more. She still wasn't sure that she'd handled Martha Jones the right way.

Brittany felt a cold gust of air from behind her, and she turned to see Nathan enter the room. "Bitter cold out there," he said, shrugging out of his coat. "Wouldn't be surprised if it snowed tonight. Scott made his trip to town none too soon."

He started toward them, then seemed to notice Brittany for the first time. "Sorry—am I intruding?" he asked, glancing toward the door as if he were thinking of leaving.

"Not at all," Johnny said. "We don't mind you comin', do we, Brittany?"

"No." She shook her head. And that was true. She might not know Nathan very well, but how could she dislike him after he'd come to her rescue?

"Have you met Brittany yet, Nathan?" Johnny asked as Nathan took a seat close to the stove.

"Yep," Nathan said, giving no hint of the strange circumstances around their meeting.

Brittany had to fight back a smile. He was keeping his word to her.

"Good." Johnny didn't seem to notice any undercurrent in the room. "Did you know Brittany's gonna be teachin' school?"

Nathan looked at her. "School?"

"Not a real school," Brittany said, feeling almost shy as Nathan's gaze settled on her. An unfamiliar feeling for her. "Just lessons on reading, writing, and maybe some math."

"That's still a good bit of work." Nathan leaned back in his chair.

"Just what I said." Johnny rose from his seat. "Coffee, anyone?"

Both Nathan and Brittany shook their heads. Nathan was still looking at her. "Where are you going to teach them?"

"Here at the Myerses'."

"Maybe you should help her, Nathan. You've got a whole heap of learnin' under your belt." Johnny took his seat, steaming cup in hand.

"Oh, no." Nathan held up a hand. "I'm not cut out to be a teacher. Evan and Maryanne were the bookworms, not me."

"You had a school where you grew up?" Brittany asked, somehow not shocked. She had noticed that his speech was an improvement on that of most westerners.

"No," Nathan said, surprising her. "My ma taught us kids at home. She was a schoolteacher before she married Pa."

"Really?" Brittany was intrigued. She opened her mouth to ask him another question but closed it as the door opened once again.

"Howdy," Clem said, stepping into the room. "She's not a gentle one out there tonight."

Brittany's eyes were caught by a paper-wrapped package in his arms. "What's that?" she asked.

"A present," Clem said, his eyes twinkling.

"Who is it for?"

"Well, I reckon it's for you if Scott's to be believed."

In a flash, Brittany left her seat and ran to his side. "Oh, Clem, let me see it. Please!"

Clem let her take it out of his arms, shaking his head. "My, my—Scott must be on somebody's favorite list tonight."

Johnny and Nathan chuckled, but Brittany was too busy fumbling with the packaging to blush. As she untied the last knot in the string wrapped around the parcel, pencils and a stack of paper spilled out onto the table, making Brittany clasp her hands together. Paper had never before looked so precious.

"Oh, Clem," she said, turning to her brother. "Tell Scott thank you for me, won't you? This is wonderful, just wonderful!"

"If you think that's good, wait until you see what else I brought you. I've got it right here in my pocket." Clem patted the front of his coat. "Take a guess."

Brittany shook her head. "Clem, I'm terrible at playing the guessing game."

"It should be easy. What else do we get from town besides supplies?"

"I don't know," Brittany said, trying to look forlorn. "Tell me, quick."

"Impatient tonight, aren't we?" Clem shook his head. "On second thought, maybe I shouldn't give you your letters."

"Letters?" Brittany felt her heart soar.

"Sure thing," Clem said, pulling three from his pocket. "Here only a month, and you've got more mail than I get in a year."

Brittany hadn't realized how much she longed for news from home until she saw those beautiful white envelopes in Clem's hand. She reached for them, but Clem pulled them back just beyond her fingers.

"Not so fast, little sister," he said, grinning. "There's something I want to know first."

Brittany frowned at him. This wasn't the time for jokes. "What?"

"Who is William Brown? And even more important, why is he writing to you?" Clem's grin stretched wider.

"He wrote?" Brittany had wondered if William really meant it when he suggested they write to each other. But evidently he had been serious. Her fingers itched to take hold of his letter; she hadn't realized how much she missed him until that moment.

"That doesn't answer my question. Who is this young whippersnapper who's writing letters you're so happy to receive?"

Brittany caught a glimpse of Nathan and Johnny's faces. She realized that they were paying close attention to her conversation with Clem and obviously found it quite amusing. Brittany's face heated.

"William is only a friend," she said, trying to ignore their audience.

"A friend, hmm?" Clem quirked one eyebrow. "How old is this friend of yours?"

"Twenty-three."

"Yep, just what I thought." Clem shook his head.

"Clem!" Brittany glared at him. "He's Pastor Brown's son. Do you remember the Browns?"

Clem thought for a moment. "I can't say I do."

"They're a very nice family. Pastor Brown is always willing to help out with whatever is needed. And his wife, she's such a sweet woman, one of Aunt Ida's dearest friends."

"And what about this William fella? What's he like?" Clem asked in a tone that made Brittany wonder if he was still joking or if he was serious now. Her cheeks warmed even more.

"He's–he's very nice," she said. "You'd like him a lot. He's studying to be a minister and will be graduating this year. He's a very kind, considerate man, and he's been one of my closest friends since we moved to Des Moines."

"A minister, you say?" Clem nodded slowly. "That's not too bad."

"Can I have my letters now?" Brittany asked, trying not to sound sarcastic.

"Guess you passed the test." Clem handed the letters over to her. "Although I wouldn't mind at all reading that letter from your William."

Your William. Brittany's jaw clenched. Even here in Wyoming Territory, she couldn't escape being paired with William.

Brittany grabbed her coat and marched toward the door.

"Where are you going? I just got here," Clem called after her.

"I'm going to read my letters. I'll see you tomorrow." Brittany thrust her arms into her coat and opened the door. As she glanced back, she found all three men watching her with matching grins on their faces. "And for your information, *all* of you, William is a friend and nothing more," Brittany said, glaring, especially at Clem. But she couldn't close the door fast enough to block out Clem's snort.

The walk through the cold back to the Myerses' helped to cool her cheeks and calm her thoughts. Clem was such a tease. That was one thing the years hadn't changed about him. Back when they were just children, Clem would sometimes tease until Brittany hit her limit. Usually Brittany would run crying for Mama. But she remembered one time in particular when, rather than running as Clem expected her to, she spun around and slapped him square in the face, sending him tumbling to the ground.

Brittany shook her head, wondering how Mama ever managed to put up with the two of them. But the funny thing was, while Clem himself might tease her to the point of tears, he would never tolerate any other boy picking on her. On more than one occasion, Clem had gotten into trouble at school for fighting other boys who teased her. That protectiveness of her was one thing that hadn't changed either.

And yet in both the teasing and protecting, Brittany had always known Clem loved her. Those were just his ways of showing that love. And Brittany knew that even when she was mad enough at him to tackle him, she still loved him as well.

Brittany pushed open the door to the Myerses' house and shrugged out of her coat. The room was empty except for Lars and Brenna, seated at the table with the checkerboard spread between them.

"Where are the Myerses?" Brittany asked, hanging up her coat.

"In bed," Lars said, moving one of his pieces. "Your turn, Brenna."

"After you finish that game, come to bed," Brittany said, heading toward her room.

They both nodded without looking up.

Brittany entered her room and, lighting the lamp, sat down on the edge of the bed with her letters in hand. Sure enough, one of them was addressed to her in William's neat handwriting. The other two were from Aunt Ida. Brittany carefully opened William's letter first.

Dearest Brittany, it read.

I miss you. I know that even if you were still in Des Moines, we wouldn't see each other since I'm now at seminary, but knowing that you won't be waiting for me when I come home for Christmas break makes me miss you even worse. I'm warning you that if you don't come home at the end of this year, I will hop on the first train west and bring you back here where you belong.

Brittany smiled even as her eyes filled with tears. Christmas was going to seem strange without seeing William.

She scanned through his letter, reading about his studies, the activities he participated in at the seminary, and news about the rest of the Brown family.

I hope and pray that you are fitting in well in Wyoming Territory. William closed. *I'm sure you are learning many new lessons, maybe some that you hadn't intended on learning. I admit to having done some research about the territory and ranches there, and it sounds rather primitive to me. Remember in all things, Brittany, that God is in control and that He never lets you slip from His care, not for one moment. Know that I am praying for you each and every day.*

Your friend,

William Brown

Lessons. If only William knew. Or perhaps best that he didn't know about some things. Brittany folded his letter and set it aside, reaching for one of Aunt Ida's.

But Aunt Ida's letter failed to bring her any encouragement. It was a long letter. Filled with how much Aunt Ida missed her and Lars and Brenna, of how she was getting older and her time might come at any given day. After all, Brittany's parents had both been gone for years and she was older than both of them. And of how she thought Brittany ought to have stayed in Des Moines and married William. The letter ended with a plea for her to return home if at all possible, and Brittany set it down, feeling irritated with her aunt. Returning to Des Moines wasn't as simple as Aunt Ida thought. She had agreed to stay for a year, and stay she would, come what may. Brittany frowned at the letter. Surely Aunt Ida couldn't think that living in Wyoming Territory was easy for her. She had no idea of how different life was here than in the city.

Brittany hugged herself against a wave of homesick that followed on the heels of the letters. She was adjusting to life in the West, but it wasn't home, and just then she would have paid dearly for one day back in Des Moines.

CHAPTER
17

Brittany was ready and waiting when the first of her new students arrived on Tuesday. Makeshift benches had been set up around the room to provide ample seating for all who came. Paper and pencils sat waiting to be used on the kitchen table. Brittany had pulled out Lars and Brenna's two slates as well, and a couple of books—the Bible being one of them. As she stood beside the kitchen stove looking around the room, she was all too aware of the pitiful lack of materials her budding school faced. But Brittany determined to make do with what she had. *I do wish I had a blackboard for the wall,* she thought wistfully. It would make teaching easier if she could write things out for everyone in the room to copy. But there was no use wishing for what she didn't have.

Allie Bryan and her son Billy were the first to arrive, freshly fallen snow blowing through the door along with them.

"It's a mighty cold day," Allie said, stamping the snow off her boots on the rug by the door. "I thought that today bein' the first day of school and all, I'd leave the youngest with Kate and bring Billy over myself. Billy's feelin' a bit shy just now."

Billy looked more than just a bit shy. He looked scared stiff.

"That's understandable." Brittany offered the small boy a smile. "Why don't you come and pick out a seat? You may have any seat you want since you're the first one here."

Billy looked up at his mother, and Allie said, "Go on. I'm right here, and I ain't leavin' just yet."

Billy only clung to her hand tighter.

"A bit shy," Allie said again, trying to disentangle her hand from his.

"I'm sure he'll be fine before long," Brittany said with a confidence she did not feel. She knew that many school children struggled with first-day jitters but had hoped none of her students would be scared. Before now, she'd never had trouble with children warming up to her.

"Maybe I'll stay for a bit, iffen that's fine with you." Allie turned the question into more of a statement.

"That would be just fine," Brittany agreed. She was tempted to ask if Kate's children would be coming today, but she restrained herself.

A group of four children arrived next, two boys and two girls. They stopped in the doorway and looked around the room as if not quite sure they were where they ought to be.

The Joneses, Brittany thought, stepping forward to greet them.

"Come in and set your coats in the corner over there," she said, amazed at how alike the four siblings looked with their dark hair and dark eyes. "I'm Miss Haines, your teacher."

The two girls and younger boy dipped their heads in a nod and headed toward the corner without meeting her eye, but the oldest stood in front of Brittany, grinning. "Boy!" he said. "I don't know why you had trouble gettin' hitched. City fellas must be worse fools than I thought. *Is* it true that you came here just so you could git hitched?"

Brittany stared into his laughing dark eyes, completely taken aback. "I–I beg pardon?"

The boy shrugged. "Just repeatin' what Ma said. She says you couldn't find a man back East to take you, so you came here to snare one." He brushed past Brittany and joined his siblings in the corner before Brittany could even catch her breath.

Snare a man? Brittany was horrified. Anger with Martha Jones for thinking such things of her, and even worse, spreading them abroad, made her clench her jaw. The nerve of the woman!

Lord, please grant me patience. Help me not let such rumors get me worked up, Brittany prayed, forcing herself to take a deep breath. Hoping that neither Allie nor Mrs. Myers had overheard the boy's comment, she passed to the front of the room to get her books—and herself—in order.

Brittany kept an eye on her watch as the minute hand moved closer and closer to two, the agreed time for her lessons to begin. Still, Kate's children failed to arrive. The Jones children, Allie and Billy, and Lars and Brenna all found places to sit and fidgeted restlessly, waiting for her to get started. Brittany was about to give up hope on the Bryans arriving and begin her lessons without them when the door swung open. Everyone turned and looked as Carson and another well-bundled little girl entered the room together. The two children paused just inside the door.

"Howdy," Carson said, looking around the room. "Pa said it was all right for me to come. Sarah decided to come along, too. She's six." He motioned to the girl beside him.

Brittany smiled at both of them. "I'm glad you could come, Carson, Sarah. How are you this afternoon?"

"Good," they both said, shrugging out of their coats. It appeared they were alone.

"Are your siblings here with you?" Brittany asked, trying to keep her heart from sinking.

"No," he said, sliding onto the bench next to Lars. "Guess they weren't much interested in learnin'." His blue eyes found Brittany's, and he added, "But *I'm* interested, *very* interested. And so is Sarah."

He nudged his younger sister, and she nodded vigorously, her blue eyes not leaving Brittany.

Brittany caught the Jones children exchanging swift glances, and her heart sank even farther. So now they knew that Grant Bryan's children were not coming to her lessons. Surely she wouldn't lose them as well, would she?

It was for Carson's sake that she forced a smile to her lips. Lips that would rather crack than turn upwards.

Brittany opened the lessons with a passage from the Bible and prayer. She wasn't sure how much attention her students paid to the reading but knew it was what *she* needed to calm herself and release her mind from the worries that threatened to strangle her.

"Now, let's have everyone go around the room and introduce themselves," she said when her amen had faded away. She nodded at Brenna to start.

Brenna was more than happy to oblige. She stood and rattled off her name and age, adding, with plenty of emphasis, that Brittany was her sister, so everybody better listen up. Brittany wasn't sure whether to thank Brenna or scold her, so she nodded for the next person to go.

Around the room they went, each of the nine students saying their names and ages. The oldest of the Jones children, Charley, was eleven, Brittany discovered. The sparkle lurking in the corner of his dark eyes cautioned her to watch him closely. Something told her there might be more going on in his head than could be seen at first glance.

At ten, Abe was the next of the Jones children, followed by nine-year-old Eva, and seven-year-old Grace. As Grace stood to introduce herself, Brittany noticed she wouldn't meet anyone in the eye and that she stuttered over her words. *Does she normally stutter, or is she just nervous?* Brittany wondered.

When the introductions were over, Brittany let out a deep sigh. Time to get down to business. This was going to prove a challenge, she realized, looking at the row of faces before her. How to teach all of these children of different ages the same basics without making the older children feel embarrassed or the younger children feel overwhelmed? Perhaps it was a good thing she only had a few students. Each of them was going to need her help and attention. Apart from her siblings, of course. And that was good because she was going to need their assistance as well. *At least I don't have to teach any of these children their numbers,* Brittany thought, reminding herself to be grateful for even small blessings.

"So how'd it go?"

Brittany dropped into the chair nearest the stove, feeling completely drained. "Not well," she said to Johnny. "Not well at all.

Teaching that handful of students had been one of the longest two hours of her life. All the students had been restless, obviously not used to sitting still for any length of time, and even worse, they had been bored. Brittany had them go over the alphabet several times, encouraging them to work hard and memorize it quickly. She had gone over a few of the letters, demonstrating how to write them and what sound each letter made. On another day they would learn to do some simple sums, but for today, Brittany figured their minds could hold only so much new information.

The interruptions during her lessons had seemed endless, especially at first. She spent some time teaching them to raise their hands when they had a question, rather than just blurt out whatever was on their minds and interrupt everyone. But then, everyone's hands seemed to be in the air more than resting in their laps as they should have been. Abe had to use the outhouse, Charley had to go check the horses, Eva was thirsty and needed a drink, and now Charley had to use the outhouse. The constant stream of interruptions put Brittany's patience sorely to the test.

"Givin' up on your idea, then?" Johnny asked.

"Giving up?" Brittany repeated. "Why I'm just getting started. Tomorrow will be better, I'm sure," she added, trying to sound confident.

Johnny only raised his eyebrows.

CHAPTER
18

Things did not get better.

Brittany couldn't remember ever being as exhausted as she was by the time she reached her second Thursday of teaching. As she stood looking at her makeshift schoolroom, she had to restrain tears. It wasn't the work that made her feel so weary. It was the discouragement. Despite hopes that things would improve, it seemed her school was going from bad to worse. The Jones children had failed to show up after the first day of lessons. They seemed to care little about learning, what with their fidgeting and longing stares out the window. It appeared they wanted nothing more than to escape her and her teaching. But they still made up half of the school and to have them drop out, possibly for good, was a blow.

None of the other Bryan children came, despite Brittany's hope that they would change their minds. Each day Carson and Sarah trudged through the door alone, Carson's attempts to convince his siblings to join him unsuccessful. And to make things worse, Sarah had been home with a bad cold during Tuesday's lesson. So it had been only Carson, Billy, Lars, and Brenna sitting at the kitchen table. They hadn't even needed to pull out the makeshift benches.

"Is it really worth your effort?" Mrs. Myers had asked Brittany yesterday after their lessons were over. "You're putting a lot of time into this for just a couple students."

"Of course, it's worth it," Brittany said, trying to ignore her own smothering doubts. "A couple students have as much right to learn as an entire roomful."

Mrs. Myers said nothing more, but her skepticism weighed more heavily in the room than any number of words could have.

This is worth it, Brittany told herself now as she looked around the empty room. It was discouraging at times, yes, but she was investing in her students' entire lives. Perhaps they didn't fully appreciate that now. But someday maybe the things they were learning would save them from being fleeced by a crook in a business suit. Or it could lead to jobs that would have been inaccessible had they not been given an education. Perhaps they would come to know the Lord by being able to read His Word. *This* was worth *that.*

The door blew open, and Carson entered the room. "Howdy, Miss Haines," he called, shrugging out of his coat. "Cold out today."

"Hello, Carson." Brittany forced herself to smile. "How's Sarah today?"

"Still awful stuffed up, but she's getting better. I reckon she'll be able to come with me next week."

"I'm glad to hear that, and I'm glad you could come today."

"I'd come if I had to crawl all the way here," he said, plunking down in a seat at the table and pulling out his alphabet chart.

Brittany smiled. He was one determined boy. Carson worked harder at learning than any child she'd ever met before, intent on learning as fast as possible so that he could read a "real" book soon. His enthusiasm was contagious, and Brittany felt her despair fading away like clouds before the sun.

The door opened again, and to Brittany's surprise the Jones children filed in. They mumbled a hello and took off their coats without a word of apology or explanation for their failure to come the last two days. Brittany decided to let it pass.

Carson set aside his paper and went to visit with the Jones boys and Lars. Brittany felt the heavy shroud of discouragement slipping away. *Thank You, Lord,* she thought, grateful beyond measure that the Joneses had returned. Perhaps there was hope for her school after all.

Allie Bryan was the last to arrive, the baby in her arms and Billy trailing reluctantly behind her.

"Thought we were gonna be late," she said, stamping the snow off her boots. For the first couple of days she had come, presumably to make Billy feel more at ease, sitting with him during the lessons "just for today." Now she had dropped that phrase and simply came, bringing her littlest one as well so that Kate wouldn't need to watch him. Allie drank in Brittany's lessons with far more interest than her five-year-old son, her interest rivaled only by Carson. Brittany was happy to have her come. She was, in a way, another one of her students.

"We're going to need the benches today." Brittany looked around the full room. She saw Mrs. Myers standing in the doorway of her bedroom looking around the room as well, and when their gazes met, they both exchanged a smile. So much for a deserted schoolroom.

The boys were quick to volunteer to set up the benches, and within minutes Brittany's schoolroom had been expanded to fit everyone. She was ready to begin teaching.

"Please take your seats, everyone," she said, going to the front of the room and picking up the Bible for their daily reading. She flipped through the pages as everyone noisily took their seats, opening to the Psalm she had chosen the night before.

A sudden yelp brought her head up in time to see Carson, always a model student, leap out of his seat so fast that his chair tumbled backward onto Charley Jones behind him. Carson's hands held the seat of his pants, and the room tittered.

"Carson, what is it?" Brittany asked, frowning the room into silence.

"Nothing, Miss Haines," he muttered, his face red. He picked up his chair and slid onto it again. Brittany thought she saw Charley smirk.

Brittany walked over to Carson and, lowering her voice, asked, "Do you want to talk about it in private?"

"No, ma'am." He didn't look at her. "It was nothing."

Brittany glanced at Charley, and this time knew she saw him smirk. She turned on him. "Charley, do you happen to know anything about this?"

He stared back at her with wide eyes. "Me? No, ma'am. Carson was probably just clumsy."

Brittany looked back at Carson, certain that he wasn't saying all he knew. Lars, sitting on the other side of Carson, made a little movement that caught her attention and pointed almost imperceptibly beneath Carson's seat. Brittany had no clue what she was supposed to find there, but she obediently stooped to look.

There, lying on the floor, was a bent pin. Brittany picked it up, the pieces beginning to fall neatly into place. "Charley, do you happen to know what this was doing under Carson's chair?" she asked, holding it up.

Charley shook his head, his face straight but his eyes gleaming.

Brittany felt anger rising up in her. It was obvious that Charley was the one who had put the pin on Carson's chair so that he would sit on it. It was even more obvious that he was lying to her.

Brittany turned to Carson. "Carson, did Charley put this pin on your chair?" she asked point-blank.

Carson's face tightened. "It really weren't nothing to worry about."

"Did he, Carson?" Brittany was determined to get to the bottom of this.

The minutes stretched as Carson stared at the table. At last he sighed, and his shoulders fell. "Yes, ma'am."

"I see." Brittany spun around on her heel. "Come with me, Charley."

He rose from his seat and leisurely followed her to the front of the room, giving Carson a dirty look as he passed by. In her planning to teach, Brittany had never thought of how she would keep order in the schoolroom, nor had she even thought of needing to keep order. But now it seemed only natural to reach for the ruler. It angered her that a boy as big as Charley would mistreat a younger boy. That was something she would never allow in her classroom. Never.

"Hold out your hand," she told Charley, taking a deep breath and reminding herself to discipline with love for him in mind, not anger.

Charley did so, eyeing her warily. Brittany raised the ruler and brought it down hard on his hand, twice. Charley didn't wince, but his cheek twitched.

"Go sit down, please," Brittany said in a softer voice, lowering the ruler. "And after this, I hope you will never play such a prank again."

Charley stomped back to his seat, his shoulders stiff and his head held high. Brittany returned the ruler to its proper place, feeling sick at heart. She had just disciplined her first student, and if Charley's behavior was any indicator, her trouble with him was not over yet. She picked up the Bible again, feeling a deeper appreciation for teachers than she'd ever before felt. Teaching was not by any means a picnic.

The day had started on a bad note that hung in the air during the whole two-hour lesson, and various little pranks kept popping up. Brenna's braid was yanked when she rose from her chair, Billy got hit with a spitball, Carson tripped and fell when he left his seat. Brittany suspected there were even more pranks she wasn't informed of. She was dead sure that Charley was the instigator behind the mischief, but she couldn't catch him in the act, and he refused to confess. With each prank that passed without the prankster being discovered, Brittany could feel her frustration mounting. None of the students in the room wanted to be known as a tattler, and if they had evidence against Charley, they kept it to themselves.

Besides that, Brittany had to take extra time to work with each of the Jones children individually. They needed to review what had already been learned and then go over what was missed during their absence. It cut into the time she would have spent working with the whole class, and Brittany had to remind herself to keep calm and be patient as she worked with them.

"Do you remember any of the letters in the alphabet?" Brittany asked Grace, sitting down beside her after a trying session with Charley that set her teeth on edge. He was taking out his resentment of the punishment he had received by acting dumb and asking meaningless questions that cut further into her valuable time.

Grace shrugged her thin shoulders.

"Can you try to remember?" Brittany asked, keeping her smile intact only by sheer will.

Grace shrugged again.

"How about we say it together?" Britany said, sighing. She started off but stopped when Grace didn't join in.

"Grace, say it with me," she said, turning her request into an order.

"I don't know it." Grace stared back at Brittany.

"Try." The single word sounded clipped to Brittany's own ears.

Together they began reciting the letters, but halfway through, Grace burst into tears. "I don't know it," she nearly wailed.

"Grace." Brittany took the girl's hands. "I only wanted you to try. I don't expect perfection." *How did this start? I was trying to be very patient.*

Grace continued to sniffle but agreed to study the letter chart that Brittany gave her. Brittany moved on to see how Billy and Allie were doing, wondering how two hours could be so long.

Brittany couldn't deny her relief when she glanced at her watch and the two hours were up. Finally she could say, "Class dismissed."

All the students jumped to their feet and ran to fetch their wraps. Brittany saw Carson stumble and almost fall as he passed Charley. But in the tangle of children, she couldn't tell if Charley had tripped him on purpose or not. Brittany chose not to say anything.

"You had a hard day," Allie said as the room cleared of children. She lowered her voice. "Charley's the one causin' all the trouble, you know."

"I know." Brittany rubbed the tight muscles in her neck. "But what can I do if I can't catch him *doing* the mischief?"

"He needs a good trip to the woodshed—that's what."

"And how am I supposed to get him there? He's almost as tall as me, and at least as strong."

"Say the word, and I'll gladly jump up and help you haul him out there." Allie gave a determined nod.

Brittany smiled despite her weariness. "Thank you, Allie. I'm glad I can count on you."

"Anytime." Allie struggled to juggle the baby in one arm and button Billy's coat with the other. Brittany stepped forward.

"Let me take the baby," she said, holding out her arms.

Allie handed him over without hesitation. "Thanks."

It had been too long since Brittany had held a baby. She swayed back and forth with him, her smile earning one in return from the little boy. *I wonder if I'll ever have a baby of my own,* she thought, holding up a finger for the baby to grasp. Her mind leaped to William faster than she could blink, and Brittany found herself wondering if he loved babies like she did. Come to think of it, she couldn't remember him ever spending any time around children, not even Lars and Brenna. He was an only child with no younger siblings, and whenever he spent time with her, he never paid any attention to Lars and Brenna. Somehow she couldn't picture him holding a baby.

"Brittany!" The door burst open, and all peace fled as Brenna flew into the room. "Come quick! Charley and Carson are fighting!"

"Charley and Carson?" Brittany's heart did a little flip. Passing the baby back to Allie, she ran for the door, snagging her coat off the wall on the way. She could hear shouting as she hurried onto the porch, and in a quick glance, she saw the boys surrounded by a ring of children cheering on their fight. Picking up her skirts, she ran down the steps and through the snow to the group of children.

"Stop it!" she called as she neared them. "Carson and Charley, stop fighting right now!"

The children's shouts died down, and Carson's fist lowered. But Charley wasn't finished. He took a step forward and slammed his fist into Carson's face, knocking the boy to the ground. Charley jumped on top of him and pinned the writhing boy down.

Brittany ran to the boys' side. "I said, stop it! Stop it right now!" she screamed. She grabbed Charley by the collar of his coat and jerked him backward off Carson.

"What is the meaning of this?" Brittany asked, breathing almost as hard as the two boys.

"He started it!" Charley's bloody nose and swelling eye gave his face a savage look.

"I did *not* start it!" Carson glared at him, wiping at his own bloody face.

"Yes, you did!"

"No, I didn't, you liar!"

"'Liar'?" Charley made a sudden lunge at Carson, catching Brittany off guard.

Both of the boys went tumbling and began to thrash about on the ground, grunting in pain when a fist made contact with one of them. Brittany reached blindly through the flying snow and flailing arms, trying to find a handhold on one of them.

"Boys, stop right now!" she yelled. She felt her feet slipping on the snow-covered ground, and she adjusted her position, trying to stabilize herself. She reached into the fray again, her hand closing on one of their coats. One of the boys bumped up against her, knocking her off balance again, and Brittany found herself tumbling down into the snow. A burst of cold, icy needles flew straight into her face, and Brittany came up spluttering.

"Boys!" Brittany rubbed blindly at her face. Her face burned with the cold, the little bits of ice stinging her skin mercilessly, and if she hadn't felt so mad, she would have broken down and cried right then and there.

"Oh, what have you boys done?" Allie's voice was a welcome relief. "Here, Miss Haines—just hold tight and let me help you."

Brittany felt humiliated but undeniably grateful. Allie took her face between her hands as if she were a little girl and wiped away the snow. It was a relief to be able to see clearly again.

"There now—I hope you boys are good and ashamed of yourselves, knockin' down your teacher like that." Allie wiped some snow from Brittany's cheek, then helped her to her feet.

"Would you please tell me why you were fighting?" Brittany asked, trying to brush more snow off her skirt and regain some dignity.

"Charley's been pestering me all day long," Carson burst out, desperate enough not to worry about being a tattler. "He was calling me 'teacher's pet' and a 'sissy', so I ran at him and pushed him into the snowbank."

"Charley, is this true?" Brittany turned to the older boy.

Charley shrugged and nodded.

"Carson, after this, I don't want you to use your fists for dealing with problems, but I'll let that pass for today. Now Charley," Brittany frowned at him, "you have been disrupting class all day, and I cannot overlook that any longer. Today you will need to stay and do some chores as punishment."

Slowly, deliberately, Charley folded his arms across his chest, a grin spreading across his face. "Oh yeah?" he said, his words freezing Brittany's heart. "I'd just like to see you try and make me."

CHAPTER
19

The western horizon was ablaze with color as Nathan took a seat on a log outside the barn, a broken bridle in hand. He could have worked on it in the bunkhouse where it was warmer, but he needed some time away from the other men. Especially Rueben. Today it seemed that if Nathan said "up", Rueben said "down" just to be contrary. The man managed to irk Nathan like no other. Besides, it was a nice evening; chilly, yes, but not as bad as some nights.

Nathan studied the bridle for a moment, thinking through how to fix it. He ran his thumb over the leather, the material feeling right in his hands. His pa always said that he had a way with leather and rope, something he'd probably inherited from Pa himself. As a child, he'd been convinced that there was nothing broken his pa couldn't fix, whether it was a saddle or a corral or a horse. To him, there was nothing more influential than his pa, nothing else worth aspiring to than becoming a man just like his pa. That was a tall order, Nathan realized now. One that he feared he could never meet.

The sound of footsteps in the snow brought his head up. It was Brittany coming toward him, bundled up against the cold.

"Is Clem here?" she asked, stopping in front of him.

"Sorry, haven't seen him. I think he went to visit Morgan," Nathan said, turning back to his work. He expected her to walk on, but she lingered, watching him.

"What are you doing?" she asked at last.

"Fixing this bridle." He held it up so she could see. "The leather is worn through right here, so I'm going to replace it. It should be a simple fix."

"I wish all things in life were a simple fix." Brittany sighed and sat down on a nearby log. Nathan glanced at her, noting that she looked tired. Tired and defeated.

"You've got a problem?" Nathan asked, hoping he wasn't prying.

"You could say that." Brittany dug the toe of her boot into the snow, her forehead creased in a frown. "You said your mother was a schoolteacher?"

"Before she married Pa, yes."

"Did she ever talk about any of her students causing her trouble?"

Nathan squinted at the horizon, trying to remember. The truth was, Ma had never talked a whole lot about her days as a teacher. She much preferred being a wife and a mother to being a teacher, she'd often said, giving Pa the special smile she saved for him alone.

"I don't know that she had much trouble," he said. "From what she said, the students loved her; a few of the older boys were even sweet on her."

"I envy her." Brittany's boot dug harder at the snow.

"Your students causing you trouble?"

"It's that Charley Jones." Brittany's frown deepened. "I'm not sure how to handle him, to be honest. Last week he challenged me flat out to try and make him do the chores I had assigned him as punishment for misbehavior."

"What did you do?"

Brittany gave a small smile. "I didn't do anything. I was still in shock when Allie Bryan marched right up, standing nose to nose with him, and said if he didn't get down to work that minute, she was going to tan his hide—*and* she'd tell his pa he was causing trouble, and his pa would tan his hide too."

The picture was all too vivid to Nathan, and he was hard pressed not to laugh. "So he hightailed it?"

Brittany's smile broadened. "Yes, he actually did. And I can assure you that I was very grateful. If he hadn't given in, I'm not so sure that Allie and I really could have given him a whipping."

"I'd be happy to help you any time," Nathan said. And he meant it. Humorous as the idea was of petite Allie Bryan threatening to whip Charley, the thought of Charley treating Brittany like that sparked his anger.

"I'm not sure that would do it, but thank you anyway." Brittany's smile wavered for an instant before a teasing glint leaped to her eyes. "You never caused your mother any problems, did you?"

Nathan arched an eyebrow. "The evidence is slightly incriminating."

Brittany burst into laughter, just the effect Nathan had been hoping for. He would have done a whole lot more to keep that sad look off her face.

"Seriously," Brittany said, still smiling. "Did you ever cause problems?"

"Yes, seriously." Nathan fiddled with the now-forgotten bridle in his hands. "My brother and sister loved school, but I would have rather been outside working. I wanted to be a rancher and didn't think school was all that important. But Ma was convinced that all of us kids needed a solid education even if we did live out in the middle of nowhere."

"I admire your mother," Brittany said.

"She was an admirable woman." Nathan studied her. "You remind me of her in a way."

"Me?" Brittany's eyes widened. "How?"

"Well, you both have a love of learning for one thing, and a love for children. And you both have the pluck to stick with something even when it's hard. Even when everything seems to be going against you." Nathan shrugged. "Sorry—I'm not much for words."

Brittany blinked. "I think that was a high compliment you just gave me. Thank you."

It was funny how a simple expression like "thank you" could warm a person clear through. Nathan tried to shrug the feeling aside and picked up his bridle again. The light was dimming, and he knew it was going to be harder to see what he was doing now.

Brittany settled her chin on her hand as if she were settling in for a long stay. "Nathan, do you ever feel homesick?"

"Homesick?" The unexpected question made Nathan fumble and nearly drop the bridle. "Sometimes, I guess."

Liar, his mind shouted. *Often.*

Brittany nodded, her eyes far away. "Me too. Aunt Ida would rather have had me stay in Des Moines. Sometimes I wish I had too."

"I reckon everybody feels homesick once in a while." Nathan chose his words carefully. "Do you think you'll go back? To Des Moines, that is?"

"Oh, yes." Brittany pleated the hem of her coat between her fingers. "Next September, when my contract is over."

Nathan was tempted to ask if William, whatever his name was, had something to do with that, but he held his tongue. "Clem would like it if you stayed."

Brittany shrugged. "If I'm not mistaken, he'll be married before long, and he'll be too busy with his own family to notice I'm not here."

"He'll notice. Having a family of his own might take away some of the sting of your leaving, but he'll notice your absence. A family member's leaving always creates a gap."

The look on her face said that he had scored a point. "Des Moines is still home," she said, not answering him directly.

In a way, Nathan understood. *Home* was a compelling word. But what he didn't understand was how she could consider a crowded city like Des Moines as home. It seemed to him that she could have a far better life here in Wyoming Territory with her pick of men to marry and a blue sky of clean air spread over her head. He couldn't understand how anyone could prefer a city to open land like this.

"Do you think you'll ever return to Texas?" Brittany asked.

"Texas? Oh, no." Nathan shook his head. "'Fraid I burned that bridge when I left."

Brittany pulled her gaze from the horizon and looked at him. "Does your family still live there?"

"Yes." *I think.*

"So you don't plan to ever visit them?"

This conversation was getting out of Nathan's comfort zone. "I–ah, you wouldn't understand."

"What do you mean?" Brittany's eyes questioned him.

"My family and I aren't exactly—" Nathan stumbled for the right words—"close anymore."

"That's too bad." Brittany tilted her head slightly. "How many siblings did you say you had?"

"Two. A brother and a sister."

"Maybe you should try writing to them. I'm sure they'd like—"

"My brother's dead." The words came out more harshly than Nathan had intended.

"Oh." Brittany drew back slightly. "I–I'm sorry."

"It can't be helped," Nathan said in a softer voice. *Not now, anyway.*

"How did it happen?" Brittany asked, her eyes still on his face.

Nathan stared back at her. What could he say? Evan's death wasn't something he liked to think about, much less talk about. The truth that lurked behind it ripped at his heart daily. The truth that, despite everything he believed, he had not been able to protect his baby brother from injury. And yet her eyes seemed to pin him in place, forcing him to think through the one thing in life that he tried so hard to forget.

"It was an accident." He pulled his gaze away from hers and looked down at the broken bridle instead. Broken, just like his life.

Nathan gave his head a shake, trying to clear his mind of all the memories fighting for release. The gathering shadows around them suddenly bothered him. "Might as well call it a night.

I can't see a thing I'm working on," he said, his fist tightening around the bridle.

Brittany seemed to sense the shift in his mood. "I suppose I'd best be going," she said, but seemed hesitant. Before she could make a move to leave, the crunch of footsteps made them both look up.

"Howdy!" a croaking voice called out. Able Zimmerman turned neither to the right nor to the left as he came toward them, walking with an extra swagger that gave him the appearance of a scarecrow who had just stepped off a ship.

"Howdy, Able," Nathan said with little enthusiasm. Brittany had gone rigid and stared down at her hands.

Able didn't seem to even notice Nathan. "Miss Haines, I was wantin' to see you. I wanted to ask you if you changed your mind about—"

"No!" Brittany sprang to her feet and took off running for the house faster than Nathan could blink. Both he and Able stared as she flew across the distance between the cabin and barn—as if a pack of wolves were after her. The door closed behind her with a slam that could be heard even from where they sat.

Able wagged his head slowly back and forth. "I don't understand that girl—I really don't."

Nathan glanced at the man beside him. "I'd say she seems a bit scared of you."

Able's forehead furrowed as if he were genuinely confused. "Now why would that be? I'm gentle as a big teddy bear."

Nathan chose to ignore that comment. "What brings you this way tonight?"

"Just like I was tellin' her. I wanted to see if she was amenable to the idea of marryin' me."

Nathan almost groaned aloud. Leave it to Able to just throw out what he was thinking with no beating around the bush. He didn't blame poor Brittany for being scared of the man. It would be a scary thing to be asked to marry Able Zimmerman.

"She's a feisty little thing too," Able said, his voice thoughtful. "Last time I was here she started yellin' at me. But I'll overlook that. I kinda like that dash of spice, you know?"

The more Able talked, the more annoyed Nathan felt. "Look, Able—I've got to go. It's getting late."

"Sure, sure. Guess I'll be leavin' since she don't want to talk tonight. But mark my words—she'll come around here eventually. She will, sure as my name's Able Zimmerman." Able nodded firmly.

I rather doubt that, Nathan thought.

"By the way," Able said, "you don't happen to know her first name, do you? Sure would be handy to know."

Nathan stared at Able, then shook his head, feeling more disgusted with the man than ever. Who in his right mind would propose to a girl without even knowing her first name? He was no expert on girls and courting, but he at least knew that a girl wanted the man proposing to her to know her name. He turned away without another word.

"So long, Nathan," Able bawled after him. "Just keep your ears open, won't you?"

Nathan raised his hand but muttered under his breath, "You can run me over with a herd of loco mustangs before you drag her name from me."

He made his way back to the bunkhouse, still riddled by thoughts of Able Zimmerman. As he reached the door, he noticed Rueben Pierce standing outside against the wall, chewing on a wad of tobacco. He said nothing as Nathan brushed past him, but a strange smile curled his lips upward, and a gleam appeared in his eyes.

CHAPTER

20

I *wonder if Able will ever realize that I'm not interested in marrying him.*

A week had passed since Able interrupted her talk with Nathan, and still the man plagued her thoughts. Brittany stared at the books spread before her on the table, knowing she ought to be preparing her lessons for the next day, but her mind wished to wander to anything and everything else. Resting her chin in her hand, Brittany thought back to the surprise she'd had earlier that day and smiled. When Carson and Sarah Bryan arrived for school, they had brought two more children with them. Julia, age ten, and Zach, nine, had both come with their younger siblings, deciding that maybe it was a good idea to learn to read and write. Now the only Bryan child not in school was Everett. Who was to say, maybe with all his younger siblings heading out the door to school each day, he would feel lonely and decide to join them as well.

Even Charley had been improving lately. There were far fewer pranks than in the beginning, and Brittany was starting to think that *maybe* she would actually make it with her school.

Brittany pushed back from the table and her books and crossed to the window to look outside. The shadows were lengthening, and she would need to call Lars and Brenna in for supper. She hesitated to call them in any sooner than necessary, knowing that they were off doing some unstated activity with Clem.

Maybe I'll just take a little walk and see what they're up to. The idea was too tempting to resist, and grabbing her coat, she opened the door and headed outside, not giving herself time to change her mind.

As she left the cabin's porch, Brittany lifted her face to the sky and breathed in the cold evening air, glad to be away from the house and her books. She set off down the path of trampled snow leading away from the cabin, letting her arms swing at her sides. *Why don't I set out and take walks like this more often?* she wondered. The answer was simple. She was too busy. The boredom she'd felt when she first arrived was a thing of the past, and often she wished for just a few more hours in the day.

I have to remember to take time for these kinds of things as well, she thought. Getting outside for even just a few minutes each day would help to improve her state of mind.

A sharp crack rang out from somewhere near the barn, and she spun in that direction, wondering what was going on. The sound came again, and she turned her steps in that direction, mystified.

She followed the well-worn path until she reached the barn, then stepped into the deeper snow, trying to match her own steps to the footprints already there As she reached the corner of the barn, she tripped over a log half-buried in the snow and almost fell but managed to catch hold of the barn wall and right herself.

She took a final step forward and looked around the corner, unsure of what she would find.

Her eyes fell on three figures, a man and two children—her siblings. Clem knelt beside Brenna, pointing at a box several yards in front of them. He said something, and the girl nodded, her gaze fixed on the box. Clem leaned back from her a bit, motioning Lars to move farther behind him, and as Brittany watched, Brenna raised something that glinted in the sun and aimed at the box. A shot split the air, and Clem let out a whoop.

Brittany stared, unable to believe what she was seeing. This was the kind of activity that Clem had been engaging in with the children? Target practice? What was he thinking? Didn't he realize that Lars and Brenna were only children, too young for such things?

She watched as the three of them ran toward the box, the pistol safely tucked in Clem's holster, and bent over to inspect it. Their obvious excitement sparked the anger gathering in Brittany's middle. This had to stop. Putting a firearm in the hands of such young children was just asking for someone to get hurt.

Brittany took a step forward, fully prepared to give her brother a talking to he would never forget but was stopped by a hand on her arm.

She spun around and found herself face to face with Nathan.

"Brittany, don't," he said, his tone effectively holding her in place. "I know what you're going to do, but don't."

"Can't you see what he's doing?" Brittany waved a hand toward her brother. "He's teaching children to shoot guns!"

"So?"

"So someone's going to get hurt, and just for a few minutes of worthless fun—"

"Stop." Nathan's voice cut her rant short, and though Brittany tried to glare at him, she could feel tears stinging her eyes.

"You're on his side, aren't you?" she asked, folding her arms across her chest.

Nathan looked back at her evenly. "I'm not taking sides. I'm just telling you that running over there and yelling at Clem isn't a good idea. You're too worked up."

"Why do you care?" Brittany's glare worked a little better this time.

"Well, Clem happens to be my friend, so I don't want to see him hurt by words spoken too hastily." He held her gaze. "And you happen to be my friend as well, and I don't want to see you hurt either."

His words worked like a dose of cold water, quenching Brittany's fury. "I'm your friend?" she asked, blinking.

"Of course. I sure don't want to be your enemy. I'm afraid I'd get the worst out of that." He offered her a smile.

Brittany gave him a small smile in return. She was glad he thought of her as a friend. That was how she thought of him, but until that moment she'd feared he saw her as nothing but a pest who was always causing him trouble.

Her gaze slipped in Clem's direction again, and she watched him help Lars hold the pistol steady. The sight of it brought all her anger back in full force.

"Do you trust Clem?" Nathan asked, his gaze following hers.

Brittany didn't have to think through her answer. "Of course. But—"

"Then trust him now. Clem's a wise, responsible man. And knowing him, he gave those two a good safety lesson before even thinking of putting the pistol in their hands. If it were George or Little Joe out there, you might have some cause for worry, but not with Clem."

His words sounded rational, but Brittany still wasn't convinced. "Lars and Brenna are too young for firearms."

"Are they?" Nathan arched one eyebrow. "They're smart kids and good about listening. They might be too young to shoot unsupervised, but as long as Clem's there to make sure they're doing it safely, what's the harm? My pa taught me how to shoot when I was six."

Brittany blinked. "And your ma agreed?"

"Well, not really." Nathan's eyes shadowed. "Ma was always—overprotective. She was a good woman, but she worried too much. Didn't want us kids to scratch ourselves or get a bruise, but that's the way we learn best sometimes. I wonder if some lessons would have been learned easier and without such a high cost if we'd been allowed to fail on smaller things." He shook his head. "Don't be like her, Brittany."

Brittany frowned. "I thought you already said that I was like her."

"Yes, and that's good—with most of her qualities. But you have to let Lars and Brenna take risks sometimes. Shooting a gun with Clem is a risk, but not a very big one. Life's full of risks, and you have to choose which ones are worth putting up a fight about and which ones are acceptable. Don't be overprotective. It leaves a kid feeling smothered, like you're giving him no room to breathe."

Brittany sent another glance toward her siblings, weighing Nathan's words. *Was* she overprotective? Nathan seemed to think she was.

"How long has Clem been teaching them to shoot?" she asked.

Nathan hesitated, his eyes dropping to the ground. "A few weeks now."

A few weeks? Brittany couldn't help but feel hurt. None of her siblings had breathed a word about the lessons to her. Was she really so difficult that they had decided to say nothing rather than risk getting into an argument with her?

She looked toward her siblings again, then squared her shoulders and turned to Nathan. "Well, if they've been doing this for a few weeks and no one has gotten hurt, I guess it's okay."

She watched Nathan's shoulders relax, and his face light up in a smile. "I think so too," he said. "It's getting chilly out here. Maybe we should go see if Johnny has his coffee pot on."

Brittany opened her mouth to protest that it was almost suppertime and that they ought to wait, but then stopped. "Let's do that," she said, unable to keep from smiling. She felt as if she'd just accepted an offer for a stolen treat.

She turned away from the three figures, still intent on slamming bullets into the crate, and almost fell over the snow-covered log again. Nathan caught her arm just in time and helped to steady her.

Brittany hoped he couldn't see her blush. She always seemed to be getting into one accident or another when he was around. "Thanks," she said, and although she didn't say it aloud, she silently added, *Friend.* It sounded good.

Brittany had to marvel at how time had flown as she turned the calendar page from November to December a few days later. The months marched by quickly now that she was teaching school. It was amazing how much time her simple lessons took to prepare and teach. She was having a hard time keeping up with everything and wasn't ahead of schedule on anything. She certainly couldn't complain of being bored.

"How do you usually celebrate Christmas around here?" Brittany asked Mrs. Myers, taking a seat at the table beside her.

Mrs. Myers looked up. "Christmas? I haven't thought of Christmas in—well, in years."

"No Christmas? Impossible. You better start thinking now, because I for one don't want to miss out on Christmas," Brittany said. "Things need livening up around here as it is."

Mrs. Myers shook her head slowly. "This isn't the city, Brittany. Things are different around here. We don't have sleighing parties or even a church service."

"Maybe we don't, but that doesn't mean we can't celebrate Jesus's birth." Brittany laid her hands on the table, palms down. "Let's think of ideas for how we should celebrate."

"You really are serious, aren't you?" Mrs. Myers shook her head again. "I don't know what Tim will say about this."

"If he has any common sense, he'll say that a party is a splendid idea."

"A party?" The word seemed to startle Mrs. Myers. "We never have parties around here."

"Yes, a *party*." The word appealed to Brittany, so she said it again. "A *party*. Let's think. We'll invite all the men from the ranch, and Johnny, of course. We should invite Morgan and her uncle as well." Brittany ticked the numbers off her fingers. "That would make fourteen people, including us. Is there anyone else you'd like to invite?"

Mrs. Myers still looked doubtful. "What do you mean when you say a party?"

"Well, we could have everyone come for dinner. Then afterward, maybe Johnny could play his banjo, and we could sing." Brittany shrugged. "That's just off the top of my head."

Mrs. Myers sighed. "I don't know about this."

"Don't worry. We'll have plenty of time to prepare for the party. I'll give my students a couple weeks off for the holidays, so time won't be an issue."

The door opened, and Mr. Myers entered the room along with a blast of cold air. He stamped the snow off his boots, muttering about the cold, and began unbuttoning his coat.

"Tim, what do you think about having a party for Christmas?" Mrs. Myers asked.

"You want a party?" Ha stamped off more snow and rubbed at the ice that had formed on his mustache. "Iffen you want a party, guess it don't matter much to me."

"Brittany thinks we should."

"What?" Mr. Myers suddenly lost his amiable tone. "What do you want with a party, girl?"

Brittany felt a little stab of annoyance. Must he frown at every idea she came up with? "Why *not* have a party? Christmas is a time to celebrate, to be with family and friends."

"Seems like a bunch of nonsense to me." Mr. Myers let out a huff.

"It would be something out of the ordinary."

"We don't need things to be outta the ordinary." Mr. Myers glared at her.

"It would give us a chance to do some real visiting with people." Brittany matched his glare.

"We do enough visiting without a foolish party."

"It would be fun."

"A party is a pointless, useless, ridiculous idea," Mr. Myers snapped. "And—"

"I think Brittany might have a good idea," Mrs. Myers broke in, a thoughtful expression on her face. She seemed to have been thinking so hard that she didn't even notice her husband and Brittany's argument.

Mr. Myers turned to look at her. "What?" he asked, his jaw going slack.

"I said, I think Brittany has a good idea," Mrs. Myers repeated. "A Christmas party might be just what this place needs."

Mr. Myers started to open his mouth, then clamped it firmly shut. His gaze flickered between Mrs. Myers and Brittany as if he thought they had ganged up on him, then settled on his wife. "Huh," was all he said.

"What do you think, Tim?" Mrs. Myers asked, confirming that she hadn't been paying attention to the argument. Brittany felt that Mr. Myers had already made his opinions abundantly clear.

"Well, uh—" Mr. Myers seemed trapped between the words he'd already spouted off against a party and his desire to agree with his wife. "I reckon you can do whatever you think is best, Eleanor."

"So you don't have anything against a party?"

"Well, I–I reckon not." Mr. Myers glared in Brittany's direction.

"Good," Mrs. Myers said, and Brittany resisted letting out a cheer. It seemed they would be having a party after all.

"I wonder if we could pull off a Christmas play for the children too," Brittany said aloud, her mind racing with ideas. Christmas brought so many opportunities.

Before Mrs. Myers could speak, Mr. Myers said, "Oh, no. One party's quite enough. You see, Eleanor, this here girl's gonna try to overrun this place with people iffen we give her half a chance. We ain't havin' no program, or we're gonna be wearin' dirty laundry and missin' meals 'cause she'll be so busy."

Brittany didn't press. Rude words notwithstanding, he might have made a point.

CHAPTER
21

The last stars were fading in the gathering morning light as Nathan threw his saddle over Loner's back. The morning was bitterly cold, a day that made him wish he could stay close to the fire rather than go out to check on cattle. But the work needed to be done, regardless of the cold or his wishes.

Nathan grabbed the cinch and was beginning to fasten it when he heard footsteps behind him. He paid them no attention until a shadow fell across the snow beside him. He glanced up to see George Maxton scowling down at him.

"Nathan, I need to ask you somethin'," he said without preamble. "Are you sweet on Clem's sister?"

Nathan jerked, dropping the cinch. "On Brittany?"

"Yeah, she's Clem's sister, ain't she?"

Nathan could feel in his bones that there was something behind George's questioning. "What put such a notion in your head?"

"Just wondered." George looked hard at him. "You spend more time with her than any of the rest of us, you know."

"Not that much time."

George's tilted his chin stubbornly. "You spend plenty of evenings with her."

Nathan snorted. "Maybe two evenings a week at the most. And that's only because we happen to be at Johnny's at the same time."

"Oh, sure. You just happen to run into each other."

Nathan was beginning to feel irritated. "I've always enjoyed spending time with Johnny, even before Brittany came, in case you've forgotten."

Ignoring Nathan's defense, George asked, "Well, do you like her or not?"

"Oh, I like her, but–but not in the way you mean." Nathan's face felt overly warm. "Besides, how I feel is none of your business, now, is it?"

"Depends." George studied him. "Iffen you do care about her, then I reckon it's my business."

"I don't see—"

"Of course, you don't. You ain't been openin' your eyes to see that maybe you ain't the only man who cares about her 'round here."

It took a moment before the truth dawned on Nathan. "You think you're in love with her?"

George drew himself up to his full height. "I don't just think so—I know so."

"But that doesn't make any sense." Nathan couldn't recall ever seeing George so much as speak to Brittany. How could he think he was in love with her when he didn't truly know her? "What makes you think you're in love with her?"

George shot him an annoyed look. "What do you think? Every time I see her, my heart starts poundin' like crazy, and I git this strange feelin' down in the pit of my stomach, and I go all hot and cold at once. You know, that kind of stuff."

"Hmm." Nathan thought quickly. "I can't say for sure, George, but it sounds more like indigestion to me."

He was rewarded with an explosion from George. "Indigestion!" he hollered, his face turning a mottled red and the veins on his neck bulging. "You quit tryin' to make a fool of me, or you're gonna be sorry, Nathan!"

"Sorry. Didn't mean to offend you," Nathan said, feeling annoyed. George was in a pretty hot temper if he couldn't even take a joke.

"You might think you got the advantage with her, but let me tell you that you're gonna be doin' some reckoning with me iffen you do care for her." George stuck his face inches from Nathan's. "Just keep that in mind, all right, Nathan? You hear?"

"I hear, all right." Nathan tried to push George back a little. "Along with everyone within five miles of here."

"Huh." George eased back a little, but the anger didn't leave his eyes. "Keep in mind that I've got my eye on you, Nathan Lindale. I'm gonna be watchin' you."

George turned and began to stomp away, but Nathan stopped him.

"George, I answered your question, so now it's your turn to answer one of mine. Where did you get the idea that I was sweet on Brittany?"

George hesitated, then muttered, "Rueben."

"Rueben." Nathan looked across the corral to where Rueben stood, forcing a bridle into his horse's mouth, swearing all the while. "Rueben. I see."

"He was just sayin' the plain and honest truth," George said, his tone defensive. "And he's a heap of a better friend than you."

He turned and stomped away. Nathan didn't stop him.

"Rueben," Nathan said again in the quiet. Anger with the man welled up inside him—anger mixed with irritation. What was the man trying to do this time? Why did he always have to make himself a thorn in Nathan's side?

When Nathan was sure that he had his emotions under tight rein again, he slowly made his way over to Rueben. Rueben had his back turned to Nathan, slapping a saddle on his mount, grumbling under his breath.

"Rueben," Nathan said, and the man spun around to face him. The surprise on his face quickly gave way to annoyance.

"What?" Rueben asked, glaring at him.

"I need to talk with you."

Rueben's gaze darted one way, then the other before he shrugged. "Fine, but you better make it quick. I'm a busy man."

"I understand." Nathan refused to let Rueben ruffle him. "I just talked with George."

"Yeah?" Reuben made an impatient movement.

"What have you been filling his head with? He told me that you said that I was sweet on Brittany Haines." Nathan folded his arms across his chest. "Care to explain?"

Rueben raised one hand. "Now, look, sonny—"

"Don't call me that!"

"Hmm, touchy, are we? If you're gonna get upset so easily, I'm not gonna waste my time talking with you." Rueben started to turn away.

Nathan stepped in front of him. "I'm waiting for an answer, Rueben. You better tell me why George has it in his head that I like Brittany."

"It's true, ain't it?" Rueben met his gaze, his eyes challenging.

"No, it's not true, and you know it." Nathan stared back at him.

"Well, I see you together a lot, and just the other day I saw how she came right out to sit with you and talk. She didn't have to do that. It was just a pity that ol' Able had to show up and ruin things." Rueben's grin changed to more of a sneer.

Nathan's fist clenched and unclenched at his side. "Would you stop meddling with things that are none of your business? Ever since you've come to Northridge, you've been trying to stick your nose into my personal matters. I don't appreciate that, Rueben, and it's high time that you quit."

"Look—I'm done talkin' with you. I don't take kindly to people who yell in my face when I've got work I ought to be doin'." Rueben shoved past him.

"You better tell me why you told George I was sweet on Brittany," Nathan called after him. "What *are* you trying to do?"

Rueben had already mounted and was spurring his horse forward.

"I'm not done talking to you!" Nathan shouted.

"But I'm done talkin' to you," Rueben said. His horse picked up its pace and carried him out of earshot.

Nathan slumped back against the corral, defeated. It made no sense why Rueben was spreading rumors that he was sweet on

Brittany. What could he gain from that? There was a piece of the puzzle missing, but search as he might, Nathan couldn't uncover it. He only knew that having enemies in the close quarters the men at Northridge shared could forebode no good. Rueben was problem enough, but now he seemed determined to turn George on Nathan as well. Nathan made his way back to Loner with the distinct feeling that things had changed, and not for the better.

CHAPTER
22

Nathan still felt confused by Rueben's actions as he walked toward the barn later that evening. He'd been trying to make some sense of it all day, but he was no closer to figuring out why Rueben was stirring up trouble between him and George. It was pointless, and it pulled both George and Brittany into a problem that was between him and Rueben alone. Rueben Peirce. He hadn't liked the man from the day he first laid eyes on him, and his dislike had only grown since then.

Nathan pushed open the barn door, light from inside spilling out to meet him.

Clem looked up from where he sat beside a lantern, huddled over a wooden board. "Howdy, Nathan."

"Howdy yourself." Nathan stepped inside, closing the door behind him. "I thought I'd help you for a while if you want."

"Sure, that'd be right nice." Clem turned back to his work.

Nathan took a seat across from Clem, studying their work as he did so. He and Clem had been working on this project for nearly a week now. It seemed they were working painfully slow, but they *were* making progress. What had been a pile of dusty boards a week ago was now pounded together to form the rough shape of a blackboard, Clem's intended Christmas present for Brittany. Nathan had offered to help him mostly out of boredom, though he wasn't sure whether Clem's work would turn out or not. Neither he nor Clem was an expert in woodworking, and while Clem insisted that he had every detail of his construction plan in place, Nathan wondered. But regardless, the hours they had spent working on the project had drawn them even closer and had afforded them some laughs over their blunders. Now they were racing against time to get the present done by Christmas.

"Where did you come up with this idea anyway?" Nathan asked Clem, running a hand over one of the boards.

"I think it came from back in Iowa; some folks were talking about a school that couldn't afford a real blackboard, so they made something like this instead. After we finish sanding it, we'll give it a coat of black paint and have ourselves a blackboard." Clem, too, ran his hand across the boards, still rough to the touch. "I hope, anyway; I hadn't figured on it taking this much work."

When their only sanding tool was their knives it was no wonder that it took them forever to get the wood at least somewhat smooth. Nathan had already gotten more splinters in his fingers than he'd ever had in his life. He frowned down at the blackboard, noticing all the rough spots and splinters of wood that still marred it. Yes, making this blackboard was a lot of work.

He picked up his own knife and set to work, glad that helping Clem had given him an excuse to avoid the bunkhouse tonight. Although if any of the men caught wind of how he was helping make a Christmas present for Brittany, he would be in for a heap of teasing.

Nathan frowned. It didn't seem right that the men could take his perfectly innocent intentions and twist them into a completely different meaning, yet he knew that's what Rueben would do given half a chance.

Nathan and Clem worked in silence. Nathan wished Clem would say something, anything that would distract him from all his troubling thoughts, but Clem didn't seem to be in much of a talking mood. And since Nathan could think of nothing but bad things about Rueben and George, he kept quiet as well.

Rueben. George. Brittany. He couldn't get them out of his mind. He wished he could have cornered Rueben into telling him why he was spreading crazy rumors about him and Brittany. He wished he could have gotten ahold of that sneaking, conniving man and told him just what he thought about all that—

The tip of Nathan's knife caught on a particularly rough spot. Before he could adjust his grip on the handle, his index finger slid forward, striking the blade's sharp edge. Letting out a yelp and dropping the knife, Nathan cupped his injured finger in his other hand and watched as blood welled to the surface.

Clem looked up. "Cut yourself?"

"Yeah," Nathan said between gritted teeth, fumbling around in his pocket for a handkerchief. He couldn't find one, so he reached up and jerked the bandanna off his neck, wrapping that around his finger instead. He knew his finger was going to hurt for a while, and that only added to his frustration with himself. It was an accident easily avoided if he'd been focused, as he should have been, on his work. *Rueben,* his mind began, but he stopped himself. It was unreasonable to blame Rueben because he'd cut his finger. It was his own fault for letting his mind wander.

"Fool knife," he muttered, turning his anger on the blade that had caused all the problems—with his finger anyway. But being upset with an inanimate object struck him as even more ridiculous than being angry with Rueben Pierce.

"You all right?" Clem asked, setting down his own piece of glass.

"I reckon so. I'm not going to bleed to death."

"I meant besides the cut." Clem's gaze met Nathan's. He was too perceptive. He realized that it was more than a cut that was bothering Nathan tonight.

Nathan shifted restlessly. He couldn't tell Clem what he had been thinking. It would be too humiliating.

Clem still watched him, making no move to continue his work. The tension in the room mounted. Or maybe it was only inside Nathan. Clem didn't look at all uncomfortable.

"Did you know that George is sweet on Brittany?" he asked at last.

Clem shrugged. "That's no surprise. I reckon 'most every man around these parts is sweet on her." He seemed unconcerned.

"Seems to me that at least some of them have nothing more than a case of indigestion," Nathan said, thinking of George in particular.

Clem burst into laughter. "Nathan, Nathan, I'm just waiting for the day you find yourself a girl. You sound mighty practical now, but if I know you, you'll be jumping over the moon if that's what it takes to woo her. When you do something, you do it with all your might."

Nathan felt more annoyed than amused. "You'll be waiting your whole life."

"Stranger things have happened."

"So," Nathan said, ready to get back to the point. "doesn't it bother you that George is sweet on Brittany?"

"No." Clem picked up his knife again. "I figure most of those fellas, including George, will be content to admire from afar. And that they'll drop interest in her after a while—if it really is just indigestion they have."

"I wouldn't be too sure," Nathan said half under his breath.

"Why?"

"Because maybe George would give up on the idea if left to himself, but he's not going to forget as long as Rueben Pierce is egging him on." Bitterness crept into Nathan's voice.

"Rueben Pierce?" Clem raised an eyebrow. "What does *he* care about George and Brittany?"

"How should I know?" Nathan ran a hand wildly through his hair. "He's working hard at driving me mad, though."

"You?" Clem stopped. "You're not saying what I think you are, are you? You're not saying you're sweet on Brittany?"

"No, I am not! Why does everyone keep telling me that I am?" Nathan scowled at him, and jumping up from his seat, began to pace.

"Well, no need to get so upset." Clem stared at him. "You just sounded kinda suspicious for a moment."

"Clem Haines, that is enough!"

"Sorry." Clem threw his hands in the air. "I should've known better. After all, you like to think you're immune from such stuff, don't you?" Nathan caught a trace of sarcasm in his voice.

Nathan made himself take a deep breath. "I'm sorry," he said, turning to face Clem. "I'm not mad at you. I'm not even sure why we're talking about this."

"*You're* the one who brought it up," Clem reminded him.

"I—" Nathan paused, realizing Clem was right. He dropped back onto the seat, feeling suddenly worn out. Nathan had never considered himself to be easily angered, but tonight he kept snapping at the littlest things. Maybe that was why he was so tired. Anger was an exhausting emotion.

"I just don't know what to do," he said in a quieter voice. "It seems as if things are starting to spin out of control."

"That's not always a bad thing." Clem resumed his sanding. "Sometimes we *need* things to spin out of control so we realize we aren't the ones in control of our lives. God is."

"This is one mess I doubt God wants to get Himself caught up in." Nathan kept his tone joking even though humor was the farthest thing from his mind just then.

Clem shook his head. "God wants to be involved in every part of our lives, even the messy parts. He wants to be our Master every day and every hour, whether things are going good or bad."

Nathan raised an eyebrow. "Really, Clem, you can't think that He wants to be in control of *everyone's* lives. Some people just aren't worth His worrying over."

"Everyone has worth in God's eyes."

"Everyone? What about someone who has done something unforgivable? Like–like killing a bunch of people?"

"There is no sin that God can't forgive. All God requires is that we truly repent of what we have done and put our faith in Jesus, trusting that He has paid for our sin. God has promised He will never cast out the one who believes on Him."

Nathan shifted uncomfortably. "Well, I just don't know about that. It sounds good, but it won't hold up in real life. I mean, if God has to forgive *everyone* for *everything,* then someone like–like a killer can just go on killing people without having to face any kind of punishment. And then the world is even worse off."

Clem studied him. "That's not the way it works. First of all, God doesn't save everyone—only those who put their faith in Him. He never forces people to accept Him as their Savior. And second, when He does save someone, He gives them a new heart so that their desires change and they wish to follow His way. No, they don't obey perfectly, not on this side of heaven, but they are working in an upward direction. And when they do sin, they no longer need to fear the eternal consequences, but they might well have to face the consequences it brings in this life. Being saved doesn't give you a free ticket out of pain."

Nathan didn't try to come up with a response, realizing that he couldn't win the argument. He was too unsure of what he believed; he only knew that he didn't believe what Clem said.

"If that's what you want to believe," he said, shrugging.

"Maybe you'd be happier if *you* believed that," Clem said, his gaze never leaving Nathan.

His words hit home. "What? Why do you think I'm unhappy?"

"I'm not saying you're unhappy. But sometimes you get this look on your face that says not all is well with you." Clem leaned forward, his voice softening. "Nathan, if you were to die right now, where would you be going?"

Nathan wanted to get up and leave but felt frozen to his seat. "I–really, Clem, I try not to think about dying."

"But there will come a day when you die. The fact that we're all going to die is the one certainty in life. Don't you want to know where you're going afterward?"

"Clem, you don't understand."

"Don't understand what?"

The air was so thick with tension that Nathan could scarcely breathe. He really should tell Clem the one incident in his life that kept him from believing what Clem said—but he couldn't bring himself to do it. Some things were too painful to be spoken aloud.

"Don't worry about me." Nathan looked away from Clem. "It's not worth your time."

"I care about you, Nathan. That's the only reason I want you to make peace with God, you understand? Sometimes a person doesn't realize how much they want peace until they've had a taste of it. I've tasted that peace, and I want you to have it too."

He really meant it; Nathan could see it on his face. Nathan felt torn. Torn between Clem's words and their logic and between his own confused thoughts and beliefs. He was willing to admit that he would rather grab onto Clem's ideas than his own. The plain truth of it was, he was miserable with his own beliefs. But he couldn't accept Clem's way of thinking. Clem made it sound simple to get God's forgiveness. What he didn't realize was that Nathan was far more messed up than anyone ever would have guessed. If there were any way to right the wrong in his life, Nathan would have paid any price to do it, but that just wasn't possible. He had learned the hard way that not every mistake in life could be repaired. Sometimes a person messed up, despite their best intentions, leaving a path of heartache and broken relation-ships behind them.

"I can't do it." Nathan shook his head.

"Ask God to help you."

"No." Nathan picked up his knife again and set to work, wincing at the pain from his cut finger.

"You don't have to work on this tonight," Clem said, watch-ing him. "With your finger—"

"It's fine." Nathan kept his eyes fixed on his work. "Life goes on whether you're hurt or not."

A truth, he reflected, that went far deeper than just the physi-cal side of life.

CHAPTER
23

The last school day for 1881 was over. As Brittany put her books away, she reflected on the past couple of months of teaching—the trials and the joys. Each of her students was making progress even beyond what she had hoped for. Especially Carson. That boy had a bright mind matched with unquenchable curiosity, and he was working hard to catch up with Lars and Brenna in their studies. Brittany's only wish was that she had more books for him to study from. More books, more materials, more opportunities for all her students. Lack of materials was her daily worry. The paper supply Scott had brought from the fort was already dwindling, despite hoarding and insisting that every square inch be used. She had even started to erase the writing on some sheets in an effort to stretch her supply. But paper could be erased only so many times, she had discovered. As often as possible, she used the two small slates she brought along from Iowa—but two slates among twelve students created difficulties of its own. *It's too bad we don't have a blackboard,* she thought for what must have been the hundredth time, but she dismissed that thought as quickly as it came. *Find joy not in the things of earth and not in your circumstances but in the things that come from above,* Mama had often said. Mama had been such a wise woman. Too often Brittany struggled to remain joyful, especially when her circumstances were far from pleasant.

"I put the benches against the wall like ya asked, Miss Haines," Charley said, coming up beside her. "Can I go home now?"

"No, you *may* not, Charley," Brittany said, emphasizing *may.* "Please take the broom and sweep the room now."

Charley groaned but did as she asked. Some things had not changed since the beginning of the school year. Charley was in trouble again, this time for knocking down Zach Bryan. He seemed to have a knack at finding trouble in whatever he did, a fact Brittany was now resigned to. At least he had gained a measure of respect and no longer openly challenged her. He didn't even throw a fit over the chores she meted out as punishment.

A knock on the door made Brittany straighten. "Come in," she said.

The door opened slowly, almost hesitantly, and a boy with reddish-blond hair and a spray of freckles on his nose entered the room.

"Howdy," he said, raising his chin a notch.

Brittany blinked in surprise, then recovered her composure. "Why, Everett Bryan, how good to see you! How are you doing today?"

The boy seemed to relax slightly. "So you remember me? I wasn't sure you would."

"Of course, I remember you. What brings you here this afternoon? Your siblings already left, I'm afraid."

"I wasn't comin' for them. Truth is—" Everett hesitated, his gaze darting to Charley, who stood listening with the broom held idly in his hands. "I was hopin' I could talk with you. Alone."

"Why certainly." Brittany turned to Charley. "You may go home now, Charley. I'll see you in two weeks when school resumes."

"Yes, ma'am." Charley offered her a salute, then ran for the door, grabbing his coat on the way.

"Have a merry Christmas," Brittany called after him.

"I will!" he said, the door slamming shut behind him.

"Now, Everett." Brittany turned back to the boy. "What can I do for you?"

Everett shuffled his feet. "Well, I—I was wonderin'—I've been doin' a lot of thinkin' lately, and I'd like to learn that stuff my siblings are learnin', only, well—" Everett hesitated, then said in a rush, "I was wonderin' if maybe there was a way so I could kinda get ahead, you know, so that I don't have to start way back at the beginning."

"Ah." Brittany understood. Everett had a sense of manly pride and couldn't bear the humiliation of starting school at a level beneath his younger siblings and his five-year-old cousin, Billy. Admitting that his younger siblings were right in choosing to go to school would hurt his pride enough.

Brittany's mind raced to come up with a solution. "How about this? I've given the other students these next two weeks off for Christmas, but if you want to get ahead, you may come over for some private lessons each day."

"I'd like that," he said, brightening. "Do you think I can get caught up?"

"That depends. If you work hard, you might catch up with Billy and some of your siblings, but you certainly won't be caught up with Lars and Brenna and Carson. You're going to have to work really hard if you ever want to catch up to that brother of yours."

"I'll take the challenge." Everett beamed. "Can I start tomorrow?"

"Yes, you *may*," Brittany replied. "Come anytime tomorrow afternoon."

"Thanks, Miss Haines," Everett headed for the door, looking as if he could jump over a mountain. "I'll work real hard—you'll see!"

"I'm sure you will." Brittany smiled as he disappeared out the door. Yes, she was convinced that he would work very hard.

That evening Brittany slipped outside to find Clem and tell him the good news. Funny, but she'd scarcely seen him at all for the past couple of weeks. Her evenings had been busy with making each of her siblings a Christmas present, but she had found the time to visit Johnny—only to have Clem fail to appear. Oh, well. If he wouldn't come to her, she would just have to go to him.

Brittany hummed to herself as she set off down the snow-packed path leading away from the cabin. Clem would most likely either be in the barn or the bunkhouse—or the cook shack. She was not eager to search the bunkhouse or the cook shack, so she turned her footsteps to the barn. *Only a few more days until Christmas,* she thought. And from the looks of it, it would be white. She found herself momentarily wishing for Des Moines and time with Aunt Ida and the Browns, especially William. Holidays were special times to be spent with friends and family, surrounded by all the comfortable, homey traditions passed down year after year. But then she reminded herself that she did have family and friends here in Wyoming Territory. And there would be a party on Christmas Day. That alone was enough to put a skip in her step.

As she neared the barn, Brittany noticed two men standing beside the corral, their thick coats making it hard to tell who they were. One of them gestured with his arm as he spoke, and Brittany thought he might be Clem.

She changed direction and briskly walked that way. "Clem," she called.

Both men turned to look at her, and Brittany found herself looking not into Clem's blue eyes but into a pair of unfamiliar gray eyes.

"Oh," she said, taking a step back. "I—I'm sorry. I thought—"

The man stared at her, seeming to have lost all power of speech. Then his partner nudged him, and he said, "H—howdy, miss. I—I'm George." He said nothing else, just stared at her some more.

"I see." Brittany glanced from him to the man beside him. "I'm looking for my brother, Clem. Have you seen him?"

George mutely shook his head.

"I know where he is." The second man shot George a glare. "He's in the barn workin'."

"Thank you, sir," Brittany said, backing away from the two. George was watching her in a most disconcerting way.

"Name's Rueben," the man said, scowling at her now. "Not 'sir'."

"Thank you for the correction, *Rueben*." As soon as the words were out, Brittany was mortified by how sarcastic she sounded. Turning away, she nearly ran to the barn, the man's coarse laughter ringing in her ears. She risked a glance behind her when she reached the barn doorway and felt her cheeks flame when she realized that George and Rueben were still staring after her.

All that staring was going to drive her out of her mind if she didn't escape. Still glancing back at them, she hurried through the barn door but was stopped when she collided with something warm and solid.

"Whoa!" a man's voice said. "Where are you off to so fast?"

It seemed that she was having a night of accidents. Brittany stumbled back a step and found herself looking up at Nathan. "Nathan," she said, feeling a flood of relief that it was only him and not one of the other ranch hands. Now that she stopped to think about it, she hadn't seen *him* in a long time either.

Nathan's gaze slipped past her to the two men standing by the corral. "They causing you trouble?" he asked, his smile disappearing.

"Oh, no." Brittany shook her head. "Really, they're fine."

"Good." Nathan's expression didn't change. "If they ever do, you make sure to tell me or Clem right away, all right?"

Why he thought George and Rueben might cause her trouble, Brittany didn't know and didn't care to speculate on. "I will," she said. "Do you know where Clem is?"

"Right here," a voice said behind Nathan, and Clem appeared in the doorway.

He broke into a grin when he saw her. "How's one of my favorite little sisters doing tonight?" he asked, tweaking her nose.

"Clem." Brittany straightened and frowned at him.

"Now don't get all in a huff thinking you're too old for me to tweak your nose. You're still my little sister. What brings you here?"

"I haven't seen you much lately," Brittany said, arching an eyebrow at him.

"I know," Clem said, making no excuses.

"What have you been up to?" Brittany asked. "Surely Mr. Myers doesn't keep you going from dawn to dusk."

"He's capable of it. He keeps us busy beyond dawn to dusk in the summer."

"But it's winter, not summer."

Clem grinned at her again. "You shouldn't ask questions too close to Christmas."

Brittany gave him a sidelong glance, wondering just what he was up to. "Fine, no questions. Not until Christmas at least. By the way, today I got a new student."

"You did? Who's that?"

"Everett Bryan."

"There now, see? Your little school is coming along real nice." Clem started to reach out to pat her head, then stopped himself. "Oh, right. You think you're too old for that kind of stuff."

Brittany hid her smile. "Everett's going to be coming for private lessons during these next couple of weeks. He wants to get ahead before joining the others."

"So I guess you're not getting much of a vacation. Unless you canceled that party you were planning?"

"Of course not. I'll still have plenty of time to prepare for that. If I'd had doubts about having a party, do you think I would have broached the subject to Mr. Myers in the first place and endured his blustering over all my crazy ideas?" Brittany shook her head at the idea. "Besides, everyone is planning on it, including Morgan and her uncle. It's too late to cancel."

"Well, Clem, did you hear that?" Nathan asked, drawling the words out more than usual. "Morgan's coming. Or have you been seeing her so much lately that you don't feel any excitement?"

"Course I'm excited to see her. I can't get enough of her." Clem jabbed an elbow at Nathan. "You, of course, wouldn't understand that since you have a natural immunity to such stuff."

Nathan shook his head and looked at Brittany. "Ever noticed that you've got an incorrigible tease for a brother?"

"I'm glad you noticed," Brittany said, smiling back at him.

"I can't believe I didn't see it before now." The bitterness in George's voice made Rueben smile. George was mad, all right, just the effect he'd been hoping for.

"And the worst thing is that he acts innocent about it." George scowled. "Fool man."

"Who's a fool?" Able Zimmerman appeared beside them, his sad-looking horse following behind.

Rueben nodded to him. "Howdy, Able."

"Who's a fool?" Able said again.

"Look." George jabbed a finger in the direction of Clem, Brittany, and Nathan. "He's crazy 'bout her."

Able squinted at them. "I don't see. Who's crazy about who?"

"Use your eyes! Nathan's crazy about Brittany!" George folded his arms across his chest. "And he's not shy 'bout it neither. He looks as if he's settlin' in to talk with her all evening."

The creases in Able's face turned down even more. "Nathan's crazy 'bout her, huh? No wonder he was so closed with his information 'bout her the other night."

"It's–it's outrageous!" George's eyes blazed. "And he's purty confident in himself too. Thinks he's far ahead of all the other men 'round here."

"He shouldn't be too sure." Able stared at Nathan in a cold, calculated way as if he were measuring him up. Rueben would have paid top dollar to know what was going through his mind.

"Maybe you should give him a little competition," Rueben said, turning to George.

George's shoulders drooped. "I've tried."

"You haven't tried that hard."

"Yeah, well, it's tough. But I'll keep tryin'." All the cockiness had left his voice, and he sounded grim.

Reuben wanted to shake the man. George stood no chance of success if he was going to be so faint-hearted. He sure talked big when it was just him and Rueben, but Reuben had witnessed tonight how tongue-tied George got in Brittany's presence. It was terrible. If George was going to act like that, Rueben might as well say goodbye to all his well-laid plans to get a reaction out of Nathan. A cowering man like George would bother Nathan about as much as a pesky fly.

Rueben's gaze slid from George to Able. He'd heard that the man was out to marry Brittany—and that his attempts weren't going so well. Able was too direct for his own good. He settled his mind on what he wanted and chased after it with all his might, not stopping to think that in his rush he might be trampling more delicate matters underfoot. But at least he tried. He was no whining, cowardly, mess of a man. He was a man who acted.

Rueben chewed on the end of his mustache, studying the man before him. Able was not a handsome man. He wasn't a young man either. But he was made of a substance Rueben needed for his plans to succeed. Maybe he'd been setting his sights on the wrong man. Sure, as far as appearances went, George was the better of the two, but when it got down to the grit that Rueben needed, Able surpassed the younger man. It was that grit that would drive Nathan crazy and make him jealous. Jealousy could bring out the worst in a man. Rueben had witnessed that firsthand. And the worst was just what he wanted out of Nathan Lindale. Everyone seemed to love Nathan, thinking him such a fine, upright young man. Nathan did a good job of giving that impression, but Rueben was dead certain the young man was hiding something. It just didn't match up; how Nathan could go from inheriting a ranch to working as a common cowpoke, and in Wyoming Territory, no less. Nor how he could have made a complete break from the family he'd been so close with when he was younger. No, Rueben was convinced that something had happened during the gap in years between first meeting Nathan and running into him again last fall. Something that Nathan was doing his best to keep a lid on. Whatever that was, Rueben was determined to ferret it out. The young man needed to be brought down a notch. He was far too cocky, too high and mighty for his own good. His whole manner was enough to make Rueben want to grind his teeth.

And besides all that, Nathan was partly responsible for destroying Rueben's most cherished dream. It would serve Nathan right to see how it felt to have a dream on the brink of realization only to have it smashed to pieces.

Yes, Rueben decided, Able was the man for the job. He would need to learn about being more, uh, sensitive in his courting, but Rueben considered himself up to the task of coaching him. It made no difference to him whether Able married Brittany; he didn't care one way or the other as long as Nathan responded the way Rueben hoped. And that was the key to it all. Give Nathan a good dose of disappointment and jealousy, and the pressure would make Nathan crack, revealing the real man inside. The not-so-perfect Nathan.

Rueben glanced at Able. He'd have to find a time to talk with the man in private. It would never do to discuss his scheming right here, with George absorbing every word, realizing Rueben didn't care about him. But no matter. There was no rush. Rueben was sure that once the job had been handed off to Able, he would execute it with a will.

CHAPTER
24

Christmas Day dawned with a cloudless sky and a fresh layer of glistening snow. Brittany stood at the kitchen window and watched as the rising sun turned the white of the snow into a glowing pink until it was impossible to tell where the land ended and the sky began. *Yet another beautiful sunrise,* Brittany thought, wondering if she would ever tire of watching the colors play across the eastern horizon each morning. The sunrises were one thing she would definitely miss when she returned to Iowa. One of the very few things.

Clem arrived shortly after breakfast, grinning wide enough to dim the sun. "Merry Christmas, Brittany. You have a little time to come take a look at something?"

"I suppose I can schedule you in." Brittany smiled. He might be trying to cover his excitement, but he was having no more success than if he attempted to tamp down one of the geysers she'd heard about up north.

"Where are Lars and Brenna?" Clem asked.

"Here!" The two children burst into the room at a run.

"Good. All of you go get your coats, quick. I've got something I want you to see."

Brittany was curious about what Clem wanted to show them, and she hurried to pull on her coat and gloves. At the last moment she remembered the gift she had made for Clem, and she retrieved the package from her sewing basket. "I'll be back in a little bit," she told Mrs. Myers before going out the door again. "Clem has something to show me."

"Take your time, dear," Mrs. Myers said over Mr. Myers's snort.

As Brittany closed the door behind her, Clem reached out and took her arm. "Come on," he said, hurrying her down the steps. Lars and Brenna skipped ahead of them, their laughter echoing in the clear morning.

"Over to the barn," Clem directed them.

Brittany gave him a sideways glance. What could be worth seeing in the barn? But then, it was Christmas morning, and as Clem would say, one shouldn't ask too many questions.

They all entered the barn together, and Brittany's eye was caught by an oddly shaped object wrapped in a blanket, propped up against the wall. She studied it, trying to guess what it was.

"That's for Lars and Brenna," Clem said. As they hesitated, he waved them forward. "Go ahead. See what it is."

The two children walked forward and pulled the blanket off at the same time. Brenna let out a squeal and began dancing in place.

"It's a sled!" Lars looked back at Clem, his eyes sparkling. "You made it?"

"Yep," Clem said, his tone nonchalant. "Every kid needs a sled, and there are plenty of hills here for you to use it on."

"Thanks, Clem!" Both of the children ran and threw their arms around him, nearly knocking him off balance.

Clem chuckled. "You're welcome, and I hope you like it."

"Oh, we do. Can we go try it out now?" Lars asked, turning to Brittany.

"I don't see why not," she said, smiling. She couldn't remember ever seeing the two of them so excited. Her heart warmed with more love than ever for her big brother; such a kind, thoughtful man to come up with the idea in the first place.

As Lars and Brenna ran out of the barn, Clem turned to Brittany and said, "Now for *your* turn. Your present is behind you."

Brittany looked behind her. Sure enough, another blanket-wrapped object stood against the wall, this one even bigger than the present for Lars and Brenna.

"Clem, you didn't need to make me a gift," she said, touched. "Just being here with you is a gift enough."

"Go on—just open it. I wanted to make you a gift, so you might as well see what it is." Clem shifted impatiently.

Brittany was eager to see what the blanket was covering, but first she pulled out her gift for Clem. "Here—take this," she said, thrusting it toward him. "It's for you."

"For me?" Clem's eyebrows rose. "Now Brittany—"

"No, Clem. Just open it." Brittany grinned at him. "Do you remember when we were children how we always opened our presents at the same time? Let's do that now."

Clem nodded. "Fine. On the count of three. One, two, three—"

Brittany grabbed the corner of the blanket and pulled. The blanket came off, revealing a sheet underneath. Mystified, Brittany drew it back and found herself staring at a wooden object, long and flat. It was black, and smooth to the touch, and—it could be only one thing! But Clem couldn't have gotten her a blackboard, could he? No, that was impossible. But what else could it be?

"A new shirt! Just what I needed!" Clem came up behind her. His voice turned hesitant. "Do you like your present, Brittany?"

Brittany turned slowly to face him. "Clem Haines, is that a blackboard?"

"Next thing to one. I couldn't get a real blackboard; that's just some boards sanded smooth and covered with a coat of paint. I did the best I could, but I know it's not perfect."

"Oh, Clem!" Brittany flung herself at him. "How did you know that a blackboard is just what I wanted? It's perfect, Clem, perfect!"

Clem disentangled himself from Brittany's embrace to look down at her. "Are you sure you like it?" he asked again, his eyes shadowed with doubt.

"Love it!" Brittany was tempted to give him another hug to prove that she meant it but knew Clem wasn't fond of that kind of thing. "You are one of the most thoughtful men on earth, Clem Haines—do you know that?"

"I'm not so sure about that." Clem smiled. "Or that I'm the only one you should be thanking. Nathan helped too. He put in about as many hours as I did on that thing."

"He did?" Brittany couldn't hide her surprise. "But why?"

Clem shrugged. "He said he'd rather do something productive with his evenings—and I did keep him busy."

Brittany looked back at the blackboard, thinking what a difference this would make in her teaching. "I don't know how I can ever thank you enough for this."

"This here shirt's plenty of thanks for me." Clem held up the blue shirt she had made for him. "I haven't had a shirt this fine since back when Ma did my sewing."

"That's nothing compared to *your* gift. I'll think of you every time I use it." *And Nathan,* she added silently to herself. Nathan. How could she tell him how much the gift meant to her? She wished she had something to give him in return, but the idea of making a gift for him had never even crossed her mind. All she was left with was a pair of empty hands.

"I'll have to tell Nathan thank you later," she said, understanding what it meant to have a heart overflowing with gratitude.

"Good idea. Just don't tell him thank you the same way you told me. He won't appreciate all the hugging." Clem's eyes twinkled.

"Clem!" Brittany could feel the heat rush straight up to her hairline.

"Aw, I'm just teasing you. Come on—let's go see how Lars and Brenna are doing with their sled."

Brittany had dinner ready and was changed into her best dress when guests began to arrive for the party. She ran her fingers down the blue fabric, glad she had an excuse to wear it for the first time since coming to Northridge. With its delicate lace collar and cuffs, the dress had been quite fashionable in Des Moines. Not that fashion made a difference to anyone here in Wyoming.

Johnny was the first guest to arrive. He entered the cabin without even bothering to knock, his banjo tucked under one arm. "Merry Christmas, everybody," he said, grinning around the room. He winked at Brittany and patted his banjo. "Wouldn't be a party if there weren't no music."

"I was hoping you would bring your banjo, Johnny." Brittany smiled in return. "Thanks for coming."

"Why, bless you, girlie—you're the one who oughta be gettin' all the thanks. You're the one who planned this whole shindig. All I did was come." Johnny winked at her once more before making his way through the maze of makeshift benches to where Mr. and Mrs. Myers sat at the kitchen table.

The ranch hands arrived one by one after Johnny, all of them well scrubbed and looking very uncomfortable. Brittany greeted each of them, feeling as if she had been placed in her element once more. She might make a poor westerner, but Aunt Ida had seen to it that she knew how to be a good hostess. Not even Mr. Myers could find fault with her on that point.

Morgan and her uncle were among the last to arrive. As they entered the cabin, their cheeks red with cold, Brittany hurried forward to take their coats.

"It's so good to see you again," Morgan said, giving her a hug. "Feels like I haven't seen you in ages."

"Then you should have stopped by if you missed me so," Brittany said, once again blessing her brother for making such a good choice in courting Morgan.

"Maybe, but I know you're busy with teaching school and all, so I hesitated to burst in on you."

"Nonsense. Stop by anytime. It's been far too lonely around here, even if I am teaching school. Sometimes a person finds themselves wishing to talk to an adult."

"I do get tired of talking to my horse. I'll try to come more often." Morgan turned to her uncle. "You haven't met Brittany yet, have you?"

"'Fraid not," the man said, his voice loud enough to be heard from every corner of the cabin—and beyond. "Pleasure to meet you, little lady. Name's Dave, Dave Norris." He held out a hand to her, his weathered face beaming.

Brittany accepted his hand and found herself being given a handshake hearty enough to send tingles up and down her arm. "I'm pleased to meet you, too, Mr. Norris," she said, flexing her hand after he released it.

"Pleasure's mine, pleasure's mine," he said. "Boy, but you sure resemble your brother. Blond hair and blue eyes must be a family trait, huh? Glad to finally meet you, especially since we're gonna be almost family. I'll tell you I might be even more anxious than Morgan waitin' for your brother to pop the question."

Morgan's face reddened. "Now, uncle. Don't rush things."

"Well, it's comin', and I don't see why you gotta be so shy about it," Dave Norris said, his voice booming in the small cabin.

Morgan blushed even more, and taking pity on her, Brittany excused herself to go check on the food.

Dinner proved to be a success, at least in Brittany's eyes. The food turned out well, and all the guests seemed to relax and settle down to enjoy themselves. The only bad thing about the meal was that she found herself seated between George and Little Joe, who both grinned at her far too much for her liking. But while it was unnerving, every time she happened to glance their way, Brittany had the impression that the two men were rather shy. By the time dinner was over, neither had mustered the courage to do more than just smile.

After dinner, Johnny pulled out his banjo, and everyone shifted to form a circle of sorts around him. Brittany used the opportunity to escape from George and Little Joe. Darting a glance around the room, she searched for Clem. When she saw him across the room squeezed in between Morgan and Dave Norris, she realized that sitting by him wasn't going to be an option.

Just as her panic began to mount, she spotted an empty space on the bench beside Nathan. As inconspicuously as possible, she made her way across the room and slid onto the seat beside him. She was saved. Nathan wouldn't blush and stutter and gawk at her all afternoon.

"Have a nice dinner conversation?" Nathan asked, glancing over at her.

"I think you know the answer to that, so I won't favor you with a reply," she said in a whisper.

Nathan's chuckle was drowned out as Johnny strummed the first chords of "Silent Night." They had no time for further conversation as everyone, both old and young, began to sing.

It didn't take Brittany long to realize that, despite their different backgrounds, everyone in the room had one thing in common—they loved to sing. Not everyone sang all the right words, and many of the men couldn't carry a tune, but that didn't stop them. Everyone sang heartily, so heartily that Brittany was sure the cabin's rafters must be shaking from all the noise. *There's nothing silent about Northridge today,* she thought, smiling.

Johnny had played a couple of songs when Brittany's attention was drawn to the door as it opened. To her horror, the one man she dreaded to see marched into the room, just as if he owned the place. His gaze swept around the room, settling on her, and a grin spread across his face. *No, Able. Don't come near me,* Brittany thought, but in vain. Able strode across the room straight toward her, not so much as glancing at anyone else in the room.

"Miss," Able said, stopping in front of her and bowing.

"Mr. Zimmerman." Brittany hoped the coolness in her voice would at least make the silly grin on his face fade. It didn't.

Able's smile stretched wider, and without so much as asking permission or excusing himself, wedged between her and Nathan and sat down, looking pleased with himself.

How dare he! Here she had chosen to sit next to Nathan, feeling safer with him than those other bumbling cowboys, and now a man far more upsetting had appeared. It aggravated her how Able Zimmerman thought he was the cleverest, most charming man around and had such confidence in his own opinion that nothing could shake it. Brittany fumed, but she determined not to let the disgust show on her face.

The rest of the afternoon was ruined for Brittany by Able's coming. His voice grated in her ears, his off-key singing sounding worse than nails on a chalkboard. Every time she glanced his way, he was staring at her, and he grinned broadly as if he were entirely convinced that she was struggling to keep from turning her eyes to his handsome face. Never once did he glance at Morgan, who was sitting securely at Clem's side. He seemed to have entirely forgotten that he had ever asked any other woman to marry him.

Brittany never thought she would be glad to see Johnny lay down his banjo but was tempted to cheer when at last he said, "Wal, I reckon we've probably done enough singin' for one day."

That was her ticket to escape the obnoxious man. Brittany jumped to her feet and hurried to the kitchen, away from Able Zimmerman. Nothing needed to be done there, but she made a show of being busy as people slowly began to leave.

"Thanks for the wonderful party," Morgan said, coming up beside Brittany before she left. "You were right. We all needed something to stir us up a bit."

"I'm glad you could come. Make sure to stop by soon, all right?"

"I will." Morgan's eyes took on a teasing glint. "How can I ever thank you enough for getting Able's attention off of me? I'm indebted to you for life."

"That man is going to drive me crazy," Brittany said, dropping her voice to a whisper. "He's *always* showing up at the worst time. He won't take my word for it that I don't care to marry him, and he just won't leave me alone!"

Morgan looked sympathetic. "I'm sorry for you. I've been there before." She reached out to give Brittany a hug. "Just hold tight and don't let him bully you into marrying him. He'd probably leave you alone if you found another man, you realize."

"No, thank you. I'll manage until I leave for Des Moines this fall." Brittany pulled back. "Have a good trip home."

"Thanks again. I'll come and visit sooner rather than later." Morgan hurried off to join her Uncle Dave.

Brittany noticed Nathan making his way to the door, and she quickly shot a glance around the room to make sure Able wasn't nearby. He appeared to be gone. Brittany deserted her post in the kitchen and ran after Nathan, catching him in the doorway.

"Nathan," she said.

He turned to look at her, along with several other men.

"Clem told me you helped make the blackboard." Brittany felt her cheeks warm. "I don't know how I can ever thank you enough. It was a perfect gift, just what I needed."

Nathan shrugged. "It was Clem's idea. I didn't do that much."

"I think you did. Thank you."

Their gazes met and held for one moment, and looking into his brown eyes, Brittany felt a sudden and unexpected—something. Before she had time to figure out what that was, a man coughed behind her and said, "Excuse me, ma'am."

"Oh, yes, of course." Brittany stepped back from the doorway.

The man had a little smile on his face, and as he brushed past them, Brittany saw him lean toward Nathan and whisper something that made Nathan redden. Before Nathan could reply, the man walked away, looking well pleased.

"That was Rueben Pierce, wasn't it?" Brittany asked, looking after the man.

"Yeah." Nathan sounded grim. "That was Rueben."

He seemed to have suddenly become restless. "I'd better go," he said, not looking at her.

"Of course. Merry Christmas."

He nodded, and settling his hat more firmly on his head, walked away.

Brittany watched him leave, wondering what Rueben could have said to make Nathan hurry away like that. She was even more confused when she turned and saw George scowling after Nathan. *Something's going on that no one's telling me about,* she thought. But she had no clue what.

After leaving the Boss's cabin, Rueben hurried to catch up with Able. It was past time that he talked with the man about his plan. He was more certain than ever that Nathan was smitten with Brittany, but he hadn't thought of what would happen if the girl fell for Nathan. That couldn't happen. It would be far more difficult for Able to catch her attention if she already had her sights on a handsome young man of her own choosing. It might even be impossible. He had to act now—and quickly.

"Hey, Able," he called out, quickening his steps as Able prepared to mount his horse. "Wait up!"

Able turned at the sound of his voice and waited for Rueben to join him.

"Able," Rueben said, reaching the man's side. "I've been wantin' to talk to you about somethin'."

"Oh, yeah? What's that?"

There was nothing like plunging right into the heart of the matter. "I noticed that you seem to care for Brittany Haines."

Able nodded, running a hand through his thinning gray hair. "Yeah, so?"

"I don't know if you noticed, but Nathan Lindale's sweet on her too."

Able's eyebrows drew together. "Can't help that. But I don't think he's got a chance. Brittany's love for me is growin' by the day."

Rueben had his own opinions about that. "Maybe. But it seems to be growin' mighty slow."

Able opened his mouth to protest, but Rueben stopped him. "Look here—if you want to win her over faster, then you're gonna have to face the truth of it. The truth is that if you don't watch sharp, Nathan's gonna steal her from you, and you're gonna be left in poor shape. That's the truth, plain and simple."

Able seemed to think over what Rueben said.

"I want to help you. I want to see you and Brittany together, honest. We can help each other's causes."

"How?" Able asked, his eyebrows drawing together. "What do you want out of me?"

"Like I said, it's simple. You want to marry Brittany, and I want to see Nathan thwarted. Me and Nathan have this thing between us, you see—" Rueben waved his hand. There was no need to try to explain his side of the plan to Able.

"Ah." Able nodded slowly. "I see. So since he wants to marry Brittany, you want me to git her instead, and that's how you want to thwart him, huh?"

"Right. I knew you were a smart man."

"But how's that gonna help me? Seems like I'm doin' all the work."

"Look here, Able—I need you to git her attention fast. Iffen you don't, there's no hope for either of us. So I'm gonna help you with that. Your problem, Able, is that you've been tryin' to go too fast."

"You say I'm goin' too fast, yet you need me to catch her attention quick-like?" Able shook his head. "You lost me."

"You're goin' to try gettin' her attention from a new angle." Rueben leaned toward him. "Iffen you listen close to me, I can just see you marryin' her in no time."

Able's forehead wrinkled in thought for a moment; then he nodded. "But what about Nathan? What am I supposed to do with him?"

"That's where I come in." Rueben smiled. "Leave him to me."

CHAPTER
25

"Done."

Brittany closed the last of her books and stretched, glad to be finished with her preparations for tomorrow's school day. School had been in session for a week now, and she was busier than ever with her twelve students—thirteen, including Allie Bryan. But it was a good kind of busy that left her falling asleep with the deep satisfaction of a day well spent.

Everett was doing well in school; he'd kept his promise to work hard and had accomplished far more than Brittany could have hoped. Charley had teased him during the first couple of days, trying to get him to make trouble. But Everett ignored him. Finally Charley gave up and set to work on his studies—probably trying to keep ahead of Everett.

Rising from her seat, Brittany crossed the room to the stove and opened the oven door. Heat and the fragrance of freshly baked bread greeted her, and after touching one of the golden-brown tops, Brittany decided it was done. Using a folded towel, she pulled the loaves out and set them on the table. As she closed the oven, she heard a firm knock on the cabin door.

"Who do you suppose that is?" Mrs. Myers asked, coming from her room, rubbing her gnarled hands.

Brittany shrugged, although she had a suspicion niggling in the back of her mind. She hurried to the door and swung it open. Her heart promptly sank. Just as she had suspected, it was Able Zimmerman.

"Evening, Miss Haines." Able sketched a bow. "I hope I'm not imposin'. Would now be an acceptable time to visit?"

This wasn't the first time Brittany had heard the request from Able. Since the Christmas party he had stopped by three times, each time asking *most* politely if he could come in for a visit. There was something puzzling about the man. He had gone from being in her face all the time to behaving like a well-mannered gentleman. He had even dropped the references to marriage. It left Brittany wondering what exactly the man was scheming. His manner may have changed, but his eyes still had the same look of self-confidence, as if he already knew he would be successful—in whatever he was trying to do.

The whole thing made Brittany uneasy. She wanted to tell him that now was not a good time to visit, that there would never be a good time, but the hostess inside her would not permit that.

"Of course, Mr. Zimmerman." Brittany forced a smile. She swung the door open wider to let him in and stepped back as he entered the cabin. He certainly was dressed up tonight. He wore a newer-looking green shirt with a leather vest over it, his chaps were dust-free, and the belt holding them in place was polished to a shine. Even his hat and boots had been cleaned up, and his hair slicked down to the side.

"Mr. Zimmerman, how good to see you," Mrs. Myers greeted him. If she, like Brittany, felt annoyed by his visit, she kept it from showing. "What brings you here tonight?"

"Just thought I'd stop by for a friendly little visit." Able gave another bow. Brittany wished he would leave off with his ridiculous-looking bows.

"How nice." Mrs. Myers beamed. "I'm sure my husband will be in shortly. Won't you stay for supper?"

Able perked up. "Why that'd be right fine."

"Good." Mrs. Myers seemed to have no qualms about talking with Able. She carried the conversation on smoothly, setting both Brittany and Able down at the table with her. Brittany chaffed at being forced into the man's company, but she had no excuse to leave the room.

After a few minutes, Brittany began to enter the conversation despite herself. When he wasn't boasting, she found that Able could be interesting. And it seemed he was trying to keep the conversation pleasant, speaking so politely that Brittany had to wonder if this was really Able Zimmerman or merely a look-alike.

"So have you decided yet that you like Wyoming Territory?" Able asked her.

Brittany tensed, unsure of how she should answer the question. "It's not that I dislike it here. It's just that I love Iowa more, and my family is there."

"You have family here too."

"Well, yes, but—"

"And you seem to be gettin' along with folks around here real well."

"But—"

A knock at the door interrupted her, and jumping to her feet, Brittany hurried to answer it. *Perfect timing,* she thought. The questions were getting too pointed. Whatever Able was driving at was most likely best left unknown.

Brittany pulled open the door and was startled to find Nathan standing there. The expression on his face told her something was wrong, and her heart gave a little flutter of fear. She knew him well enough to know that he wouldn't have stopped by just for a friendly visit.

"Brittany," he said, sounding out of breath as if he'd been running. "I need you to come. There's been an accident."

"An accident?" Brittany felt as if the air were suddenly knocked out of her lungs. "Who?"

"Lars."

The world seemed to tilt, and Brittany grabbed at the door frame. "Oh no, not Lars. Please, Lord, not Lars!"

She was faintly aware of Nathan's hand on her arm, its warmth and strength a lifeline in her panic. She had to draw herself together. She *must,* for Lars's sake.

Drawing a deep breath, she looked up at Nathan. "What happened?"

He studied her as if he weren't sure that she was truly okay. "Lars was knocking down icicles from the barn roof. One fell and hit him," he said, his voice more controlled now.

Brittany inhaled again. "How bad?"

"He's got a nasty looking gash in his forehead. He's at Johnny's now."

"Then let's go." Brittany straightened and turned away from him. "Just let me get my coat."

"We can wait a minute if you need," Nathan said, watching her with concern.

"I'm fine. Lars needs me." Brittany pulled on her coat, then remembered Mrs. Myers and Able. She turned to the two of them, whose expressions told her they'd overheard everything. "Stew and fresh bread are ready for supper," she said. "Don't wait for me. I'm not sure when I'll be back."

"Of course, dear. Do what you must," Mrs. Myers said, her forehead furrowed in concern.

"Sure, sure," Able said, but his face clouded over. As Brittany hurried outside, she saw him send Nathan a dirty look before the door closed, a look that reminded her of Charley Jones when he was having a bad day. She glanced at Nathan; he didn't seem to have noticed.

"Clem isn't here now," Nathan said as they set off at a quick pace toward Johnny's. "Hopefully he'll be back soon, but there's just no way of knowing."

"Oh." Brittany felt a stab of sharp disappointment. Here she was with Lars hurt, maybe even dying, and Clem wasn't around to offer his support. *At least Nathan's here,* she reminded herself. That thought was incredibly comforting. If Clem couldn't be here, there was no one she would rather have than Nathan.

"Do you think Lars will be all right?" Brittany dared to ask him.

"I'm sure of it."

"I don't know what I would do if something were to–to happen to Lars. Or Brenna. I'd never hear the end of it from Aunt Ida. She was against this trip from the beginning, and she'd say this just showed how right she had been." Brittany sniffed back tears. "Maybe she *is* right. Maybe it was a bad idea to think I could bring two children here. I should have been keeping a closer eye on him, at least. If something does happen to him, I don't know how I'll ever forgive myself. I should have—"

"Brittany, look at me." Nathan stopped abruptly and turned her around to face him. "Don't do that to yourself. This is not your fault—you hear me? It is *not.*" He gave her a little shake for emphasis. "You can't keep Lars and Brenna sheltered from every risk, not here and not in Iowa. Accidents happen everywhere. Don't let anybody tell you this is your fault; I know you. You've done your best to protect those two, and if any accidents happen, it's not because you've been careless." His voice softened. "Guilt's a nasty thing, Brittany, and you don't want to get yourself tangled up in it. Believe me."

Brittany stared at him, hardly able to make out his face through the tears. But his words rang clearly, their force reaching through the haze of fear that had settled around her. She swallowed hard, then nodded. "I understand."

"Good." Nathan patted her arm and turned away. Brittany looked down, wondering why it suddenly felt so warm, but Nathan was already walking toward Johnny's. She hurried to catch up with him, pushing aside all thoughts except for Lars.

Together Nathan and Brittany climbed Johnny's cabin steps, and Brittany fought to get her emotions under control again.

"He'll be fine," Nathan said, opening the door for her. Brittany nodded but wondered.

She stepped into Johnny's cabin, her gaze darting around the room in search of her little brother. Her eyes fell on him, lying on Johnny's table, unmoving. Johnny bent over him with his back to her, holding a rag against the boy's head.

Brittany swallowed hard, unable to move forward, afraid of what she might find. She sensed Nathan behind her, and gaining strength from his presence, she inched her way across the room to Lars's side.

Johnny nodded his greeting to her and shifted so she could get closer to Lars.

Bracing herself, Brittany stepped forward and looked into Lars's blue eyes. "Hi, Brittany," he whispered. His face was pale, and he had been crying, but he looked far better than Brittany had expected.

"Lars." Brittany's voice broke. "Are you all right?"

"I got a cut." He shrugged.

"It's not bleeding so bad now." Johnny lifted the rag, exposing a ragged, gaping wound. The rag was soaked with blood, such bright, red blood that Brittany felt the color drain from her face.

"Head wounds always bleed a heap," Johnny said, noticing her horror.

"Is he—is he going to be all right?" Brittany asked, her voice sounding strange to her own ears.

"Why, sure he will," Johnny said. "He'll be right as rain in no time."

"Thank God." Brittany sank down into one of Johnny's chairs, feeling weak with relief.

"Lars hardly cried at all," Brenna said, coming up beside Brittany and putting an arm around her. "Just a little when the ice hit him and when Nathan carried him in."

"I wasn't crying," Lars mumbled.

"Yes, he was. He was sobbing," Brenna said importantly.

"No, I wasn't." Lars paused, then added, "Well, not much, anyway."

"But I would have cried too if I was bleeding like that," Brenna said, coming to her brother's defense. "He got blood everywhere, even on Nathan's shirt."

Brittany darted a glance at Nathan. Sure enough, his blue-checkered shirt had several bloody stains on it. She felt her face go even whiter, if that were possible.

Nathan seemed to decide Brenna had done enough talking. "Come here, Brenna," he said, scooping her up in his arms. "I've got a job for you to do. I want you to go outside and watch for Clem. Tell him to come here right away when you see him, okay?"

"Sure!"

"Are you sure you can handle such an important job?" Nathan asked, only the tiniest of smiles giving away his teasing.

"Of course!" Brenna squirmed, and Nathan set her down. She ran, and pulling on her coat, scurried out the door.

"That'll keep her busy for a bit." Nathan turned back to Johnny and Brittany.

Johnny was still inspecting Lars's cut. "This is a purty bad cut," he said, shaking his head. "I think it's gonna need stitches."

His gaze turned to Brittany. It took a moment for the look's meaning to sink in.

"Oh, no!" Brittany jerked back in her seat. "I can't do that!"

"Why not? You know how to sew."

"Shirts and dresses and quilts, yes, but not humans!"

"It's the same concept."

"I don't want stitches!" Lars said, his voice edged with panic.

Johnny ignored him. "You're probably the best sewer 'round here, Brittany. Mine ain't even worth considerin'." He pointed to his elbow, where a patch was held in place by a few large, uneven stitches. "And I doubt any of the boys can beat that."

Brittany sent Nathan a desperate look. He shook his head. "Don't look at me. I'm no better than Johnny."

"Iffen it don't get done right, it's gonna scar for sure," Johnny said, his eyes still fixed on her. "It's up to you, Brittany."

Brittany looked helplessly from Johnny to Nathan to Lars. It seemed there was no escape. Either she had to do it, or it wouldn't be done, at least not well.

She quickly blinked a couple of times. "I'll do it."

"I don't want stitches!" Lars howled louder now.

"Quiet. Your sister's gonna do a fine job," Johnny said, and Brittany had a feeling the words were meant to reassure her more than Lars.

"I already got a needle and thread set on the stove to boil," Johnny said almost to himself. "Ought to be ready soon."

He turned to check on it, and Lars's protests turned to all-out screams. Brittany winced. This was hard enough without Lars putting up a fight.

It was Nathan who moved to Lars's side to calm him. "Relax, Lars. Stitches aren't so bad. It'll be over in no time and you'll be able to run around with Brenna good as ever." He talked on, rubbing Lars's arm in soothing circles, and Lars's screams lessened until there was only an occasional hiccup.

Brittany couldn't make out most of what he was saying, but the sound of his voice helped calm her as well. She closed her eyes, trying not to think of the ordeal ahead, and let his voice play in her ears instead.

"Here we are," Johnny said, turning back to them with needle and thread in hand, and Brittany's calm was broken.

Brittany accepted them, her stomach clenching in a nervous knot. Her fingers were shaking so badly that preparing the needle and thread for sewing was difficult. *Lord, please be with us all,* she prayed, turning to Lars.

Lars's eyes went wide at the sight of the needle in her hands, and he began to howl again. This time Nathan's voice was not enough to calm him.

"He's not gonna make this easy on us." Johnny shook his head and looked at Nathan. "Do what you gotta to keep him still."

Nathan nodded. "You ready?" he asked, looking at Brittany.

She swallowed hard and managed a slight nod. She moved to Lars's head, and Nathan took Lars's hands in his, pinning the boy down. Lars gave a terrible scream.

"Don't worry 'bout him," Johnny told Brittany, lifting the rag from Lars's cut. His wound looked even worse up close, and that was after Johnny had cleaned it up as best he could. The ice had got him good.

"Go ahead." Johnny nodded encouragingly to her.

Taking a deep breath, Brittany leaned over and carefully put in the first stitch. And another. And another. Lars kept screaming, but Nathan kept him still enough that she could keep stitching. Brittany knew that one sweep of Lars's hand could do a good deal of damage. *I wonder what Mama and Aunt Ida would say if they knew all their sewing lessons were being used to stitch up a nasty cut to the forehead,* Brittany found herself thinking. Thinking of the horrified look on Aunt Ida's face was enough to make her smile. But realizing what *could* have happened brought a rush of tears to her eyes. Brittany pushed aside any thought beyond making tiny, even stitches as fast as she could.

Brittany had never been more relieved than she was when she reached the end of the cut. "Done," she said, knotting and snipping off the excess thread.

"Well, least we know his lungs weren't injured," Nathan said, releasing his hold on Lars. The boy's screams gave way to whimpers, and Brittany let out a breath of relief at the quiet that fell.

It was in the quiet that Brittany heard heavy footsteps bounding up the porch steps. The door burst open, and Clem ran into the room, Brenna at his heels.

"I came as fast as I could," Clem said, breathing hard. "How is he?"

"You're just in time to carry him back to the house," Johnny said. "He's doin' fine."

"Thank God." Clem sagged back against the wall. "I'll tell you, I haven't run so fast since–since I don't know when. Don't you scare me like that again, you hear, Lars?"

"I hear," Lars said, not cracking the slightest smile. Everyone chuckled, the sound a welcome relief after all the evening's tension.

"We can just be thankful that icicle hit his forehead and not one his eyes or nothin'. That ice can be dangerous stuff; you best not be messin' around with it any time soon," Johnny said, waving a finger at Lars.

"I won't," Lars said, his voice firm with conviction.

"You look better," Brenna spoke up. "Your forehead's not bleeding all over anymore."

"Brittany made me get stitched."

"She did?" Clem said. "Let me see."

Clem crossed the room to Lars's side and took the boy's head between his hands, squinting down at him.

"Well, I'll be," Clem said. "You sure do have some fancy stitching up there. You've got some sister, Lars." He grinned at Brittany.

"But I didn't get to see it." Brenna looked from Nathan to Brittany. "You shoulda waited for me. Maybe this was my only chance to see somebody get stitched up." Her lip came out. "It's not fair."

"I'm a hopin' you *never* git another chance to see somebody git stitches," Johnny said, tugging one of her braids. "Maybe we shoulda had you stay to help your poor sister, though she did do one mighty fine job."

"You did," Nathan said, looking across the table at Brittany. "You did a great job, far better than any of us could have."

His praise sent warm tingles all the way down to Brittany's toes. "I couldn't have done it without you, Nathan," she said, unable to pull her gaze away from his brown eyes.

"Then I guess we make a good team," Nathan said, looking deeply into her own.

CHAPTER
26

"It was good seeing you, Clem." Morgan mounted her horse in one fluent motion and flashed Clem a smile that made his heart jump.

"Pleasure's mine. I'll stop by sometime in the next couple of evenings." Clem tipped his hat and took a step back as Morgan turned her horse and took off down the ranch lane. She made one fine figure up on a horse, all her movements at one with the animal. She was a beautiful woman, his Morgan was, both inside and out.

The sound of Cookie's dinner bell rang through the evening air, and Clem walked toward the cook shack, whistling. Not only did he have a good job here at Northridge, but he also had family now, and, of course, Morgan. Just a few months ago, he hadn't dared to hope that she would pay him even the slightest bit of attention, and now here they were courting, with things going smooth as pudding between them. Life couldn't be going any better.

Clem met Nathan leaving the barn and he waited for him.

"Was that Morgan you were talking to?" Nathan asked without preamble, reaching his side.

"Yep." Clem could feel a grin tugging at his face.

"So, any wedding plans yet?"

Clem rolled his eyes. "We're still getting to know each other. Can't rush things too fast."

"True. By the way, how's Lars doing?"

"He's doing good, completely back to normal, I'd say. It'll take Brittany a little longer to get back to normal, though. I think the whole thing was harder on her than Lars. She fusses over him, but I keep telling her the boy is fine." Clem shrugged. "She'll accept that eventually."

They reached the cook shack and climbed the steps. Clem glanced about the room as they entered, noticing they were among the first to arrive. He moved into line and dished up his plate, poured a cup of coffee, then made his way to a place at the table. The cook shack's setup wasn't fancy, just a long table with two benches on either side, Cookie's stove at one end of the room, and his cot at the other. The room grew cramped as more men gathered; none of them ever stayed any longer than necessary. There were better places to visit than in the shack's tight quarters.

Rueben and George took a seat across from Clem and Nathan. Rueben paid no attention to Clem, but his eyes lingered on Nathan, a little smile curling his lips. Something was obviously going through the man's mind, and Clem wondered uneasily what it was this time.

It didn't take him long to find out.

"Say, George," Rueben said, turning to his friend. "You wanna know what I heard the other day?"

George was quick to take Rueben's bait. "Wal, sure Rueben, what's that?"

"I heard that Nathan was playing nurse for the Haines boy. Of course, we both know why he'd be doin' that."

"Oh, sure." George glared at Nathan. "That's so he can gain points with his sister. Quite handy."

"Nathan Lindale knows how to play it smart." Rueben gave Nathan's name a little twist that plainly said what he thought of him.

"Oh, he's smart, all right," George agreed.

What are those two trying to start? Clem wondered. Something in his bones told him that their intentions were not innocent. He glanced at Nathan. It appeared Nathan's attention was fixed solely on his plate, but Clem knew him well enough to recognize from the way he had gone rigid that he didn't like this conversation at all.

Little Joe took the seat next to George, his eyes darting around the table from one face to another. He obviously felt the tension as well.

"Nathan's in deep if he's willing to even play nurse to get her attention," Rueben said, his eyes never leaving Nathan. "Real deep."

"Pass the salt and pepper." Little Joe's voice cracked.

He had to repeat it before Clem realized that the salt and pepper were in front of him. Without a word, he slid them to Little Joe.

"If I've said it once, I've said it a hundred times," George said, his voice rising a little louder. "Nathan oughta remember that he can't be thinkin' he's got a claim on her when he don't. Nothin's set in stone yet, and this is by no means over. He ain't won her yet."

Clem felt Nathan twitch beside him, but all Nathan said was "Salt, please."

Little Joe passed it to him, then looked at the pepper still in front of him. Clem saw his eyes dart toward George, and a smile suddenly lit Little Joe's face.

"You wanna know what I think? I think the only reason Brittany spends any time at all with Nathan is because she can't help it." George was thoroughly warmed up to the subject now. "Because she can't politely say no to bein' near him. You see, Nathan *presses* himself on her."

Clem watched with interest as Little Joe slid George's coffee cup closer to himself, one wary eye on George all the while. He began to unscrew the lid of the pepper shaker.

"You know, I bet she don't even like him all that much," George said, his face reddening. "Not when he's always in her face makin' her pay attention to him. I bet she don't like him one bit more than any of the rest of us. I bet she likes him even *less* than us."

Clem felt annoyed. Here, a man who knew nothing about Brittany was putting words in her mouth, when he, her brother, was sitting right at the same table. Did the man think Clem knew nothing about his sister's interests?

He watched as Little Joe lightly sprinkled George's coffee with pepper, then peered into the pepper shaker and dumped the rest of its contents into George's cup. He gave the coffee a quick stir and pushed it back into place, keeping a careful eye on George. But George didn't even notice, and Clem had to hide his smirk. George was in for a little surprise.

"And all that just goes to show that you shouldn't be too confident in yourself. 'Cause I can guarantee that you ain't the one she's gonna end up with, Nathan," George said, addressing Nathan directly for the first time. "She ain't yours, so you best just keep back and not be layin' no claims on her, you hear?" He brought his fist down on the table with a loud thud that made the dishes clatter.

"Of course, Nathan can't help how he feels," Rueben said, his voice sympathetic, but his face saying he was anything but. "Poor Nathan. You gotta feel sorry for him. He ain't got a chance at marryin' Brittany, but he's already in deep. Now maybe if he owned his own ranch, he'd have a better chance—"

Nathan seemed to have hit his limit. He jumped to his feet so fast that he almost took Clem over with him.

"Look—if you have something you want to talk to me about, make it private, all right?" He stared at Rueben, not George. "I don't know what I ever did to make you think I care about Brittany. She can marry any man she wants, and I'll be downright happy for her!" He swiveled his gaze around to George. "And for your information, I don't force my attention on her. I don't try to win points with her. I don't do any of those ridiculous things you've accused me of." Nathan stopped abruptly, then turned and walked toward the door. "I see what you're doing, Rueben, and I don't like it!" he threw back over his shoulder. Then the door slammed shut so hard that the cookhouse walls shuddered.

The room went still with Nathan's leaving. Clem couldn't recall ever seeing Nathan get upset like that. Never. He was glad he wasn't in either George or Rueben's shoes. It might take a lot to make Nathan mad, but when his wrath was stirred up, it was something to be feared.

"Well," Scott said, breaking the silence. "Seems like there are a few people here tonight who missed their calling and shoulda been lawyers."

Cookie guffawed, but Clem saw nothing funny about the situation. He knew Rueben and Nathan had some burr under their saddles, not that Nathan had ever said much about it. But it was there nonetheless, and Clem could see that the friction building up between the two of them was not lessening. Time didn't heal everything, and in this case only seemed to make a deeper, more impassable rift between the two of them. Nathan wasn't one to let some man's comments get to him like that, and Clem guessed that Rueben Pierce was the only man on earth who could get under Nathan's skin the way he had.

"Guess the kid's just touchy tonight." Rueben's smile plainly said that he knew he'd scored this battle.

"Reckon so." George took a long gulp of his coffee, then quickly slammed his cup back on the table, coughing.

"That stuff's nasty!" he gasped, eyes watering. "What'd you do to the coffee tonight, Cookie?"

"Me?" Cookie drew himself up to his full height. "Me? I ain't done a thing different than usual, and iffen it don't please you, you can just git your sorry self out of here and make your own coffee from now on."

"No, no, it's fine," George said hurriedly, and to prove his point, took another drink.

He went into another round of coughing, pounding on his chest, and Scott said, "I don't know iffen it's the coffee or what, but he's got somethin' wrong with him."

"Well, nobody else seems to be sufferin' none," Cookie said. "And they're drinkin' the same stuff. I reckon it's just George."

Little Joe mumbled something about the privy and ran for the door, his face nearly as red as George's. Clem didn't even try to hide his grin. George sure had deserved that tonight. Too bad Little Joe couldn't have done it to Rueben as well.

CHAPTER

27

The snow crunched beneath his boots as Nathan dismounted Loner in front of the barn. Another long, cold day was over. Here it was only the end of January, and already he was tired of winter. He dreaded the thought of more cold and snow but knew it could be well into May before they saw the last of winter's blizzards. He'd always preferred heat to cold, which made it rough living this far north. One more positive thing about Texas—the weather was a far sight warmer than it was here.

Nathan heaved a deep sigh. He ought to be done feeling homesick for Grand Forks, Texas. It had been ten years since he'd left, more than enough time to get over the hurting for home.

Nathan shook his head and set to work unsaddling Loner. He thought back to the night before; the memory made him grit his teeth. How could Rueben have been so callous, going on about him and Brittany in front of everyone like that? He'd never felt so humiliated in his life. The worst thing was, nowadays he wasn't sure how he did feel about Brittany. The more time passed, the more he admired her. She was a kind, brave, selfless young woman, one he might have considered marrying if he was in a position for that. But he wasn't. So he couldn't care for her any more deeply than as a friend. He couldn't marry her, and he was inviting certain heartbreak if he did fall for her. Their two worlds simply wouldn't mix.

One of these days a young man was going to come around, a good, hardworking, solid young man, the kind of man she deserved, one who had the means to take care of her, and they would fall in love and get married. And Nathan would be left out in the cold. He wanted to feel happy for her, as he'd said with as much conviction as he could muster the night before. And he was willing to wish her all the best in life, but that didn't mean he might not hurt. Still, his resolve was set. Nothing must change between them. She deserved a far better man than him.

But not Able.

Nathan tightened his grip on Loner's saddle. Able had been hanging around the place too much lately. Even more remarkably, he'd cleaned himself up, dressing nicer than ever and polishing up his manners. There could only be one reason for that: Brittany. The man had never been so set on one woman, and Nathan had no doubt that the man had courtship on his mind. Just the thought of the man marrying sweet Brittany was enough to make Nathan feel sick to his stomach.

But he'll never be able to pull off a marriage with her, he thought, a reminder he repeated often lately. Brittany was smarter than to fall for a man like Able, and if by some chance her thinking became clouded and she did agree, then Clem was sure to set her straight.

But Nathan still struggled to keep calm and not interfere. Something about such dogged determination made Nathan uneasy and feel as if more was brewing than met the eye.

Nathan dropped Loner's saddle on the ground and turned his horse loose. He thought back to what Rueben had started to say last night before Nathan cut him off. *Now maybe if he owned his own ranch he'd have a better chance—*

It meant nothing to the other men in the cook shack, but it meant everything to Nathan. And Rueben knew it. The single sentence rang with truth. Suppose life had turned out the way it should have? Suppose he had inherited his pa's ranch as he was supposed to? Suppose he'd never left home. Suppose he were still there, right where he belonged, helping his pa, teasing Maryanne about her callers, playing checkers in the evening with Evan—

You sure are trying to torture yourself tonight, he thought.

But it was true. Had he inherited his pa's ranch, everything would be different. Then he could have fallen in love with Brittany and had no reason *not* to ask her to marry him.

The cold bit at Nathan, driving to his very bones, but he lingered there, unwilling to face the other men quite yet. Who knew what trick Rueben might pull tonight? Nathan might as well put him off a little longer.

Rueben. Nathan wished he'd never met the man. Not here or in Texas either. The man was good at causing trouble wherever he went.

At last Nathan stirred and, picking up the saddle, made his way to the barn. He hoped he wouldn't meet anyone, but as he entered the barn he heard a rustling in the tack room that told him his wish had been denied. Everything seemed to go contrary to him lately.

Nathan walked back to the tack room but stopped outside as he heard a strange sound, as if someone were half-singing, half-mumbling under his breath. It didn't sound like any of the other Northridge men, but it stirred a long-buried memory somewhere deep in Nathan's mind. Where had he heard that sound before?

Nathan stepped into the room. A man, his back turned to Nathan, was setting his saddle down against the wall. As he turned around, Nathan caught a glimpse of his weather-beaten face, and he knew. He drew back, a little gasp catching in his throat. Jeb Hawkins! What was he doing here? Last Nathan had seen of him, he was working on Nathan's pa's ranch at home in Texas.

Nathan's heart began to pound like crazy, so loud, he was sure Jeb Hawkins could hear it. Nathan would have turned around and lit out of there, but Jeb had already noticed and was coming toward him.

"Howdy there," Jeb said, no recognition in his voice. "You work here?"

"Yes." The single word was almost more than Nathan could manage. The light was dim here in the tack room, dim enough to hope that Jeb still wouldn't recognize him. Under different circumstances, he would have been delighted to see the old man who had served his pa faithfully for so many years. But just now he was the last person Nathan wanted to see.

He brushed past the man to set his saddle where it belonged, wishing Jeb would leave. He should have known that was too much to hope for.

Jeb lingered in the doorway. "I'm Jeb Hawkins," he said, confirming what Nathan already knew. "I'm on my way to Montana. Got a brother up there who's been doin' mighty poorly, so I told him I'd come and help him out fer a spell. Purty country comin' through here, but awful cold. How can you stand workin' all winter in this cold?"

"You get used to it," Nathan said, keeping his back to Jeb. It was a mistake to say that.

"Say, are you from Texas?" Jeb asked. "You sound like it."

"Ah, yes." Everything inside Nathan begged the man to turn around and leave. If this conversation kept up much longer, Jeb was going to recognize him, and it would all be over then.

"What part are you from?" Jeb asked. "I've been workin' in Texas near all my years as a man, and I know the area fairly well."

"That so?" Nathan said, not answering his question.

"Shore thing. So where're you from?"

Nathan's hands felt sweaty. He *couldn't* answer Jeb's question. He'd know, then. But how could he put the man off?

Then he made another mistake. He let himself look at Jeb for one brief second.

Nathan saw the recognition flash across Jeb's face. For a moment the man seemed paralyzed. Then the shock disappeared, and the man's face turned grim. With a couple of quick strides, Jeb crossed the room to Nathan.

"Nathan Lindale, what on earth are you doin' here?" Jeb asked, his voice losing all its easygoing friendliness. He took Nathan by the shoulders and gave him a good shake. "I thought you was dead, boy; we all thought you was."

Nathan had no excuses. "I'm sorry."

"Sorry? You better be! Don't you realize what a dumb thing it was to run off like you did without a word to no one? And at such a time as you did?" Jeb gave him another shake. "You hurt your pa good, you know. Iffen you weren't full-grown now, I'd give you a whippin' myself."

"I'm sorry," Nathan said again, the words weak to his own ears.

"You oughta have known better than to disappear like you did, never lettin' on where you was headed. Why didn't you come back? Or at the very least write a letter?"

"Would it have done any good?" Nathan pushed Jeb's hands off his shoulders. "It wouldn't have changed anything."

"Changed anything? Course it woulda changed things. Your folks have been worried sick wonderin' whatever happened to you. Maryanne, too."

Nathan stared at the ground, conflicting thoughts churning through his mind. He could imagine his ma was worried. And Maryanne. But Pa? Nathan winced and shook his head.

"Pa doesn't care," he muttered, refusing to look at Jeb.

"Your pa? You're kiddin' me. Course he cares. You're his son, and—"

"I failed him." The words hurt with their truth. "I failed him badly. After everything, I really don't think he wants to see me again."

"You're kiddin' me." Jeb stared at him, then wagged his head slowly from one side to the other. "I think you're underestimating your pa. Why, that man has one of the biggest hearts—"

"They're better off without me," Nathan cut in. He didn't need Jeb to tell him about his own pa. "Look, Jeb—the past can't be changed. I admit I made a terrible mistake that day I left, and if I could, I'd go back and change everything so that no one got hurt, but that's not in my power. So the way I see it, let's just try to forget about it all. They have their life without me, and if

I went back, it would just reopen wounds best left untouched. They don't need me."

"But what about *you?*" Jeb's gaze prodded deeply at Nathan. "Don't *you* need *them?*"

The question threw Nathan for a moment. He could handle Jeb's anger, but his care for him? Nathan wasn't sure what to think of that.

"I've been living without them for ten, almost eleven years. I guess I can manage." Nathan didn't mention that the years had by no means been easy on him. Those first couple of years he'd thought he was going to die from homesickness.

Jeb continued to shake his head. "I still think you're makin' a mistake."

"Seems that I'm good at making mistakes."

"You don't have to make this mistake. Just contact your pa—"

"No!" The single word exploded from Nathan. He made himself take a deep breath to calm himself before continuing.

"No," he said in a quieter voice. "I can't do that."

Jeb said nothing, just looked at him through narrowed eyes.

"I just can't," Nathan stumbled on. "It wouldn't work. It would cause too much pain, and–and–" He paused. "Do they really think I'm dead?"

"They don't know what to think. How could they when they never heard anything from you?" Jeb's gaze didn't leave his face. "They don't talk about you too much nowadays. Guess it hurts too much."

"See? Me writing or going home would only make things worse."

"I think it might be just what they need to take care of the pain."

Nathan was tired of hearing what Jeb thought. "I'm not going home, and I'm not writing. And there's no need for you to mention that you ran into me here, all right?"

Jeb's silence frightened him.

"Jeb, you won't tell Pa that you saw me, will you?"

"I'm not gonna be helpin' my brother forever." Jeb looked past Nathan. "I told the Boss I'd be back to work for him in a few months. Michael's the best boss I've ever had, and more than that, he's a friend. How could I look your pa in the eye, knowin' where his boy is but not tellin' him? I've gotta do what's best for your pa, Nathan—and you."

"If you were trying to do what's best for me, you wouldn't tell him." Nathan could feel his panic rising.

"Would I?" Jeb met Nathan's gaze. "I care about you, honest. I've known you since you was only about knee-high, and I watched you grow up all those years. I wouldn't purposely do anything to hurt you. Maybe you don't think so now, but I think it'll be best for you in the long run to clear things up with your pa."

"We can't clear things up. It's too late, Jeb!"

"I don't think it is." Jeb turned and began to walk away.

"Jeb! Stop! You can't tell Pa!" Nathan felt sheer desperation. "I'll do anything if you won't tell him, Jeb! Please!"

Jeb looked back at him. "I can't do that, Nathan," he said, his voice quiet but edged with determination. "I won't write to him; I'll let you have a chance to do that yourself. But when I git back to Texas, I will be tellin' him."

Then he turned and left.

CHAPTER
28

Supper that evening was one of the most uncomfortable meals Nathan had ever endured. He found himself sitting across from Jeb, and each time he looked up, his gaze tangled with the man. He knew that Western hospitality made it so any visitor passing through had the right to stop at a ranch and expect food and a place to sleep. He didn't begrudge that, but he sure wished Jeb had found a ranch other than Northridge to bunk down for the night.

When Jeb left the table after supper, Nathan rose as well and followed him outside. The two of them fell in step together, their breath forming silvery clouds in the cold air. Neither of them spoke until they were a fair distance from the cook shack and any snooping ears.

"So Rueben Pierce works here too, huh?" Jeb asked as they passed the barn.

"Yep."

Jeb chuckled. "From your tone I take it he ain't changed much?"

"Not on your life. I can't figure out why that man's got to be so nasty."

"I can't say for sure what goes on in Rueben Pierce's head, but I'd say it's a matter of pride and jealousy." Jeb stroked his mustache.

"Pride and—jealousy?" Nathan raised his eyebrows. "Why would Rueben be jealous?"

"His brother, Dallas, is downright crazy about your family, you know. Maybe he feels that you've stolen his brother from him."

Nathan snorted. "That's unreasonable."

"Nobody ever said jealousy was reasonable."

Nathan let a moment of silence pass before daring to speak again. "Jeb, you know what we were talking about earlier?"

"I ain't forgotten, Nathan. And I ain't changed my mind neither."

Nathan felt a stab of frustration. "So you won't reconsider?"

"Nope."

Nathan stared at Jeb. "Then I guess that's it."

"I guess so." Jeb looked back at him evenly. "Unless you want to write to your pa yourself."

"Not going to happen." Nathan spun away on his heel and started to walk away, unable to believe what was happening to him. After all these years. Years of struggling to make a place for himself and trying to escape all the haunting memories of his past; now, he had to run into one of his pa's most faithful employees. Jeb just didn't understand. Michael Lindale might have a big heart, but every man had a limit to his forgiveness, and Nathan hit that years ago.

"Nathan." Jeb laid a hand on his shoulder, stopping him. "Look at me."

Looking into Jeb's face was the last thing Nathan wanted to do, but he didn't resist as Jeb turned him around to face him.

"You still feel responsible for what happened that day, don't you?"

Nathan gave a short laugh. "Only because I am. There's no one else to blame for what happened. It was all my fault."

"That's a heavy burden to carry around." Jeb's voice softened. "What really *did* happen that day, Nathan?"

Nathan shook his head, taking a step back from the man. "No. I try not to think about it."

"You might find it helps to talk about it."

"Nothing ever helps, and you already know what happened."

"Not really." Jeb shook his head. "I know what the result was, but you're the only one who really knows what happened that day."

They reached the corral, and both of them leaned against the wooden fence. Nathan gripped one of the rails, thinking back to a time when life had been the next thing to perfect. He'd had loving parents, two younger siblings who adored him, and a head full of dreams—of becoming a rancher just like Pa. Things sure had been simple back then. Until—

Nathan sighed, letting his head rest on the corral's top rail.

"You know that I loved Evan. I always thought of myself as his protector, his main line of defense, and I couldn't stand to see anyone or anything hurt him. That might be part of the reason why Rueben and I don't get along. Rueben tormented Evan, and whenever I caught him at it, I tried to make him pay. I thought there was nothing on earth that could stop me from keeping him safe."

Nathan closed his eyes, still able to recall every detail of his younger brother's face. A smattering of freckles, the lock of unruly brown hair that hung over his forehead, a smile that lit up his laughing dark eyes, identical to Nathan's own. He swallowed hard, feeling as if he were going to be crushed under the weight of all those memories.

"He thought the world of you." Jeb's voice broke the silence that stretched between them. "A person could tell just by looking at him or hearing him talk about his big brother."

Nathan clenched the rail harder. If he didn't go on now, he might lose his nerve entirely. "The spring that I was twelve, Ma and Pa decided to take a trip into town for supplies. Maryanne went with them, but Evan and I decided to stay home. Ma—well, you know how Ma was. She always expected the worst to happen, so she always kept us kids under a tight rein. She gave us a list of rules longer than a lariat. Things we couldn't do while she was gone, including everything from swimming to riding our horses to using our pocketknives. She worried too much."

"Only because she loved you."

"Yeah, I realize that now. But at the time, all those rules chaffed at me until they about drove me crazy." Nathan sighed. "After Ma and Pa left, I took Evan down to the corral. He hadn't heard the rule about not taking the horses out while they were gone, but I knew it was wrong. Ma and Pa always told us to obey whether they were present or not, but I was knot-headed. Thought it was a ridiculous rule that we couldn't take our horses out. Guess I wanted to prove that I was old enough that I didn't need a list of rules to follow. Pa always said I was a natural with horses—thought I'd be able to handle any problems that might come up. Figured it wouldn't hurt just once."

Nathan drew in a slow, painful breath, reliving the scene from ten years earlier when he and Evan sat on top of the corral, watching their pa's horses.

"How about we ride double?" Nathan had suggested. After all, taking out one horse wasn't as wrong as taking out two, was it?

Evan dipped his head in agreement, just like Nathan expected him to. "Which horse should we take?" Evan asked.

"How about—Hot Foot?"

"Hot Foot?" The lift of Evan's eyebrow said more than words.

"Sure, why not?" Nathan knew Evan didn't like Hot Foot. He was a young horse with plenty of spirit and a good deal of speed. Evan got scared when a horse so much as threw its head in the air, but Nathan liked a horse with spirit. This horse had one of the smoothest gaits of all the horses on the ranch, and he was good looking as well. Yes, he was a little skittish, but how could he learn not to spook without being ridden? It was all an adventure to Nathan.

"Trust me," he told Evan. "I know what I'm doing."

"Fine." Evan shrugged his slight shoulders and grinned. "But remember that I wasn't the one who suggested we ride that crazy horse—and you get to be in control of him."

Nathan blinked quickly, pulling himself back to the present. He squared his shoulders and looked straight ahead, not daring to so much as glance at Jeb. "We rode Hot Foot out to the pasture and messed around for a while. We must have spent at least an hour out there. Hot Foot was doing okay, and I got careless—stopped paying close attention to our surroundings. Just then, a tumbleweed rolled in front of him, and he spooked. Evan fell off—" Nathan struggled to continue. He hated thinking about that terrible moment when he jumped off Hot Foot's back and ran to his little brother, screaming his name.

"Evan hit his head on a rock when he fell. He was so still, and pale, and–and he wouldn't wake up." Nathan's voice shook. "I didn't know what to do. I couldn't bear the thought of leaving him there alone, but he needed more help than I was able to give him." Nathan closed his eyes. "Leaving him behind was the hardest decision I've ever had to make. It was the one time that I couldn't protect him. I rode like the wind for home and got Dallas Pierce to help me. I kept telling myself Evan was going to be fine. I couldn't believe any differently, or I'd lose control."

Nathan thought back to the moment he and Dallas reached Evan. Dallas dismounted and ran to his side, Nathan following at a slower pace, watching as Dallas bent over the boy.

"Will he be all right?" Nathan asked.

Dallas didn't move or respond.

"Will he be all right?" Nathan asked again, his heart pounding.

Dallas turned to look at him. The tears running shamelessly down his face froze Nathan's heart even as he said, "He's dead, boy."

Dead. The word still rang in Nathan's ears. He tightened his fist on the Northridge corral. "He died. He was only nine, too young to die, and it was all my fault." The agony of it pressed down on him, threatening to smother him with its force.

"You might've made a bad decision, but it ain't your fault that he died. We both know you would never would hurt Evan on purpose." Jeb reached out and touched Nathan's arm. "It ain't your fault, Nathan."

Nathan shook his head. "Yes, it is. Even Pa said so."

"Your pa said it was your fault?"

"Oh, you better believe it. After he got home and found out what had happened, he just fell apart. I've never seen him so angry. He yelled at me—and Pa never yelled at me before. Never." Nathan's jaw ached from clenching it so tightly. "He said he thought I was more trustworthy than to deliberately disobey him. And he said he couldn't take highhanded rebellion like that, especially not when it cost him his son's life. He said he was disappointed in me—" Nathan stopped and looked at Jeb, the pain from remembering wrenching at his heart. "Have you ever seen my pa cry? Well, after he got done yelling at me, he just–he just broke down. It was far worse than the yelling."

Nathan rubbed a hand across his face, fighting to regain control of himself. "I couldn't take it. I ran and ran and kept on running. I could never go back. I failed Pa and killed my brother, I–"

"Nathan, stop. You can't do that to yourself."

"Easier said than done. I wish I could forget about everything that happened, but just when I think I'm moving on, the memories come flooding back and it's worse than ever." Nathan rubbed harder at his face. "It's been ten years, Jeb. I think that if healing were going to come, it would have come by now. I don't think I'm ever going to be able to get over Evan's death."

"Nathan—" Jeb began, then stopped.

"It's all right. You don't have to think of any comforting words. They might sound good, but they don't help." Nathan looked sideways at the man. "Now do you see why I can't patch things up with Pa?"

Jeb studied his hands, his shoulders rising in a sigh. "I understand better why you left, and I know you're hurtin'. But your Pa's hurtin' too. I don't think either of you will be entirely right until you make up."

Nathan stared at him. "You're joking. You can't seriously think after everything that's happened that Pa's going to forgive me. For your information, I already told him I was sorry, several times. They went right over his head."

"People ain't always thinkin' straight when they're grievin'. Give him another chance, Nathan."

"The problem isn't that *I* won't give *him* another chance. The problem is I don't think *he* will give *me* another chance. Why should he? I already failed him once. What's to keep me from failing him again?"

"Why don't you let your pa be the one to decide if he'll give you another chance or not? How can he give you another chance when you won't show your face to him?"

Nathan looked down. The answer didn't need thinking through. The truth was that he was terrified at the thought of facing his pa again. The memory of the last time he saw his pa was burned too powerfully in his mind. He couldn't bear another rejection. He was already hurting, and another refusal from Pa would be too much.

"I don't see how this is your business," Nathan said, his voice low but hard as iron. "Just forget you ever saw me, and forget we ever talked about this."

"For the last time, I ain't keepin' secrets from your pa. I'm sorry you feel the way you do, but I'm gonna tell him." Jeb's voice was just as firm as Nathan's.

Nathan turned away from the man, fighting to keep his temper under control. He kicked at the snow with the toe of his boot, making it fly in all directions, powerless to resist him. Struggle as he might, it never seemed he was able to get on top of his circumstances. He couldn't stop Evan from dying. He couldn't stop Rueben from coming to Northridge. And now he couldn't stop Jeb from telling his pa where he was. Powerless, all right. Despicably powerless.

Somehow Jeb had missed the point of Nathan's story. Pa *couldn't* forgive him. Nathan had wronged him too badly. The relationship was broken. Just as it was impossible to build on a foundation beyond repair, there was no way to rebuild this relationship. It was a lost cause.

Then a sudden thought struck him. Straightening his shoulders, Nathan swung around to face Jeb. "Fine. Tell Pa if you must. He isn't going to do anything."

Jeb raised his eyebrows. "What do you mean?"

"He doesn't have to feel responsible for me anymore since I am twenty-two, and he doesn't care about me anymore, so there's no reason for him to come after me now. I hardly think he's going to travel all the way here from Texas just to say he's still mad at me." Nathan met Jeb's gaze evenly. "Tell him and see if he does anything."

"You don't think your pa loves you after what happened?"

"Of course, he doesn't. I killed his son." Nathan had thought the words so many times that he should have been numb by now, but somehow they still managed to cut at his heart like a whip.

"That's crazy talk. Of course, Michael still loves you." Jeb folded his arms across his chest as if preparing for an argument.

Nathan didn't have the emotional strength to fight anymore. "Just see what he does when you tell him you saw me." He turned to leave, feeling much as if he'd been trampled by a herd of rampaging longhorns. "He won't do anything."

That should have liberated Nathan from the dread of Jeb tattling on him. He didn't *want* his pa to come after him. But he couldn't explain the devastation sweeping through him.

"I think you're wrong. A man doesn't just lose his love for his son." Jeb's voice was quiet but rang with conviction. "Just you wait, and we'll see which of us is right."

CHAPTER
29

"Miss Haines! Miss Haines! You gotta come quick!" Brittany looked up from the clothesline to see a man barreling toward her, his arms flailing in the air. His hat nearly fell off, and he clamped it down with one hand but didn't slow his pace or stop hollering her name. Something was obviously wrong.

Dropping the wet shirt she had been hanging out to dry, she started toward him. "What is it?" she asked, but he didn't seem to hear her. Maybe he was making too much noise to hear anything besides himself.

"Miss Haines," the man gasped out when he reached her at last. "You gotta–come!"

It was Little Joe, she realized. He seemed terribly worked up about something.

"Hurry, Miss Haines," he said, panting around each word. He grabbed her arm and started to pull her along with him. "He said–to git you. We don't know–what to do!"

Brittany tried to pull her arm away from him, but he held on tight, determined she wouldn't escape. "You gotta come!" he said again.

"Little Joe, what is going on?" Brittany planted her feet firmly, refusing to move. "Talk sensibly, please."

Little Joe gulped in a deep breath of air. "Boss is hurt."

"Mr. Myers is hurt?" Brittany blinked, her annoyance with Little Joe giving way to concern for her employer. She couldn't say she was overly fond of the man, but she didn't want to see him injured.

"Yeah! We need you fast!"

"We?"

"Me and Cookie."

"Why do you need *me?*"

Little Joe looked at her blankly. "I dunno. I just helped the Boss into the cook shack, 'cause, you see, iffen you got a problem, you bring it to Cookie, and he can patch you up one way or another. But Cookie, he takes one look at the Boss, and he says to me, 'Little Joe, we need help. Go git Miss Haines.' So I lit out of there, 'cause that weren't a time to be askin' questions." Little Joe shrugged. "I dunno why Cookie needs you, but iffen I was you, I'd hurry along. You don't want to git on the wrong side of Cookie."

"I see." Brittany tried again to free her arm from his grip. "Could you please let me go?"

"You'll come?" Little Joe asked, eyeing her as if he thought she might try to make a run for it.

She wasn't sure about many things, but one thing was certain: if she was needed, it was her duty to go. "Of course. Now let go of me!"

Little Joe released his grip on her. "Come on. We don't got any time to lose." He set off for the cook shack at a quick pace.

Brittany had to nearly run to keep up with him. "What exactly is wrong with Mr. Myers?" she asked his back.

"You'll see" was his only answer.

Brittany was out of breath by the time they reached the cook shack. Little Joe charged up the steps and bawled through the door, "I got her, Cookie!"

"Bring her in," Cookie said, his voice muffled.

Little Joe turned back to Brittany, nearly losing his balance on the steps. "He says to come in."

Brittany climbed the steps without replying. Despite the serious situation, she was tempted to laugh at Little Joe. He was so oblivious to his own clumsiness.

Her eyes took a moment to adjust to the darkness of the cook shack. She could make out a single long table with benches on either side of it. Next to the stove at the end of the room a man was lying on the floor, his leg stretched out in front of him. She swallowed hard. It was Mr. Myers. His face was contorted in a grimace, and he refused to look at her.

"What happened?" Brittany asked Cookie, who was kneeling on the floor beside him.

"Good—you're here," he said, "Git another rag off the table for me, won't you?"

Brittany did as he asked, grabbing a ragged old cloth from the table and handing it to him.

"What happened?" she asked again.

Mr. Myers only grunted, so Cookie said, "He busted up his leg—that's what."

"It's broken?"

"Naw, just ripped up purty good. I hear you put in good stitches."

He stared at her, and Brittany immediately caught the hint.

"Look." She folded her arms across her chest. "I am not a doctor, and I do not make it a habit to give people stitches."

"That's good. I don't need a sawbones. I need a stitcher."

Brittany felt an urge to stamp her foot. "Well, what did people do when they needed stitches before *I* came here? Or is this a new epidemic that has never been heard of until recently?" Brittany let a note of sarcasm enter her voice.

"We made do—that's what." Cookie looked back where Little Joe still hovered in the doorway. "Little Joe, show her your arm."

Little Joe walked over to her, a bit of a swagger in his steps, and pulled up his sleeve, revealing an angry scar that ran down half of his forearm. Whoever had sewn it had done a terrible job. The scar was jagged, with raw-looking pink edges. Brittany quickly looked away, grateful that she was the one who had stitched up Lars. He had healed nicely, and his scar was scarcely noticeable now, unlike Little Joe's.

"You can see I ain't so good with a needle," Cookie said. "And my thinkin' is, why should I make a mess of the Boss's leg when there's someone here capable of doin' a right fine job?"

Brittany sighed, knowing what her duty was. "Do you have a needle and thread?"

"All ready for you."

"You'll have to hold your leg still," she told Mr. Myers.

"Iffen he don't, I'll hold it for him," Little Joe called out.

"Unnecessary," Mr. Myers said through gritted teeth.

"Not very happy, are we?" Little Joe grinned, ignoring Mr. Myers's glare. With his boss helpless on the floor, Little Joe seemed to have lost all fear of him.

Brittany took the needle and thread from Cookie, feeling like an expert after her ordeal with Lars three months before. At least Mr. Myers wasn't screaming and fighting her. And at least this time she felt in control of herself, despite the fact that her assistants were far less supportive than Johnny and Nathan.

As she knelt down beside Mr. Myers, he glared at her. "No embroiderin' nothin', all right? Just plain stitches, girl."

"Aw, that's no fun," Little Joe said. "I think you'd look real good with a purple violet on your leg." He laughed at his own lame humor.

Brittany blocked him out and concentrated on her work. Mr. Myers held still for her, frowning heavily enough to make the sun think twice about shining. Brittany worked quickly, and within minutes she finished and handed the needle back to Cookie.

Cookie glanced at her work and nodded. "Good."

"Sure is." Little Joe bent down close to look. "Boy, those are little stitches."

Mr. Myers cleared his throat noisily, and Little Joe backed up. He grinned at Brittany. "Iffen I ever need stitches, I'm comin' to you. I see why everybody's so crazy to marry you. You sure are a handy lady to have around."

A handy lady? Brittany struggled to keep in check the laughter that suddenly wanted to escape. "Thank you," she said, not daring to look Little Joe in the eye.

Mr. Myers studied his leg a moment before pulling his pant leg back down over it. He gave a quick nod. "Looks all right."

It was a high compliment from a man as sparsely worded as Mr. Myers. The simple words were all the praise Brittany needed. Both the compliment and the satisfaction of a job well done made Brittany's heart sing as she left the cook shack and returned to the laundry still waiting for her at the cabin.

Brittany felt both joy and sorrow when May arrived. Joy because it meant the end of winter and no more blizzards. Sorrow because it brought the end of the school year. She had loved teaching her students over the winter. Their twice-a-week coming had been a ray of sunshine through the long days of snowstorms and isolation. But that season was over, and it was time to tell her students goodbye. Summer brought with it extra work, and her students were needed at home.

On the last school day they held a program and invited everyone from the area to come. Brittany expected that the parents would attend and maybe a few others, but she was taken aback by just how many people did show up. So many that they couldn't fit everyone inside and had to move the program outdoors. The change in plans added to the pre-performance jitters Brittany already felt, but she reminded herself to take it all in stride.

Despite the tension beforehand, the program went off without a hitch. Charley and Abe told the audience about the founding of America. Julia recited a poem she had memorized, and Carson read aloud a story that he had written by himself. All the children put on a skit that Allie had helped them put together, and to finish off the program, the younger children sang a song that made even a couple cowboys in the crowd roughly brush their sleeves across their eyes. Brittany was proud of how well each of her students did and considered the program a success. The thunderous applause that followed her students' performance agreed with her.

But the day's crowning moment came after the program when the crowd had mingled, taking the rare opportunity to visit with one another. As she passed by Mr. and Mrs. Myers, Brittany overheard her name and paused to listen.

"That girl sure has a way with kids. She made a heap of progress with them in just a few short months," Mr. Myers was saying. "No real, licensed teacher coulda done better, and he woulda demanded pay too. But that girl, she just gave all of herself and never asked for no payment or nothin'."

His words shocked Brittany, and she wondered if it was possible that after months of trying she had finally gained Mr. Myers's approval. She didn't even mind that he still failed to call her Brittany, always referring to her instead as "that girl." The way he had just said it made it sound almost endearing.

Before the day was over, Allie Bryan shouldered her way through the crowd over to Brittany. "I hope you realize just how much this winter has meant to me, to all of us," she said. "I've never learned so much in my life, and neither have the kids."

"The pleasure was all mine, Allie," Brittany said, and meant it.

"Is there any way we could convince you to stay and be our teacher next year too?"

"I can't stay." Brittany shook her head. "I'm going home early this fall."

"You say you can't stay." Allie gave Brittany a scrutinizing glance, then reached out to give her hand a pat. "Just remember—home's where the heart is, and sometimes our hearts change on us when we ain't watchin' close. Think about it, honey. Is your heart still in Des Moines?"

Before Brittany could think of a response, Allie turned and walked away. *What does she mean by that?* Brittany wondered, staring after her. *Does she think that my heart is no longer in Des Moines but here in the West?*

The idea was laughable. She had never intended to stay here in the "wild West"—why would she have changed her mind? She would be miserable spending the rest of her life anywhere but in Iowa.

Brittany shrugged the idea aside. Her plans remained unchanged, and come fall, she would be leaving on the east-bound stage for Fort Laramie. She refused to allow anything to stop her.

CHAPTER
30

"Brittany! The cows are eating your laundry!"

Brenna's shout made Brittany set down the plate she was washing from supper and run to the doorway, wiping her hands on her apron. Only a few minutes before, she'd sent Lars and Brenna outside to take the laundry off the line, a job she wouldn't have thought would offer much excitement. But evidently her two siblings had managed to find just that.

"Eating my laundry?" she said. "What cows? What are you talking about?"

"Mr. Myers's cows!" Brenna yelled. "Hurry, Brittany, or you won't have any laundry left!"

Brittany still didn't understand. She might not know much about cattle, but she did know that fabric was not a normal part of a cow's diet. Still, the situation sounded serious, so she let Brenna grab her hand and pull her down the steps and around the side of the cabin where the clothesline stood.

She stopped short. Brenna was right. A group of cattle milled about the yard, their sharp hooves cutting into the August grass and speckling the yard with dozens of pockmarks. Some wandered idly around, sniffing at the grass, but several gawked at her clothesline. One cow sniffed at Lars's trousers. Another cow rubbed its neck against one of the clothesline posts, making the laundry on the line dance. A young steer with an impressive set of horns stood staring at a sheet flapping in the breeze. He snorted and pawed at the ground.

Brittany stared at them. She had been in Wyoming Territory for nearly a year, but she had never seen the cattle this close up before. The livestock, excluding a few horses kept in the corral, roamed free-range, so they rarely came up to the ranch like this. Sometimes in the morning when she came outside, Brittany found signs that the horses had spent the night near the cabin, but never the cattle. The cattle preferred to keep away from people most of the time.

"They sure are big," Lars said from where he leaned against the cabin, watching the cattle.

Brittany murmured in agreement. For a minute the three of them stood watching the cattle, intrigued. But then Brittany's attention was caught by the steer. He was getting a little more worked up over the sheet now, and his snorts had taken on a challenging note. He pawed at the ground, sending clumps of dirt and grass flying, then all at once made a run at her laundry flapping in the breeze. His horns hooked onto the sheet, ripping it clean off the line, and he let out a bawl of fury.

Brittany was horrified, then angered. How dare that filthy, disrespectful beast take her clean laundry and wreck it like that? It was no easy job to scrub the laundry clean, wring out the excess water, and haul it out to the line. These cows had no right to come and trample her yard and laundry underfoot like this!

Brittany didn't even stop to think. She ran at the cattle, waving her arms and yelling, "Get out of here! All of you, get!"

They took off running before she was anywhere near them, their heels flying and their bellows splitting the air. All, that is, but the steer. Somehow the sheet had gotten tangled around his horns, covering his whole head and eyes, and he remained behind in the yard, making enough noise for a herd of cattle.

Lars and Brenna came to stand beside Brittany, staring at the steer.

"Oh, boy—what do we do now?" Lars asked.

"Do?" Brittany gritted her teeth. "Do? Get my sheet off him, of course."

Both children's eyes widened.

"And how do we do that?" asked Brenna.

"Well, we–we–I don't know. Come on, both of you. This can't be too hard; we'll figure it out as we go."

Brittany marched toward the steer, her mind racing to think of the best way to corner him. Lars and Brenna trailed after her with some uncertainty. Neither of them seemed too excited about the job ahead of them.

The steer seemed to sense they were coming, and he took off running, faster than Brittany had expected. She managed to cut him off before he could escape to the open range, and wheeling around, the steer took off toward the barn, bawling at the top of his lungs.

"Don't let him run past the barn!" Brittany shouted to Lars and Brenna. But her call was unnecessary. The steer veered neither to the left nor right as he neared the barn, and Brittany winced as he crashed into the wall. The wall shuddered from the force of the blow, and for a moment the steer seemed stunned.

There was no time to waste feeling sorry for the blind brute. Darting forward, Brittany grabbed at the loose end of the sheet and tugged. It was stuck. She pulled desperately at it, not caring whether she ripped the material or not as long as she got her sheet back. The steer let out a moan, shook his head, and recovering from the impact, wheeled away from the barn toward the corral. He took off running, knocking Brittany over in his hurry, and sent her sprawling in the dust.

Brittany would have cried if she weren't so angry. Instead, she clenched her teeth and picked herself up off the ground. She had to keep trying. The steer could not run around with the rest of the herd with a sheet over his head. Besides, they were bound to get it off of him soon. Weren't they?

Lars and Brenna kept the steer from running past the corral and turned him back toward the house. He dashed under the clothesline, hooking one of Brittany's aprons along the way. Brittany waited for it to flutter harmlessly to the ground, but it didn't. She groaned. Now the insolent beast was decorated with both a sheet and her apron. This had to stop.

"Brittany!" Mrs. Myers appeared in the bedroom window. "What is all that racket out there?"

The steer let out another bawl before Brittany could reply. Mrs. Myers's gaze turned to him, and her mouth opened wide in surprise.

"What on earth?" Mrs. Myers stared at him, then at Brittany. "What did you do to that poor creature?"

"Me?" Brittany's hair had slipped out of its neat bun and was sliding down her neck onto her shoulders. And when she brushed at the dirt on her dress, her fingers snagged on a rip in the skirt.

"Me?" she said again, tears of anger, frustration, and helplessness springing to her eyes "I did nothing to that—that *thing*, and I hardly consider him a 'poor creature.' He was vandalizing my laundry!"

Mrs. Myers's face twitched; then she began to laugh. "Just look at him. Vandal or not, he's terrified!"

Brittany looked at the steer. He did look rather frightened—maybe even terrified. He reeled about beside the cabin, wandering in aimless circles and crying pitifully. All the tough bravado he had exhibited toward the sheet was gone, and he looked more like a calf, away from its mama too long.

But Brittany hardened her heart against him. "If he hadn't messed with my laundry, he wouldn't be in this mess. And one thing's sure. He's going to give me back my sheet! I'm not about to watch him make off with it."

Brittany started toward him, calling for Lars and Brenna.

She focused her attention on the steer, mentally going over the best way to corner him. She heard footsteps from behind and said, "Stand by the corner so he doesn't get past us and out with the herd."

"Yes, ma'am," a voice deeper than either Lars or Brenna's replied.

Brittany whirled around and found herself looking into Nathan's brown eyes. They were twinkling, and she felt her face turn bright red.

"Nathan, I—I didn't know you were here."

"So corner of the cabin, hmm?" Nathan turned and went where she had directed.

Brittany felt humiliated. She hadn't meant to order him around like that; she had thought he was Lars or Brenna. Why, he certainly knew much more about cornering cattle than she did!

Before Brittany could regain her wits, the steer took off again, not toward Nathan but her. Too late she tried to block him, but he ran past as if she weren't even there. Brittany tripped and again found herself on the ground.

She felt a childish urge to bang her fist on the ground from pure frustration. No matter how she tried, that steer kept getting the best of her!

Nathan appeared at her side and held out a hand to help her up. He was smiling wider than Brittany had ever seen him smile before; actually, he almost looked as if he were enjoying himself!

"It's all right; we'll get him," he said as if he had guessed her doubts. "Let's try to drive him into the barn, where we can work with him in a smaller space."

He pulled her to her feet, then motioned Lars and Brenna over to them. Brittany felt grateful that he was taking charge. She'd already proven she was no match for this animal.

Nathan positioned them all to be the most effective in driving the steer into the barn. The steer kept up a steady stream of bellows, probably getting tired of not being able to see. At Nathan's signal they all began to move forward, slowly closing in on the helpless beast. He ran toward the barn, but after all the trouble he'd given Brittany, she didn't set her hopes on him going in right away. Oh, no—knowing that creature, he would cause as much trouble as possible before relinquishing her sheet.

The steer reached the barn, bumping into the side. He began to trot alongside it, and Nathan sent Lars to the end of the wall to head him off if he didn't go through the door. The rest of them began to move closer, tightening the human circle around him.

The steer stopped short just a couple of feet from the door. *Here it comes,* Brittany thought, waiting for him to wheel away from the barn and try to break through to freedom.

Brittany was watching the steer so closely that she wasn't looking where she was going. Neither was Brenna, evidently, and they collided. Brittany swerved to keep from stepping on the little girl and lost her balance. For the third time, she found herself on the ground—and all because of that witless steer!

She jumped to her feet again, but the steer was already going through the door. Or rather, running. She barely glimpsed his tail before he was in, probably terrified by her and Brenna's tumbling about.

Nathan ran in after him, slamming the door shut. The yard fell quiet, and Brittany began to pray that Nathan would be able to deal with that—that brute. Maybe that's what she should have done first—prayed. She realized that not even the actions of a simple cow were within her control.

Brittany waited impatiently, straining to hear any sound from inside the barn. All was quiet. Too quiet. She was almost ready to go in there and see if she could help when the door opened, and Nathan appeared with both sheet and apron in hand. He stepped aside, and the steer charged out, bawling as if he'd just come face to face with the butcher.

"How did you ever get it off him?" Brittany asked Nathan, deeply impressed.

"Wasn't too hard after I got him cornered." Nathan looked after the steer, and Brittany saw his face twitch.

"What?" Brittany looked after the steer as well. He was galloping for freedom, still bawling with all his might. "What?" she asked again.

"Just look at him." Nathan pointed after him. "He looks whipped. Why, he's even got his tail between his legs."

It was too much. Brittany didn't even try to keep her temper in check. "Why does everyone feel sorry for that miserable creature? He's a filthy, dirty cow, and he just ruined a perfectly fine evening, vandalizing my laundry—"

A burst of laughter from Nathan cut her off. Brittany spun around and stared at him, watching as he fell back against the barn wall, laughter shaking his whole frame.

"I don't see what's so funny," she said, shocked by his laughter. Had he been Clem, that would have been one thing, but Nathan? Brittany felt victorious if she could make him smile, let alone laugh.

"I've been in cattle country–all my life," Nathan gasped. "And I've heard cattle described a whole lot of ways, but never as-as–vandals!"

He laughed even harder, and Brittany was powerless to resist joining him. Not because she found it funny that a cow had tried to rob her, but simply because Nathan's laughter was infectious. Soon they were both laughing so hard they could scarcely stand.

"This isn't a ruined evening," Nathan said at last, still battling laughter. "I haven't had so much fun in I don't know when. Just the look on your face as you went after that steer, Brittany. He looked as decked out as a Christmas tree, but you looked so serious." He laughed again.

"I guess it must have looked a little funny." Brittany had to agree that the evening no longer seemed ruined. Not with all this fun. She began to laugh once more. "That steer was one of the most cowardly thieves I've ever heard of. This incident is probably going to take away his confidence for a while."

"At least where apron-clad women are involved."

They fell into another round of laughter, collapsing against the barn wall. Now that it had started, they couldn't seem to stop. Just when Brittany thought she had her laughter under control, she caught Nathan's eyes, and the laughter spilled over again. Nathan seemed just as helpless.

"Ahem!" a voice said, and they both whirled around.

"Clem." Brittany blinked, startled by her older brother's sudden appearance. She knew he'd been at the Norrises that evening, but she hadn't expected him home so soon. The expression on his face said he thought they were out of their minds, and she felt another giggle threatening to escape.

"What on earth are you up to?" Clem asked. As he stared, Brittany remembered the rip in her skirt and messy hair, now completely freed from its hairpins and tumbling down her back. Then Clem's gaze slid to Nathan, sheet and apron still in hand.

"The cow stole Brittany's laundry," Brenna spoke up on their behalf. Neither she nor Lars seemed to have caught Brittany and Nathan's case of laughter. "They had to chase it to get it back."

"Lot of work for a bit of cloth," Nathan said, still grinning as he handed the laundry over to Brittany. "Looks like you'll have some mending to do."

Clem's eyebrows arched toward his hairline. "Why chase the cow when you could have just roped it and been done with it?" he asked, looking at Nathan.

"And miss all that fun?" Nathan chuckled again. "You missed out on one mighty fine evening, Clem."

Clem still looked uncertain, obviously taken aback by their hilarity. "Thanks, but I had a fine evening as it was. There was something I wanted to tell you both."

His tone was enough to make Nathan and Brittany put a stopper on their laughter. "We're listening," Brittany said.

Clem suddenly seemed nervous. He looked down at the ground and drew a circle in the dust with the toe of his boot. "This evening—" he began, but his voice cracked, so he paused and cleared his throat.

"This evening," he began again, voice steady. "I proposed to Morgan." He looked up at them, a smile playing around his lips. "She said yes."

"Oh, Clem! That's wonderful!" Brittany ran to his side and gave him a hug.

Nathan reached out to shake Clem's hand. "Congratulations."

"What's 'proposed' mean?" Brenna asked.

"It means he asked her to hitch up with him," Lars said in a whisper loud enough to be heard from the other side of the barn.

"Oh. I know about that," Brenna said.

"What's a tyke like you know about proposals?" Clem asked, grinning. He was at ease once more.

"Me and Carson did a proposal." Brenna pulled herself up importantly. "He said he liked me, so I said we should get married, and he said sure."

"Brenna!" Brittany was shocked, but a look from Clem warned her to keep quiet.

"Don't you think you're a mite young to be getting married?" he asked Brenna, keeping a straight face.

"We're not getting married now," Brenna said with great patience. "But we will soon as we're old enough. We decided on the last day of school, and he said he'd marry me even if he had to go all the way to Des Moines to get me."

"Huh." Clem flashed Brittany a grin. "That's one determined boy. I reckon Brenna's future is pretty well settled, so you better resign yourself to it."

Brittany wasn't sure how to respond, but Nathan was already pulling the conversation back to Clem's announcement. "When are you and Morgan getting married?" he asked.

"Not sure, exactly. It's already August, so I thought we'd wait to head into the fort for the ceremony until after the round-up and cattle drive. I reckon it'll be in early October when I get back from Cheyenne."

"But I won't be here in October," Brittany broke in.

"Then stay a little longer. What will one month hurt?"

"I can't. Suppose we have an early winter and we get snowed in? Then I couldn't go back to Des Moines, at least not comfortably, until next spring."

"So? Would that really be so terrible?" Clem tilted his head to one side.

"Aunt Ida is expecting me."

"She could wait a little longer."

"My contract with the Myerses ends in September."

"I doubt they'd mind if you stayed on longer. I bet they'd be downright glad to keep you as long as possible."

"That isn't the point." Brittany frowned at him. "I *want* to go back to Des Moines, sooner rather than later."

Brittany watched the darkness fall across Clem's face, his forehead furrowing in a frown. "Why?" he asked. "Why on earth do you want to go back to that jam-packed, crazy-busy place? Stay here, Brittany. This year has gone too fast, and I'd love more time with you and the kids."

"You think I don't want more time too?" Brittany flung the words at him. "I've loved this time, but it has to end at some point. This isn't easy, but I have to go home."

"Is Des Moines your home?" Clem asked, his words an eerie echo of Allie Bryan's. "You could make your home here. You fit here fine; you've got friends and family. What else do you want?"

"Civilization! Lars and Brenna can't grow up here. I'm not going to let them stay and grow wild like all the other rough west-erners around here—" The moment the words left her mouth, Brittany wanted to take them back. How could she have forgot-ten that Nathan was still here listening to every word she said? He had grown up in the West and was a genuine westerner, though he wasn't rough by any means.

Clem stared back at her, the lines of his face tight. "Fine. Go back East if you must. I won't bring this up again."

He spun around and walked off, his shoulders rigid. Brittany wondered if she ought to call after him and apologize, but for what? She had meant every word she said. Well, except for the rough westerner part. *You could have been kinder with what you said,* a little voice whispered, but Brittany ignored it, shoving it down before it could twinge her conscience further.

She risked a glance at Nathan, but he was staring at the ground, probably feeling awkward at witnessing a family fight. The expression on his face was unreadable, but he definitely wasn't laughing now.

How was it that a madly running steer could turn an evening into a memory to look back on and laugh over for a lifetime?—Yet bitter words could ruin an evening and make a person want nothing more than to escape to a private corner and weep? *And why does everyone keep questioning whether Des Moines is my home? Of course, it's home. I've never belonged here, but in Des Moines,* Brittany sighed. If only she could make everyone understand her desire, her *need,* to go home. Brittany had enjoyed her visit to Wyoming Territory, more than expected, but was more convinced than ever that she wasn't cut out to be a westerner.

CHAPTER
31

"I think our plan is working."

"You do? Good, 'cause it don't seem that way to me just now." Rueben scowled and kicked at a clod of dirt, breaking it into a dozen tiny pieces. "It don't feel like we've made any progress over these last several months, Able. None at all."

"Now hold up. We are too makin' progress. It's just been so gradual you ain't been seein' it." Able waved a finger at him. "I've been visitin' Brittany every week since January, and it's the middle of August now. And I've done what you told me to, and I ain't said nothin' about marriage. I really think she's comin' to care, Rueben. She's too modest to give much sign that she is, but the feelin's are there all right. Don't you think I've waited long enough to ask her again?" The expression on his face turned pleading, like a little boy begging for a cookie.

Rueben tossed Able's question about in his mind. He knew Able was growing impatient with the waiting, and he couldn't blame the man. Time was running out on them. Two more weeks were all that remained of August, and come September Brittany would be leaving. If they were going to make a move it had to be soon.

But that wasn't the only thing bothering him. Nathan wasn't responding to Able's courting the way Rueben had thought he would. Rueben had been watching him closely and noticed Nathan tense up when the other men commented on how smitten Able was with her, but he didn't seem inclined to do anything about it.

Rueben wanted more from him. He wanted Nathan to be downright angry about it. He wanted Nathan to come riding to her rescue as though it were his duty, not just stand aside waiting for things to play themselves out between Able and Brittany.

Able wanted to marry Brittany, of course. And Rueben would have no greater pleasure than to help in the destruction of Nathan's dream. His goal was something no one else would care about, but for Rueben, its success would bring deep satisfaction. He and Nathan had a long history between them shaped by a dozen fights too minor to remember the cause, but the bitter words had left their mark. What was more, Nathan and the whole Lindale family had turned his brother Dallas against him, ruining his dream. It was high time that one of the Lindales lost a dream.

Rueben clenched his teeth. He'd had dreams when he was younger: dreams of owning his own ranch, getting rich, being a man of power—at least in his own world. Dallas caught that dream as well, and together they had laid out plans for that ranch, *their* ranch. They'd both worked like crazy, biding their time, waiting for the day when they would be the ranch owners and not mere hirelings.

Then Dallas took a job at Michael Lindale's ranch, and things started to fall apart after that. Dallas began to change, becoming a little quieter, a little more thoughtful, nothing that concerned Rueben at first. But when Dallas began to swear less and talk religion more, Rueben had to wonder about his older brother. And as the Lindales began to dominate his conversations, Rueben became alarmed. It seemed he was losing interest in their ranch, their dream, and he talked instead of his admiration for Michael and how good his wife was to the ranch hands. Of how cute their kids were.

"I could be happy working on Michael's ranch for the rest of my life," Dallas said once.

"But what about our ranch?" Rueben asked.

Dallas laughed. "I don't really care much about that anymore. Don't you think it might git a bit lonely at times, Rueben?"

"Life can be lonely wherever you are. This ranch is our dream, Dallas."

Dallas's reply chilled him. "Is it?"

There were arguments and heated debates between them, but nothing had convinced Dallas that a ranch with Rueben was better than working for the Lindales. At last out of sheer desperation, Rueben decided to take a job at the Lindales' for himself, just to see why Dallas was so hooked on them.

He was disgusted from the start. Michael was far too goody-goody for Rueben's liking, yacking away about religion whenever he had half the chance. His wife was just plain old sickly-sweet. And the kids? Oh, they were little terrors! Especially the boys. They asked question after question until Rueben wanted to shake them and knock their heads together. Nathan was the worst. A glare would settle the younger one, but Nathan? That boy refused to be cowed by anything. And if he thought his younger brother wasn't being treated right, he took it upon himself to take care of the offender. Maybe that had been the root of all the contention between them. That and the irritating resemblance Nathan had to his father, both in looks and actions. Rueben couldn't lash back at his boss, but the boy was another matter. Anyhow, something went wrong between them from the very start.

Things didn't get better between him and Dallas either. In fact, they grew increasingly worse. Dallas kept singing their praises; he had only good to say about the Lindales and only criticism for Rueben. And he did not budge his position on the ranch. Rueben grew more irritated with each passing day. And just like that, a rift had formed between them. That rift stretched wider and wider until it was like the Grand Canyon, utterly impassable.

And finally the day came when Michael paid him with the ultimate insult—he fired him. It started with a rebuke from Michael over the way Rueben had been acting toward his boys. His words sent the fire burning in Rueben's middle soaring sky high, and he started yelling in response. One thing led to another, and almost before he knew it he had slammed his fist into the boss's face.

He was fired on the spot, and Michael told him to "grab your stuff and git."

Heaping injury onto the insult, Dallas sided with Michael. He actually agreed that the best decision was to fire Rueben. And with no trace of sorrow, Dallas stood, unmoving, in front of the bunkhouse, watching Rueben ride down the lane. Rueben hadn't seen his brother since, but the picture was still firmly fixed in his mind, along with the knowledge that because of the Lindales, he had lost Dallas.

He'd held tightly to the hurt, letting it fester and grow deep within him for years, wishing for revenge, but knowing it would never come—

Until he ran into Nathan.

Rueben let his gaze wander past Able and around Northridge. Yes, it was Nathan who had stolen Dallas from him. A thousand times he'd caught himself wishing to ask Nathan about Dallas, ask if he was still working for Nathan's pa and if he was well. But Nathan never brought it up, and Rueben was too proud to ask "the enemy" anything. Rueben still wondered how the young man had ended up here in Wyoming Territory, so far away from home, but Nathan kept his lips shut about that too. Something had happened. Rueben was sure about that, and if he could just get to the bottom of it, Rueben was certain he'd get his revenge. Something was paining Nathan. He'd seen that look on his face the evening Jeb Hawkins had visited. Jeb knew what it was, but when Rueben tried to draw it out of the man later that evening, he'd clamped his mouth shut and told Rueben to mind his own business. Whatever it was, Rueben wanted to know. That was the key to get Nathan. And Rueben's victory, though private, was one he would relish.

"So when can I ask her?" Able asked, his whiny voice pulling Rueben back to matter at hand.

Rueben glared at him. "I don't know. Figure it out yourself. If you think she cares for you, then go for it."

Able looked hurt. "You're supposed to help me."

"I have been. Just remember my tips on acting polite, and you'll do okay."

Able brightened. "So I can ask her now?"

"I guess." It was a gamble. If the girl accepted him, Rueben was sure Nathan would be riled into action. But if she didn't, then he had just played his last card.

Then a thought struck him.

"Hold on!" He grabbed Able's arm as if the man were going to escape and ask Brittany that very minute. "Wait a little longer. I just had an idea."

Able frowned. "How long? You can't make me wait forever."

"I just need a couple more days," Rueben said, turning the idea around in his mind. "I just need a couple of days to make my move, and then the girl is all yours."

CHAPTER
32

"Dave Norris went into the fort yesterday and brought back the mail with him," Mrs. Myers told Brittany. "He stopped by this afternoon while you were outside. There are two letters for you over there." She nodded toward the table.

"Good." Brittany scooped up the two letters and scanned their return addresses. One from Aunt Ida and one from William. She raised her eyebrows, surprised that William had written again. She'd sent him only one letter, and that had been way back in the fall. He was proving to be more faithful than she'd thought he would be.

As she tucked the two letters into her apron pocket, Aunt Ida's on top, Brittany's mind flitted to Clem. They had struck an uneasy truce after their fight, and true to his word, Clem had not spoken again about her staying. Brittany was relieved to have the issue behind them, although she suspected that Clem was still hoping she would change her mind. He should have known better. Once she made up her mind, she allowed nothing to change it.

The good thing was that the cattle drive would be a little later this year, so Clem would be here to tell her goodbye. Only two weeks remained of her time in Wyoming. Only two precious weeks. Brittany was determined to enjoy them and not let her leaving cast a cloud over these last days with Clem.

Mrs. Myers cleared her throat. "I got a letter back from my niece." She held up a white slip of paper covered with delicate writing.

Brittany knew that Mrs. Myers had written to her niece a while back, asking her to come and help out at Northridge. "What did she say?" Brittany asked, glad to think about something besides leaving.

Mrs. Myers's smile twitched. "You aren't going to believe this, but she's already on her way. She'll be here in two days."

"Good! Then I'll get to meet her before I leave. I'm sure you must be excited for her to come."

Mrs. Myers hesitated. "Yes. I've kept in touch with her mother through the years, but I've never met Amelia. I hope we'll get along."

"Mrs. Myers, I believe you could charm a bear." Brittany crossed the room and planted a kiss on Mrs. Myers's wrinkled cheek. "I'm sure you and Amelia will get along well."

"Perhaps, but—" Mrs. Myers sighed. "I'll miss you, Brittany. This ranch hasn't been the same since you and your siblings came. Why, you're like family to me, even more than Amelia. Isn't there any way you could stay?"

Brittany sighed. Here it was again. She was getting tired of people trying to persuade her to stay.

"No." Brittany shook her head. "No. I'm a city girl at heart, Mrs. Myers, and—"

Mrs. Myers laughed. "A city girl? Not you, Brittany."

Brittany wanted to argue that, but Mrs. Myers was already continuing.

"You know, Brittany, when you came, Tim and I thought for sure you'd be just like the other girls we hired. Scared to get your hands dirty, fussing over the primitive conditions out here, trying to convince us to end your contract so you could get married." Mrs. Myers smiled at her. "But you did none of that. You dug right into the work, and you found even more ways to bless not just us but also the neighbors. You've left a mark here, Brittany, and you'll be in our hearts long after you're gone."

Brittany felt a sudden rush of tears. "The blessing has been all mine. I've learned so much, and I've come to love all of you so." She stopped, afraid that if she continued she would break down.

"Speaking of love," Mrs. Myers's smile turned mischievous. "Maybe you don't want to stay and work for us any longer, but surely you aren't going to get away without finding yourself a husband."

Brittany felt her cheeks flame. "Oh, no. I don't think so."

"Why not? There are plenty of fine men around here. Able would marry you." The twinkle in her eyes deepened.

Brittany shook her head. Marry Able? Why she'd sooner die! But she had to admit that he had improved since their first meeting.

"What about that young man your brother gets along with so well?" Mrs. Myers asked, unwilling to let the subject drop. "Let's see—his name was Nathan, wasn't it?"

"Nathan?" Brittany was even more shocked by that idea. "Oh, not Nathan. He's not a believer, and we're just friends. Nothing more."

"Hmm." Mrs. Myers looked disappointed. "I'll have to keep thinking, then."

Please don't. Brittany decided that an escape might be her best defense against Mrs. Myers's matchmaking. Muttering something about being back soon, she slipped out the door and drew a deep breath of the cool evening air.

Marry Nathan Lindale? The thought had never occurred to her. Well, not really. He was a fine, upright young man with a charming Texas accent, but facts were facts. He didn't care about her like that—and she didn't care for him either. And besides, he wasn't a Christian, and Brittany could never consent to marry an unbeliever. Marry Nathan Lindale ha. Why the sun would sooner rise in the west than that would happen. Besides, what would Aunt Ida say? Oh, but she would be horrified! She would wag her head and give Brittany her sad I-told-you-so-look and would never say a civil word to Nathan, one of those "barbaric westerners."

She wouldn't even give him a chance to prove himself. For some reason, that thought bothered her.

Brittany shook her head, clearing her mind of the uncomfortable thoughts. She leaned against the corral, the place her feet had carried her while she was deep in thought, and glanced around. No one was around—a good thing since her cheeks still burned—and she reached into her pocket where the two letters waited. She took out William's first, feeling another wave of confusion as she looked down at his strong, perfect handwriting. Perfect. That described William to a tee. He always looked perfect, he always behaved perfectly—and today, for some reason, that annoyed Brittany. Looking back, she wondered just how open she and William had been with each other during their years of friendship. In Des Moines they had always met during polite social functions where the talk never wandered to inner struggles or failures. There were no mishaps to bring out the worst in a person. Society ruled that it was too cultured to speak of the "dirty" stuff of life; all the events were too perfectly planned to allow for mishaps. *Perfect.* There was that word again.

Brittany gave her head another little shake, wondering why all these unsettling thoughts were coming to her now. She opened William's letter slowly and scanned down the page. He seemed busy with social engagements and demands, the sort of things she had just been criticizing.

What is wrong with me? Brittany wondered, pausing to look up at the color-washed evening sky. Soon she would have her wish and be back in Des Moines where she belonged, yet here she was contrasting Des Moines social functions with life out west. She thought of the school program months before, when the crowd *so* exceeded their expectations that they had to move it outside. According to Des Moines society, she should have considered the event a fiasco, what with everyone, including the guests, hauling around chairs and benches, rearranging the food table to make room for the extra dishes. But it had been fun. Maybe all the shuffling had actually helped some of the guests to relax, to loosen their collars, and let themselves act normal. And they'd all had such a good afternoon. One thing about Wyoming Territory was that while parties might be few and far between, when everyone did get together, there was no shortage of laughter and fun.

I wonder what William considers our relationship to be, Brittany thought as she turned back to the letter. His writing style seemed a bit warmer than in his last letter, and he admitted right out that he'd realized absence does indeed make the heart grow fonder.

Surely he doesn't consider us a couple. The idea alarmed Brittany, but she pushed it quickly aside. No, that couldn't be the case. It was his mother and Aunt Ida who had paired them together. William considered her merely a friend, which was why he had taken the time to write to her. True friends always went the extra mile, and William simply wanted to make sure that she didn't get lonely or feel forsaken out in the Western wilderness. That was all there was to it.

Rueben's luck was with him. After supper he came around the corner of the barn and saw Miss Haines standing by the corral, all alone. Great. It was just the opportunity he'd been hoping for.

He made a beeline toward her, double-checking to make sure that no one was lurking in the shadows, especially not her older brother. But no, now that he thought of it, Clem had taken off after supper for a visit with his fiancée, so the coast was clear on that score.

The girl was so involved in reading the slip of paper in her hand that she didn't even notice him. He stopped a few feet away from her, and keeping his voice casual, said, "Evening, Miss Haines."

She startled and shoved the letter into her pocket, her face turning just a bit red. "Why, Mr. Pierce, how good to see you," she said, giving him an obviously forced smile.

"Same, Miss Haines. Say, is Nathan around?"

"Nathan?" Her face reddened even more. "I haven't seen him. Why?"

"Well, the two of you seem to be together often enough—" he let his voice trail off.

Brittany pursed her lips together. "I don't know where he is," she said, her voice quiet but holding an edge. "So if you're looking for him—"

"Naw, I'm not lookin' for him." *You're the one I need right now.* Rueben drew in a deep breath. It was time to drive to the point. "Miss Haines, I feel that it's my duty to warn you about somethin'."

He could see the surprise flicker across her face. "Oh?"

"There's something about Nathan I think you should be knowin' before you commit to anything with him."

Now a spark leaped into her eyes. "Mr. Pierce," she said, putting great emphasis on his name. "I am *not* committing to anything with Nathan."

"Really?" That was good news.

"Nathan is a fine man, but—" Brittany paused.

"But there's something off about him, huh?"

Brittany glanced at him, the expression on her face saying she had not been thinking along those lines. "Something off?"

"Well, sure. Don't tell me you hadn't noticed. He hides it well, all right, but there are some things that don't make sense about him. Has he ever told you about his growin'-up years?"

"Not much."

"Ah. You see, I knew Nathan from way back when he was a kid—used to work for his pa down in Texas. The Lindales had a nice spread, and everyone knew that Nathan was gonna be the one to inherit it. That whole family was real close, real clannish, always lookin' out for each other." Rueben paused. "But now Nathan's here up north workin' for another man, which don't make sense iffen he could be runnin' his pa's ranch. And he don't keep in touch with his folks neither. Strange, given how close they all were."

Brittany looked away from him but said nothing.

"I've got to wonder why Nathan left home in the first place," Rueben said. "He ever told you?"

Brittany shook her head. "He has a right to privacy," she said, as if that should end the conversation.

"It's strange—that's all. I'm sure he's got something he's hiding, but of course, he won't 'fess up to it."

Brittany seemed restless. "Mr. Pierce, I really think—"

"I think the strangest thing of all is that he seems to have broken things off completely with his family. He and his parents seemed to get along right well. And his little brother? Why, those two were inseparable. I'm only surprised that Nathan got away without the kid tagging along at his heels."

A funny look crossed Brittany's face. "Nathan told me his brother was dead."

Evan Lindale was dead? The words threw Rueben for a moment. "Are you sure?"

"That's what Nathan said."

"Huh." Rueben's mind raced. Somehow Evan's death seemed like another piece of the puzzle, but turn the information about as he might, he couldn't see how it fit into the picture.

"Well, at the very least it would have devastated him," he said almost to himself. "He was positively devoted to that kid. He downright babied him."

Brittany stiffened. "Mr. Pierce, I really don't like this conversation." She attempted to move past him.

Rueben blocked her way. "Just one more thing. Iffen you ever do change your mind about Nathan, you best be diggin' some answers out of him first. Wouldn't do to be marryin' a man with a shadowy past."

Brittany planted her hands on her hips. "I don't see how that's your business, Mr. Pierce."

"Anything that has to do with Nathan is my business."

"Well, maybe you should stop *making* it your business." Brittany glared at him.

"And I don't see how that's *your* business."

"Mr. Pierce, please get out of my way," Brittany said, her chin lifting. Her tone made Rueben all the more reluctant to let her past him. He would let her go in his own timing, not because she ordered him to.

"What are you doing, Rueben?" a voice suddenly said behind him. Rueben whirled around and found himself face to face with Nathan himself.

"What are you doing?" Nathan asked again, the look on his face foreboding trouble.

"Just havin' a little talk with Miss Haines here." Rueben refused to be the first to look away.

"Look, Rueben, you leave her alone, hear?" Nathan leaned closer, his eyes flashing. "I won't stand for you pestering Miss Haines. Whatever problems we might have are strictly between you and me, Rueben, so quit trying to drag others into it."

Rueben squirmed and decided that it was time to flip the coin on Nathan and put him on the defensive. "Oh, yeah? What are you going to do?" he asked. "You might be sweet on her, but you can't keep her from talking to other people."

Nathan's face colored. "I told you to stop making a mountain out of nothing," he hissed in reply. It was obvious that Brittany's presence disconcerted him.

"So you don't care about her? Tell her," Rueben said. Now that was brilliant. If Nathan said he did care, he would crash into a stone wall when Brittany refused him, but if he said he didn't, well, there was no chance Brittany was going to listen to him after that.

"Tell her," Rueben said again as Nathan clamped his mouth shut. "She wants to know the truth." He stepped back a bit so that he could see both of their expressions. They both looked uncomfortable, all right.

"I don't care about her like that!" Nathan burst out, not looking Brittany in the eye. "Now get out of here, Rueben."

"Sure, I will," Rueben said, but he made no move to leave. As worked up as Nathan was, Rueben knew he had him in his clutches at last, and he wanted to savor his victory. And he couldn't resist making one final attack.

"By the way, while you're feeling so honest, you might want to tell Brittany why you left Texas."

Nathan glared at him. "I said get out of here!"

"Try to make me. Now come on—be honest, Nathan. Why'd you leave home? Was it because Evan died?"

Rueben hadn't been sure if he was on the right track or not, but the way Nathan's face suddenly drained of color told him he'd struck home, all right.

"How'd you–who told you Evan died?" Nathan asked. His whole face radiated anger, but something else flickered deep in his eyes. Surely it couldn't be fear?

Out of the corner of his eye Rueben saw Brittany shrink back against the corral. She was realizing now that it had been a mistake to tell Rueben.

"Well, how'd he die?" Reuben asked, pressing closer to Nathan. "Was it your fault?"

"No!" Nathan burst out, then looked guiltier than ever.

"Was it your fault?" Rueben asked again. He and Nathan were standing nearly nose to nose now.

He saw Nathan swallow once, then again. "That's not your business."

"I see how it is. Evan died, and everyone blamed you, even your folks, right?"

The look on Nathan's face confirmed that he was right.

"So that's why you ended up here. You ran away so you wouldn't have to face everyone's condemnation. You ain't really as good as you first appear, are you?" Rueben leaned back a bit. "I knew from the start there was somethin' you weren't ownin' up to."

"Rueben Pierce," Nathan said through gritted teeth. "You are the meanest man that ever walked this earth."

"Least I didn't kill my brother."

Rueben watched the red creep up Nathan's neck and into his face. Nathan stared back, and Rueben saw him clench his fist and draw it back. Rueben braced himself for the blow, thinking that maybe—after all, he'd forced Nathan to confess right in front of Brittany—he deserved a punch.

But then Nathan stopped, and his fist dropped limply at his side. Without a word, he whirled around and walked away from them, his shoulders rigid but his jaw working.

"Nathan!" Brittany called after him, finally finding her voice. She started to run after him, but Nathan didn't look back at her.

"No, I don't want to talk right now," he said without so much as glancing her way, and Brittany stopped, the hurt evident on her face.

Both Reuben and Brittany watched in silence until Nathan disappeared around the corner. Rueben let out a whoosh of air. "Well, sure wasn't expecting that."

Brittany didn't reply. Rueben glanced at her, and without warning she burst into tears and took off running toward the Myerses' cabin.

Rueben stared, startled by her reaction. His goal hadn't been to hurt *her*, just Nathan. And hurt him he had. The pain in Nathan's eyes as he turned away told him that.

He should have been feeling triumphant. He should have been rubbing his hands together in glee over his long-awaited victory. But he wasn't. Instead, he kept thinking how awful it must be to be blamed for his brother's death. Why if it were him and Dallas—

He had to stop this. Nathan was his enemy, for goodness sake! He'd needed to be brought down a little. He had asked for it.

CHAPTER

33

Nathan spent the next day in agony. The whole conversation with Rueben kept replaying in his mind, haunting him with every step he took. Without a doubt, Brittany was disappointed in him. He was disappointed in himself. And Rueben was no doubt gloating. Nathan made a point of avoiding him, sure that he would fly to pieces if Rueben made one comment about Evan. Rueben had him by the throat with that information, all right, and knowing Rueben, he would make the most of the opportunity.

Rueben sure never learned about not hitting a man when he's already down, Nathan thought that evening as he left the cook shack. Rueben had kept quiet during dinner, but Nathan was on edge, waiting for the next blow. He rubbed a hand over his face, then tilted his head from one side to the other, trying to release some of the tension from his neck. All this extra stress and worry was taking a toll on him. It didn't help that he hadn't been able to sleep last night, despite the hard physical work he'd put in the day before. How was it that the mind could be going at such a high speed that it overpowered even physical exhaustion?

The truth was, Nathan was more tired than he'd ever felt in his life. Tired of hurting other people. Tired of his failures. Tired of his own helplessness. He was tired of constantly butting heads with Rueben and fighting battles that he never failed to lose. He was just plain tired of *himself.*

Nathan heaved a deep sigh that rose from the toes of his boots upwards. Try as he might, he was never good enough. Always, circumstances got the best of him and left him worse for the wear. Was it simply bad luck?

He saw Johnny sitting out on his porch, Bible in hand, and decided that a visit with Johnny might be just what he needed. As long as Brittany wasn't around. That would be uncomfortable, to say the least.

Nathan made his way toward Johnny, trying to act casual. A quick glance showed that Johnny was alone, so taking the steps two at a time, Nathan climbed onto the porch and eased himself into the chair alongside Johnny's.

Johnny looked up from his Bible and broke into a grin. "Why, Nathan, good to see you. How's it goin'?"

Nathan debated whether he should be honest or give the polite response of "good." It took him only an instant to decide. Honesty, of course. Since when had he been anything but honest with Johnny? Besides, if he didn't talk honestly with somebody, the pain and conflict trapped inside was going to drive him mad.

Nathan stared straight ahead, studying the horizon. "To say it's going awful is an understatement."

"How so?" Johnny asked, the simple question prompting Nathan to open up.

"You know that Rueben Pierce and I don't get along well, but here lately, he's been taking some especially hard jabs at me."

Johnny listened in silence as Nathan told him about the night before. How Rueben had driven him to tell Brittany that he didn't care about her. How Rueben had ferreted out Evan's death somehow and had made Nathan admit that it was his fault. He even told Johnny about snapping at Brittany, saying he didn't want to talk to her, which wasn't entirely Rueben's fault. Nathan still felt embarrassed about that.

"Time seems to make Rueben only grow worse, and he's getting to be unbearable now." Nathan hesitated before saying aloud the thought that had been niggling at him. "I've been thinking that maybe I should quit here at Northridge."

"Quit?" Johnny's eyebrows rose. "Don't you think that might be running away from your problem?"

"What's the point of staying when I can't win? I can't stand to hear him say Evan's name, and knowing Rueben, he will." Nathan ran a hand through his hair.

Johnny studied him. "Nathan, let me tell you something. You can't outrun your troubles. Did running away from home solve your problems?"

Nathan shifted uncomfortably. "Well, maybe not solve, but at least I don't have to look at my pa every day and see the disappointment in his eyes."

"You might argue this with me, but I'm thinking had you stuck it out, he would've come around eventually. Son, when you run, you drag your troubles right along with you and add new ones on top of that. The reason you can't stand to hear Rueben say Evan's name is because you can't git past your guilt over what happened to the kid. That's a problem that running didn't help. And your problems haven't lessened any over the years, have they?"

Nathan had to admit that they hadn't. "But if I quit, I won't have to be around Rueben."

"So what happens when you run into another Rueben in your life? Do you run yet again?" Johnny shook his head. "Nathan, you have to face your problems head-on and quit tryin' to run from them."

"But how am I supposed to deal with Rueben?"

"Forgive him."

Nathan stared back at Johnny. "Forgive him?" He gave a bitter laugh. "Do you realize all that man has done to me? He doesn't deserve my forgiveness."

"This ain't about whether he deserves it or not, Nathan. It's about you. You need to forgive him and let the past go."

"That's impossible! You can't seriously think that if I just walk up to Rueben and say, 'Rueben, I forgive you for all that nasty stuff you said and did,' then everything's suddenly going to be fine, and Rueben will stop trying to tear me down at every turn? That's the most ridiculous thing I ever heard!"

"That ain't what I said." Johnny's voice was even. "The change won't be in Rueben, though that would be something to praise the Lord for. The change would be in *you*, Nathan. Anger and bitterness have a way of grabbin' a person and hurtin' them far worse than the person they're upset with."

Nathan shook his head. "Impossible," he said again.

Johnny watched him. "Let me ask you something, Nathan. Have you forgiven yourself for what happened the day Evan died?"

Nathan jerked around to face him. "What's that got to do with anything?"

"I see. What about God? Have you accepted His forgiveness?"

Nathan wondered what Johnny was trying to drive at. "Johnny, do you really think God would want to forgive me when my own pa couldn't?"

"So you can't forgive Rueben, you can't forgive yourself, and you can't accept anyone's forgiveness. Nathan, you have a far bigger problem than you realize. You have a forgiveness problem."

Nathan blinked. "Well, what do you want me to do, then?"

Johnny was quiet for so long that Nathan thought he wasn't going to answer him.

"This ain't about what *I* want you to do, Nathan," Johnny said at last. "It's about what *God* wants you to do, and do you really want to hear that?"

Nathan hesitated. Did he?

"I guess," he said, shrugging.

"Do you really?" Johnny asked, looking at him hard. "I've tried to tell you before, Nathan, but you wouldn't listen."

Nathan stared at a crack in the floor. He knew Johnny was right. Whenever Johnny tried to talk about God before, Nathan had always changed the subject or cut him off. He hadn't wanted to listen to such talk. But now he was to the point where he was willing to take any advice, anything that might lend him a ray of hope. "I'll listen."

"With your mind and your heart?"

"With my mind and my heart. But I'm telling you, Johnny, I don't think God can save just *anyone.* There's something wrong with a God who would want to save someone as messed up as me. I mean, after all the things I've done, He *can't* love me. Either that or He doesn't really know me."

"So you *have* given God some thought, have you?" Johnny cracked a smile. "You had me fooled. But let me tell you this—He knows you. He knows everything you ever did, and He knows you better than you know yourself. And more than that, He loves you. Iffen He didn't love you—and all of the rest of us broken, miserable sinners—He never would've sent His Son to carry your sins to the cross for the punishment you deserve to pay." Johnny reached out and squeezed Nathan's hand. "Now, let me tell you about something called grace."

CHAPTER
34

The sky had filled with stars and the moon had climbed high in the sky by the time Nathan made his way back to the bunkhouse. *Grace.* The word still rang in his mind. He'd heard it before and had even tossed it around himself a few times, but until tonight he'd never really understood what it was.

Nathan looked up at the sky, filled with the wonder that finally, after all these years of heartache and running, he could experience true forgiveness. Johnny had helped him to see that things weren't really as hopeless as they seemed and that the only thing holding Nathan back from forgiveness and salvation was himself. Grace wasn't something he could earn. And he knew for sure that he didn't deserve it. But the offer was there regardless of his own unworthiness, and Nathan was now willing to accept it.

Nathan breathed deeply, feeling as if he'd been cleansed from the inside out. For the first time since Evan's death, he finally felt released from the guilt of what happened. He still missed his little brother. He knew guilt might try to regain a foothold. But through Christ it would not overcome him again. Not as long as he kept his mind centered on what Jesus had done and not on his failures.

His mind drifted to his pa, and he wondered if just maybe Johnny was right. Had his pa found it in his heart to forgive Nathan? The idea kindled a spark of hope in Nathan. Anyway, he intended to ask again for forgiveness. The worst Pa could say was no, and then Nathan would let it rest, satisfied that he had done all he could

He would have to talk to Rueben—and Brittany. And Clem would be delighted to know as well. Like Johnny, he'd been trying for years to tell Nathan the truth.

He had a lot to make up for but would make a fresh start, with the Lord's help, beginning tomorrow.

First thing next morning Nathan wrote a letter to his parents asking for their forgiveness. Work started at the crack of dawn or before, so a short letter would have to do for now. As he sealed the envelope, he wondered what their reaction to hearing from him after all these years would be. Eleven years had passed since he left, and they hadn't heard a word from him—unless Jeb had made it back to Texas and told them about their long-lost son. They still had plenty of reason to be upset with him.

It's in the Lord's hands, Nathan reminded himself, tucking the letter away. Next time the mail went out he would send it, along with his prayers that it would be the beginning of a bridge, spanning the rift that years and circumstances had created.

Evening came before he had the opportunity to talk to Rueben. Nathan found him alone in front of the barn and, swallowing the fear of what he might trigger, made his way over to him.

"Wal, would you look who we have here?" Rueben said as he drew near. He appeared no different than usual, scornful expression and all. "It's one fine man who kills his brother and jilts a nice young lady."

Nathan took a deep breath, warning himself not to react with an angry reply. "I'm glad to see you, Rueben," he said, meeting his gaze. "I wanted a chance to talk with you."

"Oh, yeah? So what do you got against me this time?" Rueben folded his arms across his chest.

"Nothing." Nathan kept his voice even. "I wanted to ask you to forgive me. I–I haven't treated you very well, Rueben. I've been angry and bitter and grudging, and I–well, I'm sorry about that. It was wrong of me to act like that toward you."

Rueben stared at Nathan, his mouth opening and closing with no words coming out. He looked as shocked as if Nathan had hit him in the forehead with a rock.

"I just wanted to ask your forgiveness, and–I guess that's all I was going to say." Nathan stumbled to a stop. "See you later."

Nathan turned and walked away, feeling better than he had in a long while. Johnny was right. His words might have no effect on Rueben, but they gave him a release from all the past grudges between him and Rueben.

Strangely, he felt even more frightened facing Brittany than Rueben. He hadn't seen her since that terrible evening two days before when he told her he didn't care for her. Now that he might have lost even her friendship, he had to admit to himself that he cared about her, all right. Perhaps that was why he was so scared. If she said that she didn't want to talk to him again, it would hurt far more than Rueben could ever hurt him. Maybe he and Brittany could never be anything more than friends, but be that as it may, he wanted a chance, even though he'd given her plenty of reason to deny him.

Nathan found himself brushing at a smudge of dirt on his pants and smoothing down his hair as he climbed the Myerses' steps. He paused at the door, gathering his courage together before raising a hand to knock.

The door opened before he was prepared. Brittany stood there, a smile on her face, the lamp behind her casting a soft glow.

Her smile dimmed when she saw Nathan. "Nathan." She hesitated, emotions playing across her face. Nathan thought he detected uncertainty, uneasiness, and something else. Could it be relief?

But then all those emotions fled, and her grip on the door tightened. "What's wrong?"

"Wrong? Nothing's wrong."

"You're sure?" She lost some of her tension.

"Yeah. Why would anything be wrong?"

"Well, the only time you ever come here is when there's an accident or a problem of some sort."

Nathan could have kicked himself for scaring her like that. It was a poor way to start this conversation. "I was wondering if you had time to talk."

"Oh." Brittany glanced over her shoulder, then back at him. "I suppose."

She stepped out onto the porch and shut the door behind her. Nathan thought she looked wary.

He took a deep breath. "I want to tell you that I'm sorry. About the other night."

"Oh, that. It was nothing, Nathan," she said a little too fast.

"It was something to *me*." Nathan struggled to find the right words. "I'm sorry that I hurt you. I shouldn't have snapped at you like I did, and–can you forgive me? Please?" He willed her to see that he meant what he said.

"Oh, of course, I'll forgive you–for whatever there is to forgive." She gave him a slight smile. "I'm sorry too."

"You? Sorry? For what?" Nathan's confusion turned each word into a question.

"I shouldn't have told Rueben about–about your brother." She looked pained. More evidence that he had truly hurt her. "I didn't know he would—"

"Brittany, it's all right. It was coming anyway. You didn't do anything wrong." The expression on her face twisted his heart.

He took another breath and looked away. "The problem wasn't that Evan died. The problem wasn't even that I was the one to blame for it. Johnny explained to me yesterday that the real problem was a lack of forgiveness, and he was right." He looked back at her. "I've been living all these years rejecting forgiveness, God's forgiveness, and I realize that now. Johnny helped me work through it, and I've laid my burden of sin and guilt at the feet of Jesus. He's my Lord and Savior now, and from now on I intend to be a different person—"

He stopped short as Brittany let out a little cry and threw her arms around him. She stepped back from him almost immediately, but whatever else Nathan had planned on saying flew from his mind.

"Oh, Nathan, that's wonderful!" she said, her face alight. "I've been praying that would happen."

"You have?"

"Oh, yes. You couldn't have given me any better news, Nathan." Her smile warmed him clear through.

Looking down at her, Nathan found himself tempted to blurt out right then and there just how much he really cared about her. More than cared. Loved her. But he restrained himself. He had told her not more than two minutes ago that he was a believer, and now he expected her to be ready to take his word for it and commit the rest of her life to him? Without even seeing the changes he intended to make in his life now that he followed Christ? And how was he supposed to provide for her if they were to get married? His pockets contained little more than dust, and he sure couldn't move her into the bunkhouse with him.

And yet would circumstances be any different by the time she prepared to leave? They were down to a matter of days now, and time was running out on him. Was it possible for a man to convince a lady to marry him in such a short amount of time? Even without all the barriers in their way? And what about her distaste for westerners, men like him? Would she be willing to even consider staying here and spending the rest of her life with a westerner?

The more Nathan thought, the more tangled the situation became. It seemed there was nothing he could do besides hold his tongue and pray. He needed more time to lay some plans, but did he have that time? The way things were going now, he was going to have to stand by and do nothing, absolutely nothing, as she rode away for Des Moines in less than two short weeks.

CHAPTER
35

Will this journey ever end?

The man stared out the stage window at the tree-less, sage-dotted land and resisted the urge to groan. If he never had to travel again, at least by anything but horseback, he'd die a happy man. He'd been on the road for days, making a journey he was by no means certain would be successful. But he knew he couldn't live with himself if he didn't make the effort, so here he was, trekking across hundreds of miles on what some might call a fool's errand.

Not that he considered his mission that. No. If he believed that for a moment, he never would have exchanged the comforts of home and family for this rocking, bouncing, monster they called a stagecoach.

The driver had said they would arrive at Fort Laramie, Wyoming, at around one-thirty, claiming that to be good timing. But for a man who had been traveling for two weeks by every contraption except his own two feet, even a couple more hours seemed unbearable.

Have patience, he told himself, two words he'd repeated countless times on this journey. Taking his mind off their snail-paced progress, he turned from the window and looked around the interior of the stage. There sure was an assortment of people crammed in today. Three cowboys on the back seat kept passing a bottle to each other. A whiskery old fellow sat beside him saying no more than an occasional grunt. Across from him was a young lady wearing her fingernails down to nothing by the way she was chewing on them. And a young man dressed in a fashionable-looking suit sat next to her.

Michael Lindale shifted on his seat, his slight movement making the young man's eyes turn to him.

"Where do you get off?" he asked Michael.

"Fort Laramie." The name was blazed in Michael's mind. That and the name "Northridge Ranch".

He thought back to the day Jeb Hawkins had returned to the ranch with the news that he'd seen Nathan in Wyoming Territory. After years of silence, wondering what had happened to his son, whether he was even alive and regretting his own thoughtless words, the news had been almost too much to take in.

"You're sure it was him?" he'd asked Jeb several times.

"Oh, no doubt about that," Jeb had said. "Only a Lindale could be as stubborn as that boy."

"And you think he's still there?"

"Boss, I ain't got a clue. For all I know, he could've taken off the very day I left. But I can tell you one thing he ain't comin' home on his own. He's still broken over what happened to Evan, and he's dead sure that you never could've forgiven him."

From the moment Jeb told him the news, Michael had known in his heart that he would be leaving for Wyoming to find his boy. He'd lost count of how many times through the years he'd berated himself for the way he'd acted the day Evan died. He'd been outraged by Nathan's disobedience and blinded by grief, and he hadn't thought through what he said to Nathan. He'd let the words spill out, wanting Nathan to realize the high cost of his disobedience. Of course, Nathan was a smart boy, and he'd already figured out long before then that he'd done wrong. And knowing Nathan, he was heartbroken over what had happened. One thing Michael knew was that Nathan never would have hurt Evan on purpose. Never. And a thousand times over, he'd wished that rather than yelling at Nathan, he'd taken the boy in his arms and told him that he forgave him despite the wrong he'd done. Maybe then he'd never have lost him.

The look in Nathan's eyes as he'd yelled haunted Michael to this day, and more than anything, he longed for a chance to right the wrong that had happened so many years before. He loved that boy dearly, and nothing ever had or could change that. Now he could only pray that his trip would be successful and he'd find his son again. And he knew that Christy and Maryanne were praying too, waiting eagerly to hear how everything turned out.

"So where are you going?" Michael asked the well-dressed young man, forcing his attention back to the present here in this dusty stage.

"California," the young man said.

Michael frowned. "But this isn't the route to California."

"I know. I'm making a bit of a detour on my trip." He smiled. "I'll be stopping at Fort Laramie as well."

"I see," Michael said, although honestly he didn't. "Why are you heading to California?"

"I was ordained a minister not too many months ago, and I'm traveling to my first church in San Francisco."

"San Francisco. That's a pretty big city, I've heard. You know anyone there?"

"No. But I will soon. And," the young man drew a deep breath, "Lord willing, I'll be bringing a wife with me."

"Oh?" Michael glanced from the young man to the lady beside him, who was still nibbling on a fingernail. "When do you intend to be married?"

The young man caught Michael's glance between him and the woman, and his face blanched, then turned bright red. "Oh, no," he said, putting a little more distance between himself and the young woman. "We–she–the woman I intend to marry lives on a ranch outside of Fort Laramie. That's the reason for my detour."

The young woman reddened as well, and she pressed against the wall even more tightly, staring down at her shoes.

"Pardon me for the confusion." Michael tried to hide his smile at their consternation. He looked at the young man. "I'm sorry, but what was your name?"

"William. William Brown."

"Well, William, I hope you and your fiancée get it all worked out."

William's face reddened even more. "Uh, she's not my fiancée–yet. I haven't had a chance to ask her yet."

"Oh." Michael scolded himself for jumping to too many conclusions too quickly.

"She came here about a year ago, and she's been helping an elderly woman, mostly so she can be with her brother. But her contract's up here in a matter of days, and I intend to marry her then."

"Have you seen her since last year?"

"Well, no." William shifted on his seat. "But we wrote to each other–a few times. And we've always kind of had an understanding that we were going to get married. My parents and her aunt expect it."

"Hmm." Michael wondered how the young woman herself felt about it all. It sounded to him as if the couple was being forced together. "You said she lives outside of Fort Laramie?"

"Yes."

"Do you know where the ranch is?"

A flicker of uncertainty crossed his face. "Well, no, but I guess it can't be too hard to find."

Michael wondered if the young man realized just how spread-out ranches could be and how broad the definition "outside of" was.

"Anyway, I have the name of the ranch." William patted his pocket. "It's Northridge ranch, owned by Tim and Eleanor Myers."

"Northridge!" Michael jerked upright in his seat. "That's where *I'm* going!"

"Northridge!" The young woman sitting next to William jerked upright as well. "I'm going there too!"

Michael swiveled his gaze to the young woman. "Why are *you* going there?"

"Eleanor Myers is my aunt," she said, her face flushed. "Her hired help is leaving, so she asked if I would come and help out."

"That would be Brittany," William broke in. He might as well have said "*my* Brittany."

"What is this?" The whiskery fellow beside Michael spoke for the first time. "A sightseeing party to this here ranch in the middle of nowhere? Am I missin' out on somethin'?"

The humor of the situation struck Michael, and he began to laugh. "Well, I'll be. What are the chances of three different people ending up on the same stage at the same time headed for the same ranch?"

Neither William nor the young woman seemed amused. "Excuse me, but what was your name?" William asked, turning to the young woman.

"Amelia Burton." The woman looked overly hot in her high-collared, lace-trimmed dress. It was made of heavy material, probably quite fashionable but out of place on such a warm day. "I'm from Boston."

"Ah. I'm from Des Moines."

Amelia sighed. "I already miss the city. This land is perfectly barren, and so–so uninhabited. I do hope my uncle and aunt live near the fort. I can't imagine living too far from town. But I am looking forward to seeing all the little calves out in the pastures this spring." She brightened. "My uncle has cattle, you see, and I'm sure they must be adorable."

Michael barely restrained himself from rolling his eyes as William gave a murmur of agreement. He thought about saying that cattle sure didn't look too adorable when they were bearing down on you like a locomotive when you were trying to brand their calves. But Amelia was already on to something else. Oh, well. Might as well let her dream a little longer. He was just glad that he wasn't in Tim and Eleanor Myers's shoes.

The stage pulled up in front of the Rustic Hotel at one-thirty, right on time. Michael stepped down, grateful to have his feet on solid ground once again and to have Amelia Burton silent once more. She'd spent the remainder of the trip talking with William Brown about city life, with her doing most of the talking. Her voice was starting to give Michael a headache.

But now he watched as she stepped forward to meet her uncle, seeming to shrink under the man's unsmiling expression. "Uncle Tim?" she said, glancing around as if hoping there were some mistake.

"Amelia." He gave a short nod.

Amelia turned around, presumably for moral support. "That's William Brown," she said, jabbing a finger at him. "And that's Michael Lindale, and they're coming with us too."

Michael cringed, wishing she'd just let him introduce himself in his own way. "Pardon me, mister," he said, stepping forward. "I'm Michael Lindale, and not to be an intrusion, but does my son Nathan work for you?"

Tim Myers stared back, studying Michael as if measuring him up. Evidently he was satisfied with what he saw. "I don't know whether he's your son or not, but I do got a Nathan Lindale who works for me."

Michael released the breath he'd unconsciously been holding. "Good. I was hoping to talk with him."

Tim grunted. "My ranch is a half day's ride from here. You got a horse?"

"No, but I can get one from the livery."

Tim grunted again. "Iffen you can be back here in half an hour, I reckon you can come along with us."

"What about *me?*" William asked. He looked pleadingly at Michael. "Can you help me get a horse too?"

Michael looked back at the young man, noting his suit, polished shoes, and slicked-down hair. He looked so out of place standing in front of the tumbledown Rustic Hotel that Michael felt sorry for him.

"Ever ridden before?" Michael asked.

"No, but I can learn." William raised his chin a notch as if to bolster his courage.

Michael had to hand it to him that he was determined.

"Be back in half an hour," Tim said again, then motioned for Amelia to follow him.

As Michael walked away toward the small fort, William at his heels, he wondered what exactly he was getting himself into. The last thing he heard from the young woman behind him was "A horse? Oh, please, no, not a horse! Anything but a horse!"

Yup, he had to wonder what he'd gotten himself into.

He wondered even more when the four of them set off down the road to Northridge. Neither William nor Amelia had ever ridden before, and they needed all the help Tim and Michael could give them. Amelia seemed frightened of her uncle and clung to Michael, wailing for him every time her horse gave a little stumble or snort. Tim stuck to riding alongside William, a task Michael envied of him. William was a much better sport about the whole thing, and besides that, he didn't burst into tears like Amelia. The woman was a nervous wreck. If Michael got even a little ahead of her, she started screaming for him to wait and not leave her behind. Her voice was giving him more than a headache now.

This is the worst leg of the trip yet, Michael thought as the sun dipped low in the horizon, and they were still making painfully slow progress. He loved being on horseback; it was as natural to him as walking, but with these two—

Tim tried to hurry them up, but his efforts were futile. William tried, manfully, but his horse was getting the best of him. And Amelia? She screamed if the horse went faster than a walk and cried for Michael to help her before the horse killed her. More and more, Tim sent Michael sympathetic glances, even as he edged farther away from Amelia.

Darkness fell and still they struggled on.

"How far to the ranch?" Michael asked Tim, coming up alongside him after a time.

"Were I by myself, I woulda been home by now." Tim squinted through the darkness. "You know that big rock we passed here a spell back?"

Michael nodded, then realized Tim couldn't see the movement in the darkness. "Yeah?"

"That marks about the halfway point to the ranch."

"What?" Michael had hoped they were doing better than that. He was exhausted after all the strain of the journey and the sleepless nights on the stage. All he wanted was to curl up somewhere and sleep for a couple of weeks. And they were only a little over halfway there!

"Well, best keep a move on it then," he muttered, spinning his horse around as Amelia shrieked his name for what must have been the hundredth time.

Michael lost track of time as they pressed on over all kinds of terrain; hills, plains, creek beds. The night took on a chill that stood in stark contrast with the afternoon's blazing heat, and Michael was soon shivering. *I sure do hope Nathan actually is at the end of this road,* he thought. It would be unbearable if, after all this struggle, Nathan disappeared on him yet again. A real disappointment.

"I think we've gone about as far as we can for one night," Tim said at last, riding over to Michael. Near as Michael could tell, it was past midnight. "It's still a couple hours ride to Northridge, and that's iffen you're a good rider. And I don't know if you noticed, but those two have been slowin' down, *even more*, this last hour."

Michael had noticed. They had been going slowly before, but now they seemed to be crawling.

"I know the rancher who lives over yonder." Tim nodded to a shadowy outline of buildings that Michael had failed to notice. "Dave Norris will let us stay overnight."

"Sounds good to me." A part of Michael was tempted to leave the others and ride ahead, but common sense told him that was unreasonable. It was the middle of the night, and Nathan wasn't even awake. Not unless he was crazy like them, and that would have to be pretty crazy.

"Bed sounds mighty good," Michael said, turning in his saddle to hurry Amelia along.

Chapter
36

I wonder why Amelia Burton and Mr. Myers aren't here yet.
Brittany peered through the early morning gloom, worrying over what might have happened to them. They should have arrived by now, and knowing Mr. Myers, he would have made it back as quickly as he was able. And yet here it was hours after they should have been safely home, and still there was no sight of them. At least Mrs. Myers was still sleeping, so that was one less person pacing the floors.

Brittany turned back to the stove, where breakfast was cooking, and tried to turn her attention to something besides Mr. Myers and Amelia's nonappearance. Her mind jumped instantly to Nathan, a troublesome habit it had developed recently. Her heart still sang whenever she thought of their conversation two nights before when he'd told her that they were now fellow believers. The joy of it more than made up for the hurt of the days before.

She kept remembering the look on his face after she'd said that he couldn't have given her any better news. It was a look that had set her heart pounding, both with fear and excitement. She'd held her breath, waiting for him to speak, watching as he opened his mouth—then promptly shut it. He never did say exactly what he'd been thinking, just looked down at his feet, then changed the subject by asking if she still planned to leave on September first.

She hadn't wanted to talk about her upcoming departure, but she'd dredged up a smile anyway and said that, yes, she would be leaving on the first. And Nathan had simply nodded, not even saying that he'd miss her.

Brittany gave her head a fierce shake. Why *should* he tell her he'd miss her? Her leaving wasn't going to affect his life much. Work on the ranch would still go on, and he'd be busy with the upcoming cattle drive. Probably too busy even to think of her. If only she could push him out of her mind so easily.

Brittany poured some pancake batter onto the pan, wishing that they had butter to put on top of them at breakfast. It was too bad that with all the cattle Mr. Myers owned, none of them were milk cows. She remembered when she first arrived and innocently asked how much milk they got on the ranch. Mr. Myers had exploded.

"None," he'd said. "We ain't a milking parlor here. We raise beef, not milk, and if I made any of the boys milk one of those critters out there, I'd be left without a single hand by sundown."

Milk was not a commodity around here, she'd learned, although she still didn't see why everyone had such an aversion to the idea of milking a cow.

Brittany set the bowl of pancake batter down onto the table. She heard the sound of boots on the porch, and her mind instantly jumped to Mr. Myers and Amelia. *It's about time,* she thought, hurrying to open the door for them.

But as she opened the door, she found not Mr. Myers but Able Zimmerman.

"Miss Haines." He doffed his hat to reveal gray hair thinner and stringier than ever. "I couldn't wait to talk to you. You got a minute?"

"Uh—" Brittany looked from the stove to Able. "I suppose, but it'll have to be fast. I'm cooking breakfast right now."

"It'll only take a minute, one minute."

Brittany stepped outside and closed the door so that their voices wouldn't wake Mrs. Myers or the children. She wrapped her arms around herself against the early morning chill and nodded for him to begin.

"Miss Haines." Able twirled his hat around in his hands. "I reckon you remember the day we first met."

Brittany nodded. She doubted she would ever forget it, the day of her first proposal.

"Well, I gotta admit, I was too quick that day, askin' you to marry me. Rueben helped me see that."

Rueben? Brittany felt herself stiffen. What did Rueben care about Able's attempt to marry her?

"Miss Haines, Brittany, I've kept quiet for a long spell, waitin' for you to come to love me, and in that time my love for you has grown a hundredfold. I know you're plannin' on leavin for the city here in a few days, but I want to ask you to reconsider. Please, Brittany, I love you, and I can't imagine spending the rest of my life without you."

Brittany stared back at Able, horrified. She had thought Able was over his romantic notions. But he'd been biding his time, waiting for her to come to love him?

"No. Oh, no." She stumbled back a step, her back hitting the wall of the cabin. "Mr. Zimmerman, I—"

"It's just Able, darlin'."

"Mr. Zimmerman, I–I never dreamed you felt this way. I—"

"Course I did. I've loved you like nobody else ever will. Ever." He grinned at her. "Come on, now—tell me you love me and will become my little wife."

Brittany felt as if she were being smothered slowly but surely. "Mr. Zimmerman, I'm afraid you've read things wrong. I don't care for you in that way—"

"Pooh." Able waved his hand. "You're too young to understand how you feel. Trust me, darlin'—I know how things are between us, and I'm older and wiser than you."

"Actually, I *do* know how I feel," she said with all the firmness she could muster. "I do not wish to be your wife. I don't love you like that." Nor did she have the respect that a wife should have for her husband. Let alone trust or admiration or love!

"You've deluded yourself." Able's grin remained undimmed.

"I don't think I have."

"Sure, you have. Don't you feel something when we're together?"

She sure did, but it was more of a nervous, on-edge feeling rather than love. "Mr. Zimmerman, I cannot and will not marry you."

"Can't?" Able's face went cold. "Are you engaged to someone else?"

"No, but—"

"There! You can marry *me*, you see?" The self-confident grin returned to his face.

"No, I can't marry you because I do not believe we would have a healthy marriage were I to agree to be your wife." Brittany

338

stopped him even as he started to interrupt her. "Marriage is not a decision to be made in a moment. It lasts for life, and I will not marry a man unless I intend to commit the rest of my life to him. I can't put the rest of my life in your hands when I am afraid of you and don't trust you. Nor can I ever consent to marry a man who doesn't share my beliefs in the Lord."

"What are you talkin' about? I believe in God."

"That's good, but knowing about God is a far different thing than knowing *Him*. I want to marry a man who lives each day of his life in constant awareness of the Lord and who relies on the Lord in every choice he makes. I want a man who belongs first and foremost to the Lord, not a man who only prays to God when he finds it convenient."

Able stared at her, then threw his head back and laughed. "You think you'll really find a man like that? Some weak, womanly man that'd be. Look—here in the real world we gotta use our brains and brawn to push our way through to success, not just fall flat out over every little thing, hoping that the God up in the clouds will bend down and help. I'd feel downright sorry for you marryin' such a man."

Brittany lifted her chin slightly. "That is my choice, Mr. Zimmerman, so I ask you to please leave now."

A completely different look came to his face now. "Don't tease."

"I'm not teasing. I'm serious."

"Look." He took a step closer to her. "I've been waitin' for you, lettin' you have some time to think through this, but you can't think I made all those trips here through the cold last winter and all the busyness this summer for nothin', huh? You're supposed to marry me."

"I never told you I would!"

"Then why'd you lead me on?"

"I did no such thing!" Brittany wished he would back up a little. "You never said a word about marriage. You never even asked if you could court me!"

"Course not! We had to sneak around your contract, you see. But you knew what we was doin'—I know you did—so now stop bein' coy and tell me you'll marry me."

"Leave!" Brittany realized she was shaking. "Leave this moment!"

"You gonna make me?" Able didn't move, just grinned at her lazily. "I know Myers ain't here right now. Who's gonna make me leave?"

Brittany's heart pounded even more wildly, realizing that he knew Mr. Myers wasn't home.

"I'm ain't goin' nowhere without you." He took another step closer.

"Hold it, Able," a different voice said. "I'd advise you to move back real slow and easy-like and get out of here if you know what's best for you."

Brittany looked behind Able, where the voice was coming from. Nathan! He stood at the bottom of the steps, his hands hanging loose but his body tense as if he were prepared to charge onto the porch and tackle Able if that was what it took to get the point across.

Able whirled around, his attention diverted from Brittany. "I know what you're doin'!" His face reddened to the tip of his long nose. "Rueben told me all about you, and let me tell you that *you're* the one who better clear out of here!"

Nathan stood without budging. "Don't make this difficult, Able," he said, his voice low and controlled but with an edge of warning to it.

"You want her for yourself, I know, but you ain't gonna be gettin' her!" Able shook his fist at him. "She's mine, and I'm not goin' to let you sneak off with her! You can just forget you ever laid eyes on her, Nathan Lindale, and quit your troublemakin', 'cause she ain't marryin' you!"

"That's neither here nor there." Nathan looked back at him evenly. "The point is that she has chosen not to marry you, so I'm giving you two choices. Either get out of here, or I'll *make* you get out of here."

"Somebody's gettin' out of here, but it ain't me!" In two strides, Able crossed the porch to stand in front of Nathan. His whole frame quivered. "Get out of here while you're still in one piece Lindale."

"Don't do anything rash, Able." The lower Nathan's voice got, the more dangerous he sounded.

"Get out of here!" In a flash, Able swung his fist at Nathan, but Nathan ducked it.

"I'll teach you!" Able drew his fist back for an all-out attack.

"Able, knock it off!" another voice rang out, and Brittany swung around to see none other than Rueben Pierce standing not far behind Nathan. She was sure her jaw must have dropped. Rueben was the last man she'd expect to appear in her defense.

Able's fist fell, and he stared at Rueben. "What are you— why—?"

"Nathan's right." Rueben moved in closer. "The lady has spoken, and it's time for you to git."

"You—you can't do this to me!" Able seemed stupefied by the sudden attack from his ally. "I thought you was my friend!"

"Git," was all Rueben said.

Able's gaze slipped from Rueben to Nathan, then back again, his face staining bright red. "So that's the way it's gonna be," he said in a voice that was almost a hiss.

His right hand went to his side, and whipping out a pistol, he pointed it at Rueben. "Git out of here, both of you, before I have to use this!"

Rueben didn't move. "Put it down, Able."

"No! I said git out of here!"

Brittany could see that neither Rueben nor Nathan had a gun with them, putting them at an obvious disadvantage.

"Are you gonna git or not?" Able asked, swinging the gun from Rueben to Nathan.

Nathan didn't flinch, but the sight of the gun aimed at him made Brittany feel weak. Just one movement of Able's finger, and Nathan would die.

Lord, please help us! Rueben and Nathan were only trying to help me. Please send us help—

A sudden idea sent something like a jolt through Brittany. Of course! Why hadn't she thought of it sooner?

She glanced at Able, but his attention was still centered on the two men in front of him. Slowly, silently, Brittany crept along the wall to the door. Just two more steps, then one, and then her fingers closed around the door handle. Keeping an eye on Able, she turned the handle and pushed the door open just enough to slip through, praying that the door wouldn't squeak or the movement catch Able's attention.

Another step and she was inside. She reached above the door where Mr. Myers kept his rifle and pulled it down, carefully keeping her fingers back from the trigger. The wooden stock felt smooth and cool beneath her fingers—and dangerous.

Pointing the barrel of the gun at the floor, Brittany slipped outside again. The three men were still in a deadlock. She had the impression that Able didn't really want to shoot Nathan or Rueben, and he was trying to use the gun merely to cow them. But it wasn't working, and Brittany feared that his fingers were going to slip on that trigger.

"Mr. Zimmerman." Her voice sounded high pitched but otherwise steady.

Able glanced back at her, then stared at the gun in her hands. "What are you doin'?"

"I asked you to leave, as did these men." Brittany stared hard at him, feeling a trickle of sweat run down her neck despite the cold. "Please leave now, Mr. Zimmerman."

Able stared from her to the gun. Then his lips curled into a sneer. "A woman of your delicacies wouldn't use that thing, now, would you?"

Brittany hoped he couldn't see how terrified she truly was. "Sometimes drastic circumstances call for drastic measures."

Able's eyes went cold as he looked at her, and it was all Brittany could do to keep from flinching.

"I take back what I said." Able glared at her. "I wouldn't marry you iffen you was the last woman on earth. You little spitfire—"

Able spewed off several other uncomplimentary names and swiveled the pistol around at her. Brittany's heart lodged in her throat at the sight of the gun's eye pointed at her, but then Nathan made a mighty bound up the steps and grabbed Able by the collar of his shirt. Able's pistol went off, the bullet whizzing harmlessly past Brittany and slamming into the wall of the Myerses' cabin.

"Let go of me!" Able fought under Nathan's grip, but Nathan didn't relax his hold.

"You miserable, cowardly villain!" Nathan tightened his hold on Able, giving the man a hard shake.

Able writhed and rammed an elbow into Nathan's side, then kicked at Nathan's shins. Nathan still refused to let go of him, and Brittany thought he was trying to get the pistol out of Able's hands.

Then Able flung his head backward, smashing it into Nathan's face, and Nathan let out a muffled yell. His hold on Able slipped, and breathing heavily, Able half turned around, smashing his balled-up fist into Nathan's face.

Nathan staggered back a step, still gripping Able by the collar, and Brittany gasped as he stepped right over the edge of the porch stairs into thin air.

He fell backwards, still holding onto Able and dragging him down with him. The two men hit the ground with a terrible thud, Able landing on top of Nathan.

Brittany let out a half-smothered scream as Able rolled off Nathan and aimed the pistol at him. Before he could fire, Rueben leaped forward and slammed into the man, knocking the gun from his hands.

"You've gone too far, Able!"

"Don't kill me!" Able raised his arms to protect his head from Rueben's blows. "I didn't kill anybody!"

"You sure *could've!*" Reuben said, not letting up on his attack.

"What's going on?" yet another voice thundered out. Brittany whirled around. Mr. Myers! And *three* other people?

Rueben looked away from Able just one second, long enough for Able to gather his legs beneath him and take off running across the yard toward his horse.

"Don't you ever show your face around here again!" Rueben hollered as Able threw himself onto his horse. "And if you do, you'll be dealin' with me!"

Able needed no further warnings. He tore off down the lane at a gallop.

"What's going on?" Mr. Myers asked, his eyes narrowed.

Brittany glanced at Rueben, who still looked mad as a fighting rooster. Then she looked at Nathan, lying at the bottom of the porch steps, making no effort to get up. And when she looked at the gun in her own hands, she realized what a sight they must be.

Her gaze snagged with the eyes of a young woman on a horse, obviously Amelia Burton, and the expression of pure horror and disapproval on her face confirmed Brittany's realization.

The door of the cabin opened, and Mrs. Myers appeared in the doorway, a robe pulled on over her nightgown and her head still covered in a nightcap. She was coughing, and Brittany gasped as smoke trailed out of the open door along with the smell of something burned.

"My dear," Mrs. Myers said around her coughing. "I believe you left something on the stove."

"My pancakes!" Brittany's hands flew to her face. "Oh, my! I'm so sorry!"

Mrs. Myers looked around at everyone, her eyes settling on the gun in Brittany's hands. "What's going on out here?"

It was all so ludicrous that Brittany started laughing. Everyone turned to stare at her, and then she realized with dismay that she was actually crying.

CHAPTER
37

For several minutes after falling off the porch, Nathan had no clue as to what was going on around him. The fall knocked the wind clean out of him, and Able tumbling down on top sure hadn't helped. That man might be skinnier than a bean pole, but he had some weight, and he packed a powerful punch. His face hurt like fire after Able's blows, and he could taste blood.

As he began to catch his breath again, Nathan was aware of somebody raining down threats on Able. It sounded almost like Mr. Myers, but that wasn't possible. Mr. Myers wasn't home yet. He also heard someone crying and thought it sounded like Brittany. He felt his anger at Able kindle once again. How dare that man try to force Brittany into marrying him! And what's more, the man had pointed a gun at her! That fact doubled his rage. He longed to give Able a thrashing he'd remember for a long while, and he would, too, just as soon as he caught his breath.

He heard a man's footsteps coming toward him, and he struggled to sit up, but it seemed to take a lot of effort. He couldn't even get himself propped up on his elbows before the man reached him.

The man dropped to his knees beside him and reached out to touch his shoulder. "Nathan?"

Nathan felt a sudden jolt run through him. He could have sworn— But no, that was impossible.

The man's face filled his vision, and Nathan's heart pounded double-quick. The face that hovered over him, the lines of it drawn in concern around worried eyes, was his pa's. Impossible! His pa was miles away in Texas, not here at Northridge.

Nathan shut his eyes, blocking out the face, then slowly opened them again. He was still there, unmoving. *I have to be dreaming*, Nathan thought, but the hand on his shoulder was warm and solid, and Nathan's heart was still pounding hard enough to be heard from the bunkhouse.

"You all right, Nathan?" his pa asked, Texas accent just as heavy as ever.

No, he *wasn't* all right. He feared he was losing his mind. Everything rational told him that it was not his pa here at his side, but his eyes said that it had to be true. The face was just as he remembered it, a few more lines, the hair a little grayer, but still the same. And the voice— Nathan shivered. That was his pa's voice, all right.

"Pa?" Nathan hated the way his voice shook.

"I'm here, son." Michael eased back a bit, some lines on his face smoothing. "You all right?"

"I think so." His face hurt like crazy, but he didn't think there was anything much wrong with him besides that. If he could just stand up, he would be fine.

His eyes caught with his pa's, and another shiver coursed through him. Pa didn't look angry. He didn't look accusing either. But he did look serious, and Nathan could feel himself start to shake. *There's nothing to be scared of,* he scolded himself, but his body wouldn't listen.

Nathan was the first to look away. He struggled again to sit up, and without a word, his pa slipped a hand behind his back to help him. *What is he doing here?* Nathan wondered, finally accepting that his pa was indeed here, though it still made no sense.

"Nathan, are you hurt?" Brittany appeared behind Michael. She seemed more composed now, and she had set down the gun.

"I'm fine." To prove it, Nathan pulled himself to his feet. He felt a little dizzy, but he wasn't sure if that was from getting hurt or from the shock of seeing his pa again, and he didn't intend to let on about it.

"You're bleeding." The expression on Brittany's face told him that he must look pretty awful.

Nathan shrugged her concern aside. "I'm fine," he said again, fully conscious of his pa still beside him. "Where's Able?"

"Gone. Thanks for coming when you did. That man—" Her shiver said more than words.

Mrs. Myers called to her, and she turned away before he could reply.

Michael shifted, and Nathan looked at him. Or rather, at the top button of his shirt. He didn't want to meet his pa's gaze.

"Is there somewhere we could talk?" Michael asked.

Nathan nodded and motioned for his pa to follow him to the barn. His heart began to race again, and somehow, even though his hands were sweaty, his mouth felt dry.

They walked in silence for a moment before Michael said, "Your nose is still bleeding." He reached into his pocket, and pulling out a handkerchief, handed it to Nathan.

Nathan mumbled his thanks and started to put it against his face when he saw the corner of the handkerchief. There, embroidered in delicate letters, was the brand of his pa's ranch. It had been so long since he'd seen it, or his mother's needlework, that it gave him a start for a moment. It seemed a pity to ruin her work, but he pressed it under his nose anyway. The handkerchief had his pa's own special scent, and without warning Nathan felt the back of his eyes begin to burn.

A heavy silence fell between them, a silence Nathan had never experienced with his pa before. This silence was heavy with years of absence, years of pain and heartache, years of regrets and wishing, bitterness and grief. Nathan tried to think of a way to break the silence, but he couldn't form the right words. He'd always been confident, both as a boy and a young man, but all that confidence fled from him now.

"I suppose you're wondering why I'm here," Michael said at last.

Nathan took a guess. "Jeb?"

"He told me you were here, yes."

Nathan took a deep breath. There was only one thing he could say. "Pa, I'm sorry. I'm–I'm sorry about everything. I shouldn't have disobeyed you, and I shouldn't have run away, and—" he paused, struggling to overcome his emotions enough to continue. "I'm so sorry about Evan. I didn't mean to hurt him."

Michael shook his head slowly from one side to another. "You already asked me to forgive you."

"I know." The burning behind his eyes grew stronger.

Michael heaved a deep sigh. "Nathan, I was wrong. I shouldn't have yelled at you like I did, and I should have told you that I–I forgave you." He turned to look at Nathan, his eyes glistening.

"Can you forgive *me*? You weren't the only one who did wrong that day." He laid a hand on Nathan's arm. "I love you, son."

Nathan stared at him, uncomprehending for a moment. Then everything inside him seemed to break open at once.

"Oh, Pa." Tears that he could not stop blinded him as he fell into his pa's open arms. "I thought you hated me after what happened."

"Nothing you could *ever* do could make me hate you," Michael said, and Nathan realized that he was weeping as well.

It was several minutes before Nathan pulled back, trying to get himself under control again. "So what brings you here to Wyoming Territory?"

"I told you. I was looking for you."

"For me? That's the only reason you came here?" Nathan couldn't hide his shock. It was a long, arduous trip from Texas to Wyoming Territory. He knew from experience.

"It was worth it." Michael looked deeply into his eyes. "I have a feeling my prodigal won't be running off from me anytime soon."

"Lord willing, I'll never run again." Another tear leaked out despite Nathan's struggle to restrain it. "Not more than a few days ago, Johnny explained to me how useless running is. He also explained what grace means, and I finally understand what it means to accept God's forgiveness." He smiled tentatively. "Do you know that I actually have a letter at the bunkhouse that I was going to send to you and Ma with the next mail?"

"You were?" Michael reached for him again. "Then God answered my prayers. He has been working in your heart. Do you know that I was scared stiff the whole way here that you weren't even going to talk to me?"

"I can't say as I blame you. I've been pretty stubborn, all right. Just ask Johnny or Clem."

"You've been living here the whole time?"

"Pretty much. And I've been miserably homesick."

"Then why didn't you come home? Did you really think I was never going to forgive you?"

The look of pain in Michael's eyes made Nathan's own heart ache. "I'm sorry, Pa. I—"

Michael stopped him. "It's all right, Nathan. You don't need to keep telling me you're sorry. Let's just try to forget about the past and all those hard years."

Nathan nodded. That sounded just fine with him.

Michael looked down, pushing at a clod of dirt with the toe of his boot. When he looked up, his eyes held an expression Nathan couldn't read. "Would you consider coming back to Texas with me?" he asked. "I'd like it if you came home."

Nathan was caught off guard. "You would?"

"Of course. Our family isn't complete without you."

It was like the words out of a dream. Nathan found himself nodding. "Sure. I'll come home. But I'll have to talk with the Boss first. I believe he's planning on me for the cattle drive coming up, and I might not be able to get away for another couple of months. I can't leave him shorthanded."

"That's my boy." Michael smiled at him, a smile that warmed Nathan clear through. "Your ma's going to be real glad to see you again. Not to mention Maryanne."

"Is Maryanne still as much of a tease as ever?" Nathan asked, smiling despite the pain as he realized how many years he'd missed out on.

"Would she be Maryanne if she didn't tease? I think her fiancé gets picked on the most nowadays, though."

Nathan started. "Fiancé? Little Maryanne?"

"Not so little now. She's eighteen, going on nineteen."

About Brittany's age, Nathan realized.

"I've lost track of the years." Nathan forced a laugh. Unexpectedly, a little edge of uncertainty crept in on him. He could picture Maryanne only as the little girl with flying braids and dancing eyes. But she had grown up during the years he'd been gone and had undoubtedly changed. And if not even his little sister had remained unchanged by the eleven years he'd been gone, how many other changes had taken place at home?

He pushed his feelings aside before he could dwell on them. The important thing was that Pa was here—and had forgiven him. Jeb had been right, after all. Despite all the chances Nathan had given his pa to forsake him, Pa still loved him.

Brittany felt that she finally had herself in hand when Mr. Myers helped Amelia Burton off her horse and up the porch steps. She knew she didn't look her best and that her face must be tear-streaked, but given all that happened this morning, that fact didn't bother her like it might have earlier.

Amelia didn't look at her prime either. Her emerald green traveling dress was rumpled and dirty, her hair was coming loose from its bun, and the frown on her face gave her a pinched look.

"Amelia, how good to see you," Mrs. Myers said, but her smile wavered. "How was your trip?"

"Awful." Amelia shook out her skirts. "We had to travel long into the night, and we finally stopped at this tiny little cabin to spend the rest of the night there. And traveling by horseback, oh, but it was awful!" She shuddered delicately.

Mrs. Myers murmured something sympathetic, but Brittany's attention was caught by a man behind Amelia. The young man was struggling to untangle his foot from the stirrup, and as he looked her way, her heart jumped into her throat.

"William!" Brittany ran towards him, unable to believe her eyes. "What are *you* doing here?"

"Hello to you too." William freed his foot, then turned his full attention on her. His face was furrowed in concern. "Brittany, what just happened back there?"

Brittany bit her lip. "There was a man, Able Zimmerman, who wanted to marry me, and he was too pushy, so Nathan and Rueben tried to make him leave. That's all there was to it."

William frowned. "Do things like this often happen around here?"

"Oh, no! Usually it's very quiet."

William shook his head slowly. "Now, Brittany," he said, taking on a tone as if he were scolding a child. "I don't think your aunt would like to know that such things are going on out here. And as your friend, I must advise you against remaining in such a place where you are in peril."

"But I'm *not* in peril. I'm just as safe here as I am in Des Moines." *Maybe even safer,* she thought. Here at Northridge she knew everyone, and she knew that each of the men, whether polished or rough, would gladly come to her rescue if necessary. Wasn't that just what Nathan and Rueben had done?

William opened his mouth again but was cut off by the sound of someone running toward them.

"Brittany, are you all right?" Clem stopped in front of her, taking her by the shoulders and staring down at her. "Rueben told me what happened."

"I'm fine," she said.

"Good." Clem crushed her against him in a tight hug. "If I ever get ahold of that man, he's going to wish he'd never been born."

"Clem, violence won't solve anything." Brittany's words were muffled against Clem's shirt.

"I still can't believe that cowardly wretch would do such a thing." Clem released his hold on her. "I'll try to restrain myself, little sister, but if Able knows what's best for him, he'll be steering clear of me."

Brittany stepped back from him and smoothed her hair, trying to regain a semblance of dignity. "I suppose you don't remember William Brown from Des Moines?" She motioned to William.

Surprise flickered across Clem's face, but he quickly regained his composure. "Can't say that I do. A pleasure to meet you, William."

"And you as well." William accepted his offered hand. "Brittany has told me quite a bit about you, all of it good, of course."

"She's mentioned you too." Brittany feared that Clem would choose now, of all times, to do some teasing, but to her relief he kept his mouth shut.

"So what brings you here?" Clem asked.

Brittany watched William closely, just as eager as Clem to hear his answer.

"I'm going to be pastoring a church here out West, and since I was passing through Wyoming Territory, I thought I would visit a certain friend of mine." William smiled at Brittany. "And anyway, her aunt asked me to check on her if at all possible."

"I see." Clem's gaze turned to Brittany, and much to her disgust, she could feel the heat blazing its way up her neck and to her face. She just knew what Clem was thinking, and it gave her an unsettled feeling, much like how she had felt when Aunt Ida and William's mother were matchmaking in Des Moines.

Clem turned back to William. "So you're a pastor, you said?"

"Yes. I was ordained a few months ago."

"Hmm." Clem seemed to be thinking quickly. "How long are you staying?"

"I suppose that depends." Somehow William's eyes caught Brittany's, and the look in them warmed her face even more.

"Well, since you're here, maybe Morgan and I should think about getting married sooner. It would save a trip to the fort, and we could have more of our friends at the ceremony. Besides," Clem said, grinning, "I wouldn't be at all opposed to getting married sooner."

William nodded. "I could certainly do that if you wish."

"I'll have to talk to Morgan, but if we were married in a week, would that work for you? Or do you plan to leave sooner?"

William tilted his head, then nodded once again. "A week should be fine."

Brittany smiled, hardly able to keep from dancing in place. It seemed that she would be able to attend Clem and Morgan's wedding after all. And William intended to stay for at least a week, giving them plenty of time to catch up with each other.

Her eyes snagged with William's, and he smiled too, telling her that he shared her joy. But then her gaze slipped past him, straining in the direction that Nathan had disappeared. The man he was with looked so much like him that he had to be his father. She caught herself and shook her head. What was she doing? It made no sense for her to be looking for Nathan while in the company of one of her very dearest friends on earth.

CHAPTER
38

Nathan studied the checkerboard in front of him and frowned. "This is the last time I go easy on you, young man." He wagged a finger at Lars. "You've got me trapped but good."

The boy grinned, obviously pleased with his success. "Go on. Make your move."

"You sure do enjoy beating me, don't you?" Nathan eyed the board, then carefully moved one of his pieces.

Lars began shaking his head. "Shouldn't have done that." With a quick move of his hand, he jumped three of Nathan's pieces and swiped them off the board. "Crown that one now."

Nathan stared at the board again. He sure hadn't seen that one coming.

Nathan moved another one of his pieces while stealing a glance across the porch at William Brown and Michael. He wouldn't have said that he was a great checkers player but he knew he could play better than he had tonight. The problem was, he was trying to listen to the two men on the other side of the porch, and he wasn't giving the game much of his concentration. He shrugged. At least he was making Lars happy.

"Your turn," Lars said, and Nathan looked down just long enough to move another piece.

William Brown. He sneaked another glance at the man and saw that he had changed into a new suit, a little wrinkled but otherwise in good condition. Nathan didn't usually think much about a man's looks. But now he studied William, noting his blond hair, his blue eyes, even the perfect shape of his nose. Nathan was pretty sure that William was what most women would consider handsome. And on top of that, he had impeccable manners and a friendly, easygoing character that made it hard for Nathan to dislike him. Until he thought of Brittany.

If Brittany loves William, then you ought to just step back and be happy for her, he told himself, but it was easier said than done. Just the sight of the man churned his stomach.

"Your turn again," Lars said. He followed Nathan's gaze. "You might do better if you stop watching William."

Nathan felt the heat rush to his face. Was he so obvious that even a nine-year-old boy could figure out what he was thinking? He stared down at the board and refused to let himself look in their direction again. But watching the board was about as discouraging as watching William. He was playing a failing game. Just as, he feared, he was playing with William.

With his attention back where it belonged, Nathan began to gain some ground again. Lars's pieces were all over the board, speckling it like a red rash, but Nathan managed to eliminate a few of them without losing any more himself. He was concentrating so hard on the game that he didn't hear footsteps behind him.

"Who's winning?" Brittany asked, and Nathan jerked around. She stood just behind him, looking at the board over his shoulder.

"Me," Lars said, shaking his head. "Nathan's mind isn't all here tonight."

Nathan flushed again, but Brittany laughed. "Is that your excuse for him or his excuse for himself?"

"Mine, but I think Nathan agrees with me."

Brittany laughed again, then turned away from them. "William, do you want to take a tour of the ranch?"

"Sure!" William jumped out of his chair.

"I want to come too!" Brenna jumped up from where she sat on the steps with her doll.

"Of course, you can," Brittany said, but Nathan noticed the slight frown that creased William's face. So he didn't like the idea of Brittany's little sister coming along, did he? Didn't he realize that the children were a part of Brittany and that he wouldn't be able to marry her without the children coming along?

Brittany started to descend the steps but then stopped and looked back. "Pardon me. Do you want to come along, too, Mr. Lindale?" She was looking at Michael, so Nathan knew she wasn't talking to him.

"No, thanks." Michael smiled at her in return. "Nathan already showed me around earlier, and my old legs tell me they'd rather stay where they are right now."

Brittany nodded, then looked at Nathan. "Nathan?"

William really had a pained expression on his face now, and Nathan was tempted to say that he'd be delighted to go along. Instead he found himself shaking his head. "No, thank you. I'm going to see this game through and beat Lars."

Lars grinned. "Not going to happen if you keep on like you are."

Brittany nodded again, and Nathan decided it was his own wishful thinking that made her look disappointed.

"Come on, William," she said, leaping off the last step. "If you want to see Northridge by anything but moonlight, we'd better hurry."

William took the steps two at a time and caught up with Brittany in two long strides. They fell in step with each other as if it were the most natural thing in the world.

Nathan stared after them, his emotions in a tumult. On the one hand he felt frustration with William. But that was tempered by knowing it wasn't William's fault if Brittany loved him more than Nathan. His own feelings for Brittany added to the struggle. He loved her, and the idea of losing her to another man right before his very eyes was a bitter prospect. William seemed like a fine man, a man who would treat Brittany like the treasure she was. But where did that leave him? He couldn't imagine ever caring for another woman as he did for Brittany.

Lord, he prayed, feeling as if his burden were about to overwhelm him, *help me. Help me to remember that You are sovereign over all things and You know who is best for Brittany to marry. Help me to accept whatever Your will is in this and to be willing to step aside for Brittany's happiness if I must. Help me to have wisdom, and help Brittany to have wisdom as well.*

He hesitated, then added, *And please, be with William too. If he is the man You have chosen for Brittany, please smooth the way for him and bless him.* He resisted the urge to throw in his own pleas that William somehow, miraculously, would change his mind about Brittany so Nathan would be the one she married. No, he couldn't order God around. He had to trust that He would work all things out as He willed, even if that involved pain for him.

"Your turn," Lars said, and Nathan looked down at the board. He was down to only a couple of playing pieces and was in a bad position. Again.

Without a word Nathan moved one of his checkers. As he looked up he happened to catch his pa's eyes. He was studying Nathan, and Nathan wished he knew what was going on in his mind.

"So what do you think?"

Brittany studied William's face, her heart sinking as she saw none of the love or appreciation for the land that she had come to feel over time. His face was blank, and as his eyes traveled over the ranch spread below them, a slight frown furrowed his forehead.

"It's small," he said. "And, well, it would be vastly improved by a coat of paint on everything. And a bigger house to replace that little hovel the Myerses live in."

Hovel? Brittany felt a stab of irritation with him. "It's big enough for five people. Who needs a big house anyway? It's just extra space to clean."

"Well, at least you wouldn't be cramped together like animals." William's words held just a touch of heat.

"In case you hadn't noticed, animals have as much room out here as they wish. They're free-range."

"That's another thing. Everyone around here just lets their animals run wild. Is it pure laziness that keeps them from building fences?"

Brittany felt her temper rising, and she cautioned herself to keep her tone kind. "Most ranchers have too much land to economically put up that much fence. And do the cattle do any harm roaming free?"

"It's just–different."

"Different isn't always bad." *He doesn't understand how things work here, so don't be snappish with him.*

She decided it was time to change the subject. "So you said that you were going to be pastoring a church here in the West?"

He nodded.

"That's good. Life here is different than back home, but I know you're going to love it after you've been here a while. At first I disliked how open the land is and how far it is from town, but that isn't so important now. I think Wyoming is beautiful, and even more, I've found out what it means to have true friends who will stand with you through thick or thin." Her mind flitted to Morgan, encouraging her to start a school. To Allie, getting ready to tackle Charley on her behalf. And Mr. Myers, who just that morning had shocked her by saying, his voice gruff, "You know, girl, you're a gem. Shore will miss havin' you here." And there was Johnny, with his gentle smile and free advice; and Nathan, who was always, it seemed, coming to her rescue.

"The people here have such a heart, William. You should be here when we all get together. We might not do it often, but when we do, no one's left feeling lonely. The feeling here is so different from the city. No one cares if you break society's rules, or how you look, or what you wear. They just accept you as you are. After you meet more people I'm sure you'll understand what I mean."

William stared at her for a moment, then began to laugh. "You misunderstand. My church is in San Francisco, which will definitely have a different feel than here in Wyoming."

It was Brittany's turn to be surprised. "Oh."

William laughed harder. "I wish you could see your face. You look so disappointed."

"You're sure you want to go to a city?"

"Of course. I'm a city boy, and that ride here to Northridge cured me of ever wanting to live in the country." He looked at her with raised eyebrows. "I thought you were going back to Des Moines."

"I am."

"Then why such strong sentiments against the city and such praise for life here?"

His question caught her off guard, and unexpectedly she heard Allie Bryan's voice whisper in her ear, *Is your heart still in Des Moines?*

Brittany shrugged, trying to rid herself of such unsettling thoughts. "Both places have their benefits, I guess." She turned away quickly, not wanting William to read her mind. "Let's go back. It's getting dark."

Brenna raced ahead of them, her arms full of wildflowers, leaving William and Brittany to make their way home at a slower pace. They fell in step together, and Brittany felt her shoulders relax again. This felt more like old times when she and William went for Sunday walks, always getting along well together. She couldn't understand why the two of them kept bickering tonight.

They were nearing the barn when William suddenly said, "Oh, disgusting!"

"What?" Brittany stopped.

"I just stepped in some—droppings of some kind." William wiped his shoe on the grass, his face screwed up in disgust.

Brittany looked at his shoe. "Looks like horse droppings. That's too bad, but at least it wasn't a cow pie. Those are even more of a mess."

William didn't answer, just continued wiping his shoe on the grass.

"You can wash it off when we get back," Brittany added. "It *does* come off."

"This is one of the problems of your open range," William said with a bite to his words.

Brittany's irritation flared once more. "For pity's sake, William, Wyoming isn't the only place with horse droppings. There are horses in the city as well, and naturally droppings follow the horse."

"Well, at least they're kept off the boardwalk."

"This isn't a boardwalk, in case you hadn't noticed. Around here you might say that we are the ones invading the horses territory. If you don't want to step in any droppings, keep an eye on where you're walking."

Brittany started to spin away from him, but William stopped her by putting a hand on her arm.

"I'm sorry, Brittany. I didn't mean to make you upset. This is just—" He paused, then awkwardly finished, "different."

Different. There was that word again.

Brittany made herself take a deep breath, letting out her frustration. "I'm sorry too. I didn't mean to get angry with you. It's just—I wish you would give this place a chance. You're right about it being different. It isn't the city, but it has its own merits, and I wish you would be more open to them."

William appeared to think for a moment, then gave a brief nod. "Fine. I'll try to see it through your eyes while I'm here, but you might have to help me sometimes."

"I'd be happy to. I *am* glad you're here, William. It's good to see a familiar face again."

William's customary smile returned in full force. "And I'm glad to see *you* again. Let's not waste any more time arguing while I'm here, all right? If we don't quite see eye to eye on something, let's just drop it and talk about something else. We've been apart for so long that we surely have plenty of other things to talk about without declaring war on each other."

Brittany smiled back. "That sounds good to me. I never have been able to win against you."

"Are you sure?" William tucked her hand in the crook of his arm. "As I recall, I've never been able to make you change your mind about anything. Not even what flavor of ice cream to get."

CHAPTER
39

Michael made his way to the fringes of the gathering, bumping shoulders with innumerable strangers along the way. It seemed to him that the whole community must have turned out to celebrate Clem and Morgan's wedding this evening. Nathan had introduced him to as many people as possible, but there were just too many names to remember. Even as the names entered one ear, they slipped out the other. No matter. He was enjoying himself despite being in a crowd of mostly strangers.

He spotted an unoccupied bench away from the crowd and sat down on it with a sigh, glad to get off his feet. He let his eyes wander through the crowds, searching until he found the one person he was looking for: Nathan. Brenna Haines had sweet-talked him into dancing with her; remarkable since Michael knew how much his son hated to dance. Now he could see them weaving through the other dancers, Brenna standing on the toes of Nathan's boots. Michael smiled. Nathan would make a good father someday. If he found someone to marry.

His eyes continued to follow Nathan, and for what must have been the one-thousandth time, he breathed a prayer of thanks that he had found his son again. The past week had been one of the best of his life, catching up with his son and working through the difficulties that an absence of eleven years and numerous heartbreaks bring. There were times when Michael could plainly see his little boy in Nathan, the boy with unquenchable confidence, a fine sense of humor, and complete adoration of his pa. But other times he found himself watching Nathan, like now, wondering just how well he really knew his son. Nathan had grown up over the years, and there were marked differences in him. He was a little quieter, a little more thoughtful, not so quick to throw all caution to the wind. He was a man now, and at times Michael had to wonder if they could reclaim the years.

"Mr. Lindale, do you mind if I join you?" Brittany Haines appeared beside him.

Michael smiled at her and moved over on the bench. "Of course. Have a seat."

She sat down with a sigh. "This feels good."

"Had enough dancing?"

She shrugged. "For the moment. I've been going all evening, and a breather seems good right now."

Michael had noticed that she was in high demand tonight. Every time she stopped dancing, a line of young men immediately formed, vying for her attention.

"Where's Nathan?" she asked.

"Your little sister convinced him to dance with her."

Brittany laughed. "Little girls sure do have a way of getting what they want."

"Speaking from experience, they have a way of getting a man to bend over backward for them if that's what it'll take to make them happy."

"That's a perfect way to describe it."

They fell to watching the other dancers, and Michael picked out the few people he knew by name. He saw Clem and his new bride go by, and William with Amelia Burton. Michael slanted a glance at Brittany, but she didn't seem to notice.

"There was a time I thought Clem was never going to find himself a wife," she said, her eyes on her brother. "It seemed one day he was talking about what a bother girls were, and the next, here he is getting married." She shook her head. "Funny how things change."

"How old is your brother?"

"Twenty-two."

Twenty-two. That was a year younger than Nathan.

Michael stole another glance at the young woman beside him. He and Nathan had talked about many things over the last week, but not marriage. Nathan acted disinterested, but Michael had noted the way he watched Brittany and how the expressions played across his face when she was around—especially if William was there too. And Michael could see signs that trouble might lie ahead. Two young men smitten by the same young woman was just asking for someone to get hurt. It wasn't Brittany's fault. She treated them both in an impartial way that made Michael wonder if she even noticed their interest.

Michael leaned back slightly. He would be glad to accept the young woman into his family if that's the way things went. She was kind and sweet and godly, everything he could wish for Nathan to find in the woman he married. But there was William. During their conversation on the stagecoach, William had made it sound like marrying Brittany was a sure thing. Michael wondered now if perhaps he had spoken too confidently too soon. But what did *he* know? William and Brittany seemed to get along well together.

It was a prickly situation, and one Michael didn't feel he could speak about with Nathan unless he brought it up first. But he had been praying, and that, perhaps, was the most important thing he could do just then.

Michael pulled his attention back to Brittany. "So where will your brother and his new wife be living?"

"They'll be living at the Norris ranch. Clem and Morgan's uncle are going to be partners."

"That's a good opportunity for Clem."

"And Dave Norris couldn't be happier about it. He and Clem get along well, and he says that it's about time a younger man stepped in to take over part of the ranching."

"I understand." Michael had realized himself lately that he wasn't getting any younger.

"Clem told Mr. Myers that he would be willing to keep working for him until the cattle drive is over since Mr. Myers was planning on him for that, but Mr. Myers said he didn't mind if Clem quit right now. He said he can find another man to fill in easily enough."

"It'll be good for him and his wife to spend their first weeks together."

Brittany nodded. "That's what they think. And I'm glad they had their wedding before I leave. I was afraid that I wasn't going to be here for it."

"When do you leave?"

"Just a few more days now." Brittany sighed, her gaze wandering about the crowd. "I'm going to miss it here."

The music paused, and as dancers rearranged, Michael saw Nathan pressing through the crowd toward them.

"How do you keep up with that little sister of yours?" Nathan asked Brittany, sitting down on the bench beside her.

"How did you get away from her?" she asked in return.

"Carson wanted to dance with her. Mark my words—those two are going to make a match of it one of these days."

"Could be. Carson is the kind of young man who finds something for his hand to do, then goes after it with all his might."

Nathan grinned at Michael. "Brenna informed us all a few weeks ago that her and Carson 'did a proposal' and are getting married when they grow up."

Michael laughed. "The things kids come up with."

At that moment his eye fell on one particular man in the crowd, none other than Rueben Pierce. Michael watched him, still finding it strange that with the whole country to roam, Rueben and Nathan had ended up working on the same ranch. Nathan said little about the man, but enough for Michael to know that the two of them had a difficult time getting along.

He felt himself tense as the man passed in front of them, but Rueben did nothing more than tip his hat to them and murmur, "Good evening." As he disappeared into the crowd, Michael glanced at Nathan. He, too, seemed to have been braced for the worst and stared after Rueben, his eyebrows knit in thought.

"That's one difficult man to understand," Brittany said, putting Michael's very thought to words. "He was the last person I would have expected to stand up to Able last week."

Nathan nodded but said nothing, still lost in thought. Before Michael could ask about it, Nathan suddenly said, "Speaking of Able, did you hear that he's selling out?"

"Selling out? Why?" Brittany asked.

"I guess that's obvious enough. Able's a coward at heart, and he's looking to be out of here before word spreads too far about that little incident last week. Don't know where he plans to go, but then, I don't really care long as it's a good distance from here. Or Texas," Nathan added almost as an afterthought.

"How big is his ranch?" Michael asked.

"Not as big as the Myerses' or the Bryans. And he doesn't have as large a herd, either, but it would be a good buy for someone starting out. Long as they fixed up the house." Nathan made a face. "It's a miracle Able never froze in that cabin."

The musicians announced one last dance, a reel, and Michael noticed several young men aiming toward Brittany. Nathan didn't move, and Michael decided to take matters upon himself.

"Why don't you two go along and dance?" he said. "I'm content to stay just where I am."

For a moment Nathan didn't seem to realize he was talking to him. Then a look of shock and something like panic crossed his face.

"Oh, no!" Nathan held up a hand. "I'm terrible at dancing. I—"

"Come on, Nathan." Brittany jumped up from her seat. "Stop making excuses."

"I'm not! I'm telling you the plain and honest truth." Nathan's eyes sought Michael's, pleading with him to grant him an escape.

But Michael took no pity on him. "Get along. If you can dance with Brenna, you can do it with Brittany."

"That's different," Nathan said almost under his breath.

"Well, if you really don't want to dance with me—" Brittany began.

"No, it's not—" Nathan stopped, shooting Michael one last glare. In one motion he rose to his feet. "Fine—let's go." He looked as grim as if he were being led to his own execution.

"Nathan, really," Brittany said. "If you don't want to—"

"No, come on." Nathan took her arm. "Just don't look at me if your feet are bruised tomorrow."

How can anyone enjoy dancing? Nathan felt as if he were going to break a sweat at any moment as he and Brittany joined the other couples lining up for the reel. He just knew that he was going to mess something up. The reel was a fairly simple dance, but that knowledge did little to ease his mind. If he did make a mistake, it would make him look even worse.

Nathan made sure that he and Brittany got a position at the end of the line so that he had plenty of time to warm up before they took their turn as the head couple. Johnny raised the bow of his fiddle, Grant Bryan took his place as the caller, and the music began, making Nathan's stomach twist into a knot.

Just keep calm. This isn't hard, he told himself, moving forward as Grant called to "Bow to your partner." He turned Brittany on the right-hand swing, then on the left. Linking hands, they circled clockwise, and Nathan risked a glance at Brittany's face. Judging by the way her eyes sparkled, she was enjoying herself. He stumbled and stepped on her toe, but even that failed to dim her smile.

"Sorry," he whispered.

She just laughed. "Nathan, you look like you're being tortured."

"Sorry."

"Sorry? For what? Smile and don't worry about making a mistake. You dance better than you realize."

But not as well as William, he tacked on. He'd watched William earlier, and what he saw left him thinking that if Brittany were to judge them based on their dancing, he would be a goner for sure.

Nathan kept an eye on the couples ahead of them. He and Brittany moved steadily closer to the front of the line until, at last, it was their turn to lead.

The call came to reel the set, and Nathan felt another attack of butterflies as he and Brittany parted to hook elbows with new partners. Brittany might laugh over getting her toes stepped on, but Amelia Burton might not be so gracious. He vowed to pay even closer attention to his dancing.

Nathan suffered his way down the row, grateful when, at last, he met up with Brittany again. They sashayed down the middle together, then parted on the call to "cast off." They met at the end of the line and linked hands to form a bridge for the other couples to pass under, and then it was over. The music came to a close, and Nathan breathed a deep sigh of relief. He hadn't done as badly as he thought he would, and getting away with just one dance in an evening was pretty good. Although *no* dancing would have been better.

Brittany looked at him, a smile playing across her face. "Sorry to make you go through such an ordeal."

"It wasn't an ordeal." Nathan's honesty got the better of him, and he said, "Well, not much anyway."

All around them, people began to gather their children up to go home, calling their goodbyes to one another. Both Nathan and Brittany remained where they were, silent, and Nathan wondered if she was just as reluctant as he was for the evening to end.

"When will you leave for Texas?" Brittany asked, her eyes still on the crowd.

"I don't know. After I get back from the cattle drive, I guess."

"Your pa will stay here that long?"

"No." Nathan shook his head. "I think he's getting anxious to get home to Ma and Maryanne. He'll probably be leaving soon, and I'll follow later on."

"Do you find that the closer it comes to leaving, the more you realize how much you'll miss it here?"

Her question caught Nathan off guard. He'd never even thought of missing Wyoming Territory. He'd never liked it here; it had seemed more like a prison away from home than anything. But now he looked around him, realizing for the first time that he was going to be leaving this land behind and the people he called friends.

"I—I guess I hadn't thought about it," he said.

One of Brittany's former students waved to them, and they both waved back. Nathan felt his heart constrict.

"I guess I *will* miss it here. I'll especially miss the people, people like Johnny and Clem—" Nathan let his voice trail off, but the thoughts kept coming. He *was* going to miss it here. Now that he knew he could return to Texas, Wyoming Territory didn't seem so imprisoning. Somewhere along the line his feelings for the place had changed without his knowing it.

"I'll miss it too," Brittany said, her smile wavering. "I'll miss teaching school, and I'll really miss my students. And the Myerses, they've become special to me as well—even Mr. Myers. I've found that he's not really as gruff as he seems at first. And I never thought I'd be saying this, but I'll miss riding Major too. We've worked out most of our difficulties by now."

Nathan looked down at her, wondering how she could think of Des Moines as home when she fit in so well here. Amelia Burton didn't fit here like Brittany. Amelia refused to set foot near the barn, and she looked down her nose at the men who worked for her uncle, considering them far beneath her. She wore dresses fashionable enough to go on an outing in Boston but entirely unsuitable for everyday work. If she was a sampling of what city people were like, Brittany would never be able to cope in such a place.

"I suppose you wouldn't think of staying?" he asked, careful about how he phrased the question. He didn't want to cause a flare-up the way Clem had just a couple of weeks before.

Brittany seemed to think about how to respond. "I love it here, but I love Des Moines even more."

He noticed her glance toward William, and he wondered if there was a flicker of doubt that crossed her face. If only she would realize that she and William did not seem to complement each other. Just watching them, William in his fine suit and Brittany in a simple dress, showed that. If she married William, he would undoubtedly treat her well, but would he really understand her?

And if William couldn't understand her, could the people of Des Moines or San Francisco?

"You belong here," he said, and with all his heart he meant it.

His words made her eyes widen. She started to speak, then seemed to change her mind. "Thank you."

Someone called her name and murmuring goodbye to Nathan, Brittany hurried away. He watched her go, and once more he whispered, "Lord, let Your will be done."

CHAPTER
40

You belong here.

Brittany pondered Nathan's words as she sat on the Myerses' porch an hour later. The yard was deserted now, and after all the noise earlier the quiet seemed deafening. The Myerses, Lars, and Brenna had gone to bed, and while she knew that was where she should be, Brittany felt too wound up to even think of sleeping. Here on the porch with nothing but the moon for company, she couldn't bother anyone with her restlessness, and she was free to sort through her thoughts in private.

Far away she heard the lonely howl of a wolf, and she shivered, not from fear but more from a sense of being in harmony with the nature around her. To live in nature's own backyard gave a person all kinds of experiences. Experiences she couldn't have in Des Moines.

Brittany frowned, wishing she could stop the plague of doubts she'd been feeling lately whenever she thought of Des Moines. Rather than the joy she'd expected, she felt dread. How was it possible to dread going home? Home was the one place where a person was supposed to feel safest, the most secure, the most natural. And yet those *weren't* the feelings she had about Des

Moines recently.

"Mind if I join you?" William appeared at the bottom of the steps, making her jump.

"William, I didn't see you coming."

"Sorry." William took a seat on the top step, leaning back against the support so that he could look at her. "Can't sleep?"

"I didn't even try."

"Me neither. There's nothing like a party to get a person's blood pumping."

They both fell quiet, and Brittany heard another howl in the distance. The silence between them felt strained, and it quickly threatened to become awkward.

"You know, you've changed, Brittany." William stared at his hands instead of her.

"What do you mean?" Brittany felt they might finally get to the heart of whatever had been standing between them since William's arrival.

"Well—" William hesitated. "Take the first day I came here, and you were standing on the porch with a gun in your hands. That isn't the Brittany I know."

"I was only doing what was necessary." Brittany felt herself stiffen. "I don't even know how to shoot a rifle."

"But that's not it. You just seem more—well, countrified."

"Countrified?" Brittany sat up. "And that's a bad thing?"

"I didn't say that! It's just—" William sighed and raised his hands. "See, we can't even talk like we used to. I wasn't trying to pick a fight with you."

Brittany eased back in her chair, but tension still seemed to crackle in the air between them. "I'm sorry for getting upset, William. What *were* you trying to say?"

William fiddled with a button on his jacket. It was a long moment before he looked at her, the usual twinkle in his eyes gone. "I suppose you know that my mother and your aunt have always wished for us to marry?"

"Yes." Brittany wondered why he was bringing it up.

"I wanted that too," he said, the words coming in a rush. "I had plans, Brittany. I was going to wait to ask you to marry me until after I was ordained, done with school, and then we would be married and go to our first parish together. I loved you, Brittany."

Brittany stared back at him, feeling immobilized by the shock of his words.

"Then you said you were leaving for Wyoming Territory, and I was in anguish. I wanted to beg you to stay, but I couldn't get the words out. Since it was only for a year, I decided to keep quiet about marriage until you returned, and I wrote to you, hoping you wouldn't find someone else while you were away. And I prayed a lot. Then, of course, I graduated and got my first church, and the only thing lacking in my dreams was you. So I came here to ask you to marry me."

"William," Brittany broke in. "I never thought—"

"No, I know you didn't. That was one of the things I loved about you. You were never like the other girls who looked at me as just a boy they wanted attention from. You saw me as a *person,* and even more than that, you were my friend, and you made me love you without even trying." William heaved a deep breath. "Brittany, if that's the way I felt, why can't we seem to get along?"

His question hung in the air. Brittany blinked back tears that suddenly wished to form. "I don't know. I never dreamed of marrying you. I always thought of you more as–as a brother."

"A brother?" William's eyebrow quirked.

"That's how I always felt."

"Hmm." William seemed to think for a moment. "So I take it that if I were to ask you to marry me now, you would say no?"

"I–I would have to decline. I simply can't marry my brother."

William's lips twitched. "That's one way of putting it."

Brittany felt some of her tension release. He didn't seem devastated by her refusal.

"I've been thinking lately—" William drummed one finger on his knee. "You're different, Brittany. It's not bad, just different. Or maybe you've always been this way and I just didn't see it. You seem much braver than you ever were in Des Moines. Something happens and you run to meet it. And you don't seem so concerned about what others think; 'society,' as you say. You seem to fit in with the people here, and I find that surprising. These people aren't the most cultured, you must admit, but you—" William stopped. "Do I make any sense?"

"I think so." Brittany's mind raced. Nathan's words whispered in her mind again—*you belong here.* Could that be true? She thought of all the things she had done while here in Wyoming, things that wouldn't be allowed in Des Moines. She rode horseback. She taught school to children who would otherwise have no opportunity to learn. She played doctor and put in stitches, and she chased cows from her clothesline. And even more surprising, now she realized that the things she loved most in Des Moines were the simple things. Gathering around the supper table with family and friends, working in Aunt Ida's garden, helping neighbors in need. Those were the things she enjoyed on the farm as a child and what she enjoyed now in Wyoming Territory.

"I do belong here," Brittany said, amazed. But even as she made that revelation, the satisfaction gave way to despair. "But it's too late! I'm leaving for Des Moines in just a few days!"

"Who says you have to?" William asked.

"Well, the Myerses already have Amelia here to help them, and I told Aunt Ida I was coming." Brittany clenched her hands together until the knuckles turned white.

"Talk it over with the Myerses. See if there's any way you could stay. And as both a pastor and a friend, I suggest you pray. If God wants you here, He will make a way for you to stay."

"I guess you're right." Brittany relaxed again. "But what about *you*, William? What are *you* going to do?"

"Do? Go to San Francisco, of course. I'll talk to Michael Lindale tomorrow and see when he plans to leave. I can't imagine traveling all the way to Fort Laramie by myself, but if he intends to stay longer than a few more days, I might have to do that." He grinned. "But I can tell you, I'm praying he'll be ready to go. I'm afraid my horse might get the better of me without him there."

"I'm sorry you traveled all this way for nothing."

"For nothing?" William rose and stretched. "That's not the way I see it. You're still my friend, and I'm glad I was able to see you again. Your aunt will also be glad to hear that you are doing well. And Brittany, I think you're right. We aren't meant for each other."

Brittany smiled. "I'm glad you feel that way."

"This journey has really grown my faith. I've realized that rather than trying to get God to approve of who I wanted to marry, I should have let Him make the decision in the first place. It sure would have made for a lot less anxiety."

Brittany understood. That was a lesson she was trying to learn herself.

William paused. "So if you aren't going to marry *me*, is there someone else on your mind?"

Brittany stared at him. "I didn't turn you down because of someone else. I—"

"I know—we don't fit. But some people seem to think highly of you around here, and I just wondered if you returned their feelings." William grinned. "What about Nathan? He seems like a good man."

Brittany felt a jolt run through her at Nathan's name, and she felt the heat rise to her face. "He doesn't care for me like that."

"Are you sure?" William made a move to leave. "Then why has he been treating me with icy politeness and staring at you like he was afraid you might disappear into thin air on him?"

"I think you're seeing things."

"I don't." William descended the steps. "Remember, Brittany. Pray. God knows where He wants you and who He wants you with."

Brittany stared after him, her thoughts and emotions churning. Did Nathan really care? And did she want him to care? William didn't know Nathan the way she did. How could he possibly know what Nathan was feeling when she herself couldn't guess?

Besides, Nathan had already said he didn't care for her, and he wouldn't have changed his mind in just a few weeks.

Brittany wrapped her arms tightly around herself as the questions whirled. Then, following William's advice, she bowed her head and began to pray.

CHAPTER
41

Nathan couldn't shake the sense of depression that clung to him as he worked the next day. Normally the beauty of creation around him chased away whatever gloom he was feeling. But today the beauty only reminded him that soon he would be leaving all this behind. Brittany's talk of missing Wyoming Territory had made the reality of leaving truly register for the first time, and now he couldn't stop thinking about it. He'd expected that the closer it came to leaving, the more anxious he would feel to get home to Texas. He had been pining for home all these years, and it was only natural that he would want to get there as soon as possible.

But that wasn't how he felt. Instead, his heart was heavier than it had been in a long while. And he had trouble falling asleep the night before with all the uneasiness suddenly swooping down on him. He couldn't even lay a finger on what was troubling him, except that whenever he thought of Texas, the pictures in his mind were blurred, unclear. It puzzled him. Always before, he'd been able to vividly picture his pa's ranch and the area around Grand

Forks, but not so now. He couldn't even remember the last time he'd had a dream about Texas.

And the things he did remember made him feel even more uneasy. Faces of people he'd known rose up to haunt him. Evan, and the Nelson boys who lived on the next ranch over. Mr. Hanson, a bachelor who frequently stopped by for dinner and a chat with his pa. Evan was gone, of course. Pa told him that both of the Nelson boys were married with families of their own now and that Mr. Hanson had sold his ranch and moved away. Time marched on, and nothing remained the same in its wake. It seemed that everything he remembered about Texas had changed, and it left Nathan feeling shaken. Could he fit in again in Texas, or had he changed too much?

Nathan reined Loner in and stared across the land. The only ranch visible from this side of Northridge was Able Zimmerman's. And even then, Nathan could just barely make out its shadowed shape in the distance. Not that he cared to see it any closer. Able had not done well at keeping up with the repairs, and the ranch was in deteriorated condition. One look at the cabin showed that he hadn't been a good builder in the first place.

Nathan looked beyond Able's ranch to the horizon and felt his heart dip even lower. He was going to miss it here. Somewhere along the line he had come to think of Wyoming Territory as home. Maybe it wasn't Texas he had been missing so much, but rather his family. And now he was restored in his relationship with his pa, he found that he was content right here—in the heart of cattle country in Wyoming Territory.

I don't want to leave, he realized. The thought failed to surprise him. He had been steadily working toward that conclusion for some time now.

But he couldn't stay. He had no choice. Pa was getting older, and while he still had more energy than most men half his age, he couldn't keep ranching by himself forever. The day was coming when he would need some help, and as his only remaining son, Nathan felt the responsibility fell to him. Besides, he'd already told his pa he would go, and he hated to back out on his word. Perhaps this was one way for him to try to make up for the past. Nothing could bring back the years he had lost by running away, but he could at least be there for him now.

He sighed and urged Loner forward again. He'd best just forget about how he felt. Even if he did stay here, he was going to lose a dream. He didn't make much as a cowboy, and while he had a little money stashed away, it wasn't enough to buy even a small piece of land. And if he couldn't own his own ranch, how could he ask Brittany to marry him? He would be working for someone else. And even supposing they could have their own house, he'd be working long hours away from her. There was just no way to get the best of all things.

And he couldn't even confide in his pa about all the doubts assailing him. Michael would feel bad, and it was no use piling all his woes on him when there was no apparent answer to the dilemma. It would be best to just keep his mouth shut and enjoy his time in Wyoming Territory while it lasted.

After supper Nathan left the cook shack and headed to Johnny's, where Michael was staying. But he stopped short as his eyes fell on his pa and William talking together on the porch.

Instantly his frustration with William flared. Couldn't the man be content with stealing Brittany from him?

Right on the heels of his anger he felt repentant. Brittany wasn't his to claim, so William couldn't be accused of stealing her. And Nathan couldn't claim all of his pa's attention either. If William wanted to talk with him, what was wrong with that? Michael seemed to like William well enough, and maybe, if it hadn't been for Brittany, Nathan would have too. As it was, he felt as if his face were going to crack from all the smiles he'd been forcing in William's presence lately.

He began to walk toward them, taking his time about it, not in a hurry to talk to William again. He was still nowhere close to them when William rose and, shaking Michael's hand, turned to leave. Nathan couldn't resist letting out a breath of relief. He wouldn't have to put up with William after all.

William headed toward the Myerses' cabin, passing Nathan along the way. He smiled, seeming unperturbed at seeing him. "Nice evening, isn't it?" he said.

"I suppose." Nathan forced yet another smile. In truth, he felt hot, tired, and dusty—and defeated. William was undoubtedly going to visit Brittany yet again while lately Nathan couldn't seem to find the time to say more than a handful of words to her. If he was that lucky. Some days he didn't even see her. It seemed that on every point Nathan could think of—dress, manners, dancing, visiting—William had him beat.

"Well, I'll see you," William said, realizing Nathan had no intention of saying anything else. He walked on, whistling, and Nathan had to fight back a wave of bitterness. He stood no chance against the man.

He turned back to Johnny's and quickened his pace, trying to forget about William and the million other worries threatening to drive him out of his mind. He took the steps two at a time, and Michael looked up from his writing.

"You look tired." He patted the seat next to him. "Long day?"

"Long enough." Nathan dropped into the chair his pa motioned to. "What're you writing?"

"Just a letter to your mother." Michael tapped the end of his pencil on his knee. "Although I'm not sure that it'll make it home before me."

Nathan felt his heart sink. "You're leaving soon?"

"I just talked to William, and he was wondering when I plan on leaving. He's eager to get on to San Francisco, and he was hoping I could travel to the fort with him. We decided to leave day after tomorrow."

The words were a blow. Nathan had known his pa would be leaving, but it seemed too soon to let him go. He swallowed hard before speaking. "I suppose you need to get home."

"I've been gone longer than I intended. There will be things to catch up on, and Maryanne's wedding is coming up in just a couple of months. I don't suppose you will be home in time for it?"

"I don't know. I can try—" Nathan still struggled to believe that Maryanne was really getting married. It was a change that unsettled him.

He shrugged his thoughts aside, afraid that if he kept pursuing that line of thinking, Michael was going to guess something was wrong.

"So William's planning on leaving?" Nathan hoped his pa would offer more information.

"That's what he said."

"Did he say if he's planning to—?" This question was harder to get out than he'd thought it would be. "Is Brittany going too?" He could feel the heat climbing his face, but he couldn't stop it.

"He didn't say." Michael kept studying the horizon, not his son, much to Nathan's relief.

Her contract is up by now, so if she doesn't go to San Francisco, it's to Des Moines. She's leaving either way. That thought joined all the others clawing at his insides.

"Have you talked to Brittany about how you feel?" Michael asked, still not looking at him.

Nathan felt a jolt of shock. "How—?"

"I guessed. She's a fine young woman, and I can see why you care for her."

Nathan pondered his pa's words for a moment. "So I guess I'm pretty obvious?" He was mortified to think that Brittany— and William—might have guessed how he felt.

"No, you hide it well. But I know you, Nathan, and you couldn't fool me for too long." Michael looked at him, compassion in his eyes. "Want to talk about it?"

Nathan heaved a deep sigh. "It's no use. She doesn't care that way."

"You asked her?"

Nathan stared at Michael. "Asked her? Of course not! She's in love with William!"

"But she didn't tell you that." Michael shook his head. "How can you be so sure about that if you never asked her how she felt about you?"

"Because—because—she said flat out that she would never marry a westerner. She didn't want Lars and Brenna to grow up to be like one, and she wants to go back to civilization rather than staying here in the wilds." The words spilled out, the memory stinging even now. "She said all that not too long ago."

"And are you sure she meant it?"

"Of course, she meant it. Brittany Haines never says anything she doesn't mean."

"But we all make mistakes, and maybe she made a mistake in saying that. From watching her this last week, it seems to me that she likes westerners well enough."

Nathan refused to budge on his position. "Anyhow, that was even before I told her that I didn't care for her. It was a mistake, but—" He shook his head. "And then there's William. He's so much better than me. How could I ever hope that she'd choose me over him? I mean, his life is planned and in order—" Nathan stopped, overpowered by his own helplessness.

"Nathan," Michael leaned forward. "One of the most important things in any relationship is honesty. I think you need to be honest with her about how you feel. The worst she can say is that she doesn't care for you in that way."

"I don't know."

"Trust me. You need to talk to her."

Nathan said nothing, but in his mind, he could picture it all too clearly. He would pour out his very heart to her, but Brittany would reply that she already loved another, William. And then she would feel bad, and he would feel even worse, wishing he'd kept his mouth shut.

"There's one more thing I wanted to ask you about," Michael said, interrupting the awful scenes running through Nathan's mind. "Do you want to return to Texas?"

Nathan slanted his pa a sideways look, wondering if his memory was slipping. "You already asked me, and I said yes."

"I know. But I wondered if that was still how you felt after you had some time to think about it."

Nathan's mouth felt dry, and his mind began to race, all his mental arguments from earlier kicking into full gear.

"I know things are different now, going back to Texas, and watching you last night, well, I realized that you fit in well here. You're probably having a hard time leaving. And after being away from Texas for eleven years, I wondered if you really did want to go back, or if you said yes too quickly."

Nathan stared at him, convinced that his pa must be a mind reader. "I like it here," he said, cautioning himself to be careful. "But I know you need help, and being with family again will be good." He stopped, afraid of betraying his true feelings.

"Being together as a family would be good. But about the help, that depends. Won't deny I could use your help, but you can't let that be what makes your decision. Maryanne's fiancé will be taking over part of the ranching, something we'd agreed on before Jeb told me you were here. There's still plenty of work for both of you, but if you'd rather not, I don't blame you."

His words sent Nathan's mind whirling. *Pa doesn't need my help?* The thought brought both release and a feeling of being lost. If his pa didn't need him in Texas, then he was free to stay. But what kind of a life would that be? He'd already thought through his options earlier, and none of them appealed. But now the thought of returning to Texas had lost whatever attraction it held before his pa's announcement. Maryanne's fiancé was undoubtedly a fine man, but three could be a crowd. He and Michael had already worked things out between them, and Nathan hated to barge in and demand that he be worked into the equation as well.

"So *do* you want to return to Texas?" Michael asked.

Nathan swallowed hard, torn by all the decisions. "I don't know. At first I was dead sure I wanted to return to Texas. I dreamed of Texas for years, longed for it. But then something happened, and I realized that maybe this is home to me more than Texas." Nathan waved an arm toward the land and color-painted sky behind him. "Pa, I can't figure out *how* I feel anymore."

"Have you been praying?"

"Yes, but I still feel no closer to the answer."

"Maybe this *is* His answer," Michael said softly. "I would love for you to come back to Texas with me, but more than anything I want you to be happy. You seem at peace here, and I've been wondering if maybe it would be a mistake for you to return to Texas." He shifted in his seat. "Have you thought at all about buying Able's ranch?"

"Able's ranch?" Nathan's shock rang in his voice. "But his ranch is in deplorable condition!"

"You could fix it up. I talked with Myers today, and I agree with him that its price will probably go low, given the shape it's in, and Able bein' in such a hurry."

The more Nathan thought about it, the more the idea appealed to him. But there was the matter of money. No matter how low the ranch might go, he knew he wouldn't have enough money.

His pa must have sensed his hesitation. "I rode past it today, just out of curiosity, and I know it will take a lot of work, but I think you're up to it. I say that you better give it some thought and make up your mind sooner rather than later before someone else takes it."

The conflict inside Nathan heightened. He knew what he had to say, but how he wished there was another way! "I'm afraid I can't buy it," he said, not meeting his pa's gaze.

"Can't?"

Nathan squirmed, hating to admit just how little money he had. "Working as a ranch hand doesn't make very much, and I don't have the money for such a big investment."

"I see. But if you did have the money, would you buy it?"

It seemed like useless dreaming to Nathan, but he answered honestly. "I guess I would. Like you said, I think it will go low, and it wouldn't take too long for it to pay the buying price back, not since it's already stocked with cattle."

"So you don't want to go back to Texas." Michael nodded slowly. "Tell you what—I say you use what money you have, and I'll cover the rest of the cost to buy the ranch."

It took a moment for his words to sink in. "Pa!" Nathan jerked upright in his chair. "You can't do that!"

"And why not?" Michael looked back at him evenly.

"Because that's a lot of money!"

"I figure I can spend my money as I wish. But how about this. You're a lot like me, Nathan, and I know that you won't feel that it's entirely yours unless you've paid for it. So you buy it, and when it's doing well and making a profit, you can pay me back some. But I want part of it to be a gift. You can consider it your inheritance." Michael smiled.

Nathan couldn't shake the feeling that it would be wrong to take such a generous offer. Especially considering how just a few weeks before, he and his pa had not even been on good terms.

"I don't deserve this," he said, his voice cracking despite himself.

"Remember what I said? No more dwelling on the past." Michael leaned forward and laid his hand on Nathan's knee. "Consider it a gift of love."

Nathan couldn't speak around the lump in his throat, but he gave a single nod, accepting his pa's offer, generous as it was.

"Guess we better be speaking to Able then." Michael gave Nathan's knee a slight squeeze. "And remember—talk to Brittany. Honesty above all else."

Nathan nodded again, his mind still spinning with all the new thoughts. "Pa, could you–would you mind praying with me?" he asked, feeling a desperate need for something solid to cling to.

"There's nothing that could make me happier," Michael said.

CHAPTER
42

Brittany couldn't keep from breaking into song as she went about her chores two days after her talk with William. Her future was still hazy, but she had talked with the Myerses, and they were delighted when she asked if there were any way she could stay longer. She felt guilty imposing on them like this, but Mrs. Myers told her, "Child, you're family to Tim and me, and we've been heartbroken at the thought of you and the children leaving."

Brittany glanced doubtfully at Mr. Myers, unable to connect him with "heartbroken".

He cleared his throat noisily. "Knowin' you, girl, you'll find plenty to do to earn your keep, and we'll be the ones who end up blessed by your stayin'."

Amelia seemed relieved by her staying as well. She was obviously used to the finer things of life and struggled with the daily grind of work. And Clem, well, when she first told him she was staying, he couldn't seem to take it in. After she repeated herself, the news struck, and Clem whooped loud enough to draw the attention of everyone on the ranch, then spun her around until she demanded that he put her down.

She was happy, and she knew Lars and Brenna were as well. The two children looked ready to cry with relief when she told them the news. Now she just had to find a way to break the news gently to Aunt Ida. Aunt Ida was not going to be happy. Brittany almost feared that she would hop on the first train west and travel to Northridge to bring them home. Brittany wouldn't put it past her, even if she was in her sixties. Aunt Ida would be especially upset when she heard that Brittany and William were not getting married. The benefit of sending the news by letter was that Brittany wouldn't have to be there when the fireworks went off.

Her feelings of deep-seated peace came in full force as she stood on the porch that evening, the ranch spread out in full view before her. This was home. How could she ever have disliked this land? And how had she come so close to leaving it behind? The thought made her shiver and breathe a prayer of thanks that she had seen her error in time. She only wondered how some, like William, could leave with no desire to stay.

She saw Nathan leaving Johnny's, and she waved. He waved in return; then, changing course, he came toward her instead.

Brittany could feel her smile widen even more. It seemed like forever since she'd talked with Nathan—*really* talked with him, not just said, "Hello," "How are you?" or "Nice evening." She had started to wonder if he were avoiding her.

"Do you have a few minutes?" Nathan asked, pausing at the bottom of the steps.

"Of course, I do. Come have a seat." Brittany motioned to the chair beside her.

He climbed the steps onto the porch but didn't sit down. He leaned back against the railing, fidgeting with his hat. It wasn't like him to be nervous, and questions began to rise in Brittany's mind.

"How's work?" she asked, thinking that some small talk might put him at ease.

"Well—" He fidgeted some more. "Actually, as of today I'm done working for Northridge."

"What?" Brittany stared at him. "You're fired?"

"No." Nathan smiled, seeming to lose some of his tension. "I quit."

The pieces fell into place. Michael was leaving with William tomorrow, and obviously Nathan had decided to go with them. A feeling of devastation swept through her. Here she had just decided to stay, and Nathan had come to tell her goodbye.

He was watching her, and Brittany knew that she had to act happy for him. She forced a smile but felt it wobble. "That–that's good. I'm sure your pa is glad you can go back to Texas with him."

Nathan frowned. "I'm not going to back to Texas; I'm staying here."

"Here?" Now Brittany was confused. "But you just said you quit."

"I did. I'm going to be running my own ranch now. I bought Able out today."

The news sank in. "You bought Able's ranch? But I thought you were returning to Texas."

"I was, but I've been praying and have realized that Texas isn't home anymore."

He's staying. The thought made Brittany's heart sing, and afraid of betraying her elation, she tried to think of something to say that would pull the conversation to safer ground. "How does your pa feel about you staying?"

"He could tell that my heart was here even before I did, and he's given me his blessing. It will take some work to get Able's, I mean *my*, ranch into shape, but it will come."

Brittany smiled and nodded, still scarcely able to think past her relief that he wasn't leaving.

Nathan cleared his throat. "Brittany," he said, the anxiety in his voice not matching the joy she thought he'd feel with the deed to a ranch in his hands. "I was wondering—could I ask you a question?"

Since when did he need her permission to ask a question? "Yes, of course."

Nathan kept his gaze fixed on a crack in the floor rather than her. "I know this isn't any of my business, but are you and William intending to get married?"

Brittany stared at him but couldn't read the expression on his face. "William? Oh, no—that would be a disaster. William is a dear, but we both realize that we don't fit together as anything more than friends."

He stole a glance as if not sure whether to believe her or not. "You're sure?"

Brittany couldn't hold back a laugh. "Of course, I'm sure! Why, this last week William and I have had more arguments than we ever had before."

"Arguments?" Nathan's gaze lifted to meet hers. "I thought for sure you were in love with him."

"I've always loved William, but only as a brother. And William has come to realize, too, that his love for me is different than a husband and wife's." Brittany felt her heart start to pound a bit faster. Was he asking out of idle curiosity, or did he have a deeper intention? "Besides, William is leaving tomorrow."

"I thought you might be going with him." Nathan drew a deep breath. "So if you don't care for William—" He paused, struggling to find the right words.

Brittany's heartbeat quickened still more, sure he could hear it from where he stood.

"I don't want you to go back to Des Moines," Nathan said, the words coming in a rush. "I know you said that was what you wanted, and I thought it would be best if I kept quiet and didn't pressure you into a decision, but I can't stand it any longer. I know I fall far short of men like William, but I love you, Brittany; have for a long time. And if you just give this land a chance, I'm sure you'll never want to leave. So if you give me a chance too, I will do my best to be a good husband to you—and I'll love you always. Would you please just think about marrying me? I can't stand to see you go."

He loved her and wanted to marry her? Brittany hadn't realized how much she wanted to hear those words from Nathan until that moment. She wanted to hug the words tightly to herself and treasure them, letting them sink in slowly, but the look on Nathan's face told her that his suspense was mounting with each passing second.

"I'm not going back to Des Moines," she said, handling first things first. "One thing William's coming has confirmed for me is that I belong here, not in Des Moines, and that I love Wyoming."

He relaxed slightly. "You'll stay?"

"I'll stay," she said. "I'm surprised Clem didn't tell you."

"Somehow he neglected to share that news." Nathan studied her face, his eyes still shadowed. "And would you be willing to consider marrying me?"

"I'll marry you as soon as you like." Brittany was unable to keep a smile from spreading across her face.

"You will?" Her response seemed to take Nathan by surprise.

"I will." Brittany blinked back the tears that momentarily blurred his features. "I thought you didn't care."

"And I thought you and William were headed for the altar. You'll never know how miserable I've been, Brittany."

"You should have talked to me sooner. I could have eased your mind on that score."

"Well, I guess it's a lesson for both of us. From now on, let's make an effort to always be honest with each other, all right?"

"Always," she whispered in return.

Brittany could hear Lars and Brenna's laughter as they played behind the barn, and she heard a snort from a horse in the corral, but most of all she could hear her heart singing with joy. Nathan loved her, and she loved him. Nothing had ever seemed so right before. She was sure her heart must be filled up, pressed down, and overflowing, so powerful was the love she felt.

"When can we be married?" she asked, mentally rolling around the name *Brittany Lindale.*

Nathan thought for a moment. "Well, I need a couple of days to get the cabin into livable condition," he said, his forehead furrowing. "But I think the sooner the better."

"Do you suppose your pa and William would be willing to stay a few more days?"

"Never hurts to ask." Nathan's smile pulled one from her.

He moved closer and knelt down in front of her, his face becoming serious again. "But are you sure you don't want more time to think about this? Marriage isn't something to rush into, and I've been thinking about this for months now. If you need more time—"

"You've felt this way for months?" Brittany stared back at him. "I never would have guessed. You hide things too well."

"I'll try to be honest with you from now on, remember? Now back to my question—do you want to wait a while before we get married?"

"I've been praying about this longer than you might think," Brittany said. "What use would waiting be? I already know how I feel about you, and I'm convinced there is no man to whom I'd rather commit my life. I'm sure of my decision."

Nathan studied her, then finally accepted that she was telling the truth. "I can have the cabin ready in two days if I work hard. What do you say we get married in three days?"

"Three days," Brittany repeated. "Sounds perfect."

"Are you sure? If you'd rather have a little more time—"

"No." Brittany smiled at him, marveling at how irresistible his brown eyes were. "I love you, Nathan."

EPILOGUE

Three days later Nathan and Brittany were married, surrounded by more family and friends than Brittany would have thought possible given such short notice. William took the role of minister, as composed as if he'd been performing weddings all his life, not just twice. Clem stood in what should have been their father's place, and when William asked, "Who gives this woman away?" Clem's voice cracked slightly as he said, "I do." Morgan stood up as Brittany's bridesmaid, and Michael stood beside his son as his best man.

But from the moment her eyes met Nathan's, all the onlookers seemed to fade away, and there was only him. He smiled, a bit shaky, but his eyes said he loved her more than words could express. And that was all she needed to know.

A party followed the ceremony, and as one friend after another hugged and congratulated her, Brittany wondered how she had ever thought of leaving these dear people.

"See, I knew you would end up stayin'." Allie Bryan gave her a hug. "You were too much a part of us to leave us behind."

She stepped back to turn her gaze on Nathan. "You better take real good care of this girl, you hear? She's a treasure."

"I know." Nathan slipped his arm around Brittany's waist and smiled down at her. "She's the greatest treasure I could hope to find."

"Hey, Miss Haines. Er, Mrs. Lindale." Carson grinned up at her. "Iffen you're stayin', will we be havin' school again this year?"

Brittany hadn't thought that far ahead. "Well, I do like teaching—" She looked to Nathan for affirmation.

"I think that's a fine idea," Nathan said. "If that's what you want to do, Brittany."

Brittany smiled down at Carson. "Then let's plan on it."

"Yahoo!" Carson yelled, then tore off through the crowd, hollering, "Hey everybody! Miss Haines, I mean, *Mrs. Lindale*, is gonna be our teacher again!"

Allie beamed after him. "That's good news, all right, but you make sure and give yourself plenty of time to adjust to bein' married before you plunge into another school year. We'll wait long as we need to."

"I will," Brittany said, giving the woman another hug.

Brittany's biggest shock came when Rueben Pierce appeared and offered his congratulations. She could see the surprise flicker across Nathan's face as he shook Rueben's hand, but he recovered himself quickly. There was no apology for the pain he had caused in the past as Rueben walked away, but Brittany sensed that the trouble between him and Nathan was over. It wasn't Rueben's way to say he was sorry, but judging from how he had gone out of his way to be friendly, he was done causing problems. It was yet another chapter closed in their lives.

Later, waving goodbye to the few remaining guests, Nathan and Brittany mounted Loner and Major, a gift from the Myerses, and turned them toward home. Clem and Morgan were taking Lars and Brenna home for the night; Morgan had insisted.

"You and Nathan aren't going to have much time to your-selves caring for those two," she'd said. "Take this night as a gift from Clem and me."

And Brittany had relented.

Nathan and Brittany rode slowly to their new home, enjoying the beautiful fall evening and all that had happened in the last few days. Michael and William were heading home the next day. Brittany wished there would have been more time to get to know her new father-in-law. But he was hoping to make another trip up sometime in the next year or two, this time with Christy and Maryanne. It was something to look forward to and took some of the pain out of parting.

As they rode up the lane of their new ranch, Brittany thought she'd never seen such a beautiful sight. The setting sun cast a red-dish glow over their cabin, softening some of its roughness and giving it a cozy look. Brittany knew that Nathan had been work-ing hard on it the past couple of days, and his efforts showed. The cabin no longer looked as if it might tumble down in the slight-est breeze, and while it still needed more work, she was ready to think of it as home.

They stopped in front of it, and Nathan jumped down, flip-ping the reins over the hitching rail. He came around to Brittany's side and held his arms out to her.

She didn't hesitate and slid off Major's back into his arms.

"That's my girl," Nathan said against her hair, but he didn't set her down. Instead, he swept her into his arms and carried her toward the house.

"What are you doing?" Brittany clung to his neck, laughing.

"Carrying you across the threshold," Nathan said, grinning down at her.

"But I've already been in and out of that house several times." Nathan had shown her around the place, and then she had come back to clean up after Able's sloppiness and Nathan's construction and to arrange things the way she wanted.

"Now, darlin', don't go ruinin' the fun," Nathan said, laying on his Texas accent heavier than usual and making her laugh.

He carried her up the steps and through the door, then slowly set her down without letting go.

"Did I ever tell you how much I love you?" he asked, touching her chin with one finger.

"I don't mind you telling me again." Brittany smiled up at him.

"I love you, Mrs. Lindale." He dipped his head down and kissed her, his arms pulling her close.

Brittany felt breathless when he pulled back. "I love you too, Mr. Lindale."

"We're home at last, Brittany."

ABOUT THE AUTHOR

ALENA MENTINK is a Nebraska author who enjoys mixing history with fictional characters to create a story for God's glory. Alena lives on a farm outside Stromsburg with her parents and seven siblings and is currently writing a novel set near her home in Polk County.